Praise for Leanna Ellis's
Elvis Takes a Back Seat

"Leanna Ellis takes a back seat to no one. So put on your blue suede shoes and come along for a most entertaining ride to Memphis—and to the healing place closest to the heart."

Debbie Macomber
New York Times #1 best-selling author

"Heartwarming, funny, delightful. . . . I was floored by the way this book made me feel. *Elvis Takes a Back Seat* is first-class entertainment."

Romance Reader At Heart

"Brilliant! Charming! I absolutely adored it! *Elvis Takes a Back Seat* is an emotional journey well worth taking. I laughed, I cried, I sighed in contentment. Leanna Ellis is a gifted writer."

Lorraine Heath
New York Times best-selling author

"*Elvis Takes a Backseat* is full of surprises, drama, and humor, just like the King of Rock 'n' Roll. Welcome to a talented storyteller and a fun, deep, unexpected book."

Kristin Billerbeck
Author of *What a Girl Wants* and *The Trophy Wives Club*

"Absolutely brilliantly written. . . . This book has everything a good read should have: some tears, a little witticism, meaningful connections, a few good belly laughs, and hugs."
TCM Reviews

"A charming and heartfelt story of three women recovering from loss and on a journey of discovery. Claudia, Ivy, and Rae will curl up inside your heart and stay with you long after you've put this book down. I loved this book from the first page to the last."
Sharon Mignerey
Author of *Shadows of Truth* and *Too Close for Comfort*

"This book is gritty and real and full of hope, faith, and redemption. Leanna Ellis raises the level of contemporary faith-filled fiction. All I can say is, 'Thank you. Thank you very much, Leanna!'"
Lenora Worth
Author of *Fatal Image* and coauthor of *Once Upon a Christmas*

Leanna Ellis

LOOKIN' BACK, TEXAS

B&H
PUBLISHING GROUP
Nashville, Tennessee

978-0-8054-4697-5

Published by B&H Publishing Group,
Nashville, Tennessee

Dewey Decimal Classification: F
Subject Heading: MARRIAGE—FICTION \
FAMILY LIFE—FICTION \ PARENT AND
ADULT CHILD—FICTION

Scripture quotation is taken from the Holy Bible, New
International Version (NIV), copyright © 1973, 1978, 1984
by International Bible Society.

Publisher's Note: This novel is a work of fiction.
Names, places, and incidents are either products of the
author's imagination or used fictitiously. All
characters are fictional, and any similarity to people
leaving or dead is purely coincidental.

1 2 3 4 5 6 7 8 • 12 11 10 09 08

"Therefore everyone who hears these words of mine and puts them into practice is like a wise man who built his house on the rock. The rain came down, the streams rose, and the winds blew and beat against that house; yet it did not fall, because it had its foundation on the rock. But everyone who hears these words of mine and does not put them into practice is like a foolish man who built his house on sand. The rain came down, the streams rose, and the winds blew and beat against the house, and it fell with a great crash."

Matthew 7:24–27 (NIV)

To Gary.
Always.

1

S uz." Static crackles over Dad's voice. "I need your help, sugar beet."

Phone in hand, I turn toward a bank of windows in my kitchen. Yellow sunshine pours through as I look out at the shades of blue undulating with the waves of the Pacific Ocean. "What can I do, Dad?"

"Your mother . . . she's gone off the deep end this time. Maybe you can talk some—" His voice cuts out. The distance between California and Texas seems further with every second I wait.

"Dad?" I pull the phone away from my ear, check the electronic window to see if we still have a connection. It seems so. "Are you there?"

"—can't blame—" His voice returns, then is gone again, giving my heart whiplash like when my son, Oliver, who is learning to drive, steps on the gas then, in quick succession, the brake.

I try to piece Dad's words together to make sense of

what is happening, and find myself mentally stretching out a hand in an effort to brace myself. Maybe that's what prayer is. My gaze shifts to a framed picture of a sand castle my son once built on the beach near our house. The empty silence on the phone makes my stomach tighten. "Dad? You're breaking up. I can't—"

"—drag you—this, but—"

Static once again takes over, then fades into nothing. Silence throbs in my ear. As if I could reach out and touch my father, I straighten the corner of the white wooden frame holding the picture of Oliver grinning in front of a spectacular, if not lopsided, castle. His footprints crisscross the scooped-out moat. The towers behind him lean and sag, their foundations melting under the encroaching waves. But still, the castle stands. Barely. I straighten the framed picture, remembering those simple, uncomplicated days of sun and surf.

"Dad?" I try again, my voice peaking in desperation. "What's wrong?"

I turn as my husband, Mike, walks into the kitchen, his feet slapping the ceramic tile floor. His tan, lean chest is bare, his hair damp from his shower. He carries an empty coffee mug in his hand, looking for a refill.

"Dad called." The receiver now shows the call has been disconnected. I click the off button but hold onto the phone in case Dad calls back. "I lost him."

Mike's arm is warm, comforting as it wraps around me, strong and secure, but I feel a trembling begin deep inside as he kisses my neck. "Something wrong?"

I nod, distracted by Dad's distress call, lost in a memory of my own. When I was in high school, I sat on the back porch of my parents' home with my father and patted his shoulder. "She didn't mean it, Daddy."

His head bowed low and his hands pressed together

2

between his knees. The lines in his face looked deep and cragged. His shoulders were rounded.

"I know," he said, his voice fracturing. "She means well. But . . ."

That's all he ever said. *But*. The word, heavy and bulky, sat there between us. He always stopped with *but*.

"What's going on?" Oliver plops down at the kitchen table and pours Toasted Oats into a bowl. "Has Grandma called the sheriff again?"

"I don't know exactly." I pour more coffee into Mike's mug.

"Think her neighbor is after those flies again?" Humor laces Mike's words as if a punch line is forthcoming. Whenever I get exasperated with Mother, Mike seems to have the tolerance of a saint or a comedian looking for new material.

I begin to fill the coffeemaker, scooping ground beans, pouring water. A little Gevalia and I'll be smiling again soon. "It was more than Mr. Ned swatting flies, Mike." Mother always has good, solid reasons for whatever she does. "He was on his front porch naked."

My husband's mouth pulls sideways into a wry grin. He likes hearing the goings-on of a small Texas town, says it's more interesting than the L.A. of his childhood. Family dynamics are fascinating to him since he grew up without one. "So what would you have done?" He nudges me playfully in the side. It's the subtle question I've often asked myself, wondering if I'd react like Mother. "Gotten binoculars?"

That makes me laugh. "Mr. Ned is ninety-two. With no teeth."

"Not your type, eh?" He kisses me quick, like lightning, and heat shimmers along my nerves.

"Why couldn't Britney Spears live next to Grandma and Grandpa?" Oliver opens the fridge and pulls out the milk carton.

Smiling, I reach for the plug on the coffeemaker, but it's already in the wall socket, so I flip the switch. Immediately it belches, and wet, goopy grounds pour out over the carafe. A tiny gasp escapes me, and Mike reaches over to shut off the machine.

"I wondered what you were doing. You already made coffee."

"I knew that." But some part of my brain must have fractured. I'm not sure what I was doing, why I was making another pot of coffee when the carafe was half full already.

"Your dad's call must have upset you more than you realize. Here, let me fix it." He pulls the machine across the granite counter toward the sink and starts dumping grounds down the disposal while I mop up the mess on the counter with paper towels.

Then the phone rings again. I leap for the receiver. But this time it's not my father. Instantly, though, I know it's about the situation back home because of the area code and the Texas accent on the other end of the line. "Something's not right with a woman who can't shed a tear over her dead husband."

Linda Lou Hoover, known as the woman who sucks up information better than any vacuum cleaner, pauses for emphasis. When I realize the *widow* she's discussing is my mother, my heart gives a jolt. I get off the phone as fast as I can and punch in the number for my parents' home, my fingers trembling.

"Mother?" I say when she answers, trying to push down the panic that threatens to detonate inside me. "Mrs. Hoover just called."

"Oh, you should know better than to listen to her."

"What's going on?"

She sighs heavily into the phone as if the question is as exhausting as lifting one of the fifty-pound feedbags Daddy sells to local feed stores.

"Has something happened? To Daddy?"

"Not yet."

Her words feel like a hard slap. Heat burns my cheeks. Behind me, I hear Mike turn the water off in the sink. I can sense him watching, waiting. "What do you mean?"

"Your father . . . well, he . . ." There's another long, drawn-out sigh. "I suppose you'll find out soon enough."

My heart begins a labored beating. "Is Daddy . . ." I hesitate, scared to even voice my fear, ". . . dead?"

"Depends on who you're asking."

"I'm asking you, Mother!"

"To me, he is dead. But don't let that trouble you. He's alive and well enough to still be a nuisance."

I probably should let the conversation go as small-town gossip and another argument between Mother and Daddy. It's not the first and most probably won't be the last. I weathered a few squalls of hurricane proportions when I grew up. Once Mother threw all of Daddy's clothes out on the lawn. She had, what she thought, good reason. Another time she cordoned off part of the house, designated each side his and hers. It was to make a point. But I stood on the line, not knowing which side to lean toward, tugged one way by Mother's demand for loyalty, tugged the other by my father's soft heart. Another time Mother was convinced Daddy had a lady friend out of town and tracked her down, only to learn that Ida Mae was a prize-winning hunting dog Daddy had purchased without Mother's consent and was keeping her in Marble Falls till he could figure out how to break the news to Mother.

Mother always has a good reason for the things she says and does. Daddy doesn't mean to be thoughtless or irresponsible. Daddy is just Daddy. Mother is just Mother. Which amounts to oil and water some days, peas and carrots others.

Maybe that's all this is, some misunderstanding. Nothing out of the ordinary. Maybe Linda Lou Hoover has lost some of her suction on gossip, letting bits and pieces slip away. But I can't forget my father's call for help. So I call the airlines for a ticket home to Luckenbach.

It's been ten years but feels like a lifetime since I breathed Texas air. We've offered to fly home for holidays, but Mother and Daddy (mostly Mother) always insist on coming to California. Frankly, it's easier that way. Less hassle with presents, especially when Oliver was little and Santa brought bulky toys like a train table or cardboard rocket ship. Besides there are more activities to keep us occupied in Southern California. Mike thinks my folks have a penchant for Mickey Mouse, but sometimes I get the feeling they just don't want me to come home.

THE FOLLOWING AFTERNOON I'm standing on the front porch of my parents' home. The windmill behind the house creaks in a slow turning motion. Mother surprised Daddy with the kit one Father's Day in the early '80s. She thought a windmill added charm and atmosphere to the house. During the process, Daddy slammed hammer against thumb and lost his nail. Now the wheel looks like my parents' marriage— weathered, worn, and nearly busted.

I glance around at the gently rolling hills where I grew up. The house is not in Luckenbach proper. There is no proper in Luckenbach. The town was established as a trading post in 1849 and hasn't changed much since. The sign outside of town still reads "Population 3." The days here are long, the nights longer. The place is sometimes jokingly referred to as Lookin' Back, but reminiscing is not my favorite pastime.

Luckenbach sits in the hill country outside Fredericksburg, within spitting distance of several peach orchards and wineries. The latter might be the reason it's a favored spot among retirees and bikers. Waylon and Willie made the town famous, but if someone's GPS system goes on the blink, they might blow right past the turnoff and never realize it.

Where I grew up is not quite a neighborhood but more of a hodgepodge of houses located near one another, their styles a mishmash of brick, wood, siding, and stonework. Some neighbors built their houses themselves, not bothering with contractors. The Lindseys down the crooked gravel drive lived in a full-sized tepee for three and a half years while they built their house brick by brick. Each home sits on five or more acres. That much real estate would be obscenely expensive in California. But here in the hill country of Gillespie County land is cheap (unless oil is bubbling beneath) and hearts are humble. Most are anyway.

For some reason today cars jam the narrow lane leading up to my parents' limestone ranch house and are parked in no particular pattern on the front lawn. It looks as if Mother is throwing one of her famous parties. Folks in Luckenbach and nearby Fredericksburg and Stonewall are known for thinking up any excuse to party, whether it's celebrating Waylon Jennings, Chester Nimitz, or mud daubers. Mother may be difficult to tolerate as a neighbor (and even as a parent at times), but no one gives a party like Betty Lynne Davidson, the resident Martha Stewart. Everyone who receives a coveted invitation is certain to come.

But why today? When I spoke to her on the phone from California, she didn't say anything about preparations for a party.

"You know your mother," Mike said when he dropped me at the airport midmorning. "No telling what's going on." Now I wish he were here with me, supporting and encouraging me—and guarding my back.

Bracing myself for the unimaginable, I knock on the door of my childhood home. Through the paned windows, the Texas drawl I've worked so hard to eliminate from my own speech mingles, male and female, in low tones I can't decipher. The house is awfully quiet for a party.

I suddenly have the urge to run back to my car. Can I make it back to Austin in time to catch a flight home? Maybe Mother's mellowed with age. I toss up a quick but fervent prayer for an extra dose of love. And patience. And self-control. And—

The door opens. The weather stripping makes a sucking sound, and Mother's serenely smiling face comes into view. When the realization hits her eyes that it's me standing here, there's a brief flutter of shock, then panic. It's only a flash, here then gone. Most people who don't know Mother would miss it. She recovers quickly, her smile remaining intact. Always. It's the way she trained me.

With a glance over her shoulder, she whispers to someone I can't see, "Excuse me, will you? Oh, yes. I'll be right back. No, no, I'm fine."

Mother is always fine. Unflappable. I didn't inherit that trait. On the outside I might seem fine, but on the inside I'm usually a wreck. My ability to hide my insecurities and fears has taken years to develop.

She squeezes through the partially open door and closes it quickly behind her. She may have inherited the German bone structure and coloring with blonde hair and blue eyes, but she isn't big-boned or sporting the pounds from too many potatoes. Still, she is formidable. Mother takes my arm and leads me along the front porch to the swing, then stops as if repositioning our greeting. "Why, Suzanne!" Her accent is good and thick as white sausage gravy. She gives me a brief hug, and I catch a powdery whiff of Chanel No. 5. Her smile is unwavering, but all my senses go on full alert. "What are you doing here, dear?"

"I'm concerned, Mother."

"About what?" A tiny wrinkle appears between her carefully plucked brows, then she erases it just as quickly, jerking her chin, opening her eyes wide and innocently.

"After I talked to you. And, well, before. When Mrs. Hoover called and said you weren't acting . . . well, she said—"

"Sugar, you know you can't believe anything Linda Lou says. She could kill somebody with that tongue of hers."

Which is exactly my point. Mrs. Hoover usually has her facts straight. She could have been a police detective. Or a spy. But she prefers uncovering neighbors' dirt to overseas travel. However, there's no winning an argument with Mother, so I take a different tact. I am after all the peaceful mediator.

"And I spoke with Dad."

Her eyes narrow, suspicion making her pupils contract to tiny pin pricks. "What did he say?"

"He asked for my help."

She places a fisted hand on her hip. "Whatever for?"

"You tell me, Mother." Direct confrontation, I learned at a young age, is never a good idea with my mother. This is as close as I dare. "It's not like I show up unannounced on your doorstep every day. Why aren't you asking me inside the house? What's going on here?"

"In there? Why, it's much nicer out here, don't you think?" The constant wind is unable to ruffle my mother's magically stoic hair, and the sun's heat and my gaze don't seem to wilt her defenses either.

"It's hot," I say, fanning myself with the sleeve of my airline ticket, well aware the hill country has been in a drought for the past few years. Even now, the evidence is clear with the dry, brittle grass of midsummer.

"Well, you're just accustomed to those ocean breezes." Which is true. The wind here brings only more heat.

A car door slams behind me. Mother glances toward the parked cars. She hisses through her teeth. "Hazel Perkins, of all people."

Mother's closest friend carries a white plastic cake container. Her purse dangles at her arm, knocking against her ample hip. She takes short steps, picking her way across the lawn, stepping carefully over a hose that snakes across the grass. She looks ten years older than Mother, who keeps up her appearance better than most A-list Hollywood stars.

Mother grabs my hand and squeezes my fingers. For the first time, panic registers fully in her blue eyes like a jackpot in a slot machine. "Don't say a word."

"What?"

"Smile. Be polite."

I've heard those words most of my childhood. Nothing apparently has changed. But the obedient child in me nods, trumping the grown-up, mature me who is tired of games that are invented for appearance's sake. Mother always aimed to keep a perfect house, a perfect family. This was her idea of 'keeping up with the Joneses.'

"Hello, Hazel!" Mother gives a friendly wave.

Honor your mother and father, I remember, *that your days may be long upon the earth.* I better call Mike because my days are about to get decidedly shorter.

"My word," the older woman with yellowing gray hair huffs coming up the steps, "it's a scorcher today." She's wearing an orange straw cowboy hat, a tangerine orange top, and burnt orange capris. She even wears strappy orange sandals. "And it's only the end of June. What will it be like in July? I don't even want to think about August."

"Too hot for decent folk," Mother replies.

Hazel gives Mother a one-armed hug as she balances the cake pan in her other hand. "Just can't believe it about Archie. Why, I only saw him two days—"

"Yes, yes," Mother pats her friend's shoulder. "These things happen. You remember my daughter, Suzanne."

"Suzannah Lee! My word, it's been years! How long has it been since you've been home?" She grabs me with a strong but flabby arm and hugs me close. She smells of Aqua Net and coconut. A second whiff tells me the latter is the cake. "You came! Betty Lynne said you couldn't. Your husband needing you with all those important clients and lawsuits and such. But I knew you wouldn't miss—"

"Hazel," Mother interrupts, "we should get you inside before you pass out."

Her eyes mist over, and she blinks profusely. She props the cake container in my hand while she pulls out a crinkled tissue from her shiny orange purse. "I'm so sorry about your daddy." She blows her nose. "He was a good—"

"Hazel," Mother's tone is more forceful, "you better get that cake inside before this heat melts the frosting clean off."

"You're so right." She squeezes my arm. "I see you've just arrived." She glances down the porch at my suitcase sitting forlornly outside the door. "You need to get settled in, talk things over with your mother. There will be plenty of time for us to talk later, sugar. I wanna hear all about your fancy life out in California. You've been the envy of all the gals stuck here with their ranching husbands and lazy, good-for-nothin' boyfriends."

She waddles down the porch with her cake and purse. Mother and I stand together, looking like a proper pair during a difficult time. When she enters the house, I turn on Mother and whisper, "You ready to tell me what's going on? Or should I walk into that house and find out for myself?"

She gives a heavy, resolved sigh and crosses her arms over her chest. "I suppose you're going to find out soon enough."

She takes a breath, shifts her shoulders as if she's not completely comfortable carrying this particular burden.

"I killed your father."

"What?" The breath leaves my lungs, and I sit down hard on the swing, which wobbles and sways precariously. "But I talked—"

"Oh, not literally. Good grief, Suzanne. More . . . figuratively. He's alive and kicking." She purses her lips as if perturbed that she has to explain herself. "Unfortunately. The good Lord will have to take care of Archie in his own good time. Still, I killed him off in my own way."

I try to grasp what she's saying. My mind feels like my son's dartboard, with random words thrown at it, jabbing into me. "What are you talking about, Mother? You're making no sense."

"As far as I'm concerned your father is dead. That's what I've told everyone. We're going to have a fancy, highfalutin funeral. Then I'll be a widow—respected, envied even, with the rest of my life before me."

It takes me a moment to process what she's saying. I can hear my husband whispering in my mind, "Competency hearing." I can imagine Daddy shaking his head in consternation. My good friend Vivien would say, "Prozac."

The old, awkward, uncomfortable feelings come flooding back. As a child I felt like I was slapping glue on our family, trying to hold us together. Peacemaker was my middle name. I've stuck the pieces of my family back together before, and I can do it again. That's why I'm here.

"But," my voice wobbles like the wooden bench beneath me, "what about Daddy? Where is he?"

Mother lifts a narrow shoulder, her indifference as cold as ice. "He left town. He left me, if you want to know the truth of the matter. But to me, he's dead as an armadillo stretched out on the highway."

"Mother!" I reach for her, feeling her pain.

But she steps away. "Your father decided yesterday, after

forty-six years of marriage, that he didn't want to be married any longer. To me, I suppose. And he left." She snaps her fingers. "Just like that."

"But why? What happened?" My parents always argued. But no one ever left.

"Does it really matter? If he doesn't want to be near me, I am not about to beg him to stay." She relaxes her arms, then smooths out the wrinkles on her blouse, her attitude toward Daddy's departure and the demise of her forty-odd years of marriage as inconsequential and irritating as a crinkling crease in linen. "I asked him what exactly I was supposed to do, what I was supposed to tell our neighbors, friends, folks at church. He said I could tell everyone he was dead as far as he cared."

Her words hit me like a flat pancake in the face. The shocking heat gives way to a cold, clammy feeling. "He said that?"

"He said there's nothing left in this town he can't live without. He was leaving and moving far away with . . ." She clamps her lips together as if trying to hold back a flood of emotions. "Well, let's just say he plans to skedaddle and leave me here with all the disgrace and gossip. Isn't that just like him? Leaving me here to clean up *his* mess! Like it's a pair of dirty socks that needs washing. Well, I've cleaned up after him for forty years. Not this time. I just decided I wouldn't do it. But it was his idea anyway. I am not about to be humiliated by his untimely departure."

A cold, lumpy fear settles in my stomach.

Most of my friends worry about the teenage years, when their kids rebel and get into trouble. Oliver's a good kid, and my worry is minimal. But I worry more about the geriatric years, the difficulty my parents will cause. Now I know.

Once again, I stand on a line between Mother and Daddy, not knowing which way to lean. Suddenly the wind ceases and I feel only the heat of the sun bearing down on me.

Before I can ask more, Mother says, "I refuse to be a divorced woman."

Her gaze shifts toward the corner of the front porch. Way up high, nestled against the wall and ceiling is a mud dauber's nest. It's a brown-clay, cylinder-shaped lump. "Drat," she says and goes after the broom. A minute later, she aims the wooden handle and whacks the nest, her anger now aimed at the poor defenseless insect.

The thwacking of broomstick against wood echoes along the porch. Several whacks and the home finally crumbles and falls at Mother's feet. She flips the broom around, each movement sharp and precise, like a military exercise. Even as she sweeps the remains from the porch and into the bushes, I know she can't sweep away the anger and hurt she is feeling and the devastation Daddy has brought to our family. This, I realize, is going to take more than a little glue; this might take a miracle.

Mother props the broom in the corner. Patting her hair, which still hasn't moved, she takes a deep breath. "There. So it's not my fault. It was your father's idea. At least widowhood is respectable—"

"But, Mother, maybe Daddy said that in the heat of the moment."

The front door opens. Mother stops the conversation with a hand on my arm. An old high school buddy of mine, Estelle Rodriguez, pokes her head outside. She looks the same, only plumper, her brown cheeks round, her long black hair glossy and full. "Mrs. Davidson? You doin' all right out here?"

Did she hear the assault on the mud dauber's nest? Or is the sound of my family falling apart so loud? The foundation of my life shifts, and I feel it crumbling beneath my feet.

Then she sees me. "Oh, my! It's Suzannah Banana!"

As she rushes out the door, Mother pinches my elbow and whispers, "Be nice now."

That's code for "keep your mouth shut." So I smile, clenching my teeth. "We'll discuss this later, Mother."

"There's nothing to discuss," she whispers back in an equally pinched way.

Then I'm engulfed in a hug by Estelle and swept up by my past. I'm not sure God heard my earlier prayer, so I toss up another quick S.O.S.

2

*H*onor. I need to look that word up in the dictionary and think about the implications. In the meantime, without my Webster's or Bible handy, I'm winging it.

"This isn't right, Mother," I whisper while standing in her kitchen. Her guests are in the other room, milling about quietly as if an actual wake were in progress. Without looking, I know Mother's pots and pans are stacked neatly and methodically in cabinets beneath the stove top, just as I know her counters have been cleaned and Cloroxed daily. Everything in its place.

Flower pots, vases, knickknacks, and bowls overflowing with peaches take up each corner and line the shelves above the cabinets. The bright colors and jumbled patterns à la Mary Engelbreit make me dizzy. Or maybe it's this whole bizarre situation that has thrown off my equilibrium.

"This can't work out, Mother. You have to tell the truth! I know you're angry and hurt, but there must be another solution. Daddy's not dead, and people are going to find out!"

17

"No, they won't." She glances over her shoulder as if she were nervous that someone in the next room might hear, yet her outward demeanor is calm and collected like a real-life deodorant commercial. "Now keep your voice down. I've taken care of everything."

She starts to turn away, but I grab her arm, pressing insistently into her flesh. "But what if Daddy decides to come back?"

Mother pats my hand. "He won't. Your father always does what he says."

"He said he'd never leave you either. Wasn't that in your wedding vows? 'Nor forsake you'?"

Mother's eyes narrow into tiny slits of anger. "He said he wasn't coming back."

I'm trying to make her understand how unrealistic this plan is. I know she's wounded. She wants to save face, maintain her dignity. Maybe I can make her think this through and realize what a reckless idea it is. "What if he does?"

"He wouldn't dare." Her tone has a cutting edge, as if she would use her butcher knife with Julia Child's precise and unflustered style if he did.

I reach for my cell phone. "Let's call him." My fingers tremble as I punch in the numbers. "We'll talk about all of this. We'll figure out another solution."

A memory of Daddy sitting on the front swing draws pain like a nurse drawing blood. "Your mother," he said, his voice resigned, "is one of those women that's always striving, always trying to make things better than they are."

"Makes it pretty icky for the rest of us though."

"Sure 'nuff."

Mother's hand presses into mine, forces me back to the present. Her fingers are cool and firm as she takes my cell phone and closes it. "Stop this nonsense."

This nonsense? Maybe the hurt has so colored her vision that she can't see the ramifications of her charade. But if she were to admit the truth now, then everyone would be understanding.

"You can work things out, Mother. Maybe you and Daddy could see a marriage counselor together." Or a psychologist. Or psychiatrist. Whichever prescribes medication. Serious medication.

"I am not going to go spill my dirty laundry in front of some stranger. Or worse, someone here in town."

I know for a fact that there are no mental health professionals in Luckenbach. Although medication in the form of liquor is offered on a daily basis. But Fredericksburg . . . surely there's a professional counselor or trained medical personnel who could help.

"But, Mother, this is wrong." Not to mention irrational and insane.

"Maybe," she says. "Maybe not."

"It might even be illegal." Maybe the threat of jail will scare her onto the straight and narrow. "Have you thought of that?"

"I'm not breaking any laws. I didn't actually *kill* Archie. That would be breaking a holy commandment. But believe you me, he sorely tempted me."

"Isn't lying one of the Ten Commandments?" Surely she can't argue with God on that one.

"God understands that I've been wronged." Her emphasis on the last word resonates like a misplaced note. She turns her back, folds a dish towel in half, then again, and a third time, leaving a fat lump on the counter. "But if you feel that way, then maybe you should go back to California. I wouldn't want you to be a part of anything illegal."

"Mother—"

"But if you stay to help me through this difficult time of loss"—she pauses for effect, neatly sidestepping my question like Savion Glover—"you can help me write the obituary."

At that exact moment, the kitchen door swings open, and Mrs. Hoover barrels in. She has a pug nose, perfect for sniffing out things that aren't her business, and tiny lips pressed into a perpetual pucker. "Am I intruding?"

I'm sure there is nothing better she'd like to do than overhear a private conversation or intrude in a family matter.

"Yes," I say at the same time Mother says, "No." We glare at each other for a moment, a tiny standoff. I can feel the blood pumping through my temples.

I squelch the irritation I've always felt toward Linda Lou Hoover. Because her snooping could be, this time, our salvation. If she does overhear that my father is alive, then no doubt Mother will have to alter her plan.

Mother is the first to break the awkward silence with a trilling laugh. "Maybe you can help us, Linda Lou."

"Oh?" Mrs. Hoover accepts the invitation and moves farther into the room. She wears a full blue-jean skirt with a wide conch belt around her bulging middle. She leans forward slightly, walking as if sniffing out the scent of gossip lurking around every corner. Her beady-eye gaze bounces between us as if she's hoping for the inside scoop, some morsel of discord to go with a side of ice cream.

"We need help on the obituary."

I lean back into myself, watching Mother, letting her set her own trap if she won't listen to reason.

"Why, of course. I'd love to help." Mrs. Hoover bustles around, opening and closing drawers, and finally gathers a pad of paper and pen. "You know I've done many for the paper. I *am*, after all, a professional writer."

She pushes the kitchen door open and goes into the dining room, holding the door for us. Reluctantly I follow

Mother. The friends and neighbors gathered in the living room pause their conversations and watch us as though a funeral procession were passing.

"Maybe we should go back in the kitchen," Mother suggests.

Estelle Ramirez scolds her twin girls. They both remind me of Pippi Longstocking, but with dark brown hair that sticks out in too many directions. One girl stands on the couch like it's the prow of a ship. The other twirls in the middle of the living room, wobbling off center like a top about to tilt.

"Or outside," Mother adds.

I start to mention the stifling heat, but Mrs. Hoover says, "Oh, this'll be just fine." She pats the back of a dining chair, obviously content to be in the middle of the action where she won't miss a thing. "We can all gather right here."

"Watch it." Josie Bullard, another friend from school, puts a hand out to keep one of the twins from stepping on her pointy-toed shoe. She sits with her legs crossed, her black skirt way too high on her tanned thigh for any occasion other than sitting on a bar stool. She's running her finger around the top of her coffee cup, as if she wished it were something more potent. I'm beginning to feel that way myself.

"I'd better go," Estelle calls, having wrangled one of her children. "The girls are getting tired." They seem full of energy to me. Estelle's the one who looks bedraggled. But I remember those days when my son, Oliver, was a whirling tornado of energy.

"It's bedtime. And Naldo has a hard time putting the younger ones down, much less rounding up the older ones."

"Oh, that's too bad," Mother says, moving forward with swift attention and opening the front door for her. "But we certainly understand. Thank you for the pound cake. It looked pretty." Her tone tells me the taste was less than ideal.

21

A few other neighbors make their excuses and head out the door, forming a quick processional of "Good to see," "We're so sorry," and "You take care of your mother now."

When I hug Estelle good-bye, she whispers, "I'll call you." Her daughter wiggles out from between us, knocking her head against my hipbone. "Maybe we can get together while you're in town."

"I'd like that." But I have a feeling I'm going to be busy strapping Mother into a straitjacket.

"How long are you going to be here?"

"I'm not sure." Until Daddy is resurrected? Or Mother is arrested or committed? "As long as Mother needs me."

Closing the door after my friend, I turn and lean against the wood panel. The den hasn't changed much over the years. Daddy's chair still sits beside the bay window, aimed at the twenty-five-inch television. But one thing is different. Where are the pictures of my family? There are photos of Oliver as a toddler next to a picture of Mike and me on our wedding day. But what has Mother done with all the portraits I've sent over the past few years. Maybe they're hung in other rooms.

"When is the funeral, Betty Lynne?" Mrs. Hoover asks.

"Thursday," Mother says.

I stare at her.

"That's in five days." Mrs. Hoover is the only one brave enough to speak. "I would have thought Monday—"

"You can't throw a decent funeral in less. And Archie, of course, deserves the best." Mother's voice is dry and brittle like grass ready to ignite.

Now I know what I have to do. How much time I have. Five days. One hundred and twenty hours. Seventy-two hundred minutes. It's an eternity. Yet it seems woefully inadequate. Five short days before my parents' marriage is irrevocably destroyed. Five days to get my parents in the same room, to sit them down together and straighten out this mess. If possible. A miracle, I decide, is in order. God parted the Red Sea; surely he can bring my parents back together.

I SIT AT THE DINING TABLE with Mother, Linda Lou Hoover, and Hazel Perkins. Twisting a forgotten silver fork between my fingers, I consider calling in reinforcements. Mike might be able to talk sense into Mother. Maybe he can talk to Daddy too. Thinking of my father, my chest tightens.

"Well, now," Mrs. Hoover declares, pen in hand, "there are several ways to approach an obituary."

"I like the funny ones." Josie stretches her lithe body and walks toward the dining room table.

Mother lifts a censorious eyebrow.

"I mean," Josie doesn't bother to blush, "it's always better to laugh and cry at the same time. I didn't mean anything disrespectful, Mrs. Davidson."

"Of course you didn't." Mother's tone is caustic. She has the ability to say something that, if repeated, could not implicate her. But her meaning is always as clear as one of her Windexed windows. "Why don't we start with the basic information?"

"Of course." Mrs. Hoover writes Daddy's name along the top line. "Isn't Archie's birthday in December?"

"The tenth," Mrs. Perkins adds.

Mother glances at her. "1943. His father, I believe, came home on leave from the war."

"Although that's very interesting, and I certainly like a good tidbit of gossip," Mrs. Hoover traces the comma between the date and the year with the edge of the pen, "I don't think that's a particular we can use. When did he graduate from high school?"

"He was older than me," Mother says. "So let me think . . ." She glances around the room as if the scrap of information would mysteriously appear.

"If he was eighteen," I say, doing the math in my head, "then—"

"He graduated early," Mother interrupts. "He was smart."

Was. The past tense sends a rattling chill down my spine. Josie and Mrs. Hoover look toward Mother as if anticipating a tear might sparkle in her eye.

Hazel sips her coffee. "Oh, he was that. Nobody smarter than Archie Davidson. We was in the same grade, he and I. But that was a long, long time ago."

"Would anyone like more coffee?" Mother's front teeth seem suddenly welded together.

"Do you have decaf?" Mrs. Hoover asks. "I can't drink regular this late. And I'm not supposed to drink caffeine anyway." She leans forward and whispers loud enough for someone in the next county to hear, "Cysts."

I offer a sympathetic smile.

She looks at the empty plate where she has scraped off the last bit of chocolate cream pie with the tines of her fork. "I don't think the doctor meant chocolate. That would be unbearable."

"Archie went into the army in 1961. I remember that year." Mother gets up from the table and returns to the privacy of the kitchen. The door swings shut behind her. Silence hums in the room. I can almost hear the soft clicking of the light bulbs in the chandelier.

"Don't make decaf special for me," Linda Lou hollers, then looks at me. "Was your father in Vietnam, Suzanne?"

Before I can answer, Mother pushes the door back open. "Germany," she says.

"Was that when Elvis was there?"

24

"I don't think so." The door swooshes closed as Mother disappears again.

Josie leans toward me, her perfume as heavy as her eye makeup. "Want me to spike your coffee?" She pats her purse, where I imagine there's an airline-sized bottle of whiskey inside.

In high school Josie could always be counted on to get any party going by sneaking in alcohol. I wouldn't have been able to buy it, but she always knew some older guy with a license who could and had no qualms giving it to under-age minors. But I'm not in high school anymore. And I've long since learned alcohol does not help in dealing with my parents. Keeping my wits about me is the best defense *and* offense.

"I'm okay," I assure her.

"Think I made your mom mad?"

"Sure you did." Mrs. Hoover keeps writing.

It wouldn't surprise me if that had been Josie's intention. "She's upset all on her own." Josie sticks out her tongue, but Mrs. Hoover doesn't notice. Or doesn't respond.

I hide a smile. It feels like we're back in high school. Except now I can see our attitudes as I might view them from the parent's perch. No wonder Mother never liked Josie. But I guess I know too much about Josie, her family life, and her hardships to dismiss her. Mostly I know her heart is as big as the state of Texas.

Mrs. Hoover *tsks*. "Your momma is one of the strongest women I know. Strong-willed with extra steel reinforce-ments. Don't you worry about her. Still, if she could just cry a little."

Mother comes back, carrying a tray of coffee cups and cream and sugar. She says, "Archie graduated in December of 1960."

"Here, Mother, let me help." I take the tray from her and whisper, "Did you look that up in Daddy's yearbook?"

"Called him," she says through tight lips, then louder adds, "Who wants sugar?"

"You did?" I ask.

Mother gives me a look that could silence a swarm of locusts.

"Why was 1961 particularly memorable?" Mrs. Hoover pauses in her writing and looks at Mother.

"Archie proposed to me that year. It was October. We'd only been seeing each other a couple of months. It was right before he left for Germany." A wispy look blows across her face. I can't tell if she's sentimental about the moment or regretting her decision.

"Hmm." Then Mrs. Hoover scribbles some more. After a moment or two she looks up, pleased with herself. She crosses a 't' with a flourish. "There, I'm almost done. What's your child's name, Suzannah?"

"Oliver." A reminder I need to call home. Maybe I should ask Mike to come to Texas and try to talk some sense into Mother. He would certainly know the legalities of what she's attempting to do.

"Oh, yes, of course. An odd name. Do the other kids rib him?"

Her remark shouldn't surprise me. Mrs. Hoover and Mother are known for asking questions no one in their right mind would ask.

"Always reminds me of that dark musical." Mrs. Hoover does a warbly rendition of "Food, Glorious Food." After only one line, she coughs, her cheeks reddening. "Now, let's see what we have." She begins reading. "'Archibald Lionel Davidson, born December 10, 1943; died—'"

My cell phone starts the cavalry charge, which Oliver programmed to signal a call from Mike. "Sorry," I mutter, reaching for my cell. I slide out of my chair and head toward the kitchen and a little privacy. I nudge the door into place behind me. "Hi."

"You got in okay?"

His voice brings relief and reassurance to my rattled nerves. "Yes, I'm here. And it's nuts."

"What else is new?"

"No, really. Maybe you should come and talk to Mother. She's always adored you. She respects your opinion. You could explain the legal ramifications. I know this has to be illegal somehow. And if not, then maybe you'd have some influence with Dad."

"Illegal? What is she doing? What do you want me to convince her to do?"

"Unkill my father."

I hear a sound behind me and turn.

Josie stands in the doorway close by. Too close. One of her eyebrows arches, and a slight, sardonic smile spreads across her ruby-red lips.

3

Josie grabs my arm, makes quick excuses to my mother and her friends, and takes me for a drive. We burn up a few miles in her yellow Camaro with the music (which I don't recognize) cranked to the level Oliver prefers. Josie smiles at me and laughs, her hair as wild as she was in high school. For a moment she looks just as she did at eighteen—carefree, reckless and on the verge of out of control. It's as if she hasn't grown up and I've become my mother. This is unsettling.

The wind through the open windows whips at my hair. I fist it like a ponytail in one hand to keep it from slashing me across the face. I take comfort in the seat belt strapped across my chest and lap. Before I can tell her to slow down as I would my son, Josie pulls off the highway, onto a dirt road, which then gives way to rocky terrain.

"Where are we going?"

"You don't remember?"

I shake my head and peer into the darkness, trying to spot anything familiar. But the light has given way to gray.

The trees are nothing more than shadows, their arms reaching out to us. Finally she pulls to a stop and jerks the emergency brake into place. The music shuts off, and my ears suddenly throb with the silence. Josie gets out and rummages in the trunk. I sit there and blink, allowing my heart to settle back to a nice, calm pace. When I dare to step out of the car, I realize Josie has clambered onto the hood.

"Go head. You won't hurt my car."

I'm not as worried about the car as I am the bug parts stuck to the hood and the kind of dirt that will never come out of my slacks. I lift one foot, shift sideways, hike my hip up onto the warm metal, then maneuver myself onto the hood. I don't think I'll ever be as relaxed as Josie, who leans back against the windshield, her legs stretched out in front of her.

"So what gives with your mother?"

Crossing my legs, I lean my elbows on my knees. Josie sticks a cold bottle in my hand. "Oh, uh . . ." I turn it around and realize it's not soda. "Josie, I uh—"

"Your mom is okay. Bet you never thought I'd say that, did you? It's been a long time since you were home. I bet you think nothin' much has changed. But you'd be wrong. Lots has. Oh sure, I know she doesn't like me much. But she ain't half bad. She really helped a friend of mine. Do you remember Yolanda Roberts?"

I shake my head.

"She may not have lived here when you did. I can't remember when she came. But she's cool. You'd like her. Most everybody does. When she got breast cancer, she had no insurance. And your mom, well, she went to every doc in Fredericksburg until she found someone who'd help her. She really went out on a limb. You know?"

I shift so I can see at least Josie's shadow. The brown bottle is propped against my thigh. I look up at the darkening night sky. I'd forgotten how wide the Texas sky is, how bright the stars are. In California there doesn't seem to be a place where the sky goes on forever and ever, unless you're out on the water. Among these hills of sand and limestone, the wind buffeting me, the sky becomes the ocean. I close my eyes and can almost feel the rocking of the waves.

"I'm not sure my mother is exactly helping a neighbor in need."

"Yeah, but I just wanted you to know that I'm not about to go tellin' everybody what she's up to. You know? I feel like I owe her." Josie chugs the rest of her beer and hurls the bottle up over the roof of the car. It crashes somewhere behind us against the hard ground. I cringe. My motherly instincts tell me to go pick up the glass before bare feet step on the broken pieces or tires drive over them. But it's too dark to see pieces of brown glass. Besides, I'm not about to get down off the car and wander around this rugged terrain. I grew up here and know all about prickly pear and rattlesnakes.

Is Josie still caught in the rough-and–tumble, hormone-driven, compulsive reaction syndrome of teenhood? Relief pulses deep inside me in a small hidden place—I'm glad I left. I like my life the way it is now. But there are things I miss. The solid ground, the wide Texas sky above. I know God's in control, even in this whacked-out situation with my mother. But I also know she's formidable, like the walls of Jericho. Then I remember God brought them down with the blast of a trumpet.

Why is it so much easier to feel God's presence, the rightness of my world, when I'm home in California? Is it the ocean? The family we've built? Maybe because my home-town has a lot of quirks. Or maybe because the memories of my youthful mistakes linger here. Maybe it's too easy to forget the past when I'm in California. Longing wells up inside me now. I wish I were home. With Mike. With Oliver.

Feeling out of my element, I look out into the darkness surrounding us. I don't recognize any of this terrain. It all looks the same to me anyway. The wind has bent the land-scape to its own design. Scrub brushes dot the dusty ground. The heat sucks the air out of my lungs. I miss the breeze off the ocean, the sway of the palm trees, the shelter of our home that protects me from all I fear, all I regret. Here amid the blackjack oak and hickory trees, I feel vulnerable to the winds of change, storms that blow up, heat that kills everything that isn't strong enough or resourceful enough to survive. Must be why mud daubers stick around year after year; they know how to build a solid home that can't be tossed by the wind or shattered by circumstances beyond their control.

"Where exactly are we?"

"I can't believe you don't remember!"

"It's been a while, just as you said."

"It's where we used to come and hang out. Makeout Flats."

Then I remember. Makeout Flats is an area just north of Fredericksburg, not far from Enchanted Rock, a huge pink granite dome rising out of the ground. But from here in the dark I can't see it.

"I know you came here in high school," she says, her tone holding secrets—my secrets.

"A few times." I don't want to think about Drew Waring though. I should have stopped at that particular mistake.

"Where do kids go now?" I glance around and see only patches of shadows in the dark, deserted field where we used to park.

"Oh, some still hang out here. There's also some caves nearby. Parents don't seem to care as much these days. Or maybe they just figure kids are gonna get into trouble any-way, so they'd rather it be closer to home. Don't you have a teenager?"

"Yes," I say, thinking of Oliver who is fifteen and not

yet free to drive alone. The thought brings trepidation even though he's responsible and careful.

"Is he coming in for the 'funeral'?"

"I don't think so." I sigh and rub my hand over my face. I never finished my conversation with Mike that I started in the kitchen when Josie overheard me. "There isn't a funeral, Josie. Not a real one anyway."

"So has your mom gone crazy, or what?"

"She's looking for justice. Like finding your friend a doctor." I rub my toe against my other foot, feeling gritty sand along my arch. I wish Mike *would* come. I would feel better with him here. He's better at negotiating with Mother. "You know my mother."

"Yeah, I do. She's a piece of work. I'm gonna get another beer. Want one?"

I hand her mine.

"You don't want it?"

"No, thanks."

She pops the top off with the bottle opener on her key chain.

"For emergencies," she explains. "If anyone can pull this crazy idea off, your mom can. Besides, maybe I can help."

"Oh, well, uh . . ."

"Don't worry so much. I'm not gonna tell anyone."

"That's good. Mother might kill both of us off too."

"And that would be a bad thing?" Humor laces her words. "Oh, you can trust me. I keep all kinds of secrets."

"Like what?" Then I regret asking. I haven't been in the mix of town gossip in a long while. It's way too easy to fall back into the groove of small town life. Scandals, rumors, and the like exist in California too. Attorney's wives seem to know the latest scoop and scandal before their husbands, even. But I try to stay on the outside of all that.

"Now, they wouldn't be secrets if I went around telling everybody, would they?" Her voice has a husky lilt to it.

"Am I everybody?"

"No, but you're so . . . California."

My spine automatically stiffens. "What do you mean by that?"

"I don't know."

"It didn't sound complimentary."

"Probably jealousy talking."

I crook my head to the side. Josie's a hazy shadow in the fading light. I'm not sure she can see me in the dark either.

She adds, "You got out. I didn't."

I lean back, trying not to think about the bugs smashed on the windshield. The stars fill the sky like glittering diamonds of promise and purpose. Leaving didn't seem so difficult to me, but then, I did it. Of course, I was pushed out by my mother. She told me my whole life that I was too good for this Podunk town. I never *felt* too good. In fact, I never felt good enough, like being at the fair and standing against the big measuring stick to see if I could ride the roller coaster. "Sorry, girlie too short." Too whatever. "Maybe next year."

I glance over at Josie now, seeing the outline of her shape. In some ways she hasn't changed at all. She's still curvy, still overly confident. Only the light reveals she's aged.

"Why didn't you move away?" I ask.

She takes a pull on her beer, making slurping sounds. "Thought I might leave with Robby Zimmerman. Remember him? But then he only went as far as Austin. Then there was Todd Braun. And somebody after that. And somebody else, I don't remember now." She coughs, clearing her throat that had become husky. "Just led me in circles all these years. And then I guess this is where I am. Where I'll always be."

"Is that such a bad thing?"

"Sometimes. Sometimes not. It's definitely always interesting."

It's the status quo syndrome that I grew up with—the same status quo that made me ask "Why?" when told I should sit straight and cross my legs at the ankle.

"Because," Mother would say.

"Why?" I asked when told I had to wear a dress to church when my friends were wearing cutoffs and jeans. The hose Mother made me wear were hot and bothersome.

"Because you're a lady. That's what ladies do."

"Why?" I asked about the way Mother taught me to scrub the toilet with Clorox.

"It's worked all these years. Who are you to say it's wrong?"

I quit asking why, but the questions piled up inside me. I suppose I always knew I would do things differently because I sensed something missing, something that couldn't be articulated or explained.

"You could still move away," I say to Josie, "find someplace else. Start over."

"Nah. I know people here. Know who they are. Know who I am." She juts her chin toward the west, or maybe it's the east we're facing. The moonlight glints in her eye. The true rebel of Luckenbach finds comfort in the way things have always been. Maybe I'm the rebel. "Out there," she says, "I wouldn't know for sure. Who would I be? What would I do? And I like knowing. I don't like surprises. You know?"

"It can be scary. Sometimes I wonder what others see, what they think about me. Sometimes where I live, things seem very superficial."

"Everybody's somebody in Luckenbach."

Josie laughs a gut-busting laugh at her own joke. I haven't heard anyone laugh that way in a long while, in a way that says she doesn't care if anyone hears or notices.

"It's all about who your grandpappy was or wasn't," she says. "What you drive or don't drive. What church you go to or don't go to. If you're in the VFW or the men's lodge. Or the sewing group or cowpunchers. If you play the guitar or fiddle. People are people no matter where you go." She picks at the sticker on the bottle, slowly peeling it off in one piece. "Do you have people in California lying about their husbands' being dead?"

"Well, I wouldn't say they're opposed to it." I laugh. "It wouldn't surprise me though."

"Do you have good friends out there?"

"Sure. We're mostly all transplants, all from someplace else, trying to fit in. But Mike . . . well, he's my best friend. He makes me feel secure." And yet, he doesn't know everything about me. No one does. I close my eyes for a moment, feel a gentle breeze against my face.

"You're lucky," she says.

I don't say anything. Maybe I've said too much. I don't really believe in luck. I feel more blessed, like every good thing in my life is a gift from God. But it is all so undeserved. And that troubles me.

"You don't miss it here, do you?"

"No." And I know this much is true. "All this drama is too much for me. I like my quiet life. And it is quiet for the most part." I'm not sure who I'm more upset at—Mother or Dad. "We can see the ocean from our house in La Jolla. You should visit sometime. Some days it's calm and peaceful. But I can detect ripples along the surface, so you know the potential for something powerful is there. And then the wind will churn up the waves. That's what it's like for me to come home."

Josie taps my leg with her toe. "Your mom, she's a ticket. But deep down, she really does care."

"What about your mom?" I ask, remembering the fights. More like brawls. "How is she?"

"I don't know."

"You don't keep up?"

"She knows where I am."

I reach out to Josie, then stop myself. She always hated sympathy or pity. "Where is she now?"

"Don't know, don't care."

I breathe in the warm, dry air. Is that the real reason Josie never left? Her mother knows where she is and can find her if she wants? Is she waiting for some sort of reconciliation? I know that if there is going to be a truce between my parents, then I am going to have to orchestrate it, because the battle lines have been drawn.

It's dark out here, nothing but a little moon glow. Scrub brush and old mesquite spring up from the hard-packed earth, like pom-poms dotting the ground. Makes me wonder how I sprang up out of my family.

I never wanted to be like Mother. She dominated Daddy. I always wanted Daddy to stand up to her, but he never would. Maybe this is his way of drawing the line, saying no more. But will Mother get the last word?

Mike is different from my father. He's strong but not domineering, yet I know his vulnerabilities. He's allowed me to glimpse his weaknesses, which I believe are strengths. They help him be the man he is.

"Whatcha thinking about?" Josie asks.

"How California and Texas are so different, but when you look up at the stars it's really the same."

"The shoes might be more expensive, but you can still step in—"

"There are no cow patties in La Jolla."

"I was going to say gum."

I laugh. "My husband and father are different too."
I don't voice the question reverberating in my head, pounding
in my heart: Am I different from my mother? Or am I just
like her? It's my deepest fear.

"Your dad's all right. Nice. He just needs to believe in
himself more."

"Hard when Mother's the way she is."

"True enough."

"What about you?" Who's special in her life? "Tell me
what you've been up to."

"You mean why I'm not married?"

"No." But yes. "Okay, why?"

"That seems to be what it all comes down to. Everyone
wants to know if I'm married, or if not, then why? Like that's
the only thing that matters."

"I just want to know about *you*."

"Nothing much happens here. I have a nothing job
down in Boerne. But I like this one. I like my boss. I'm the
office manager for an insurance salesman. I guess insurance is
important. We all gotta have it, don't we?"

"Sure."

"Just like we gotta have attorneys, the scourge of human
existence." She laughs.

I smile. I've heard all the lawyer jokes, usually from
Mike.

"Anyway, my boss is planted."

"Planted?"

"Married. Solidly."

"That's good." But what about Josie?

"Yeah, there's a lot of wanderers around. Those always
looking for something more, something exciting. But he's
solid. That's how come I left my last job."

"Because your boss wanted more than filing done?"

"Oh, we had an affair. But to end it, I had to leave." She sighs heavily. "Really screwed up my insurance for about three months."

"So are you seeing anyone now?" I hope it's not a married man again.

"Well, I was. He wanted more. I guess I can't figure out my type."

"What do you mean?"

"Well, a while back, I decided maybe a younger man was for me. They're less complicated. Less desperate. But they tend to buck. And I happened to pick the wrong one—a bit *too* young, if you know what I mean."

I'm afraid I do. Thankful for the covering of darkness to hide my wide eyes, I remain quiet, letting her fill the silence.

"Don't judge me, Suzanne. Don't you dare—"

"I'm not, Josie. I'm not. Really." I can't.

She shifts around on the hood of the car. I can't tell what she's doing, but the metal gives a blurping sound. "So then," she says, "I kinda liked this older man. I mean I've dated older men but not this old, not old enough to be my own daddy." She laughs again.

"What happened?"

"Maybe I'm just not the marrying kind."

"Why do you say that? I'm sure there's—"

"No, it's not that. Maybe I've been on the other end of marriage so often I don't believe in marriage anymore, that two people can stick together through thick and thin and make it work. I expect marriages to break apart like clay, crumbling after too many years."

Mike and I have been married almost twenty years now. We have a strong partnership. Only once did I fear for our marriage. But together we overcame the gulf that separated us. It's not like us to be separated by miles, and I miss him tonight. I look up at the vast stars and wish again that he were here with me.

I hope my parents can fix their marriage, but I realize I'm leaning more toward doubt.

"I've seen a lot of divorces too," I say. "Sometimes in La Jolla it seems like people change spouses as often as shoes." I fold my hand over my wedding ring, feel the cool diamond press into my flesh.

"So how have you made it work for so long?"

"I don't know. It takes work. It's not something I can do on my own. We work at it together. We both compromise." My answer is still unclear. I don't feel like an expert on marriage. In fact, I feel ill qualified to try to salvage my parents' marriage or offer advice to anyone on the subject.

"The guy I'm seeing now," she says almost hesitantly, "I've known him forever. We've never even had sex. Still, there's something there. Something."

"Something is a good start."

She laughs, then stops. She hugs her knees to her chest and sighs. "Yeah, I don't know. It's complicated."

"Maybe it's not so complicated," I say. "Maybe he'll be the one."

"Maybe we can figure out a way to get your folks back together."

"No small miracle required. I'm not even sure why my dad left. I'm not sure I want to know."

"Hmm." She slaps her bare feet together. "Seems to me the biggest obstacle is your mom. Forgiveness isn't her strong suit, is it?"

"Not exactly. But I'm not sure my dad wants to come back either. I haven't been able to reach him on his cell phone since I arrived. So I don't really know what's going on."

"Maybe your mom really did him in. Maybe the funeral isn't so fake."

I attempt a laugh. That's ridiculous. But then again, I saw my mother, saw the anger, the hurt. I can't imagine Mother doing anything that extreme. But then again, a fake funeral is pretty bizarre.

"Anything is possible, right?" She pushes against my arm, jostling me. I grab for the hood of the car. "Look at you! You went and married well."

I shift, and the hard metal beneath me pops and groans. "What did you think? That I'd end up in a trailer park somewhere?"

"I thought you'd marry Drew."

Her comment comes out of the dark and stuns me.

4

Drew

"Sheriff! You gotta see this!"

Drew looked up from the stack of paperwork on his desk. Before he could push back his chair, his deputy stumbled through the door. Sweat dotted his face. Draped over his shoulder was an enormous rattlesnake. Drew first thought, *Snake!* Second, *It's dead.*

"Lookie here." Deputy Finney's round face split into a grin. He flopped the heavy reptilian body onto the desk. He was out of breath, huffing and puffing as if he had run a marathon. "Don't worry. It's dead."

"I see that. Why'd you bring it here?"

"Got a call from Red Burnett. He wanted someone to see what a confounded thing this ol' snake was doing. Looked like it was trying its best to get to higher ground. Kept trying to creep up the wall on the backside of his house. Got caught in the wires of his air conditioner. Strangest sight you ever did see. Have you ever seen a snake this big?"

"Can't say I have." Didn't care about seeing this one. It was as big around as a pipe used by the drilling companies where Drew worked as a teenager during summer breaks. "How'd you kill it?"

"Bashed in its head." A drop of blood landed on the floor, the snake's head, as big as Drew's fist, dangled above it. "Thought I'd skin it and sell it over at the Luckenbach store."

"A snake like that could kill an elephant," Drew said more to himself than the crowd of anxious faces that had appeared at his open office door.

Drew often worried that if a real emergency ever happened in Gillespie County, Deputy Finney, better known as Flipper, would keel over from a heart attack with his cheeseburger belly. But he'd been a staple in Luckenbach for so long and was fairly reliable now that he'd sobered up. There were other deputies, but Flipper seemed to be Drew's right-hand man. Besides, young men weren't lining up to be a deputy in these parts. Austin and San Antonio were where the real action was.

The snake twitched.

Someone at the door gasped.

"Everybody out," Drew said, not wanting a wounded snake on the loose in the outer office. One of his deputies pulled the door shut.

Flipper, his eyes as big around as pie plates, yanked out his revolver.

"Wait!" Drew held out a hand then edged out of the line of his deputy's fire. "Don't—"

A blast echoed in the small room, made Drew's ears ring, and left a ragged hole in the side of his desk. Bits of paper spiraled through the air like confetti. Unharmed but now fully awake, the snake slithered off the desk onto the tile floor.

"You okay, Sheriff?" someone asked from the other side of the office door.

"Fine." Drew clenched his teeth in irritation. He kept his eye on the snake, which twitched its tail, making that hideous sound God intended to grab a man's full attention. Drew was all for listening to admonitions God might put in his path. He had discovered over the years that warnings came in all shapes and sizes. Sometimes it was the tingle that went up his spine when he approached a darkened building. Sometimes it was something the preacher said when Drew managed to make it to church on Sunday mornings. Sometimes it was just learning from his own foolish mistakes. In any case, Drew tried to pay attention. The snake certainly had his immediate attention. It faced the window, hissing at the last rays of light seeping through the blinds.

The door, Drew noticed, had inched back open. Cops and those in law enforcement were a curious lot. Someone coughed. Someone else offered to shoot it.

"Everything is under control. Y'all get on back now." Irritated at the paperwork (which would take days to redo) now scattered about his office, Drew skirted the desk, all the while keeping his eyes on the aggravated reptile.

"Sorry, Sheriff," Flipper took a step backward, his gun hand quivering. "Now it looks mad."

"Wouldn't you be?" Drew glanced at the wood splinters littering the floor around his desk. He hoped to avoid any further mess. A shot-up window would only cost the taxpayers. He looked about for a metal trash can, but this was the biggest snake he'd ever seen; no container at hand would hold it for long. He certainly didn't want it free to roam his office while he waited on some zoologist to come tranquilize it. Nope, Drew figured, there was only one solution to this problem.

"Looks like you gave it a concussion, Flipper. It seems confused."

"You mean, it's been alive this whole time?"

"Well, it wasn't resurrected."

Laughter at the door reminded Drew that an audience of office personnel and deputies were watching. His office was situated toward the back of the county building, away from traffic. "You still have that hoe in the back of your truck?"

"Maybe. Whatcha wanna it for?"

"Bustin' its head would do less damage to my office than shooting it."

"Gettin' that close might be dangerous."

"Using this bad boy for target practice isn't particularly safe either." For precaution, Drew pulled his own Glock and clicked off the safety. "Good thing it didn't wake up when you were driving here."

"I should have let Burnett skin it first. Maybe we should call a professional." Flipper's hand shook so hard his gun wobbled. "We could get one of them snake wranglers from the Austin Zoo to come out here."

"You are a professional," Drew reminded him.

"Did you hear the news, Sheriff?" A deputy stepped one foot inside the office door, caught a glimpse of the snake and backed up again. "Zoo over there had a giraffe get loose."

"What is it with the animals tonight?"

"You reckon somethin' awful's about to happen?" Flipper's jowls sagged.

"Nothin' ever happens here," the deputy at the door said.

"How 'bout Old Floyd?" Flipper glanced at Drew, then back at the snake. He quivered all over, like he was ready xto run out the door at the slightest signal. "He might come and fetch this crazy fellow. He's good at catchin' wild dogs and critters that get into houses."

"Floyd might get himself bit. I can't take that risk."

"I didn't mean to blow a hole in your desk, Sheriff."

"It's okay, Flipper."

He rubbed his temple. "I weren't thinking clearly."

"You're still upset over Archie's death."

"Yeah, yeah." Flipper backed away from the snake, which settled into a protective coil near the windowsill.

Drew pulled Flipper back another step or two. There was no telling this snake's strike zone.

"Mrs. Davidson called earlier," Flipper said. "Said Archie's body will be here Monday. Some funeral home from Austin is delivering him to the dance hall over at Luckenbach."

Drew nodded, keeping his eye trained on the tense snake. Archie Davidson had been a good man. Kind, soft-spoken. Always drove the speed limit. Always kept up his permits and such. Never one to complain or make trouble. He often said, "I'm praying for you, Sheriff. Praying for your safety." Nice to know someone cared and understood that even in a nothing-much-happening county, things could happen on this job. Accidents. Crazy things like a deputy nearly shooting his boss rather than a snake.

"You should be there. He was your best friend."

Flipper nodded. "And you should know," Flipper looked at Drew, just a quick glance, then back to the snake, "Archie's daughter, Suzannah Lee, is back in town."

The snake struck the windowsill, jabbed its fangs into the wood.

Drew squeezed the trigger.

5

Suzanne

Eventually our conversation plays out. Josie falls asleep, and night settles around us, complete with the assorted wildlife noises that always seem louder in the dark. I'm not in a hurry to get back to Mother's, so I stretch out on the Camaro's hood, enjoying the peace and tranquility of being out in the open with no expectations, no one needing my attention. Crickets chirp. Frogs croak. With my eyes closed, I drift back to simpler days when I was young and my only worry was getting home by curfew.

Mother had hated Drew. Which, of course, only made me love him more. Drew was the bad boy of Gillespie County. But I knew he wasn't bad; he was misunderstood. We didn't have a lot in common, yet there was a fierce attraction. He told me once, "You're like an angel." But my thoughts and desires toward him weren't exactly angelic.

Dating Drew was the only time I questioned going off to college. Being with him was the first time I had ever felt safe and protected, which is odd when I consider it now, because dating him only caused more problems at home and, in the end, left me far more vulnerable and insecure. Even now the remnants of our relationship remain like frayed strings running through my life.

"What are you going to do?" I asked Drew once when we were parked in his father's diesel truck.

"About?"

"When I leave for school."

I was hoping he'd say, "Come after you." Or maybe, "Don't go. Don't leave me." The summer days were dwindling. Soon I'd be leaving home. Not just leaving Luckenbach, but Texas too.

Drew hooked an arm around my shoulders. "I'm going to hit the road. Go anywhere. Do anything."

His answer didn't surprise me, but hope that we had any future began to shrink inside. "Yeah," I said as casually as I could. "And go where?"

"Wherever I want. I would have left already. But you were here."

"So will you come visit me in California?"

"Maybe."

It was enough to keep that light flickering.

I don't think it ever completely went out.

Where is he now? What did he end up doing? Does Drew still roam the roadways searching for whatever it was he needed? In many ways he was just a hurting young man with unanswered questions and more than his share of anger.

A loud rumbling jostles me from my reverie, as if the earth has been suddenly turned half a notch. The car beneath me shifts precariously. My hand slams down on the hood in a pathetic attempt to grasp something solid.

My insides sway like liquid sloshing in an unopened jar. It's the same feeling I get when sailing on the ocean. Trouble is, I'm in Texas, not on the open water. The noise subsides as quickly as it started, leaving an eerie silence. The wildlife noises have stopped. Somewhere in the dark, pebbles slide and clatter against rock.

Blinking against the darkness, I cling to the hood of the car, my feet braced on the warm metal. I feel as if I've opened a door from inside a closet and found it equally dark outside. Did I fall asleep? Have a dream? I remember being in a class at UCLA, my eyes heavy and tired from a late night date with Mike, and nodding off, jerking awake. It's almost the same feeling now. Almost but not quite. My hip has fallen asleep, so I shift my weight. The hood of the car burps.

"Josie?" I whisper. I touch the spot next to me where she used to be, before I fell asleep. I sit up, panicked. "Josie!"

I hear shuffling nearby, then a quick, sharp curse.

I press my hands flat against the hood, ready to push myself off at a moment's notice, but I remember the broken glass and wiggle my bare toes. Where are my shoes?

"Josie?"

"Yeah, yeah, I'm comin'."

"What are you doing?" I feel around for my shoes, find them up by the windshield wipers, then slide them back on my feet. Slowly working my way down the hood of the car, I set my soles on solid ground.

A dark shadow moves toward me, and I recognize her shape.

"I had to use the facilities," she says.

There are no facilities nearby, but I don't ask for details. I notice she's limping.

"Did you hurt yourself?"

"I squatted too close to a prickly bush. Fell on it." She braces a hand against the car.

"Sure it wasn't a rattlesnake?"

"I didn't have *that* much to drink. But I did feel wobbly back there."

I feel suddenly queasy myself, but the feeling passes. Nervous laughter bubbles up inside me, and I try to catch it before it escapes. Too late. "Can I do something to help?"

"Thanks for the sympathy."

"I'm sorry. What can I do? Really."

"Come on, I'll take you to your mom's."

I nod, then realize she can't see me. "Okay."

We both go to the passenger's side of the Camaro. Josie says, "You're going to have to drive."

"What? Why?"

"Have you ever sat on a prickly pear? It ain't fun."

Again laughter escapes my compressed lips. "Sorry. Okay, I'll drive."

I settle behind the wheel. She slides the key in the ignition and turns it. The headlights slash through the darkness, illuminating cacti and brambles. She leans back, her backside inches from the plastic cushion, her arm snaking across the back of the seat. Then she grins. "Feels like old times, doesn't it?"

"In a way." But not really. I'm not the same girl I was at seventeen. I'm not as naive. I'm not as foolish either. Or so I hope.

"Okay," she cranks the music, "let's go. I've gotta get home."

Carefully I put the car in gear then search the dashboard for the headlight switch. Even the bright beams are not as illuminating as I would like. I inch the car forward. "Which way?"

She jabs her thumb toward the trunk. "You can turn around back there."

Slowly, methodically, I shift from Drive to Reverse. Now I know what my son feels like driving with me in the passenger seat. Josie curses my overly cautious approach to driving this unfamiliar car in unfamiliar surroundings. When I brake too hard, her head hits the top and her bottom bounces off the seat. She hisses and winces.

"I'm sorry."

"Go faster."

"But I can't see. What if—"

"My butt is on fire!"

"Okay, okay." I push the gas too hard, and we jolt forward. "Sorry. Should I take you to the hospital?"

"I just need some Benadryl cream or something. I've got stuff at home."

"Has this happened before?" A scrub brush appears suddenly in front of the Camaro. I swerve. The scrappy branches graze the bumper.

"Once or twice. I lost my balance back there."

"Did you feel it too? Like the earth moved. What was it?"

"You drank too much. Just drive."

"But I didn't have any—"

Cranking the music louder, she starts singing some rap song. It's as if I'm riding in the car with my son, not my best friend from high school. But I notice Josie knows all the words.

With the windows rolled down, the warm summer air rushes past me, tosses my hair this way and that. I clench the steering wheel hard, strain my eyes to see a clear path. "You sure you know how to get back?" I ask.

"You can't go wrong out here. Just drive east until you hit the highway. It's just up ahead." She thrusts her foot over to my side of the car and presses down on mine. The Camaro responds, kicking up dirt and pebbles behind us.

"Josie! This isn't safe. Stop—"

"I'm dying here!"

"But—" A gaping hole in the ground rushes up to meet us.

The Camaro nosedives. I'm thrown back and forward in rapid succession. For a moment, I sit stunned. The motor misses and dies in the dust, the rap music with it. Gingerly, I rub my neck, which feels as if it's been jerked out of place. "Josie?"

"Yeah?" she moans.

I lean my head against the steering wheel and grasp it like a lifesaver. "You okay?"

"I've been better."

Sinking back into the cracked vinyl seating, I turn the key and try the ignition, but nothing happens. I open my door just to know I can.

Josie touches her forehead. "Where on earth did that come from?" She slowly moves her leg back to her own side of the car, wincing as she does. "You okay?"

"I think so." Looking back over my shoulder, I can look out the rear window straight up at the little dipper. "Did we go the wrong way?"

"No," she says with enough rancor to be a teenager.

"Well, how come we didn't see that ditch when we drove in?"

"I don't know." She curses under her breath. Reaching over, she opens her own door and hobbles out.

I put my foot outside the car. My foot waggles in the open space, my toes searching for solid ground. I stretch my leg out further. My toe bumps rock. I slide it forward, hanging onto the door, until I'm certain my footing is on solid ground. Then I ease out of the car, jumping a short way to the ground. "Josie, this is very odd. I'm thinking—"

"Well, don't. Do you have a cell phone?"

"Of course." I reach back into the car and retrieve my purse. My cell phone is in its little pocket. It feels like forever before it bleeps on, the green light looking like a phosphorescent gemstone. "It's searching for—"

"A tower. Good luck." She looks around, rubs her backside and hisses through her teeth.

"Here." I step up into the car, hanging onto the door and pushing myself up another foot. The car sways slightly beneath me. I hear the crunch of rock. How deep does this ditch go? "This is going to work." The empty words don't reassure me. There's no change in the phone, so I stretch, reaching higher. "If I could just get . . ."

"Stand on the roof."

It's not my first choice, but those seem limited. I hand the phone down to her, while I scramble and pull myself up onto the roof of the Camaro. The car shifts again, and I grab hold.

"You're okay," Josie hands the phone up to me. "The car isn't going anywhere. It's just a bit unstable."

Like my family. Like my life.

"That makes me feel so much better."

Actually it feels like the time I tried to learn to surf, except then Mike was there helping me. I wish he were here now. I wobble and bobble like I'm clinging to a surfboard, not the hood of a car that's tilted at an odd angle. "Okay, let's give this a try."

Slowly I get my feet under me and stand up in darkness. I feel like Rose in the movie *Titanic*, standing on the prow of the ship, feeling the wind in my hair. Just before the Titanic sinks and kills her greatest love. I swallow hard. "I'm not getting a signal."

"Raise your arm."

I watch my cell as I lift an arm.

"Not that one!"

Embarrassed, I switch arms. "You're not going to tell me to rub my tummy and pat my head at the same time, are you?"

She laughs then rubs at her backside. "Just hurry."

Amazingly the cell phone locks onto a signal. "Yes!" But who do I call? Mike's too far away to help. "Who do you want me to call? My mother?" How am I going to explain this?

"I know a guy who has a tow truck. 8-0-6—"

I lose the signal. "Wait."

I readjust my arm, aiming it toward the crescent moon. If I have to locate the North Star, we're in serious trouble. Slowly, I punch in the numbers Josie tells me. Then I pause at a strange whining sound. "Do you hear that? You think it could be a coyote?"

I imagine wild animals circling the car. Far ahead of me two lights bounce like balls. Josie turns in the direction I'm facing.

"Did you call 9-1-1?" she asks.

"No. I was—"

A siren shrieks, drowning my voice. A bright light hits me like a spotlight. The police car, which is actually a large SUV, zooms toward us, jouncing over the rocky terrain, careless of shrubs and brambles. It pulls to a stop in front of us, a few feet away from the jagged crack. Its headlights make me feel like I'm standing naked on a stage. Slowly I draw my outstretched arm downward. The searchlight and annoying, throbbing blue lights give a clearer view of the ground around us. Not far from where I hopped out of the car is a crevice that looks like it goes a long way down. Now I can see a jagged opening in the earth stretched outward in both directions, half swallowing Josie's car. The Camaro shifts beneath me.

A car door slams, making my head jerk toward the flashing lights. I squint against the brightness.

"What's going on here?" a deep baritone asks.

"We had a wreck, Sheriff," Josie says.

"Uh-huh. I see that." He steps closer to the ravine that I've driven Josie's car into. "Were you driving, Josie?"

"Sure thing," she lies as easily as breathing.

"Who are you?" he asks.

"You remember Suzanne, don't you?" Josie says.

"Suzannah?"

"Yes, sir," I say, remembering the sheriff from when I was a kid. Sheriff Cramer Woods had a gut like a pot-bellied stove. He could shoot one look in my direction and make me feel guilty for being honest. He steps over to the side of the car, shines the beam of his light down in the crack. "This goes down a ways. You girls are lucky. You better come down from there. It's not safe."

"Yes, sir. Okay." I drop to my hands and knees, but I'm unsure how to get to the ground. Slowly I swing my legs around, sit on the roof of the Camaro, and dangle my feet off the side. "I don't know about this."

"Here." The sheriff moves toward me, grabs my hands, and yanks me off the car. The metal scrapes my backside as I fall full against him. He grunts. He must've been on Weight Watchers for the past few years because he doesn't have a pot belly anymore. Then I look up.

It's not Sheriff Woods.

The face has a harder edge, like his lean torso. All of a sudden, like the ground rushing up to meet me, my secrets slam into me.

"Hello, Suzie Q," Drew says, his mouth quirking in that too-familiar grin.

If he calls me Suzannah Banana, I'll hit him. I don't care if he is a cop. How did that happen anyway? He was always the bad boy, the one girls loved and mothers hated. Especially my mother.

"You okay?" he asks, his hand firm on my elbow.

I cough and pull away, readjust my slacks and shirt. I feel naked and exposed, scared and unsure. Not to mention dusty. "Sure. Yes." I cross my arms over my stomach as if a chill has taken hold of me. But this chill comes from within. "Thanks."

"You remember Drew, don't you, Suzie Q?" Josie's tone is a mixture of humor and some element I don't recognize.

"How could I forget?"

"Not quite the girl you used to be, are you?" His voice is warmer than the night air.

"Things change. So do people." I stare at the badge on his chest.

He laughs. "How've you been?"

"Good." I stare at the wide brim of his hat. Who would have ever guessed Drew Waring would be wearing a Stetson? I couldn't even imagine him living in Gillespie County. The last time I'd seen him, he'd been riding a motorcycle through Southern California. And I didn't want to think about that time. I had prayed to forget. "And you?"

"No complaints."

"You're a sheriff?"

"Surprising, huh?"

I'm about as stunned as when I ran Josie's Camaro into the ditch. "Definitely."

"The guy voted most likely to get arrested in high school." Josie hobbles forward, puts a hand on Drew's shoulder.

He rubs his jaw and glances down at the ground before looking me square in the eye. "Sorry about your Dad, Suz. He was a good man."

A hefty dose of guilt pumps through me. I should admit the truth. But how? Would it somehow get Mother in trouble? Could she get arrested? And am I now a co-conspirator?

"Oh, uh . . ." I glance at Josie, wondering if she'll spill the ugly details like a kid accidentally dumping over a jar of tacks, but she only shrugs. "Thanks," I add.

"So you're here for the funeral?" His question makes the guilt I feel sharper, like a needle stabbing my spine. Before I can answer he adds, "Or are you staying longer?"

"No, that will about do it for me."

He looks at me sharply. "Have you two been drinking?"

"Who doesn't out here, sheriff?" Josie says. "Don't tell me you never—"

"Come on, I'll give you a lift home. We'll get your car hauled out of there tomorrow. Maybe."

"Maybe?" Josie protests. "What do you mean by that?"

"I'm not sure," he says. "Might be unstable around here."

I certainly feel unstable.

"What is this anyway?" Josie asks. "I've never seen it before."

"I don't know. I got a call about some kind of explosion. A loud noise. A shaking. Not to mention animals going berserk."

"Shaking? Like an earthquake?" Josie's eyes widen.

"From the looks of it, seems Gillespie County has split wide open." He stands at the crevice and shines his flashlight in both directions. "Look, it goes on some ways."

"An earthquake in Texas?" Josie wheels on me. "Did you bring this all the way from California?"

Displaced guilt, something I've always struggled with, settles on my shoulders. There are many things in my past I'm not proud of, but standing beside Drew I feel guilt push up through my insides like boiling magma.

6

Trapped with my riotous thoughts, I settle into the back-seat of the sheriff's SUV. It's like being in a small cage, or maybe a dog kennel. I have to shift sideways, press my knees against the edge of the seat in order to fit. A metal contraption separates the front and back seat, a precaution against unruly criminals, another barrier between me and my past. I want to escape but am trapped in more ways than one.

Along the dashboard a radio squawks. A computer screen glows in the darkness. There's other equipment I'm not accustomed to seeing in any car. Josie claims the front seat beside Drew and talks about nothing and everything. I feel as if I've entered "The Twilight Zone" on my parents' old Zenith television—black and white and a bit fuzzy around the edges. No snow though.

Josie touches Drew's shoulder, his arm. She seems too comfortable with him. Of course, they're old friends. But are they, or have they been, more than friends? It's actually none of my business, but the question stirs something prickly inside me, and I shift in my seat, banging my knee on the metal grid. I blame the cage, but my pain is deeper than a superficial bruise.

"You okay?" Drew watches me through the rearview mirror.

"Fine." I pretend not to notice, turn my head, look out the side window to the dark-as-only-the-countryside-can-get night.

Is he wondering if I've changed, if I remember? Out of the corner of my eye, I can see the back of his neck, his hairline, the slight curl at his nape that hints of wildness, defying the straight, starched lines of his uniform. Everything else may look the part of authority, but I know Drew's past. I know him.

Irritated at myself, I cut my gaze to the right (my eyes are about the only part of my body I'm able to move in this cramped space) and stare through the windshield streaked with bug guts and remember the destruction Drew wreaked on my life. Which I allowed.

I used to think of darkness as simply a black canvas, but I watch the desert shadows and shapes shift and deepen as we zip past. The headlights arc outward and illuminate the edges of the road that separate civilization from wasteland. It occurs to me that I'm now walking a narrow path and the slightest bobble or wrong step could send me cartwheeling into rocky, treacherous territory.

Drew Waring was that rocky overhang in my past. He almost caused my complete downfall. Perhaps he still is my weakness, an unstable precipice. Right now it feels as if I'm only hanging onto my life by my fingernails.

I remember sitting on the edge of my bed a lifetime ago. I was younger, foolish, and vulnerable. I simply sat, unable to move or think or function. I had forgotten why I'd come into the bedroom. It didn't matter. The sight of the empty bed, the spread crumpled on the end, the sheets in disarray. My energy dragged like the blanket off the side and along the floor. I hadn't touched the bed in days, not to make it, not to sleep. I hadn't crawled into it at night, sleeping instead on the couch in the den or the chair in the corner. Most of the time I couldn't sleep. Sometimes I wandered aimlessly around the apartment, lost, confused, weeping one minute, fuming the next over Mike's angry, irrational departure a few days earlier.

His face had been as hard and cold as the wrought-iron headboard. I couldn't erase the image from my mind. I couldn't escape the words chasing me.

I had challenged him. "You don't want a baby!"

"I don't want this!" He spit out a curse word that I'd never heard him use before. Then he grabbed his suitcase, already packed for a business trip to Sacramento, and left. Left.

Over the next few days I wept more tears than I could have ever fathomed. My eyes turned puffy and red. My heart felt swollen and bruised. I couldn't tell anyone. What would I have said? How could I admit that my marriage had crumbled? How could I admit my own guilt? I nursed my wounds in isolation.

I blamed myself. After all, I nagged Mike. I had wanted a baby so badly that I'd lost perspective. I had sacrificed our relationship on the altar of fertility. Forlorn over what I had lost, I wept. A dark blob of anger pulsed inside me like a ravenous creature.

Then the phone rang, jarring me out of my black thoughts. Gasping a prayer, I ran for the phone, hoping it was Mike finally calling. I'd played out many scenarios in my mind, wondering what he was doing, where he was staying. I knew he had flown to Sacramento for a couple of days' work. But when he should have returned, he didn't. So was he staying at the office? At a friend's? In a motel? Had he found someone else? Someone who wouldn't nag, who wouldn't tell him when her eggs were on the move? All the uncertainties and fears fed that angry creature lurking deep inside of me.

"Hello?"

"Suz?" The voice oozed like molasses. I knew that voice. Knew how he could soothe and cajole. Knew how he could tease and torment. Knew how he could reassure and make me laugh. And I desperately needed to feel anything but what I was feeling at the moment.

"Yes." It was a silly response. Coy. And yet brazen at the same time. I should have hung up. Okay, I should have said politely, "How are you, Drew? That's nice. I'm sorry, but I'm married." It would have ended everything and anything right then.

But I didn't.

Little decisions that seemed innocuous gathered one upon another like snowflakes, numbing me to the pain and blinding me to the potential consequences. I knew the danger, recognized the rationalizations for what they were. I made excuses. I needed a friend. God only knew what Mike was doing! Didn't I deserve a break from the stress, the grief, the strain? Wouldn't an old friend be helpful? But honestly, I knew what my intentions were.

"Drew? How are you?"

"Missing you. It's been a while, Suz."

"It has. Are you in Luckenbach or Gillespie—?"

"No, actually, I'm here in California."

"Is that a fact?"

I knew. I knew. I knew. I took that tiny side step that I've regretted ever since. Because in Drew's rearview mirror I see the same eyes I've looked at every day for the last fifteen years in the face of my son.

"WHAT EXACTLY DID you two experience out there tonight?" Drew asks.

"Like sitting on a cactus?" Josie's tone is devoid of humor.

"Like taking a dive into a ditch. A ditch I don't remember seeing on the way out there," I add, more to myself than anyone in the sheriff's SUV.

"Like a shaking or loud rumbling noise," he clarifies.

"Maybe that's what made me fall," Josie says.

"That or too much beer." Drew sniffs in her direction.

Josie slaps him on the shoulder.

"I should run you in for a DUI."

"I wasn't driving."

Drew's gaze shifts, meets mine in the rearview mirror. Tension tightens my belly. Squiggly-worm sensations wriggle across the tops of my nerve endings.

"That's not what you told me earlier."

"Put the sirens on and drive faster." Josie struggles to hold her backside off the seat.

"You want me to take you to the hospital? Say the word."

"No."

"Then I'm not breaking the speed limit."

"Not even for an old friend?"

Once again Drew's gaze shifts to the rearview mirror and mine darts away, chased by memories I don't want to face.

"Something happened out there tonight," he says. "I don't know what. But that ditch, or crack or whatever, wasn't there yesterday. And the sound of Josie backing into a cactus didn't make folks all over the county call my office in the middle of the night."

I don't want to think about it. I simply want to go home and forget trying to save my parents' marriage. I want to race back to California and reassure myself that my marriage is safe and secure.

I FEEL LIKE I'M seventeen and being escorted home by the police. It happened. Once. Just as she did then, Mother stands at the front door of her house now, pulling the sash of her robe tighter, cinching her consternation temporarily, while her frown deepens with disapproval. I know exactly what she was doing before we arrived—pacing the den, wondering where I was, conjuring up ideas and scenarios that are farfetched but occasionally hold an ounce of truth. She's been waiting for me. As she did every time I left the house as a teenager. It's not because she didn't trust my friends or boyfriends. She didn't trust me.

Two seconds before Drew comes to a complete stop in front of my parents' house, Josie throws open the door and leaps out. Drew brakes hard, throwing me forward. My hand slams against the metal cage, rattling it and my nerves. Without a backward glance, Josie barrels up the steps, brushing against my mother, and racing into the house, leaving the front door open wide behind her just as she did the car door.

"What in the world?" Mother stares after her, jaw agape. Her voice carries through the darkness. "Where have you two been? What have you been doing?"

"That girl is going to get herself in trouble some day that I can't get her out of," Drew says.

"Do you make it a habit of rescuing her?" I ask.

"Anybody who needs it." He throws the gear shift into park.

I grab the door handle but have to wait for him to unlock it. When he does, I have one foot on solid ground before I remember to say, "Thanks, Drew, uh, Sheriff."

He nods then stops me with, "Suzanne?"

I hesitate, notice he doesn't call me Suz, and look at his profile through the glass window.

"Tell Josie I'll wait out here for her and take her home when she's ready."

"All right." I don't invite him in. He doesn't seem to expect an invitation. His radio crackles and someone announces that an eighteen-wheeler hit a cow on 290.

On my way up the steps, I say, "Mother, do you have any allergy medicine or cream?"

"Well," she glances at the sheriff's car then enters her house, catching the storm door behind her, "you might look in the medicine cabinet. Your father kept some for bug bites. But he might have taken—" She stops herself. "He might have run out."

My parents' bathroom is blue and peach and smells like eucalyptus leaves. I search the medicine cabinet, catch a glimpse of myself in the mirror, the tautness around my eyes. Dad's toothbrush and toothpaste lay beside his sink. Did he forget them? Or did he buy replacements at Wal-Mart in Fredericksburg? Or does he carry a different one in his constantly packed suitcase that he uses on his weekly business trips? Finally I find a small tube of allergy-relief cream in the drawer along with tweezers and take them to the guest bathroom. Winces and groans drift from beneath the doorway. I knock twice.

"What?" Josie's irritation and pain sharpen her tone.

"Try this."

The door opens a smidgen, and I hand Josie the tube of cream and tweezers.

"Can I get you anything else?"

"No." She hisses through her teeth and slams the door. A second later comes, "Suz?"

"Yeah?"

"Thanks."

"You're welcome." I place my hand along the wooded frame of the door. The paint is smooth and cool along my palm. "The sheriff—" I stop myself, admitting only to myself that his title sounds odd in my ears, but I don't switch to his name; I prefer the distance his title affords. "He, uh, said he'd wait for you outside. Whenever you're ready."

There are a million questions I'd like to ask her about his simple readiness to help her, but I refrain. Instead, I turn toward the den and find my mother glaring at me, her mouth screwed up in a tiny knot.

I remind myself that I'm not seventeen anymore. I'm a grown-up. I don't owe her any explanations. But I know an apology will go a long way toward mending this broken fence. I should have called her to let her know I was okay and not to worry. At least my willingness to apologize tells me I don't harbor any latent teenage rebellion. "I'm sorry about all of this, Mother."

"What is going on here?" Her lips are pursed in that unforgiving way. Her anger points straight at me.

"Josie sat on a prickly pear. She'll be okay." But I know that's not Mother's concern. And I'm frankly not so confident about what will happen to Josie's car.

Ten minutes later the clock ticks on the mantel, making the only noise in the house. Mother watches through the curtains as the sheriff's car pulls away.

"It's late." Way beyond my bedtime, even Pacific Coast time. "I'm sorry if we woke you, Mother. We should get—"

"Woke me?" She jerks the curtain closed, makes the two seams line up. "I must have known you were in trouble because I woke up suddenly and realized you hadn't come home. Hadn't come home. Do you know what fear that strikes in the heart of a mother?"

"Yes, I do." Maybe the shaking sensation woke her. I prefer to think of it that way rather than some psychic connection we share. "I'm sorry, Mother. I didn't mean to worry you. But I am an adult."

"Then act like one. What were you thinking?"

"Mother, Josie and I were talking. Catching up. It's been a long time since I've seen my friends. And it got late."

"But Drew Waring, of all people. I wouldn't have thought—"

"What?" My defenses suddenly stick out like a porcupine's.

"Nothing. Nothing." She walks into the kitchen and puts on a pot of coffee. "It's not my nevermind. You're a grown woman. So you say. You know what you're doing. So you say." In other words, I don't. "You know what you're risking."

I rub my forehead as if that small action could expunge the headache carving its way into my skull. I don't need a lecture on my wedding vows right now, especially from a woman who's "killed" off her own husband out of spite. All the sympathy I felt for her earlier seems to have played out.

"Let's go to bed, Mother." My eyeballs feel like they've been scraped dry. "It's late."

"It's so late, it's early," she says. "And Mike will be here soon."

"What?" I turn and look at her. Confusion gives way to relief. "Mike? Did he call?"

"Well, if you'd been here, then you would have been able to talk to him."

She can't make me feel guilty for something I didn't do. I have enough guilt in my life and don't need to borrow extra.

Her hand flutters down the lining of her silk robe. "But I spoke to him." Ever the martyr. "He tried to reach you on your cell phone but couldn't. He was worried about your last phone call. I told him I was worried about you too. Disappearing the way you did without a how-do-you-do." She purses her lips, and I know what she's implying. "He took the red-eye."

Something twists inside me. Guilt? Fear? All silly emotions. I didn't do anything wrong tonight. No matter what Mother believes.

"He said he had to fly to Houston first, or maybe Dallas. I can't remember now. He'll be here first thing this morning. Probably in the next hour."

My hand trembles, an echo of what's going on in my heart. I touch the nearest table to steady myself. Relief injects a healthy dose of reality into my system. I'm glad Mike is coming. He will quell Mother's insinuations that I'm after Drew. He can talk candidly to Mother, and he'll confront her on all this funeral nonsense. Then we can go home. Maybe even leave on Monday as I'd originally hoped. "Does he need me to pick him up at the airport?"

"Mike said he'd rent a car. He wanted us to know, so he wouldn't scare us coming in so early. Very considerate of him, don't you think?" Her sharpened point aims right for my heart. "Your father wouldn't have bothered." She readjusts a vase, squaring it with the edge of the table. I notice she already speaks of him in the past tense. "And I bet Drew Waring wouldn't bother either." That was a quick, right hook. But I don't dodge the blow. I take it, absorb the ricocheting effect within my body. "But then I guess Mike didn't know he might beat his own wife home. Or is this how you behave in California?"

I'm not getting sucked into this argument. I turn on my heel and head for the kitchen. I rummage around in drawers and cabinets, having long ago forgotten where she keeps the dry goods, hand towels, and knives.

"What are you looking for? Not the phone book?"

"Why would I want a phone book?"

"For Drew's number. Or did he give it to you? It's probably unlisted. But you can always reach him at the station, I suppose."

I look at my Mother's spotless linoleum and consider spitting on it.

"Do you have pancake mix?"

"Well, I wouldn't keep it in a drawer. Top shelf in the pantry." She crosses her arms over her middle. She watches me, judges me, sizing me up and down. "Have you been smoking," her voice drops to a whisper, "dope? They do that over in Luckenbach all the time. I've never approved of it."

"Mother! Have you been watching too much Dr. Phil?"

"A woman is known by the friends she keeps."

"And you think Josie smokes weed?"

"I've heard things that would make the devil faint of heart."

"I doubt that."

"You still don't have better taste in friends, I see."

"Mother, please." How can walking into my childhood home turn back the years so easily, erasing the wrinkles and experience and transforming me into an adolescent again? As much as I wouldn't mind getting rid of the fine lines that have started to appear on my face, I'm not comfortable in the role of teen. I'm closer to menopause and those wacky hormonal surges than that of puberty.

"It's true," she says. "You never could see to the heart of those around you."

I grab the pancake mix off the shelf and scan the directions, the ingredients. Eggs. Water. Oil. "Maybe I see better than you think," I say.

"What do you mean by that?"

Plunking the package of pancake mix on the counter with a dull thud, I meet Mother's gaze. "No one is as perfect as you pretend."

"That's pretty obvious, I would think." She walks toward me and jabs me with a pointed finger in the middle of my chest. It feels like she's left an indentation.

The first time she did that to me was the night Drew and I were caught at Makeout Flats. I swore I would never do that to a child of mine. Anger boils up inside me.

"You just better stay away from Drew Waring. He may be the sheriff now, but he's still bad news. You can cover up a skunk's stripe, but that doesn't change the fact that he's still a skunk. And if you know what's good for your marriage—"

Laughter, caustic and spewing sarcasm, erupts out of me. "Mother, please don't lecture me on marriage when . . ." I locate my self-control and slam on the emergency brakes like a driver's ed teacher hoping to avoid a collision. Honor is harder to come by than I ever imagined.

"For your information, Miss Smarty Pants, what happened in my marriage is not my fault. It is your father's. If he'd heeded my warnings . . . but no, he thought he knew it all. Just like you. And—"

"Mother," I consider plugging my ears, but reverting back to a teenager is still better than going all the way back to elementary school, "I don't want to know—"

"Why our marriage lasted as long as it did is because of me. Or, believe me, it would have ended long before you were born."

"What do you mean by that?"

The line of her lips tightens. She jerks open the refrigerator and grabs the eggs and milk. "Does Mike like bacon?"

I watch my mother for a moment but know the "discussion" (as she would call it) is closed. Holding a cold, brown egg in my hand, I smack it against the side of the bowl.

7

"He's here." I can see the bounce of headlights as the rental car pulls into the driveway. I flick water on the griddle, and the beads sizzle and pop.

"Perfect timing. Bacon's ready," Mother says.

I ladle pancake batter in lopsided circles onto the griddle. It's an old-fashioned cast-iron griddle that belonged to my grandmother. Someday it will be mine. Although I have my own electric one.

"I'll go greet him," Mother says and starts toward the front of the house.

But I step in front of her and hand her the spatula. "Watch these for me. Okay, Mother?"

"Of course, dear."

I ignore the smirk on her face. I walk through the dining area to the front door. Just as I turn the knob, the phone jangles. The sun is barely squinting over the horizon, and already it's a surreal day. Usually my mother's house is quiet, but today at 5:30 it's more like Grand Central Station than a farmhouse in the country.

Mike walks straight up the steps, his gaze steady, intense. He steps over the threshold and into my arms. He's warm and solid and smells of stale air and a hint of Armani.

I wrap my arms around his chilled, air-conditioned neck and kiss him. He tastes of coffee and spearmint gum. Smudges of gray darken his eyes. I pull him close again, my cheek against his shoulder. "Exhausted?"

"Not too bad. I dozed on the plane." But he holds on, doesn't let go. His arms are hard like bands of iron. I want to stay like this for as long as possible. Maybe then everything wrong will right itself. "We got lost, ended up passing the turnoff and had to turn around." He takes a slow, deep breath, his chest swelling and pressing against mine. He pulls away enough to look at me. "So, how are you?"

I hold onto him as my only real answer then say, "Welcome to the Twilight Zone."

He tilts my chin upward so I meet his gaze. But before he can ask any more questions, I hear the crunch of gravel behind Mike. His words sink into my awareness. *We.* Peeking around his shoulder, I feel a catch in my chest. Oliver, looking much worse for wear, his shoulders sagging, his LA Lakers cap pulled low, trudges up the steps behind Mike, mumbles something, then heads for the living room and collapses on the couch.

"Oliver?"

"Now, *he's* tired," Mike says with a rumbling chuckle, his embrace loosening. "He had some giggly teenage girl flirting with him all the way here."

Oliver doesn't acknowledge the comment. I notice how long limbed he looks sprawled on the couch, his feet hanging off one end and, on the other end, his head propped on the arm rest.

"I didn't know you were bringing Oliver." I modulate my voice to keep my rising panic suppressed.

"That okay?"

"Well, I just would have thought he might be happier at a friend's. You know, with Tyler or Jason or . . ."

"This is family. Family is important." It's Mike's usual stance where family is concerned. Even with my wacky family.

I nod, give an uncertain smile, then reassure myself that we'll all be back on a plane Monday morning. The funeral, I hope, canceled. "Of course."

With another kiss on Mike's roughened cheek, I walk over to the couch, pull off my son's cap, slip my fingers through those short curls that never would be controlled and plant a kiss on his forehead. "Shoes off the couch. Before your grandmother—"

Mother enters, carrying a spatula like a scepter. No idle threat. Oliver immediately slides his long legs to the left and dangles his big, overgrown Nikes off the edge of her uphol-stered couch.

"The weary traveler. Travelers!" She emphasizes the plural and looks from father to son. "Here at last." Mother's apron is smooth, her lipstick bright. It's then I realize how bedraggled I must look. I never went to bed, never checked my makeup after my own flight, or even had a chance to change clothes after climbing out of a ditch with Josie. But Mother, she's dressed and ready for the day before it's even begun.

Mike steps forward. "Hello, Betty."

She hugs him like a trophy, air kisses his cheek, and pats him on his broad shoulder like she's polishing him. Mother has always adored and pampered him. From the moment I brought him home for a college weekend, she always said I had made a fine catch, as if I'd been out fishing for bass one afternoon and caught a whopper. Maybe we should have had him stuffed and mounted on the wall, the label 'Attorney at Law' engraved beneath his wide mouth.

I know what it's like when she goes to the hairdresser's. "My son-in-law won another case." Mike has given her plenty of bragging rights. "Did I tell you about the house he had built? Right on the ocean. On a cliff, actually, overlooking the Pacific. Breathtaking. Do you know the price for prime real estate like that in California? Out of this world." Let the 'Joneses' try to keep up with us. Which is how Mother prefers it.

"And Oliver! I didn't know you were coming. This is delightful. A family reunion." She swats the toe of my son's tennis shoe with the spatula. "Get up, young man, and give your grandmother a hug and kiss."

With only a slight groan, he obeys. He's a good kid, smart, conscientious and only a tad undisciplined.

"Good gracious! You might as well be a Texas boy!" Mother has to reach up to hug him. "I won't even say how tall you are or how much you've grown. Then I'd sound old and pathetic. Why do old people always tell the younger crowd how they've grown, like they weren't supposed to? What do they think? You're going to shrink? Nonsense." She pats his back. "I fixed pancakes. My secret recipe. And I'm warming the maple syrup."

Oliver's eyes widen. With the look only a starved teenage boy can manage, he heads toward the kitchen, following the scent of fried bacon.

With a satisfied smile, Mother says, "Best way to get a boy's attention. You know, Mike, looks like Oliver is going to outgrow even you."

"Watch out, Betty, you're starting to sound like one of those old people you were talking about." Mike winks. Through the open doorway, the sun catches the glint in Mike's dark hair. He can still take my breath. Even when he's tired and exhausted.

Mother laughs. Only for Mike. She shoos him toward the kitchen. "Oh, you. Probably because I am." I'm more convinced than ever that Mike can talk Mother out of all this funeral nonsense. "Go on now," she says. "Breakfast is ready." Allowing Mike to go ahead of her into the kitchen, she holds me back with her pinching fingers at my elbow. She whispers, "That was Drew Waring on the phone."

I stop, take a step backward. "What did he want?"

"*You* apparently."

"You know, Mother, it could be about Josie. Did he want me to call him back?"

"I told him not to call here. *You* are a married woman."

"Mother!" Where was she sixteen years ago? I stare into her all-knowing gaze, that motherly look that always knew when I had taken an extra cookie or hadn't really made my bed when asked. A lurking doubt lingers in the corner of my mind. Does she know everything there is to know about Drew and me? "He knows I'm married. I know it. And he's not—"

"He's a man. Therefore his scruples are under suspicion."

This time my gaze rolls right up to the ceiling. "Mother, there is nothing going on between—"

"There better not be. I will not allow it. You have a good man in there. A child you're responsible for." She aims her pointer finger at my chest, and I take a step back so she can't jab me with it again. Her mouth thins into a colorless line. "This is no way to behave."

With that, she turns on her two-and-a-half-inch heel, and I notice then she's already wearing her pumps and hose. My mother is certifiable. Maybe Mike can get her committed while he's here.

BETWEEN "PASS THE BUTTER" and "Here, have another pancake," the conversation at breakfast lags. Mike and Oliver look exhausted. I feel it. Mother, on the other hand, looks refreshed and in her element as hostess.

"We have a busy day today," Mother says. She sips her coffee leisurely as if she doesn't have a care in the world. She's ready to play cruise director on the Pearl Harbor Memorial Highway, which is not far from her home. "There will be friends and neighbors dropping by, so we must—"

"That neighbor that swats flies?" Oliver perks up at the mention of Mother's most recent tribulation. Before this funeral episode started. She had called and complained about the neighbor across the road.

"I should think not," she cuts her pancake in a grid. "Mr. Ned Peavy knows he is not welcome over here."

"Who's Ned Peavy?" Mike asks. "An exterminator?"

"A nuisance," Mother says.

"The neighbor Grandma called the cops on for standing naked on his porch," Oliver explains like he's an editor for the *Luckenbach Moon*.

"The sheriff didn't even come out. Made me so—"

"Maybe we could get you some binoculars." Mike downs the rest of his coffee.

Mother's mouth opens, but no sound escapes. Her eyes round equally.

Mike's mouth lifts at the corner with mischief, and I know he's toying with her. "You'll be footloose and single soon, so maybe you'll be in the market for a new beau."

Mother snaps her mouth shut. "I should say not."

"It's good Mike's here, Mother," I interject, hoping to steer the conversation in the direction that will most quickly get us heading back to the airport. "He can advise you."

"On what?"

"Any criminal indictments."

"Breaking the law? Mr. Peavy is the one breaking the law. Indecent exposure, *that's* breaking the law."

Mike glances at me then addresses Mother in his calm mediator voice. "I think Suzanne meant you."

"Me? What on earth do you mean? I haven't broken any law."

"What about declaring Archie dead?" He lifts the linen napkin and wipes his mouth, refolds it carefully before placing it back on his lap. It's all a play to look nonchalant, non-threatening. "Have you filed any insurance claims?" Mike reaches for another pancake. "Life insurance?"

"Of course not. That's ridiculous."

"What about filing for his social security or veteran benefits?"

"Why, no."

"I suppose Archie," Mike says, "could file a lawsuit."

Mother places her manicured hands on the table. "He wouldn't dare."

"What about perjury?" I grasp for any straw, short or long that might get us out of this.

"She's not under oath." Mike slices butter and places it atop his stack of pancakes. "But there is potential for a defamation suit."

The line, I imagine, that Mother has crossed or not yet crossed is getting harder to see. Mike is exactly the one who can make her see the ramifications of her actions.

"Where is Grandpa?" Oliver asks.

A knock at the back door makes me jump. I'm not sure if it's my nerves reacting or too much coffee.

"Why, you'd think we were JC Penney's having an 'everything must go' sale." Mother wipes her hands on her apron and opens the back door. Her smile doesn't falter, but I recognize the displeasure that tightens the corners of her mouth. "Josie."

"Mrs. D." Josie breezes inside. "Suzie Q." She casually uses the pet name Drew called me in high school. Then she turns a full-watt smile on Mike. "Well, hello! I'm Josie, one of Suzanne's friends from high school days."

He stands, shakes her hand. "I remember her telling me about you."

"I was the wild one. Wouldn't want you to get me confused with anyone else." She winks. "Oh, sit, sit. But I do love a gentleman who stands for a lady. These old-timers around Luckenbach forget sometimes. Or maybe they're just lazy."

"Or," Mother says, "the lady is—"

"Shall I set an extra plate at the table?" I interrupt.

"Women libbers," Mother says, shifting her approach, "give our men permission to be lazy."

"Josie," I move between my husband and friend, feeling suddenly territorial, "how's your—" I clear my throat while I try to think of an appropriate word, but my brain is working in slow motion. "Your backside?"

"Oh, fine." She pats the back of her jeans. "Good as new." Then she gives it a little wiggle.

I catch Mike's amused smile as he runs a reassuring hand down my spine.

"Josie," I say, "this is our son, Oliver."

"Ain't you a cutie." She sits in Daddy's empty chair right beside him. Too close. I send her a look that says my son is off limits and way, way too young. Even for her. But she doesn't seem to notice. A tinge of red splotches Oliver's face. "What are you? A senior?"

"Sophomore. This coming fall."

"Well, I would have taken you for much older." She gives him a once-over. "You're so tall. Quite the catch. I bet you have those valley girls just *oohing* and *aahing* over you all the time."

Oliver ducks his head and shoves a bite of pancake in his mouth.

"Now look, I've gone and embarrassed him."

"Only yourself, dear," Mother whispers under her breath.

"Josie," I attempt to cover Mother's rudeness, "would you like to join us for breakfast?"

"No, thanks. Maybe just coffee. You all sure do eat early over here. I don't think my stomach wakes up before noon. Of course, I didn't get much sleep last night, thanks to Suzie Q."

The name rankles but I ignore it. If I draw attention to the fact I don't like her calling me Suzie Q then she'll continue mercilessly. Mike eyes me. I give him a shrug that says I'll explain later.

Mother places a cup of coffee in front of Josie. Her motions are clipped with irritation. "Don't you have to be at work?"

"It's Sunday. I do have a slave driver for a boss, but he ain't that bad yet."

"Oh, dear. I completely forgot the day of the week, what with all the excitement!"

"Excitement?" Josie asks.

Mother glares at her. "I meant with all the company we've had." She glances up at the wall clock above the refrigerator. It's ceramic and shaped like a sun with rays pointing outward. "We still have time though."

"For what?" Oliver looks like he could use a long nap.

"Church."

Dumbfounded, I stare at my mother. It's quite an experience to watch her in action. How can she lie about her husband being dead then prance right into church? My gaze locks with Mike's. He lifts one eyebrow in amusement. Mother never seems to bother him the way she aggravates me. Maybe it's because her barbs are never aimed at him.

"Well, now, Mrs. D," Josie speaks when I can't, "I'm sure no one would say anything if you didn't show up this once, seein' you've had such a tragedy." She gives me a sly wink.

"Where is Grandpa exactly?" Oliver's voice is muffled by a mouth full of pancake.

Mother's fork clatters against her china plate. There's a moment of silence but not out of respect; it's more out of disbelief and wonderment as to how Mother will handle this. Will she really lie to her grandson in order to maintain her façade in front of Josie? Maybe it's good Oliver is here. Maybe he'll force his grandmother's hand and end this whole charade.

Mother's glaring eyes soften only slightly when they turn on Oliver. "Austin, dear. His body is in Austin."

Mike coughs and glances at me. I lean back in my chair, cross my arms, and prepare to watch my mother weave her tales.

"But—" Oliver jerks forward, his face registering pain. "Ouch!" Did Mother stomp on his foot?

"You okay, dear?" Her tone is soothing, sly, wicked, showing no more sympathy than Ted Bundy. "Don't you worry about your grandpa. It was quick." Mother dabs her mouth with a linen napkin and keeps up her pretense in front of *outsiders*. That's what she used to call neighbors and friends who weren't in our immediate family. She liked to keep family news in the family. "Within our four walls." Mother, I decided years ago, should have been in the mafia, as good as she was at keeping family secrets. "Your grandfather didn't suffer much."

"Mother!" I stare at her like I don't even recognize this madwoman.

"We must face facts, Suzy Q." Mother invokes my nickname like a subtle threat.

Facts? What facts? Fabricated facts? I imagine her scrap-booking about the fake funeral, clipping the obituary she submitted to the paper. More evidence we can show in court to secure her a nice, quiet padded cell.

"I know it's difficult." She clucks softly and pats Oliver's arm. "A semitrailer slammed into him. It was carrying pipes. One went clean through your Grandpa's windshield." She claps her hands once to show the suddenness of the impact.

We all jump, startled by her clapping and the depth of her anger toward my father.

"Mrs. D," Josie's voice is tinged with sarcasm. She seems to enjoy watching how far Mother will take this charade. "That's just awful."

Mother lifts her chin a notch. She's good at ignoring whatever she disdains or doesn't want to face. "Of course, your grandpa was wearing his seat belt. Which should have been a good thing, but it ended up trapping him." She pauses, looks at me. "Like so many things we do. And that pipe bore a hole right through him."

"Mother," a warning note infiltrates my voice. I touch Mike's arm, whisper, "Do something."

Oliver curls his lip in disgust. "If you gotta go, then—"

"Pretty much decapitated him." Mother presses her lips together as if picturing the scene in her mind. Then she smiles brightly. "But don't worry, the funeral home pieced him back together. Still, it's best to keep it a closed-casket funeral. Don't you think?" She looks around the table. "Oh, I almost forgot the pancakes. Who would like another?" She goes to the griddle but stops mid-stride. "What are *you* smiling for?"

Josie grins as if Mother just announced her lottery num-ber. "At your amazing stamina."

"Oh, uh . . ." I need to change the subject. "Josie, how'd you get over here with your car out of commission?"

"Borrowed one from a friend."

I refrain from voicing my question: Is the friend Drew? To cover my own curiosity, I explain to Mike that we had been in a slight accident. He listens quietly, his fingers templed and tapping his mouth.

Mother's eyebrows elevate. "Is that why the sheriff—" She stops herself, her mouth twisting as she wrestles with her own questions and doubts about my behavior.

"I have to wait until some geologists come over from the University of Texas and declare the area safe. Then a tow truck will have to haul my car out of the ditch."

"What exactly happened?" Mike leans his elbows on the table and looks from Josie to me.

"Were you really in a wreck, Mom?"

"Your momma was driving," Josie declares. "She can be one wild woman."

I put a hand on my son's shoulder. "No, really I—"

"Maybe the quake made me fall into that bush." Josie leans toward Oliver, rests a hand on his thigh as she pats her backside again. "I hadn't had *that* much to drink. You know, everyone's talking about the earthquake last night."

"Earthquake?" Mother clicks her tongue. "Such nonsense."

"Everyone?" Who could she have already been talking with this morning? But even Josie admits she gets around.

"Earthquake, here, in Texas?" Oliver's eyes are wide. He knows all about earthquakes as he's felt a few tremors in his lifetime.

"Sure thing." Josie touches his arm. "You should have been here. Of course, being from California you're probably used to quakes and aftershocks. Quite the excitement. Not our usual Saturday night thrill." She winks. "Did you feel the shake, rattle, and roll last night, Mrs. D?"

"No, I certainly did not." Mother stands suddenly. "The pancakes are going to burn."

"I'm not sure I felt a quake either." But I certainly feel the aftershocks this morning, as my life continues to shake out of control. "Well," I push back my chair, "can I get anyone something? More milk, Oliver?"

He gulps down the rest of his glass, then holds it out. I take it and walk to the other side of the kitchen and *clunk* it on the counter beside the griddle. Behind me, Oliver is telling about the time last fall when a quake rocked Southern California.

"Don't you think," I say in a low voice to Mother, "you're carrying this a little too far?"

"What's that, dear?"

"*Decapitation?*"

She flips a pancake. The batter splatters out along the griddle. The well-done side is darker than her normal perfectly golden brown. "No, I don't. As far as I'm concerned," Mother whispers back to me, "Archie Davidson is dead. So if you must mention him around me, please refer to him in the past tense."

Clearly I have more to worry about than saving my parents' marriage. I open the refrigerator and pull out the quart of milk. With Oliver here, I need to pick up a gallon or two at the store today. When I turn around, I notice a crack forming in the corner of the ceiling. It's a hairline fracture in the plaster. Is that new? Or has it been there for a while? It snakes across the ceiling about a foot.

"Mother—" I start to ask if they've been having foundation trouble, but Josie's voice interrupts my thoughts.

"You remind me of someone." Josie studies my son's face. What is she up to? "Something about your eyes."

"They look like Suzanne's." Mike reaches for another pancake on the stack as Mother sets it on the table.

"Well, they're the same color, all right. But no, there's something else. The shape is more like—" Josie's gaze slants toward me. She mouths Drew's name.

I drop the milk container, and a white puddle spreads like rumors across the linoleum.

8

I step out on the back porch with a cup of coffee. The strong aroma clears my head. I need a breath of fresh air, a moment from the breakfast rush and from Mother's unwavering, ever-judgmental eye. But ocean air doesn't rush to meet me like it does at home. Instead, I get a blast of Texas heat. I lean against the porch railing and stare off at the pink edge of the horizon.

My temper got the better of me this morning. Mother's pointed barbs and accusations put me on the defensive, made the sympathy I felt for her fly right out the window. How does one honor a wacky mother and a father who has deserted his wife and family? Surely God would want me to point out to Mother that her charade is wrong, that it can only cause more harm. Again I feel like I'm walking on the edge of a very high, very dangerous cliff.

I understand the humiliation of having your husband leave, the thought of friends knowing. I've made my own mistakes. Shouldn't my experience count for something good and help Mother?

My shoulders tighten. Guilt from so many years ago rises up and burns the back of my throat. It never leaves. It always lurks deep below the surface, like sulfur permeating a geyser. Now with Drew here, and Mike and Oliver having just arrived, I feel the seismic tremors. Tiny fissures in the foundation of my marriage crack and splinter.

I remember driving with Drew out to Makeout Flats when I was only seventeen. Anticipation and nerves fought for control of me. I was naive. He was a more worldly eighteen. I hadn't felt guilty for loving Drew. I knew a side of him he never showed the world. He had been tender, sweet, and gentle. He made me feel valued, special. He surprised me by being the one to stop, to put on the brakes. Shouldn't it have been me? Shouldn't I have stopped him? But even then, I wasn't strong enough.

"It's not right. Not yet, Suz," he said. "I want more for you. I want to give you what you deserve. In a nice place. Not in the back seat of my daddy's Ford."

That had been a turning point in our relationship. The rest of the summer before I went off to UCLA, Drew held my hand, his fingers clasping mine more firmly, more proprietary. He started talking about our future. He even went to church with me, sat next to me, his thigh pressed against mine. But Mother's ever-watchful eye took notice, and she intervened.

The door behind me opens. I don't turn. Mother probably needs another dartboard for her barbs since Daddy isn't around for target practice. I tighten my grip on my coffee cup. It's one of Daddy's, the one he always used. I gave it to him when I was ten. It's shaped like a big-mouth bass, the lips of the fish making the mug's rim. Mother always hated it, tried to put it in a garage sale, but Daddy stole it back.

Strong arms slide around me, pull me back against a solid

chest. Relieved, I relax into Mike's embrace, breathe in his warm, soapy scent. "How was your shower?"

"You should have joined me." He nuzzles my neck. "Where's your friend?"

"Josie left."

"Went to church?"

I shake my head. "Not Josie. She's not the type."

He's silent for a moment. I know what he's thinking, as I've heard him say it before. *There's not a "type" for God. If there was, then I wouldn't qualify.* His arms tighten before he moves away from me. "Seen hide or hair of Ned Peavy?"

I glance across the gravel road. The windows of the double-wide are open. I figure if the man wants to keep the flies out, then he should close the windows. Or maybe he just likes to swat them. "Not so far."

"There are some interesting characters around here."

"To say the least." I place the mug on the wood railing.

"How'd you turn out so normal?" he asks.

"You think I'm normal?" I give him a mischievous grin and step toward him. I wrap my arms around his neck. My fingers slide into the damp tendrils at the back of his collar. He's always worn his hair slightly longer than convention allows, giving him a roguish look, like Johnny Depp in *Chocolat*.

"Yeah, so what does that say about me?"

"Scary."

"Missed you," he whispers against my mouth, his hands bracing my hips.

"Me too." I kiss him, then hold him close, breathing in his musky scent. I wrap my arms tightly around his neck and wish we were back in our own home far away from this dysfunctional mess.

"So . . ." He sets me away from him, picks up my coffee and samples. We drink it the same—black. "What's going on with your Mother? Has she lost it, or what?"

"She's embarrassed about Daddy leaving. But of course she can't admit that. And she's angry."

"That much is obvious. And understandable."

I feel a quickening of my pulse. I've felt those same emotions. I don't want to remember, but it seems impossible to forget.

"When your mother was talking earlier," Mike says, "I thought she actually believed all that stuff about the semi and decapitation. Man, she's turning into Norma Desmond."

"That's not funny."

"You have to admit, Suz, it's good your dad finally found some gumption after all these years."

It's true. But it scares me too. If Mike ever knew about Drew . . . about . . . I know for a fact he would have all the gumption he needed to leave me. He is a man of right and wrong, of justice. But of vengeance?

Trying for a playful tone, I slap at his shoulder. "This is serious. What are we going to do?"

"Why'd your dad leave? I mean, besides her sniping? Something had to change the status quo. Did your mom do something? Or your dad? You don't just wake up one day and decide to end forty-odd years of marriage."

"Odd being the key word. Maybe you do. Maybe it's as simple as that."

"It's never that simple."

"Mother didn't say anything specific happened."

"Think there might be another woman?" His steady gaze makes the guilt squirm inside me like baby snakes writhing through my abdomen.

"No. I can't believe that. You're talking about my dad." Myriad emotions swell inside me as if Daddy has betrayed us all.

"It's been known to happen." He reaches past me, takes my coffee cup in his hands. "I feel sorry for your mother."

"I do too. But still, she can't think she's going to get away with this."

"If your dad left, well, it's not easy to be deserted." His voice dips deeper into an emotional well. He's experienced that type of abandonment. It's not a wound that heals easily. "Have you talked to your dad?"

"Not since he called. I've left him messages on his cell phone, but he hasn't called me back. Could he have left Texas? Mother says—"

"Could she have . . . done something?"

"What do you mean?"

"How angry is she? Could she have done a Lorena Bobbitt or O. J. Simpson?"

"My mother?" Mike's insinuation unnerves me. "No, of course not. She's not that crazy." Is she?

He quirks an eyebrow as if he's not totally convinced.

There's a lot I could blame my mother for, but I can't imagine she would go that far. I'm not ready to put her on trial for a crime I don't even know was committed.

Mike takes a gulp of coffee then hands the cup back to me. "So what do you want me to do?"

"Find Daddy, I guess." I lean my hip against the porch railing. I notice the white paint has started to crack in the Texas heat. Near the ceiling fan, I notice another mud dauber's nest. "We need to talk to him."

"Preferably *before* the funeral, right?"

"Before Mother is branded as a fraud."

"And arrested or made the laughing stock of Luckenbach."

"The latter would be worse. Anyway, talk to Daddy and see if he'll come home and put a stop to all this."

Mike settles his hip on the railing next to me, his thigh brushing my hip. "Your mom's in pretty deep with this charade."

"The obituary will hit the paper tomorrow."

His blue eyes widen. "What if your dad won't come home? What if she won't let him?"

"I don't know." A headache claws its way up my neck and encompasses my head like talons digging into my scalp. "We have to try. This . . . it's so deceptive. It's just not right."

"You have to know, Suz, that this might not work out the way you want. You have to consider how stubborn your mom is. And your dad, well, something has happened to him. They might not be willing to compromise, to forgive and forget. They might want to live this way."

"So you're saying we'll have to go on with this lie?"

"It's a serious possibility."

Could we find a marriage counselor for my parents? Or maybe Mike and I have been shoved in that role. Or is it too late? I once thought there was a point of no return in a marriage, but I've seen even in my own that a relationship can be saved. But both of the people involved have to want to work things out. They both have to try.

That's how it was for Mike and me. We struggled with infertility. The strain it placed on our relationship almost broke our marriage apart. But we both wanted to salvage our marriage. It wasn't easy. It practically took an act of God. But we made it this far.

The marriages I've seen crumble are the ones where either one or both refuses to work on the relationship. One person can't save a marriage by him or herself. It's like bailing water out of a sinking vessel while the other passenger sits back and watches. Or digs a hole in the bottom of the boat. Which is what Mother seems to be doing.

"Would your dad answer his cell if I called?"

"Maybe not, if he's supposed to be dead. He usually keeps his phone turned off except for emergencies. Sometimes he forgets to check for messages."

"I'll call him, see if I can't talk to him about all this." He pulls out his cell phone and punches the speed dial number. "You should come with me."

"But what about Mother?"

"She'll be all right for a couple of hours."

Nervous about leaving Mother to her own devices, I nod reluctantly. "We could meet up with her at church."

"Your mom's serious about going to church?"

"You heard her."

"I'm not sitting by her."

I tilt my head and study him. "Why not?"

"In case lightning strikes."

A slapping of a distant screen door makes my skin flinch. I jerk my head in that direction and see Ned Peavy across the road. He's standing on his porch, naked as a jaybird (as my daddy might say), and stretches his arms wide. He sees us, gives a nod and a half salute. Mike looks at me, his mouth pulling to the side in a laugh, then he waves back.

9

Drew

Sweat dribbled down Drew's back. It wasn't even noon yet and the day was hotter than a Fourth of July firecracker. He lifted his Stetson and swiped an arm across his brow. There was a time he wouldn't have been seen dead or alive in a Stetson. But now he understood its practicalities.

He had been out with the geologists all morning as they sized up the crack that had opened up Gillespie County. Already there had been calls about burst pipes, a receding pond, one lost cow, and Mildred Pierson's toilets had shot up five inches. Drew had let Flipper handle those calls. Thankfully, this being Sunday, it had otherwise been fairly quiet.

He stepped along the edge of the jagged crevice that stretched in a crooked line north and south. In some places it opened only a few inches, but the gap spread up to five feet further down, where Suzanne had creatively parked Josie's car. The geological team from the University of Texas estimated the break went down some fifty feet in places.

A few yards away, the geologists took notes and studied their equipment. One tall, lean man with a crisp western accent talked on his cell phone, while an older woman maneuvered knobs on some high-tech-looking piece of equipment.

The shrill wail of a siren made Drew turn eastward. Flipper had the squad car's lights flashing like he was on his way to a barn fire. But he drove slowly. The way the car dipped and rose across the uneven desert terrain, the movement resembled nothing more than an armadillo's waddling gait. He stopped a good twenty feet short of the crack. Drew walked out to meet him.

"In a hurry, Flipper?"

He peered over at the crack, looking like he was ready to jump back in the squad car and peel out at the sign of any trouble. "Any word yet, Sheriff, on how big the earthquake was?"

"No one said it was an earthquake. Be careful who you say that around. We don't want to start a panic. Or draw too many curiosity seekers."

"Yes, sir. You're right. You sure are." Flipper readjusted his hat, still glancing nervously toward the jagged edge. "'Course, old man Hewitt said his momma felt a quake back in the twenties. Rattled her dishes and everything. Sounds like an earthquake. Just between you and me." He stretched out his arm, pointing in the direction of the Hewitt family farmhouse that sat just over the ridge. "Lines right up. Maybe there's one of them fault lines that runs along here." He took a cautious step backwards. "What do them geologists say?"

"They're still assessing the situation."

"Could be aftershocks, don't ya know."

Already a stream of cars had come and gone as curious folks had driven out to gawk and speculate. Drew had set up barriers to keep everyone away for a while. He looked back over his shoulder where Josie's car was still stuck in the opening like a toothpick lodged in an old timer's mouth. Later, when and if the geologists declared the area safe, he would call in a wrecker to pull the Camaro out.

"You thinkin' this is what the Bible says is the 'end times'?" Flipper looked down at his boots.

"What made you think of that?"

"What the preacher said a few Sundays back, 'bout there bein' more earthqu—" He stopped himself. "Sorry. But there's been some weird happenings around here, Sheriff."

"Weird, huh? Like what?"

"Yessiree. Like, uh . . ." He nudged a rock with the pointed toe of his boot and shrugged his shoulder. "I don't know. Just weird stuff. Supernatural stuff."

Drew crossed his arms over his chest. "What are you trying to say, Flipper?"

"Nothing, just . . ." He sniffed, looked away. "I don't know. Lots of weird happenings. Like that snake. I've heard animals sense these things before we do. And you know . . ." His voice trailed off as if he wasn't sure he wanted to say what he was thinking.

Drew clapped a hand on Flipper's shoulder, tried to offer support. His deputy was grieving his friend, Archie Davidson. He didn't dare tell him he thought he saw Archie's truck at the Old Hockheim Inn this morning. Not till he had something more than false hope to offer.

"Maybe you ought to cut off early today. Go on home and get some rest."

Flipper's nose turned red. He sniffed again. Finally he cleared his throat. "I brought some lunch for the geologists. You too. I know it's early and all, but you've been out here a while."

"Good idea. Thanks." Drew hadn't had breakfast, and the one cup of coffee he swiped from the office first thing hadn't lasted long.

"Well, it was really Helen who thought of it."

Drew nodded. The weekend dispatcher had been working in the office for thirty years and was more a mother hen than officer. "Any other calls about damage?"

"No, Rodney Hedges called and said he found that missing cow. It got out on the highway. Maybe the earthquake spooked it."

Drew shot Flipper a look. "We don't know it's an earthquake. It could be the drought has dried up fissures in the bedrock. The geologists told me there are lots of fault lines that run through this area. Plus, there is the underwater aquifer."

"Fault lines," Flipper repeated. "See, earthquakes. There's gonna be aftershocks."

"Rodney's been known to have cows get out because he doesn't keep his fences up."

"Yes, sir. You're right. I'm sure you're right. But . . ."

"But?" He caught a whiff of French fries coming from the squad car's open window. "What is it?"

Flipper shuffled around but didn't answer.

Finally Drew pulled the bags of food out of the squad car and had Flipper carry the hamburgers and fries over to the geologists. He gave the crack a wide berth.

"It's not going to swallow you up, Flipper."

"Did a pretty good job on that car there."

Hiding a smile, Drew chomped down on a hamburger from the DQ.

Flipper came back, hands empty, and propped a foot on the front bumper of his squad car. "What do you think happens after someone dies?" he asked.

Lettuce fell out of Drew's burger and landed on the ground. He chewed slowly, giving himself time to think of the best way to answer his deputy. Swallowing, he finally said, "I'm no preacher, Flipper. What did you learn in church?"

"That folks go to heaven. Or . . . you know, the other place. Dependin' on . . ."

"Uh-huh. So?"

"Well, I figure Archie was a good man. He believed in God and all. So he probably went straight to heaven."

"I expect."

"You believe that, right?"

"Yes. Do you?"

"Sure. Sure. The preacher says so. And I'm gonna believe that. He's got more learnin' on the matter than I do. That's for sure." There was a silent *but* at the end of his statement.

"But?" Drew voiced the doubt when Flipper couldn't.

Flipper looked at him, then grabbed Drew's Coke sitting on the hood of the squad car and took a swig. His eyes widened and he handed the soda back to Drew. "Sorry, Sheriff."

"It's okay, Flipper." He offered him a French fry, which Flipper readily accepted. "So tell me what's got you so concerned about heaven and hell all of a sudden?"

"I don't think Archie is where he's supposed to be."

Drew schooled his surprise, hiding it behind a professional mask. "What do you mean?"

"I seen this show on TV a while back where when folks die, sometimes when it's all of a sudden, then they don't know they's dead. And they just kinda hang around."

"Like a ghost?"

"Yeah, uh-huh. Like that." He looked like he just swallowed a hamburger whole.

Drew took another bite of his burger and chewed it thoughtfully. This was getting too weird. He had heard a lot of things in his time on the force in Austin and now here in Gillespie County. He had seen a lot of crazy things. But usually the crazy things were done by people. Live people, not dead ones. Crazy as some things seem, there's usually a good explanation behind them. "You know, Flipper, something might be goin' on here that we don't quite understand."

Flipper slapped his thigh. "Exactly! You are exactly right, Sheriff."

"But don't worry. I'm going to get to the bottom of it."

"You want me to try to find one of them psychics?"

Drew frowned and rubbed the back of his neck. "What are you talking about?"

"Well on that TV show I seen, they brought in this psychic who could see dead people. Yes, sir! I know it's crazy and all. But I seen it with my own eyes. And that psychic tells that woman who was hanging out in her home after she should've been up in heaven, he tells her all kindly like that she's dead and she should go toward the light. 'Go toward the light.'"

"I don't think we need a psychic, Flipper."

"You don't?" Disappointment dragged down his features. "But I'm tellin' you. I seen—"

"I understand." Drew leaned forward, sniffed Flipper's breath. Coffee and burrito. He leaned back, clapped his deputy on the back. "You've had a shock. Why don't you go on home, sleep it off. We'll talk about it more tomorrow."

Flipper jerked at the words. "You think I made all this up? You think I've been drinking?"

"I didn't say that, Flipper, I just meant—"

"Well I ain't been drinking! I saw him. I saw Archie plain as day!"

Drew stared at his deputy for a full minute. "You did?"

His face darkened to red as if a heat wave had just swept through. Flipper looked down at the ground. "I did. I ain't gonna lie to you. I saw Archie. Like he was standing not ten feet from me." Flipper blinked. "I know that sounds crazy. I do. I been thinking it over. It is crazy. But it's true." He looked up at Drew, his eyes swimming, pleading with him to believe, to reassure him. "It's true."

Drew hadn't dismissed seeing Archie's truck. It wasn't a phantom truck out of one of those Stephen King novels. But telling Flipper wouldn't be of much help. If Drew had learned one thing through the years, he had learned to keep what he knew to himself and just listen. Interesting facts might be brought to the surface with a little patience.

"Where did you see him, Flipper?"

"Outside the Luckenbach store."

"Going in or going out?"

Flipper blinked. "I don't know."

"What else? Was he doing anything?"

"Doing? Nothing that I know of. Just standing there. Looking around. Like he ain't seen the town this way, you know? Maybe he was surprised by where he was. Maybe he wasn't even sure he was dead."

Okay, Drew didn't want to head down that slippery slope again. "Did Archie see you?"

"Yeah! Yeah! He did. He said, 'Hey, Flip,' just like it was any other Sunday." Flipper took a breath, his chest going up and down, up and down. "Imagine that. A ghost talking to me."

"Did he say anything else?"

"Uh, yeah, he said, 'You feeling okay, Flip?' I must've been pale or scared lookin'. You don't see a ghost every day of the week."

"Just Sundays, right?" Drew smiled.

"What?"

"Never mind." He set the rest of his burger on the hood of the cruiser. "What else?"

"Well," Flipper scuffed the bottom of his boot against the rocks and pebbles. "I said I was doing okay, then I asked how he was doing. Just like we was having a regular conversation."

"What'd he say?"

"He said he was fine. Just fine. Just like nothing unusual had happened. Not like he'd been dead for two days straight.

Not like he was Lazarus walkin' right out of the tomb. Which made me think, *Hey, he's been dead. What's it like?* So I asked him."

Amused, Drew crossed his arms over his chest. "You asked him what it's like to be dead?"

"Well not in so many words. I didn't wanna be rude. So I said, 'Where you been, Arch?' And he said, "Round.' So I guess he's just been hanging 'round town, floatin' around or whatever ghosts do. I asked, 'You see all right?' And he said he could. I don't know if he meant he could see everything, like what we was all doing or saying about him, or if he just meant he could see me fine. What do you think, Sheriff?"

Drew rubbed his jaw thoughtfully. "I don't know."

"Well, that was about it. Except I told him I'd been over to see Betty Lynne, paid my respects, you might say, and not to worry about her. You know, I just wanted him to know we'd all look in on her from time to time, make sure she was gettin' by." Then Flipper raised his chin a notch, his eyes widened, and he looked right at Drew. "He kinda got all weird and said, 'You stay away from her. Hear? She'll kill you just as soon as look at you.'" Flipper rubbed his hand along the butt of his revolver. "Now why you think he'd go and say somethin' like that? About his own wife? You think she's mad at me for something I done? That I didn't know I done?"

In the end Drew sent Flipper home. The first thing he was going to do was check with Austin PD about the wreck involving Archie's truck, then stop by the Old Hockheim Inn's registration desk. Then he just might have to have a talk with Suzanne. And her mother.

Oh, yes, this day was shaping up just fine.

10

Suzanne

The Old Hockheim Inn, a tavern and hotel on the opposite end of Fredericksburg, is nothing like any place I've seen in California. Mike and I need cowboy boots and Stetsons, or maybe black leather, skull rags, and a Harley, instead of our designer jeans and button-downs, which might get us shot for some novelty critter and mounted with our heads on a wall in some good ol' boy's den.

Daddy suggested we meet him here. It takes a minute for my eyes to adjust from the glaring sun outside to the darkness within. German steins and pictures of young frauleins decorate the wood plank walls, along with curling mounted horns. It's quiet inside, no traffic noise, no jukebox music of any kind. Cigarette smoke lingers in the air like uncertainty and fear. I don't know what to expect from this meeting. I don't know what my father is going to say.

"Mike!"

Sitting in a booth, a foamy mug of root beer in hand, is my father. A half-empty bottle sits in its own puddle of condensation.

"Daddy?" I regret the doubt in my voice.

"Sugar Beet!" He opens his arms, and I squeeze in next to him in the booth. "I didn't know you were coming. I thought you'd be with your mother."

"I wanted to see you." I hug him close, feel his warmth, his solid form. Tears press against my eyes, and I realize I had more doubt about his welfare than I cared to admit. Emotions bombard me from all directions. I'm not sure what to feel, what to say, what to ask.

"Thanks for coming." Daddy pats me, then reaches out to shake hands with Mike. "I appreciate y'all coming all this way."

"We're happy to help any way we can, Daddy." I keep a hand on his arm.

"Jake," Daddy waves toward the bartender, "get my daughter and son-in-law here a couple of these." To me he says, "That's all he can serve this early."

"I haven't had root beer since I was twelve." Mike slides into the booth opposite Daddy and me.

My father seems thinner than normal. Worry fuses with the other emotions stirring up inside me. He could rival Barney Fife for the Slim Jim award.

"How are you doing, Daddy?" My fingers pluck at his shirt sleeve.

"Been better."

I put my arm around his narrow shoulders, want to take him home with us, back to California, and protect him from Mother's wrath.

"Can't believe you come all the way from California."

"Wouldn't want to miss out on all this family drama." Mike grins.

"Oliver too?"

"He's back at the house with Mother. He's supposed to call us if she does anything out of the ordinary."

Daddy dips his chin downward and looks at me steadily. "Out of the ordinary is her usual."

My smile feels heavy.

Daddy shakes his head, his eyes solemn. "It's like a family reunion, and I'm not even there. 'Course, Betty Lynne would kill me if I walked into the house right about now."

"Something like that." Mike flattens his hands on the table. "So how can we help?"

Daddy's cheeks cave inward. Deep lines of regret settle around his eyes. He takes a swig of his root beer, sucks the foam off his top lip. In spite of all that's happened, he sure looks better than Mother made him out to be. Head attached and all. He's wearing his old Levis and a faded short-sleeved shirt. "These kinds of things are always hardest on the kids. And I'm sorry about that, Sugar Beet."

"But Daddy, don't you think we can fix things, patch things up between you and Mother?"

"Don't know." He presses his thumbs together, rolling them forward until the short-clipped nails meet. He pours more root beer into his mug and the bubbles swell toward the top. He shifts in his seat, his elbows bumping against the table. "Surprised me when you called this morning. It's been quiet, like I'm dead or something."

Mike and I exchange surprised looks. I turn toward Daddy. Doesn't he know what all Mother has done?

"I didn't want you kids affected by all this. Don't want you in the middle of the gun battle." It's a little late for that. "I'm sure we can get all this settled. I figure I'll lose most everything I've worked for my whole life. But it can't be helped. Betty Lynne ain't the forgivin' type."

"Daddy, we'll do whatever you want us to do. But you should know," I glance at Mike and he nods his support, "Mother's taken it a little further than you might realize."

"Gone ballistic, huh?"

Mike leans forward, his elbows on the table. "You know you're dead. Right?"

"I thought she'd kill me, for sure, when I told her." He shrugs his narrow shoulders, but he shows no sign of knowing his obituary will be in the paper tomorrow.

"I made sure my gun weren't loaded," he says, "and the knives were out of the way. If I'd stayed, it wouldn't have surprised me to find arsenic in my soup. But, Sugar Beet . . ." His eyes soften as he looks at me.

Instantly I remember the hurt welling up in his eyes when Mother would make a cutting remark. I cup my hand over his to offer some comfort.

"I had to do it. There just comes a time when a man's gotta do what he's gotta do."

I'm not sure that's God's take on things. After all, there are a lot of recorded incidents in the Bible where God instructed a man to do just the opposite of what the man wanted. In fact, most of the time that's the case. But my job at the moment is not to preach or lecture.

Jake brings two chilled mugs and two bottles of root beer hooked between his stubby fingers. He pours half a bottle, filling the mug with brown foam that spills over the top and slides down the outside of the glass and onto the table. I reach for the napkin dispenser and start mopping it up.

"Jake, this here's my daughter, Suzanne, and her husband, Mike Mullins."

The bartender, who looks like he's exhausted from cleaning up after the Saturday night partying, gives me a nod. "How do." Then he shakes hands with Mike. "Nice to know you." Jake grins, a big gold tooth shining in the front of his mouth.

"You all go ahead and talk. I gotta get ready for the lunch crowd." He ambles back toward the bar, picks up a broom, and begins sweeping the floor. "You want some music?" he calls.

"That'd be fine," Daddy calls back then turns his attention back to Mike and me. "Jake's a good friend. Known him for years. Place ain't open for business this early. But I needed a private place and knew Jake wouldn't mind. Thought it'd be better than over in Luckenbach. Your mother might have turned everyone against me there."

I hook a hand through the frozen mug's handle, wait for the foam to die down. "Daddy, what started all this? Why'd you leave?"

He looks at me from under bushy gray eyebrows. "You know your mother, right?"

Over the jukebox comes the loping melody of Johnny Cash singing "Cry, Cry, Cry."

"But," I feel my features tightening in a frown, "Mother hasn't changed. You've put up with her antics for forty years. So what did change? What made it suddenly unbearable?"

Daddy shifts his mug from one hand to another. The mug slides along the puddle of condensation like it's doing a smooth two-step.

"Another woman?" Mike voices my fear.

Daddy looks up quickly, then down again. "What did Betty tell you?"

"Nothing really, Daddy. She was pretty vague about everything." Other than the graphic description of his death by impalement and decapitation.

He takes a drink of his root beer. A bit of foam remains on his upper lip. I dab it with a napkin. Not knowing what else to say, I sip my drink too. The bittersweet flavor is hard to swallow.

I feel the pressure of Mike's shoe against the edge of my sandal, feel the weight of his gaze. When Mike walked out on me, I felt lost. I didn't react the way my mother has, but I did react in a desperate way. Ever since Mike came back, he has made it clear he will be true to his wedding vows. And I have been true. Our marriage survived much worse than what Mother and Daddy are going through now. Although Mike doesn't know that I had already broken my vows to him, and I pray he never will. But if we could survive, then I'm confident (sort of) Mother and Daddy's marriage can be saved.

"Mother drove you to this," I say, my heart as heavy as the glass mug in my hand.

"Now, Suzanne, we all make choices. Your mother is your mother. I've known how she is since the day I met her."

"Crazy."

He shakes his head. "No, she's not crazy. She's hurting. She's trying to live up to something that just can't be."

"It's pride." That's the reason I couldn't call friends or family when Mike left.

"Some of it, sure. But it's more than that." He shrugs, as if uncomfortable with his new position, his eyes downcast. His thumbnail digs into the edge of the table. "I made a decision. For better or worse, I'm stuck here. Well, at the Hockheim Inn."

"Why don't you call Betty?" Mike suggests. "Try to go back to her?"

He gives a shrug of one shoulder, his shirt pulling to one side. With a finger he makes a trail through the water on the table. "I don't know that I want to."

Disappointment presses on my chest. I'm not sure Mother wants him back either. She obviously prefers her husband dead. Not a good foundation for a marriage. "Divorce happens all the time, Daddy. But that doesn't mean it has to happen." Something inside me sharpens. "If we can stop things from escalating, maybe we can find a way, get Mother to change. If she did, would you be willing to stick it out?

"Maybe. You think your mother could change?"

"Miracles do happen."

"Until papers are signed," Mike adds, "remember, nothing is official."

"Until the lawyers show up, right?"

"Something like that. Look, Archie, I made a mistake once. I left Suzanne. This isn't news for public consumption. I tell you this because I hope it will help you and Betty Lynne." Mike's gaze is steady as it locks on me. "But that doesn't mean our marriage couldn't be fixed. Suzanne forgave me. And I bet Betty Lynne will forgive you."

My heart aches at the truth of his words but at the absence of something else. Mike has never forgiven me. But only because I never gave him the chance. That is the one thing that stands between us.

Daddy coughs.

"If we word an apology carefully—"

"Did you know what happened to Maris Cavannaugh?" Daddy interrupts Mike. "Have you heard that story?"

Mike leans back against the wooden booth. "No, I don't think so."

"Suz, do you remember?"

I give a slight nod.

"She was on several committees with Betty Lynne at the church. You know how ladies are, they have to have their committees. Our families did all sorts of things together. Trips to Oklahoma. Colorado. Dinner. Picnics. Babysitting for each other when our kids were little. Luther, Maris's husband, was a nice fellow. Maris, she was real sweet. But she went against Betty Lynne on some silly decision. Can't remember now what it was. Wasn't important then, ain't important now. But Betty Lynne and Maris went 'round and 'round. Then Betty Lynne gave her the cold shoulder. Believe you me, that can be a mighty frigid arctic blast. Betty Lynne managed to turn others in the church and community against Maris. She's got quite an influence."

"What happened?" Mike asks.

"They finally moved to Arizona. They said it was for a job Luther couldn't pass up, but I don't think so. They had deep roots here. Deep. But living in Betty Lynne's shadow can be mighty uncomfortable."

"Why didn't the preacher step in and do something."

"He was scared. Can't blame him there."

I fold my hands together. We need a battle plan. "Then we have to do something about Mother. Get her to let go of this notion about being a widow."

"She's gunning for me, huh?"

"Archie," Mike leans forward, elbows braced on the table, "she's already killed you."

Daddy starts to laugh, then stops. Emotions flicker across his face like an old black-and-white movie. "What do you mean?"

"You're dead, Daddy. She killed you off and is planning your funeral."

Daddy looks from me to Mike who nods the truth of the situation.

"You're arriving at the church tomorrow afternoon all dolled up in a casket."

Daddy falls back against the seat, his face white as if he's already a ghost.

I reach for him. "I've never seen Mother so determined."

"What has Betty Lynne done? What was she thinking?"

"She says you told her you were moving far away. Leaving town. And that you told her she could say you were dead for all you cared."

"I did?" He shakes his head as if trying to jar loose a memory. "In the heat of the moment, maybe I did. I don't know.

I was gonna . . ." He clears his throat. "My plans changed." He runs his fingers through his thinning hair. "Well, that explains it then. This morning I saw Flipper. He nearly flipped out— looked like he'd seen a ghost."

11

You can take a sinner to church, but can she ever truly be restored? At one time I would have thought so. Now I'm not so sure. Can you go too far? Push too far?

I don't like Mother's deception, but I also don't feel as if I should make the late-breaking news public. I'm still not sure which way to lean, who to support, who to challenge. My father was wrong to leave. Wasn't he? My mother was wrong to declare him dead. But what is the right answer now? How can we meet in the middle and settle this family feud?

The accordion music swells around me. But it can't block out the thoughts churning around my mind. I glance at my son, who's slouched on the wooden bench beside me. He's accustomed to an electric guitar and drums, not a polka-sounding hymn. On the other side of him is his grandmother. On my right, within reach, is Mike.

My parents' church is really just the Luckenbach dance hall. The dance hall is built like a barn. The outside windows are propped open to allow a breeze to filter through. The courtyard outside is shaded by giant trees and is only a hop, skip, and a jump away from the Luckenbach store and bar. That's pretty much the whole town of Luckenbach. It's one of a kind.

Trucks and motorcycles have assembled outside on opposite sides of the crack that now runs through the center of town. Here it's more of a sliver than the wide ravine north of town. Inside the dance hall, a small congregation of cowboys and motorcycle enthusiasts settles down as the service starts. Overhead, along the rafters, are strings of white lights which are used when the dance hall is in action. But they're dull and milky white this morning. The choir, a handful of people I've known my whole life, like my fifth-grade teacher Mrs. Piles and the barber who used to cut my hair, files in. They don't wear traditional robes of blue with scarlet stoles but are dressed simply in their blue jeans and leather.

"So what did Grandpa say?" Oliver presses his shoulder against mine.

Mother clears her throat and leans forward to grab my attention, then gives us a look that says, *Talk later when no one can overhear any confessions that might reflect poorly on me.*

Mike gives her a polite nod.

Oliver bumps my shoulder. "Can I see him?"

Mother thumps him on the knee.

I give him a nod, then glance guiltily toward Mother. Her profile is stern, her jaw inflexible. "We'll work it out."

Of course, there's the minor matter of Mother's declaring Daddy dead. Hard to hold a family reunion that way. And so there we are again. Stuck. Between a rock and a hard place. Mother and Daddy. Stubborn to the end. And who in the middle will be crushed?

A man in front of us turns and glances back. It's Al Bertron, my biology teacher from high school. I had to dissect a frog in his class. His stern expression shifts into a thin-lipped smile that is as wide as a frog's. "Suzanne Davidson." He uses my maiden name. "Good to see you!"

I pat him on the back. "Good to see you, Mr. Bertron."

The choir begins to sing. Their voices warble and waver around the notes. *"In the hour of trial, Jesus plead for me . . ."*

Doubts shift and lurch inside me. I know what I would stand trial for. Besides this weekend's deceit and fraud against the whole town, which of course I'm not exactly responsible for, but I haven't righted the wrong either. Oh, no, I have my own transgression. One that is all my own.

Josie's shocked look from this morning haunts me. How could she so readily guess? Josie is always suspicious, always searching for what lies in secret. She could easily follow in Mrs. Hoover's footsteps one day. Except Josie doesn't like to share dirt. She likes to keep it to herself. Knowledge, she says, is power.

Even now, I watch Mrs. Hoover lumber up the crooked aisle between the benches and tables. She hunches over, talking to one last person, before she scoots her way along the row in front of us, stepping on toes, bumping heads with her purse and elbows.

"Excuse me. Sorry!" Her whisper is a normal tone for others.

Mr. Bertron lets out a *whoof* of air and tilts forward sharply toward Mrs. Hoover's backside.

"Oopsie daisies! So sorry, Al. Did I hurt that bunion of yours?" Finally, she reaches an empty space in the pew, turns, gives Mother an obligatory nod, then me.

This church where I grew up is far different from our church home in California. Of course, our building is actually a church building, built for that purpose. It's a modern construction, from the simple lines of the worship center to the rocking beat of worship songs. The attire is California casual, not relaxed, kick-your-shoes-off casual like this one. Church is usually a place of comfort for me. But here my nerves feel as stripped and bare as the wooden walls.

I have long avoided coming home. Now, ensconced in my childhood room, surrounded by old neighbors and childhood friends, I find myself wrapped in the expectations and dreams I thought I had left behind and having to face my inadequacies and weaknesses. Pain swells up inside me, pressuring my heart.

I've made my place in California. I'm comfortable there. I feel safe in the cocoon Mike and I have built. But now . . . Is it all an illusion? Is it a ramshackle building on a faulty foundation, like the Luckenbach store?

I glance out the open window at the store and wonder if the earthquake has tilted it off center. A couple of bikers were wondering the same thing when we arrived. Or maybe it's just my perspective that is off.

Mike puts an arm around my shoulders and I meet his gaze, try to smile. "Do you think Mother's crazy?"

He presses his mouth to my ear and a delicious tingle races down my spine. "Prideful. But there is good news."

"What's that?"

"Your dad still loves your mother."

"Maybe. But how's it going to play out?"

"He may have to become Lazarus."

"Lazarus wasn't decapitated."

"Neither was your dad."

"It still took a miracle," I argue.

"And so will this," he agrees, kissing my cheek and joining in the chorus of the hymn.

12

The crack along the ceiling in the kitchen has lengthened to at least three feet. Beneath it, Mike works on his laptop while I help Mother clean up after lunch and sort through the food the neighbors have brought. Oliver vegges out on the couch in the den, watching some game on ESPN 1, 2, or 25. How many channels do they need for sports anyway? Sunday afternoon passes as slowly as the weathering of a rock. Conversation is impossible, as there isn't much to say without getting a mouthful of grit.

Mike and I have tried to talk Mother out of her foolishness, but determination is one of her strengths.

All my life I've watched my mother pull off events or tasks that would seem impossible to any ordinary woman, like myself. If someone said, "It can't be done," my mother would say, "Stand back and watch."

Someone on the PTA once said, "It won't work. No one will buy tulip bulbs."

"Get out of my way," Mother said to the woman in charge of the fund-raiser. She convinced the whole community that they needed tulips. The PTA raised more money that year than in any previous year. Telling my mother something can't be done just makes her dig her heels into this hard-packed Texas dirt, roll up her sleeves, and make a draw-a-line-in-the-sand stand.

It can be a wonderful asset when Mother is on your team, helping you. And she is a wonderful helper. Any one of her friends or neighbors would say so. She is the first to take a casserole, homemade and delicious, when a family member is in the hospital or has passed away. She knows how to jump in and get things organized and moving in the right direction when there's been any sort of disaster. She's a natural leader. Others look to her and are grateful for her help. But that wonderful can-do attitude can backfire on the people she loves.

Mother's favorite catchphrase when I was growing up was, "If you can imagine it, you can make it happen." She liked to say that right before she stripped the upholstery off the couch and recovered it to her liking. I try now to imagine Mother and Daddy married, happy, together until death parts them. But naturally. Not this staged death.

But Mother's determination to kill off my father has become a molehill the size of Enchanted Rock. It's supposed to take only a little faith to move a mountain, and I'm not sure I have enough. At least her imaginative plan doesn't involve my father's Winchester or the Wolfgang Puck knives she bought on the shopping network.

What's surprising to me is that she actually seems to enjoy playing the grieving widow. Although she doesn't exhibit much grief. Every time a friend rings the doorbell and brings another pineapple upside-down cake or tuna casserole, Mother recounts with the acting skills of Joan Crawford the ghastly tale of my father's demise until her current audience is cringing and gasping at the horror of it all. I must say she's clever in that she makes Daddy out to be more heroic than a victim of his own stupidity, which she could easily have done. It gives me a glimmer of hope that somewhere deep down she still loves him.

Until her anger subsides, though, there is really nothing to discuss.

"What if she pulls this off?" I asked Mike in the guest bedroom when we had a moment alone after church. "Are we going to have to pretend every time we come home that my father is dead?"

"We don't come here often, Suzanne."

I refuse to cave in to guilt or entertain the idea of continuing this farce years into the future. "What will Daddy do? Leave town? Find a new job?"

"I have a feeling she's going to dig her own grave," Mike whispered against my ear, "not your dad's."

Jarring noise from the television, the clacking of hockey sticks, the roar of the crowd, grates across my nerves. But I know it's really the silence that stretches like a bubble of pink Bazooka that has extended my nerves to their breaking point. I'm wondering just how far it will all go and, when it pops, who it'll stick to.

"Just look at that time," Mother says, folding a dish towel and hanging her apron on the hook behind the door. "Time gets away from me sometimes." She finger-curls her hair back from her temples. "We're going to be late if we don't hurry."

Frankly I'm tired of checking my watch, her clock, wondering if time moves slower in Luckenbach than in La Jolla. "Is it time for another meal already?"

"The barbecue."

"What barbecue?"

"We have to make an appearance. It would be rude not to." Mother closes a cabinet that stands ajar. "Come help me pick out what to wear. What do you think would be appropriate? All things considered."

"You want to dye your clothes black like Scarlett O'Hara?" It occurs to me this whole scenario of a make-believe funeral is exactly like something the heroine of *Gone with the Wind* would do. The first time I saw the movie, I cried when Bonnie Blue Butler died after falling off her horse. I thought it was cruel of Margaret Mitchell to kill off an innocent child. Now I realize it was probably a good decision. I know what it's like to grow up with a mother like Scarlett.

"I don't think that will be necessary," Mother says, walking past Mike and through the den. She raises her voice to combat the clatter and swoosh of the hockey game. "But I also don't want to seem too colorful. If you know what I mean."

She's colorful all right. I refrain from rolling my eyes and follow her to her bedroom. "So where are you going? What barbecue?"

She steps into the large walk-in closet. Along the baseboards her shoes are lined up in straight rows. Once upon a time Mother split the closet with Daddy. She took the left side, he the right, like a bride and groom at the altar, she told me once. But I notice there isn't one male-looking belt or jacket, not one pair of jeans, not one tie. Has she already gone through his things and taken them to Goodwill in Austin? I wouldn't put it past her. Or did Daddy pack everything when he left? Which leaves me once again sympathizing with Mother. When Mike left, he simply packed one bag. His closet held for me at least a tiny flicker of hope for his returning. But if Daddy had packed everything, then what was Mother to think? What was she to do?

I run a hand down the row of Mother's blouses, feeling the silky and starched material against my fingertips. "Where are all of Daddy's clothes?" I ask.

She sifts through the color-coordinated shirts and skirts.

Most of her collection is bright and colorful; Mother has always liked standing out in a crowd. Maybe that's why I prefer subtle tones of beige, gray, black, and white.

"Oh, he moved his things into the guest bedroom closet years ago." She pulls out a pearl-gray pantsuit that lacks her usual flair, holds it up to her. "I bought this last year for Mildred Schumacher's funeral.

"Didn't I see her at church this morning?"

"She made a comeback. But for a while we thought she was a goner." Mother looks disappointed she didn't get to wear her suit. "This will work."

"It's a bit dressy for a barbecue, don't you think? Maybe you should stay home, Mother." Not get yourself in any more trouble. "After all, you're supposed to be in mourning. Several people commented this morning about how surprised they were to see you at church, how most new widows would stay home from church. Or any other social gathering."

She narrows her eyes at me. "What ninnies! What does everyone think, that I'm going to pick up a man or get roaring drunk? Or just curl up my toes and wither on the vine?"

I clamp my lips closed. There's no talking to her when she's like this. Frankly I just want to call it a night, climb into bed, pull the covers up over my head and wake up when this nightmare is over.

She gives me a look that I recognize as not measuring up to her specifications. "Aren't you going to get ready?"

"You want us to go with you?"

"Well, it would look odd if I were to go alone."

"So we're your chaperones? In case any old widower decides to hit on you?"

She sighs. "Everyone in Luckenbach knows you're here. In fact, I'm sure it will be mentioned in Linda Lou Hoover's column tomorrow morning in the Fredericksburg paper.

Everyone will expect my family to gather around me during this difficult time."

There's no use arguing with her. I know the routine. "I'll go round up the boys," meaning Mike and Oliver. I'm sure they'll be thrilled to go to a party where they don't know anyone but my mother. I realize I still don't know where we're going, but I no longer care. Mother has a way of killing curiosity, whether it be in a cat, a two-year-old, or her own daughter. "I'll be waiting in the car," she says. She checks her hair in the mirror, dabs the corner of her mouth.

I refrain from mentioning that it could be a few minutes, not to mention it's hotter outside than the biblical lake of fire. While I prod Oliver off the couch and hand my husband a Diet Coke for a quick caffeine surge, I silently work on my own attitude. What does it mean to honor one's parents anyway? Doing what they say? Always? If so, Moses never met my mother.

There's a difference between love and aiding and abetting. So if I encourage Mother, side with her rather than Daddy, am I not also lying? Or if I swing my support to the other team, to Daddy, then aren't I encouraging the abandonment of one's commitments and responsibilities?

Fifteen minutes later I shut the door to my parents' house and try to maintain a neutral posture. How can I side with either parent? Neither is a good option. Neither seems right. But it doesn't seem right to stand up and publicly announce my father is alive and my mother is nuts.

"But where are we going?" Oliver drags his size eleven feet.

"I don't know. Just get in the car."

Mother sits in her Cadillac with the air conditioner blasting full on. She sits in the passenger seat and indicates that she wants Mike to drive.

"Can I?" Oliver volunteers, perking up at the possibilities.

"Not tonight." Mike relieves us of that stress. My nerves are worn already. The last time I closed my eyes happily, blissfully, was in California.

"What is this thing we're going to?" Oliver asks as he pours his long frame into the back seat beside me.

"An anniversary party for some old friends," Mother says, "Patty and Joe Ward. They've been married fifty years. Doesn't seem possible, but it's true. True enough, I suppose."

"What do you mean?" Mike makes the mistake of asking. "Are they not really married?"

"Or just pretending like—"

I elbow Oliver to put a stop to his next statement.

"Their actual wedding date is the end of July. But their feed mill is seventy-five years old this week. Joe's father started it. So Patty and Joe thought they'd kill two birds with one stone."

"They're killing birds?" Oliver asks with a gleam of sarcasm.

"It's an expression." Mother's words are slow, the way she speaks when annoyed by a question.

"How do you do that? Kill two birds with one stone?" My son tends to be literal, but at the moment he is about to take off with Mother's leg that he's pulling. "Does the stone ricochet off one? Go through one and hit the other?"

"Oliver," Mike says.

Mother decides she's above such nonsense and sticks to directions. "Turn right. Slow down. There's a stop sign ahead." She places a hand on Mike's arm. "Always watch along this road. We often see deer and armadillos."

"Armadillos?"

"I forget you haven't been here much." Her dig is pointed straight at me but is deflected by my cavalier attitude. I'm too tired from stress and lack of sleep to care about much at this point.

"Oliver," Mother twists around to narrow her gaze on her grandson, "you'll be a junior next year. What are your plans?"

"Sophomore." He glances at me. "Plans?"

"For college," I interpret.

"USC. Marine microbiology."

Mother blinks as if assimilating that information. She lets out a tiny huff, not of approval but reluctant respect. "Not sure how you can make a living doing that. Or maybe your daddy is making so much money that you don't need to work."

Mike laughs. "Oh, no, he'll work."

"He's very good at science," I add, unable to keep the pride from my voice and not understanding how this very different creature came from my own body. "Always has had an affinity for critters in the ocean."

Mother glances from Mike toward the road, then back at Oliver. "What classes are you going to take this fall?"

He lists a stream of classes that make my brain hurt. But I know he can handle it.

"Here." Mother shifts back to her role as navigator. She taps the steering wheel. "Turn right."

Mike looks at her but doesn't say anything. The car slows then jounces over the half-paved, half-gravel parking lot of the Luckenbach dance hall. It's jam-packed with trucks, cars, and motorcycles.

"Why didn't you just say we were coming to the dance hall, Mother?" But I know the reason. It all has to do with control.

"Remember," Mother says as Mike swings the Cadillac into a spot big enough for a Volkswagen, "try to avoid the tragic reason you've had to come to Texas. This should be a joyful celebration."

"Of cattle feed." Mike looks back at me and grins.

"Don't forget poultry, swine, rabbits, and llamas," I add to the list of feeds, not to mention all the fertilizers the Wards sell.

"And marriage," Mother adds.

"How could we forget?"

13

The earthquake and Daddy's funeral seem to be the only two topics of conversation going around the bar-becue, and I'm tired of both. I'm beginning to relate to Scarlett O'Hara—if I hear "earthquake" or "funeral" one more time, I'm going to go in the house and slam the door, fiddle-dee-dee.

I'm exhausted from giving a tight-lipped smile and say-ing "Thank you" when told how much someone thought of my father. It's hard to hide my disappointment, my concern, my fear that my family is falling apart. Maybe to others my worry looks like mourning. But I'm not sure what the dis-comfort of having to lie for my parents looks like. Like my slacks are too tight? Perhaps like my arm is twisted behind my back, but I'm not sure who is holding me hostage. Mother? Daddy? Or my own guilt and needs?

On this occasion the lights strung along the rafters glimmer bright and festive. Usually the hall is open for visitors and tourists. Five dollars at the door will get you a glimpse of an unknown singer and the opportunity to two-step. Occasionally Willie Nelson will show up with his band. But tonight it's a private function. Still, there's a band with a banjo, guitar, and fiddle.

"Don't worry." Josie surprises me. She's wearing skin-tight jeans and a racy red top that dips low enough to reveal a bit of her lacy bra.

"About what? Another earthquake, or my mother going on a killing spree?" My joke is a poor attempt to regain my sense of humor.

She laughs, tipping her head back, her teeth gleaming, her neck arched like a wolf baying at the moon. "Think the two could be connected?"

"Like how?"

"Like some deep, dark secret is coming to the surface, something so big the earth can't contain it."

"You should write for the movies."

"Only if I could get my hands on Johnny Depp."

My smile falters and my gaze veers away, searching for my husband who Josie ogled only this morning. "Good luck with that one."

"Maybe I'll come visit you in California."

"Sure," I say, but I'm not sure the invitation is as open as it was just a day or so ago. Her flirtations are natural for her but problematic for me.

She leans in close, her hand on my arm, her heady perfume wrapping around me, twitching my nose. "Don't worry. Your secret is safe with me."

My spine stiffens like an electrical shock has been shot along its length. I try to forget the look on her face when she met my son and made the connection between him and Drew. Inwardly I cringe at my defensiveness, my own anxiety twisting in me, just as Mother's has been working in her. I should say, "Thanks, Josie, for your discretion," but I don't. And

I won't. Pride comes before a fall. Was that Humpty Dumpty's problem? Am I sitting up on a high and mighty wall, about to tumble to the hard, unforgiving ground?

I can't stop myself from saying, "I didn't know I had one."

Josie's eyes narrow. In that moment secrets we shared in high school come burbling to the surface. I told her about my first kiss. She told me about her first love. I told her about my mother and father's difficulties. She told me her mom drank. A lot. I told her when Drew asked me out, when we kissed, when he took me to Makeout Flats in his father's truck. She told me about her mother's boyfriends, the ones who looked her way and came into her room after her mother passed out. Guilt is swift and sharp. Regret is slow and blunt.

"I see." Her mouth tightens then she gives me that hold-onto-your-hat smile. "Well, maybe you don't have any secrets then." She hooks her thumb through a belt loop. "You sure do have a nice family, Suzy Q."

Is there something in her eyes? Some glint of her intent? Or is it only humor at my expense?

"Thanks. I, uh . . ." I search for a way to move away from her or reach toward her. I'm not sure which. "I better go find Mike."

"You do that." She winks, her lashes weighted with thick black mascara. "I'll let you know if I find him first."

Before I can respond, she's off, swinging her backside, her red boots scooting across the wooden floor.

"DID YOU HEAR the news?"

Linda Lou Hoover, at it again, eyes me carefully and sips her lemonade.

The air is thick with the smell of smoke and tangy scent of barbecue. The honored couple, the Wards, who own the feed mill that employs my dad, assured me when we arrived, "We'll miss your father." Patty patted my hand. "No one knows our feeds the way he did." She *tsked*. "Such a shame. He was on the road so much."

Joe nodded, his Stetson shading his eyes. "Ain't nobody like Archie."

Hearing those words, I felt my chest tighten. My father is well loved.

Now, the band cues up with a fiddle and a mandolin playing a lonesome-sounding song that makes me think of infomercials selling Boxcar Willie CDs. The noise rakes across my frayed nerves, as rough and irritating as Mrs. Hoover's question.

"What news?" I ask, knowing I shouldn't.

"Well, I don't want to upset you now."

Of course she does. She'd love to upset me, so then she'd have something more to put in her weekly column. I take a long, slow breath to prepare myself. Over Mrs. Hoover's shoulder, I watch two men lifting a table and moving it over toward the wall. A folded chair that was leaning against the table tumbles over, smacking against the wooden floor.

Mrs. Hoover screeches. "What was that?" She grabs my arm. "Did you feel that? We're—"

"It's okay, Mrs. Hoover." I wipe a splash of lemonade off my arm. "It was—"

"An aftershock!" Her eyes are suddenly wild as she looks toward the exit. I imagine her elbowing me out of her way to get someplace safe.

"It was a chair," I explain. "Really. It's okay. Nothing to worry about."

She rests a hand against her heaving bosom. "Oh, my! It's so unnerving. Waiting for aftershocks or another quake. I could never live in California. You're so calm. You must be used to this."

"Not really. But that wasn't an aftershock. Just a chair." I turn her toward the men who are pushing the table into place and picking the chair up off the floor. "See?"

"Well, they should be more careful! Everyone is on edge from that earthquake last night. I wouldn't be surprised if those weak of heart don't—"

"Mom?" Oliver steps up beside me.

Mrs. Hoover frowns at the interruption, then schools her features and leans closer as if she might grab another morsel of gossip. She gives my son a thorough examination with her beady eyes. "You must be Oliver. Well, my, my. I don't know why I expected such a little boy. All of your grandmother's pictures are of you as a little boy. Suzanne, you really should get your mother new pictures of your son. Why, you're practically a man now!"

With a tight smile, I make quick introductions.

"You don't look a thing like your daddy. Guess you take after your mother. But whichever, you couldn't do badly going either way."

My nerves split like a dry, cracked nail.

"Did you feel the earthquake the other night?" Mrs. Hoover inquires.

"No. Dad and I hadn't arrived yet," Oliver explains.

"Oh, well, you're lucky. It was horrific. The most frightening thing I've ever felt in my life."

"What did you need, Oliver?" I touch my son's arm.

"You know," Mrs. Hoover continues as if I haven't spoken, "I've known your mother a long time. Your grandmother too."

"Yes, ma'am." Oliver often wanders through social gatherings we have at home for Mike's law firm. He's learned over the years to be polite and patient.

Unfortunately my manners are faltering. "What did you—"

131

"Why," Mrs. Hoover touches a hand to her wide middle, "I remember long before she met your daddy, she dated the bad boy in town. 'Course that—"

"Mrs. Hoover—"

"Oh, now, come, come, Suzanne. Surely you don't mind your son knowing you had eyes for another, someone other than his father. Of course that was long before you met that handsome attorney you married."

I put my hand on Oliver's shoulder. It still amazes me that I have to reach up to do so. "I don't think it's—"

"Well, that bad boy is now the sheriff." She pauses for effect as if eager to push whatever button she can. "Can you imagine that?" She laughs, arching her head back and mouth open so wide I can see her silvery fillings. "Life is sure full of twists and turns. 'Course back then, your momma was just in high school. We all thought she'd marry Drew. Now, don't fret, Suzanne. We all thought that. Thought you'd change your mind about going so far away to school. We sure did. The bad boy and the goody-two-shoes."

"Goody-two-shoes?" Oliver eyes me speculatively. It's not often he thinks he has me cornered.

It's easier for him to think that about me than to know the truth that hardens my stomach like a fossilized lump. "Yes, well—"

"We worried about your momma. Hooking up with such a boy. Drew had quite a reputation for breaking girls' hearts. And we didn't want him turning your momma into a wild girl."

"Okay, Mrs. Hoover," anger rises in me like floodwaters, "I don't think Oliver needs to hear old gossip." Or new either. "Oliver didn't come over here for a Luckenbach history lesson, fascinating as it is. He wanted to tell me something. What was it, baby?" Immediately I regret calling him that. I've tried to call him other manly terms of endearment, but he's still my baby. Just as I'm my father's sugar beet.

"Don't worry, Mom." He nudges me with his shoulder. "I'll keep your secret."

"It's not a secret." I sound as defensive as I feel.

He shrugs that teen shrug I've become used to. "I can't take this music." He nods toward the stage. "I'm going outside."

"Your dad might already be out there." I glance over the heads of the crowded dance hall, not seeing Mike anywhere.

"Would you like me to introduce you to the teenagers here?" Mrs. Hoover asks.

"I've already met some. Thanks."

"You have?" I'm always surprised by his resourcefulness.

"Yeah, Mom. And some of us are going to hang out. Outside."

"Okay." I'm glad he's at least found something to do. It's better than his being bored. Or hanging out with Mrs. Hoover. "Have fun." I pat his back as he heads off on his own, looking pleased to be away from Linda Lou. I can't blame him. Or maybe it's me. With the teen years comes that push and pull of connecting and stepping away. I remember my own teen years of pushing away from my parents, finding my own path. In some ways I'm still separating.

"He seems like a good boy." Mrs. Hoover watches Oliver weave his way through the crowd. "Handsome. In a different way than your husband, but still . . ."

My gaze follows him easily, as he's tall. Pride brings a smile. He's a good kid, smart, respectful, contemplative. He stops on his way to the door, and I watch him talking to someone, answering questions. I can't tell who he's talking to, then with a sideways step I see Josie. What is she saying to him? What is she asking? My nerves tighten as she leans into him, her breasts grazing his arm.

Oliver gives a nod and walks out the dance hall's door. But my gaze lingers on Josie. She turns and walks over to a table where Mike sits alone. She drags a finger along his shoulders, pulls a chair over, and sits close beside him. She's leaning into him, that flirtatious lean that every woman has attempted at some time or another but that Josie has perfected with years of practice. My nerves are as taut as the fiddle strings being plucked on the stage.

"Is he?" Mrs. Hoover steps closer to me to close the gap I've created. Her powdery perfume envelops me like a fog. The smell of her waxy lipstick makes me inch backwards.

"Is he what?" I suddenly feel vulnerable, as if all my thoughts and feelings are broadcast on my face. "I'm sorry. My mind drifted. What were you saying?"

"Are you okay?"

"Sure." I offer a smile that doesn't convince me. My gaze is pulled back toward Mike. And my friend.

Mrs. Hoover's gaze is penetrating and shifts from me toward that tiny table. That intimate table. "Oh, I see. Well, you're smart to pay attention. Josie is no woman's friend. She's always after some man."

Last night when we sat out on her car and talked, it felt like old times, and yet she was telling me clearly that she has a thing for married men. But would she go after mine? I refuse to believe that. She's my friend.

We shared a lot growing up together. We had our share of problems, but we were there for each other. Yet I clearly remember her trying to entice Drew away from me at one point. I had been grounded for something Mother didn't approve of and wasn't allowed to go out one Friday night. After Mother went to bed, I crept out of the house. My high school friends were hanging out at Makeout Flats, listening to Alabama's "Love in the First Degree" on the radio. And Josie was sitting behind Drew, on his motorcycle, giving him a back rub. He had moved into the area with his dad during our sophomore year in high school. He had been an outsider, which made him all the more attractive to the homegrown girls. Josie and Drew both denied anything was happening between them, but a tickling deep down inside me suspected that Josie had been on the prowl that night.

Now, even if she is trying to get to my husband, or tell him her suspicions about Oliver's parentage, I know Mike. I trust him. I have nothing to worry about. Except myself. And my secrets. So I give myself a mental shake, let out a pent-up breath, and focus on Mrs. Hoover.

"Josie is my friend," I say, my confidence lagging as much as my energy. "Mike is my husband. Why shouldn't they talk?"

Mrs. Hoover's gaze is assessing and crystal clear. I can see that she's seen things, knows things. But I'm not interested in her gossip and rumors. She pats my arm like I'm a simple child. "You've been through so much in the last day or so with your father."

You'll never know.

"So," she shifts from foot to foot, her stance wide to balance her weight, "I was asking about your son. Is Oliver a good boy? He seems polite enough."

I try to think of a quick way to excuse myself. At the moment I don't see anyone I know. Except Mike and Josie. And I refuse to walk toward their table and give Mrs. Hoover more food for her blender of tittle-tattle. "He is."

"Seems very considerate. I mean, coming over to let you know he was going outside. So you wouldn't worry. Not at all like some of the teens I know who say 'ma'am' like it's something dirty on the sole of their boot." She slurps her lemonade, sucks a bit of juice off her upper lip, which I notice has a shadowy mustache. "As I was saying before your son came over," she readjusts her wide too-tight belt, "I only tell you

this news that's going around because I want you to be prepared so you won't be upset by it. Why, if your poor mother
hears this, it might rattle her something terrible."

She pauses.

"It seems Flipper has seen . . ." she looks sideways then
leans toward me, her breath warm and sour on my face, "your
father."

"Okay," I say, slowly, carefully, cautiously. It's too good
to believe. Maybe this web of deception will be swept clean
at last.

"His ghost, that is."

"Excuse me?"

"That's the rumor. He's seen your father's ghost. Now
ain't that a fright?" She laughs, but it's a nervous twitter as if
she's not quite sure if Archie Davidson is going to float into
the dance hall at any minute. "I'm sorry, dear. I realize it's not
funny to you. And the thing is, everyone seems to be taking
it seriously. Can you imagine?"

I can and I'm not sure how to respond. "Well, thank you
for telling me." My mind is trapped between exhaustion and
dread. This ghost business might prove to Mother that her
shenanigans have gone too far. "I appreciate your concern for
our family."

And I make my escape, deciding to rescue Mike from
Josie's clutches. But I'm blocked once again.

"How is your mother holding up?" Hazel Perkins stands
right in front of me, a formidable barrier. Tonight her color is
green. A lime green. Her shirt, skirt and fringed cowboy boots
are all some shade of the bright color.

"Oh, she's fine, thank you."

Hazel takes hold of my arm. Her gaze is as glaring as her
outfit. "Are you sure?"

"Yes. You know my mother."

"I do. Maybe better than anyone." She looks down at the

floor, then back at me. "If I can do anything to help you and your family during this time, please let me know." She opens her mouth to speak but then seems to think better of it. Her mouth twists as if she's wrestling with something. "I . . . want to help."

"I appreciate that," I say and edge sideways, gently pulling my arm away from her heavy hand. Each act of kindness only makes me feel more guilty about Mother's ploy and my complicity. I can't understand why Mother doesn't feel the same. She seems perfectly content with all the love and concern being heaped upon her.

"Your mother is always the one to help others. When my Charlie passed on, she was right by my side, making decisions for me. I don't know how I would have gotten through it without her. And now that she's . . . well, I . . ." Her eyes fill with tears that don't overflow. She sniffs loudly. "I just don't know what to do, how to help."

I embrace her. "It's okay. Mother is fine. And I'm here."

"Yes," she pats my back, squeezes me hard, "you're here. Thank you."

I walk toward my husband and Josie. When she sees me coming, she gives me a confident smile and flounces away to dance with some biker in a faded red doo-rag and black leather.

"Everything all right?" Mike asks.

"Yes, of course."

"How long do you think your mother wants to stay?"

"I don't know. Have you seen her?"

He tilts his head in the direction of the buffet table. I give him a quick proprietary kiss but he pulls me back. "Want to dance?"

"Do you know how to two-step?"

"You could teach me."

"Okay. But first I have to tell Mother something."

"Is there a problem?" He holds onto my hand. Now that Josie is on the other side of the room, I feel more secure.

"Isn't there always?"

I sidle up to Mother and whisper, "Do you know what everyone's saying?"

"Yes," she says, picking up a square of cheese by a toothpick off a paper plate and rolling it between her forefinger and thumb. "Wouldn't you think they could offer something more appetizing?"

"About Daddy!"

She smiles, a wispy secretive smile that is way too deceptive for my peace of mind, which hasn't existed since I stepped off the plane at the Austin-Bergstrom International Airport. She pops the cheese square into her mouth and chews slowly. "Isn't it wonderful? His ghost has been spotted. I couldn't have planned that any better."

"But it's not a ghost," I protest. "It's Daddy. In flesh and blood." Maybe I shouldn't mention blood around her. She's a bit bloodthirsty these days. I don't want to give her any ideas in case Daddy does get up the courage to venture home.

"Voice down." She places a warning hand on my arm. "You don't have to worry. This is really a good thing." She acts like a child on Christmas morning playing with a brand new toy, straight out of the box, her eyes aglow with the possibilities.

"But, Mother—"

"Trust me, dear."

Said the spider to the fly.

14

Drew

The absence of a body plus no crime equaled nothing to investigate.

Drew wasn't sure what was going on over at Betty Lynne Davidson's house. Maybe the earthquake, er . . . the crack . . . had shaken loose a screw in her brain.

It should have all added up to a quiet, peaceful Sunday. But there had been more calls today than the Fourth of July celebration last year when the fireworks truck blew up.

Earlier in the day he had climbed a tree to retrieve Edna Rogers's cat.

"Spooked by the earthquake, don't ya know." She petted Mr. Whiskers and cooed at him. Those yellow eyes looked demented.

"It wasn't an earthquake, Mrs. Rogers," Drew assured her as patiently as he could, even though he had repeated the same sentence at least a hundred times. "The geologists said it could have simply been a minor shift of a fault line. Or even an existing crack widening because of the drought."

But she wasn't listening. Neither were any of the other folks. They had felt a jolt. They had seen the buckled highway. They had heard about how the crack through Luckenbach ran all the way north of Fredericksburg. Makeout Flats, as the kids called it, was blocked off for security and safety precautions. But frankly it might be better if it was available for public viewing. Rumors had spread that the crack reached from the Oklahoma border clean down to Mexico. Folks didn't care what any yahoo from over at the university had to say; they knew what they had felt and heard. And there was no ignoring the facts. Drew wasn't sure why he clung to denial. But he did. That was the sheriff's office official policy at the moment.

After a long day of answering calls related to the "incident," Drew now cruised the tiny hamlet of Luckenbach, the SUV's headlights cutting through the inky blackness. He took the long way around the dance hall, which was on the opposite side of South Grape Creek.

He had driven past the dance hall twice already. The Wards' anniversary party was still going full steam. The invitation sat on his desk. Sometimes he wondered if folks sent him an invitation so he'd attend as a guest or in a more professional capacity.

He tightened his hold on the steering wheel, turned too sharply, and the tires squealed. A spark in the darkness off to his left caught his attention. Then it was gone. But he had seen it. Maybe it was Archie, hanging out at the campfire area. Drew rubbed his tired eyes. With the grass dry and brittle from the drought, it wasn't a good idea to start fires of any kind.

Making a loop back through the parking area, then down along the highway, he pulled into the back lot. There was an empty white truck. Rick Parker's. The kid had been in trouble before. Now what was he up to? Drew radioed the dispatcher. "No, Marge, I don't need backup."

Then he stepped from the SUV and walked through the dry grass and down to the edge of South Grape Creek. The water was so low the foot bridge almost wasn't needed. Slowly he made his way along the edge of the creek and up the hill, looking for anything out of the ordinary. Everything seemed peaceful, like the choir sang about on Sunday mornings. There were other churches in the area to choose from. He wasn't sure why he preferred the cowboy/biker church. Did it have something to do with Suzanne? He hadn't let himself think about her for a long time. But ever since he had seen her the other night, he'd had a hard time pushing her out of his thoughts.

Staccato laughter punctuated the night. He rested his palm on the handle of his weapon. No reason to be jumpy. Yet caution trumped foolishness any day of the week. He followed the sounds of laughter. Female giggling created a melody and a male voice . . . no, more than one played backup.

Drew reached the top of the ridge, no longer fingering his gun but reaching for his flashlight. This should be a simple teen party to break up. He stepped to the side of a headstone, felt the soft grass beneath his boots. He just hoped he wouldn't catch the girl in the altogether. That had happened a few times in the past. He always averted his gaze, focused on the boy while the girl hastily dressed. But it made things awkward when he later had to drop by the high school or saw the girl in the community with her parents.

Dark figures ahead, shadows moving. They weren't aware of him. Two couples, he surmised. He aimed his flashlight and hit the juice.

"What's going on here?"

It always amused him to watch people scamper like cockroaches. He remembered the preacher talking about God as a light shining in the darkness. Sometimes Drew wondered if being on this side of the law gave him little glimpses into God's perspective.

One teen turned took a step outside of the spotlight, easing away from the group, starting to make a getaway.

"Freeze!" Drew hit him full with the beam. "Rick Parker, that you?"

He shaded his eyes. His shoulders slumped in defeat. "Uh, yes, sir."

"What's in your hand?" Drew walked past the circle of stones where many a campfire had been lit. Drew recognized the smoky scent and grabbed the joint. "Okay, hit the ground and spread 'em. You too . . . Lisa Boyle?"

"Yes, sir," came a squeaky reply. She blinked her not-so-innocent blue eyes at him. So much for her senior year as head cheerleader.

Drew flicked the light over the other two. The girl looked familiar. But not the boy. "Rachel Ryan? What are you doing out here?"

"I was just—"

"Move over there." Drew flicked the light to an open piece of dry ground.

"Are you gonna tell my Daddy?" Rachel whined. "You know he'll—"

"Who are you?" Drew shone the light on a kid who was still sitting with his head down. He had brown wavy hair, short and tight against his scalp. "I'm talking to you."

He didn't look up.

"Give me your name."

"Oliver Mullins." He squinted at Drew then.

Click. The name meant something to him. Had he been in trouble before? Had he brought the hash? Or had Rick provided it? "You from California?"

The kid lifted his chin then looked away from the bright

light. Drew dropped the beam to the boy's chest. The kid looked straight at him. His eyes were green like Suzanne's but larger. "How'd you know?"

Cursing under his breath, Drew flicked the light toward the ground next to Rachel. "Move over there. You're under arrest for possession of marijuana. Got anything else I should know I'm going to find when we get to the station?"

"No, sir," Rick answered.

Drew didn't believe him.

IT WAS LIKE looking into a mirror. Drew saw himself in Oliver Mullins when he was a teen . . . the same devil-may-care attitude.

The Mullins kid didn't give him trouble, didn't question or argue. He couldn't tell if the kid was scared or if he'd been this route before. Drew escorted him into a room with a simple table and chair. The kid sat as he was told. Drew took off the handcuffs.

"So how'd you get involved with Rick?"

He shrugged.

"You know him?"

He shrugged again.

"You don't have to talk to me, but I'm trying to help you out here. Rick says the weed was yours."

His head snapped up. But he remained silent.

"So did you bring it from California?"

"No." His lips were tight, barely spitting out the word.

"When did you get here?"

"Yesterday. Today. Not sure."

"Did you know Rick already?"

"No."

"How'd you meet him?"

"At that boring party."

"The Wards? Over at the dance hall?"

He nodded.

"Your folks drag you there?"

"My grandmother."

"I see. How old are you?"

"Fifteen."

And Rick Parker was eighteen. "You been in trouble like this before?"

"No."

"You tried weed before?"

"Once." The kid didn't have to admit that. Maybe he was honest. If so, that would be a plus. But Drew always waited to see how the truth played out.

"Why tonight?"

He shrugged.

"You givin' your folks a hard time?"

"No."

"You upset about your grandfather?"

"No."

That wasn't surprising. Drew doubted the kid was close to Archie. After all, they hardly saw each other. Or maybe the kid wasn't upset because he knew something Drew didn't. Maybe he could get information about Archie out of Oliver.

"It's a pretty hard thing losin' your grandpa."

He shrugged.

"Were you close to him?"

"Not really."

Drew waited.

"My grandmother—" The kid stopped himself.

"Go on."

His mouth pulled to the side. "It doesn't matter."

Drew sat on the edge of the table, crossed his arms over his chest. He wasn't sure why, but he liked this kid, sensed he was good, not a troublemaker like Rick. Maybe because Oliver

144

wasn't insisting that Drew call his dad. His big-shot attorney dad. Oh, sure, Drew knew who the kid's father was. Everyone in town knew. Betty Lynne Davidson had made sure everyone knew about her son-in-law, the high-powered lawyer. How he made big corporations tremble in their boots. What about the boy though? Was he afraid of his own father?

"I know your grandma." Drew smiled, imagining how Betty Lynne wasn't the cuddly, sweet grandma type. "Know how she can be."

"Wacko," he mumbled.

That's the second time he'd heard that in one day. He had never thought of Betty Lynne Davidson as crazy. Determined. Strong willed. Difficult at times. He had seen her operating at church, in the community, always volunteering, always handling things her way. She was the first to offer to help someone in need. She was the first to take food when needed. She could jump into a crisis situation and know what to do, and it was hard to find fault with that. He didn't like hysterics, which never helped. He had watched Archie hop-to when she said jump. She was just a born leader. Drew usually stayed clear of her though. After all, she had made it clear a long time ago that he wasn't good enough for her family.

"Stay away from my daughter," she had said to him once when he and Suzanne were in high school. "My daughter is not your type. Suzanne has plans." Plans that didn't include him.

"I'm gonna have to call your folks," he said to Oliver.

"I know." The kid had the slumped shoulders of defeat.

Drew always worried when he picked up kids what their home life was like. He never wanted to make things worse. He knew with Rick Parker, his dad had beat him black and blue. Now Rick was living on his own. He only answered to himself. But what of Oliver Mullins? He couldn't imagine Suzanne would be married to a harsh man. She was strong, like her mother, yet softer, not as domineering or controlling.

"That bother you? Me calling your folks?"

He shrugged. "You know my mom, don't you?"

Drew braced himself for the inevitable "My dad's gonna" or "My mom's gonna" shoot you/club you/sue you . . . He had heard it all.

"Yeah, I know your mom."

"I heard you dated her."

"That was a long time ago."

Oliver nodded but didn't say anything else.

"Okay, then." Drew headed toward the door.

"So what's gonna happen now?" The kid's voice had a slight waver in it. He had eyes that could bore a hole clean through. Yet at the same time he looked vulnerable, like Suzanne. Maybe that's why Drew had a soft spot for this kid.

"I'm gonna track down your folks, see if they'll take you back."

"They will." But he didn't sound cocky. "Will this be on my record?"

"You're a juvenile."

"Will it screw up my getting into college?"

Drew stared at him. No one he'd ever arrested had been worried about that. "Depends."

"On what?"

"Tomorrow you'll have to come in for a test."

"What kind of test?"

"Drug test. Urine sample. Painless."

"Why not now?"

"Not here. Over at the clinic. If we do it too soon, the traces won't show up."

"Works for me." The kid smiled for the first time.

"Need eight hours at least. But if I can't find your folks,

then you'll be sitting here all night and a deputy will drive you over in the morning."

"Then what?"

"If the results show you were lighting up tonight, then it'll be on your record. If you smoke weed again, or take any other kind of drug, if you get arrested, then yeah, I'd say it could screw up your future. But this . . . well, we'll see."

15

Suzanne

With one hand at my back and his other holding onto mine, Mike two-steps me around the dance floor. His technique is to hold me close. Most newcomers to country swing keep a good couple of feet apart in order to avoid stepping on toes. But Mike is different than any man I've ever known. He allows me to lead and anticipates my moves by the touch and feel of my body against his.

When the song ends, he twirls me around and dips me backward.

"Let's get a Coke," he says.

It's ice cold and a welcome relief in this heat. The dance hall feels like a steam bath with so many crammed inside. The crowd has grown in the last hour. It seems the whole community has come out. Folks from nearby towns have driven over. Old friends and neighbors have greeted me. Some I recognize, others not so much.

I tried to have a conversation with Estelle, but the music was too loud. And before we could say more than "we need to catch up," she raced off after one of her kids. Josie stopped beside me once, but she was either looking for someone or hiding from some guy she didn't want to face.

"Doing okay?" Mike asks.

"Managing. You?"

"Yeah. When do you think your mom will be finished making her appearance?"

I can see Mother across the room talking to the Wards. "Soon. Did you hear the latest?"

"About your dad?"

"He's turned into Casper."

"Was he friendly then?"

I laugh. "Knowing my dad, he was."

"Apparently it flipped Flipper out."

"Poor guy." Anger steams up my contact lenses from the inside. "Doesn't Mother see the harm she's causing?"

"She can only see her needs."

I know he's right because it's always been true.

Mike puts an arm around my shoulders, kisses my temple.

"So what are we going to do?"

Someone brushes past me, jostles my arm. Mike lets his arm slip down my back and guides me toward the doorway. "Let's talk outside."

When we've cleared the masses, I sit at one of the picnic tables set apart from the outdoor stage. Unique license plates have been nailed to the posts and along the back wall. "So?"

Shrugging, he leans an elbow on the grainy wood table top. "Do you think your mom would forgive your dad?"

"For leaving? I don't know."

"I don't think he did anything per se."

"The fact that he left equals betrayal to Mother."

He dips his chin with a thoughtful nod of understanding. "An unforgivable sin."

The crunch of gravel makes Mike turn toward the parking area. An older couple picks their way through the cars, trucks, and motorcycles. The man nods toward us, then they disappear inside the dance hall.

"Right now, your mother doesn't want him back."

"He doesn't seem eager to return. So what are we going to do?"

Mike draws in a deep breath, then releases it. His face is shiny with sweat. I can see wet marks on his starched shirt, which looks like it's wilted in the heat. "We have to get them in the same room."

"And then what? World War Three?"

He chuckles. "Then it's up to them." His smile fades, and he looks at me with serious intent. "And we have to accept that."

I nod, run my finger around the lip of the Coke can.

"Can you do that, Suzanne?"

"I don't know. I know that sounds stupid. I'm forty-two years old. What my parents do or don't do shouldn't affect me. But it feels like . . ." My throat closes up, clogging with emotions.

He covers my hand with his. "I know. No matter what though, it's going to be okay. You're safe. Our family—you, Oliver, me—we're okay."

"I know." But I don't. And I can't explain my fears to Mike. To anyone.

His thumb traces the edge of mine. "It's taken your dad a long time to get to this place. He's suffered a lot during their marriage. For him to have the confidence to leave . . . well, it might not be a bad thing."

"How can you say that?" I stare at him, appalled and fearful.

"Because it's the truth."

"Christians aren't supposed to walk away from their marriage."

He nods. His hand is steady on mine, not flinching or retreating. "In a perfect world. We don't live in a perfect world, Suz. I'm not saying it's right or wrong. That's not for me or you to say, is it? Maybe he's tried to make things work a dozen other ways. Maybe he doesn't know what to do anymore. Maybe this is the only way he knows how to get your mother's full attention. But whatever he decides, it's not the worst thing to ever happen."

Surprising tears burn my eyes. I blink them away.

Suddenly blue lights flash, making me squint. I hear a car door slam and the crunch of gravel again. Mike turns just as Drew walks up. He's wearing his uniform.

"Suzanne," he says, eyeing Mike, "I need to speak to you."

Uh-oh. Another serious look. He knows. He knows about Mother's charade. Did he find my father hiding out at the Old Hockheim Inn? Did Mother finally cross that faint line with her play-acting stunt? Could she be arrested? I take a calming breath, attempt a relaxed smile, but it feels awkward and flat. I squeeze Mike's hand for support.

"Sure. Uh, Drew . . . Sheriff . . . this is my husband, Mike Mullins. Sheriff Drew Waring."

The two men shake hands, eye each other. Mike knows that Drew and I dated. Once. But that's all he knows. Does he recognize the name? Make the connection? He gives no indication. No reaction. And Drew is professional in his demeanor.

"I can tell both of you then," he says.

Both of us? "About Mother?"

His head tilts slightly. Have I spoken out of turn? His pause is slow and deliberate. "Actually, I've got your son down at the jail."

Tightness seizes my chest. "What? Oliver?"

Mike shifts from foot to foot as if stepping into his professional capacity. "Why?"

"What happened?" Panic arcs through me. "Is he okay?"

"Just arrested him."

"What?" I clutch at Mike's arm.

Drew's gaze flicks across my hand, then meets Mike's square on.

"For what?"

"Possession."

"Possession of what?" My head begins to reel.

WHAT WERE YOU thinking? What did you do? What will happen now?

All of the questions Mother has flung at me over the years come back to me now, jam in my throat. I choke them back down, refuse to utter one of them as I walk into the room where Oliver is standing. First I hug him, sniffing his hair, as if that will tell me he's all right, unchanged, the same. My hand flutters about his broad swimmer's shoulders.

"Mom." He shifts away from me.

"Okay, okay." I look deep into his eyes. They're green, like mine, but shaped more like—

"If you sign here," Drew's voice is brusque, "then you can take him home."

I turn and face the sheriff, feeling a flush creep up my neckline and warm my face. I search for any sign, any recognition, but his gaze is flat, tired. "Okay."

But Mike steps forward first. With a bold slashing of pen to paper, he places our son in our custody.

"So that's it?" I glance from Mike to Drew. "That's all?"

Lines around his eyes reveal the sheriff's exhaustion. "Have him to the clinic on Fourth Street in Fredericksburg by 8 a.m. tomorrow. They'll be expecting him. The test shouldn't take long. If he doesn't show, then I'll come get him myself."

"He'll be there." Mike's voice is firm.

"Test?" I take a step toward Oliver, as if I can protect him from the unknown. "What do you mean?"

"It's a drug test, Suz." Mike takes my arm in his and escorts me toward the door.

"So what does that mean?"

"It means he'll be tested. If it comes up positive, then he'll be charged. Until then, he's in our custody."

I turn back toward Drew. Anger pumps through me. "You would charge my son?" A cold hardness forms in my stomach. "How could you—"

"It's his job." Mike's hand on my arm is firm, insistent.

What if I told Drew the truth? Would it change things? Would he decide not to charge his own son? "But—"

"It's okay, Suz. Let me handle it." Mike holds out his hand to the sheriff. "Sheriff, thanks for your professionalism."

Drew glances down at Mike's hand but hesitates to take it. His look reminds me of the same aloof, dispassionate appearance he had as a mixed-up teen. Slowly, he reaches forward and shakes Mike's hand. "All right then."

Mike gives a quick head jerk, his gaze fastened on Oliver. It's the same look he's used when we've picked up Oliver at birthday parties or play dates. It's always been our expectation for Oliver to thank his hosts. But this hasn't exactly been a party. Still . . .

Oliver moves forward at his father's bidding. I realize in that moment I've been holding onto his arm too, as if I'm afraid I might lose my grip, my hold on my son, my past, my secrets. It's hard to let go. But I do.

Oliver steps toward the sheriff, emulates his father. "Thanks, Sheriff."

"You're a good kid, Oliver."

"Thank you, sir." As real father and son shake hands, lock gazes that are so similar, so familiar to me, my heart contracts. What would it have been like to have Drew as a husband? As a real father to my son? But I know it wouldn't have worked. We were too different, Drew and I. He was wild and would have resented being tamed, being told he was to be a father. It was one situation I hadn't wanted to control or manipulate.

I knew, of course, when I figured out I was pregnant that there was a possibility that my baby was Drew's. But I was never sure until now that Oliver belonged to him. My son could have been Mike's.

Could have. Should have been.

Back then, if I had told Mike, voiced my doubts, it would have destroyed my marriage. No matter what the outcome of any DNA test. Even if the baby had been Mike's, he still would have known of my betrayal. He would have believed I was like the mother who abandoned him. I loved him too much to do that to him.

And so I kept my secret. Because secretly I feared Mike would leave me. Hearing him say it might be good my father left my mother only strengthened that fear.

When Oliver was born, I examined every inch of him, tried to discern whom he looked like. Mike? Fear made me search for images, glimpses of Drew. But frankly, he looked more like me. So I put the questions and doubts out of my mind and simply refused to think about it.

As Oliver grew, he developed more of Mike's characteristics. I have a picture of them together, Mike and Oliver, heads bent, as Mike (with more patience than I could have mustered) showed four-year-old Oliver how to tie his miniature Top-siders with secret sailor knots. Oliver's dimpled, uncoordinated fingers look small and fragile next to Mike's hands, sun-bronzed, lean, and sure. Over the years Oliver has displayed the same flirting-with-danger, nothing-can-hurt-me confidence that I love in Mike. And Drew. Or the Drew I used to know.

When Oliver was little, Mike would rock him at night and sing, "Son of a Son of a Sailor." When Oliver was older, he knew the words by heart, which reassured me that Oliver was indeed Mike's son.

Only now, looking into Drew's eyes, I am sure who Oliver's biological father is. It's so obvious. How could anyone not see the resemblance?

"Can we go?" My nerves crackle under the strain.

With Drew's nod, Oliver turns with Mike to walk out the door. I follow behind them, eager to put distance between these men, anxious to keep my secrets from becoming general knowledge.

"Suzanne?" Drew calls me back.

I turn, stare at him, have a crazy urge to make a fast getaway to the airport.

"Do you have a minute?"

"It's kind of late, Drew . . . Sheriff. I didn't get any sleep last night. And it's been . . ." I pause, words eluding me. Unease twists my insides.

He rubs his hand over his face. "Tell me about it."

"We'll be in the car," Mike says, closing the door.

I'm left alone with Drew.

He walks toward me, his steps slow and deliberate. I swallow down all the emotions that jump around inside me like pinballs.

"Look," his voice deepens to a husky level that draws me toward him, "there've been some things said about your dad."

"My dad?"

"This ghost phenomenon. I checked into some things, and I know—"

"Can't this wait?" My heart hammers. From fear he'll learn the truth about his son. From relief he didn't notice the resemblance in Oliver. From fear he knows the truth of my father. What if he asks me for confirmation? What will I say? The truth? Or will I protect my mother?

He looks at me long and hard. "Are you okay? Really okay?"

"Yes. Of course. Just tired and stressed. I was before this, and now . . ."

He puts a hand on my arm. I can feel the warmth of his touch through the sleeve of my blouse, the heat of his intensity.

"You know you can come to me if you're in trouble. Right?"

"You'd help me the way you've helped Josie?" The bitterness in my words leaves a vinegary residue on my tongue.

"You know I would."

I take a step back, break contact with him. "I do. Really. I do."

He takes a slow breath. "Okay. I guess this can wait. I'll see you tomorrow."

My breath catches in my throat. "Tomorrow?"

"In Luckenbach."

I blink at him, not understanding.

He scratches the side of his head. "The arrival of your dad's casket . . ."

"Oh! Yes, of course. Okay." How could I have forgotten?

When I reach the car, I am once again able to draw a complete breath. But my heart has trouble completing a full beat, as if it's been split into two jagged pieces.

"WELL, WHAT ARE *you* going to do about this?"

Mother sits in the front seat of her Cadillac, Cruella de Vil waiting to pounce on anything lost or innocent.

Oliver slumps farther down in the back seat beside me.

I just want to be home. Home in California. But I will settle at the moment for my room in Mother's house, and I silently urge Mike to drive faster.

"We're handling it," I say. I'm not quite sure how or what Mike and I are going to do. But I don't want Mother to think we're scrambling. Nor do I want Oliver to think that. But truly, we are. Or I am. Mike seems in control, capable, strong.

About a year ago I caught Oliver with pot in his room. We clamped down. We sought counseling. He's been a model teen ever since.

Oliver is a good kid. He's the responsible one of his group. He's diligent in his studies. He has goals for high school, college, life. So this is a curve ball we didn't expect. But we didn't expect my mother to go off the deep end either, or my parents' marriage to crumble like a three-week-old cookie. Even though all the signs were there.

"Oliver," Mother twists around in her seat to give her grandson the full intensity of her glare, "what got into *you*? What on earth were *you* thinking?"

Of course, Mother doesn't want the answers to these questions. She has her own answers. Wisely, Oliver keeps silent.

"You *weren't* thinking! That's the trouble. But you had better start or you won't make it into a decent university."

"Mother." I hope she'll stop, knowing she won't. But I have to make the attempt for Oliver's sake.

"Why, do you think your parents—"

"Did you hear Mrs. Hoover, Mother?" I lean forward, resting my forearm on the back of the front seat in an effort to shield Oliver from Mother's lecture.

She pauses. "What's that, dear?"

"Mrs. Hoover." I speak louder than necessary, as if that will derail Mother's train of thought. "Did you hear what she said at the party?"

"Nobody listens to her."

"Apparently they do." Mike takes us on the detour around the area where the highway buckled. "I heard it from several people."

"Wait till Linda Lou Hoover gets a hold of *this* piece of juicy gossip, about Oliver being arrested for possession of an illegal substance." Mother has built up a head of steam, and her momentum keeps her going down the same misguided track. "Linda Lou will chew on this for months. Chew on it like her cud. It's all I'll hear at the beauty salon. 'How's that drug addict of a grandson you have, Betty Lynne? Is he in prison yet?'"

It's always about her.

Mike grins though. I can see his reflection in the rearview mirror. "Actually, Betty Lynne, everybody's talking about Archie's ghost hanging around. Haunting the area."

"Yes, yes." Mother folds her hands over her purse primly. "That's all well and good. They believe he's dead. Which is exactly how I want it."

Silence permeates the car for a few minutes. Mike turns the Cadillac onto the country road that leads to my parents' house. The shocks jounce and bounce us with each dip and groove.

"What you're not getting . . ." Mike's grin widens as he pauses to deliver the blow.

". . . is that Grandpa *is* hanging around," Oliver finishes, a wry smile pulling at the corner of his mouth. I should reprimand him for jabbing back at his grandmother, but I can't blame him.

"What?" Mother sits straighter. She jerks around, looks at Oliver, then me, and finally Mike.

"He didn't leave." I find too much pleasure in explaining this to her and wonder if I need to repent. "Daddy's talking to people."

"He doesn't know he's supposed to be dead." Mike clicks on the high beams to illuminate the dark road ahead of us.

"Oh, heavenly hand baskets!" Mother's profile suddenly looks two powder shades paler. "Stop the car this minute. Turn it around."

"Why?" Mike keeps driving.

"We've got to get Archie out of town. Right now!"

That's one thing I don't want to see—my parents duking it out in the same room. If that were to happen, my father just might end up in the casket Mother has bought online from Costco.

"Mike?" Mother shrieks. "Did you hear me?"

He pulls into the driveway. "Yes, ma'am."

Mother glares at him. "Whose side are you on, mister?"

"My family's. We're tired. And we're all going to bed. Oliver, we'll deal with this problem in the morning."

Relieved, I smile to myself. I do like a strong man.

"WE HAVE TO be at the church—well, dance hall—in the morning for the casket to arrive." I pull down the quilted comforter and fluff the pillows.

"How did your mother pull that off?" Mike unbuttons his shirt. "She doesn't have a body, does she? Is she using a real funeral home?"

"She said she hired a hearse in Austin. I wouldn't have thought that was possible."

"Bette Moore hired one for Jerry's fiftieth birthday bash last year. Remember?" He kisses me hard and fast. "You wouldn't have killed me off, would you?"

"I hope I didn't inherit that particular gene."

Mike laughs and sits on the bed. He pulls me down beside him and begins to rub my shoulders, his thumbs making circular motions, kneading my aching muscles. I'm not used to this bed. Or the stress of being home. I can't seem to relax here.

"You're not like your mother." He's trying to reassure me.

But I suspect that I am. After all, she's lying to the whole town. I too, am a liar. The needle prick of truth pierces my heart.

"Did you have fun tonight?" I attempt to divert the conversation away from what is so uncomfortable.

"No, my son was arrested."

"I meant at the party."

"I don't think I've ever been to anything quite like it."

"Did you meet anyone interesting?" I pluck at a loose thread on the comforter.

His fingers begin to work their way up my neck. "Everyone in Luckenbach is interesting."

I can't seem to nonchalantly get around to the topic of Josie. Agitation makes me bold. "I saw you talking to Josie. She's a piece of work, isn't she?"

"I'm surprised you two were such good friends."

I shrug, guilt tweaking my stomach. I'm not behaving like much of a friend. But I push forward. Marriage is more important than a friendship. "We were different. But we cared about each other. Helped each other out. She had a rough home life. Her mom was hard on her."

"Then it's no wonder you got along."

I half turn toward him, and he stops massaging my neck.

"What do you mean?"

"You had something in common. Your mothers."

"Yeah, but hers wasn't like mine. It was rougher for her."

"Damage can be caused in different ways, but it's still painful. Still leaves scars."

"Is that how you see me? Scarred?"

"Wounded. But aren't we all? We all carry our own baggage. I brought a truckload of my own."

We've gone down the wrong path, so I detour. "So is that what you were talking to Josie about?"

"No."

I let out a frustrated breath.

"What's wrong?"

"Nothing. I just . . . you just looked like you were having fun, is all."

He pulls me backward and kisses me. "Are you jealous?"

"No." I deny the feelings roiling inside.

"You have nothing to worry about."

I feel as if I'm naked, all my scars and open wounds visible and oozing. I make a sputtering laugh to bandage myself. "I know."

"So," he kneads my shoulders again, "where'd your mother buy the casket?"

"Online. Costco ships within twenty-four hours."

"How convenient."

"Go figure. Mother said a friend of hers got a good deal, found Costco's prices to be cheaper than the funeral home's. Who buys a casket at Costco? Why do they even sell caskets?"

"Maybe," his voice dips low in an eerie way, "it's the mob."

I gently elbow him in the stomach. "This is all so bizarre. Like a TV movie. So who would take a job driving a hearse?"

Mike shrugs a broad shoulder. "Someone who needs cash?"

"Or worse."

"A drug dealer?" He grins, his cheek dimpling.

But I don't find it funny.

"I'll take Oliver over for his test," he says, wrapping his

arms around me. He pulls me back against his solid chest and rests his chin on the top of my head.

I close my eyes and try to relax in his embrace. But I fear our family is coming apart, the cracks beginning to show. "That shouldn't take too long. Why don't you get Oliver's hair cut while you're out?"

"I could use one too. We want to look spiffy for the funeral."

I rub his arm like a worry stone. "What are we going to say to Oliver in the morning?"

Slowly he stands and pulls the tail of his shirt from his slacks. "I don't know."

"Let's not go overboard. He made a mistake. But it's not the end of the world." There are worse things he could do. Like I've done. Or what his grandmother is doing. "Let's listen to him. My mother never listened to me."

"Neither did mine." Sorrow darkens his eyes.

Mike didn't have a mother. Not one that cared anyway. Mine, in her own warped way, at least cared.

He reaches for my hand, folds his fingers protectively over mine.

"We'll talk with Oliver together."

Together is how all of our problems should be handled. *Should have been* handled. It's my fault they weren't.

16

Oliver is sitting on the couch in the den, flipping channels. He's dressed in shorts, a T-shirt that says *Surf's Up*, and flip-flops. I'm glad Oliver turned out to be a boy and not a girl. It would be harder for me to react differently from Mother if I had a daughter. Besides, I never wanted to say, "Yes, you have to wear hose and a dress to church." Oliver makes that promise to myself easy to keep.

Our life in California is relatively boring, and I like it that way. Now I know why. It must be a reaction to my childhood and the chaos and turmoil I grew up in. Or maybe I'm controlling things the way my mother controlled our lives here. The thought makes my insides squirm.

"Oliver," Mike tilts his head toward the back door, "let's go."

It's already hot this morning. Or maybe it's my stress level making the temperature skyrocket. I'm accustomed to cooler mornings along the coast. This heat is relentless. With my hands clenched, I say a quick prayer that we'll say the right words to our son. Behind us, the door claps shut and Oliver's footsteps echo along the porch planks. Mike keeps moving—away from the house, past Daddy's garden, past the peach trees Daddy planted, away from prying eyes and ears of my mother—and finally stops at the foot of the windmill.

The incessant wind stirs the windmill, creating a slow, grating sound that stops and starts in an out-of-sync rhythm. I lean against the wooden tower and turn to watch Oliver follow. Mike always hoped he would follow in his footsteps to our alma mater, then into law school. But now, just getting him out of high school without a police record or a stint in drug rehab feels like a worthy goal. Mike seems calm, but I see an angry tick in his jaw. I draw a slow, calming breath.

"Yeah, Dad?" Those green eyes can look oh so innocent.

"What happened last night?"

That one simple question cuts off the childish act. Oliver sighs, crosses his arms over his chest and assumes the teenage stance of detachment. "Nothing. Really."

"That's not what the sheriff says."

Oliver stares at the dirt for a moment; his flip-flops are dusty around the edges. "I met some guy. At that party. There were a couple of girls. No big deal. We were just joking around. I didn't smoke any weed. I swear, Dad."

"Look at me."

He does.

"You've always been straight with me. Are you now?"

There's a beat of a pause that makes my hope clatter and rip through me like one of the steel blades from the windmill if it were to come loose.

"Yes, sir."

"Is this like the time with Slater?"

Oliver swallows hard. His face looks mottled, like tiny blood vessels are flaring beneath the surface. "No."

"Why didn't you just leave last night? Walk away."

"Mike," I want to step between father and son. "He said he didn't smoke anything. Sometimes—"

"Suz," Mike stops me with a hand on my arm, "he needs to answer these questions."

"But—"

"There wasn't time, Dad. The guy lit up, then the cop was there. That's all."

Silence creaks in the interval, like the unheard, unseen pressure building along a fault line. Can we believe him? Did Mike push too hard, the way my mother did in pushing me away. I ache to reach out to Oliver, to pull him close, but I force myself to resist. I know what it's like to be accused of something I haven't done. I also know what it's like to be guilty.

"Dad? Mom?"

I study Oliver's face. He's tall and handsome. I remember him as a young boy, how he cupped his hands around a frog to protect it, how he brought me a razor he broke trying to shave like his Daddy. He's always been a good kid with a kind heart, a sensitive spirit. Honest and true.

"You can tell us anything, Oliver," I say.

"I screwed up. I was bored. I shouldn't have gone off with Rick and the others. I knew that. I knew he was trouble. Do you think I ruined everything?"

"Of course not. We'll work things out," I reassure him.

Mike slants me a quelling look. "We can't promise that."

"You have connections."

Could we plead with our friends to get Oliver off whatever hook he's dangling from? Would Mike call in favors? Probably not. I know my husband. He's known for his integrity. But

I am not above such tactics. My one and only contact that could have any influence over this situation is Drew. I pray I won't have to tell him the truth to save my son's future.

"Oliver made a choice. He has to accept the consequences. No matter what they are." His gaze settles on our son. "What happens all depends on the test this morning. We're at the sheriff's mercy."

Anger flares inside me. I want Mike to say he can protect Oliver, our family. I don't want to be at Drew's mercy. What will happen if the test comes back positive, if Drew comes to arrest my son? His son? Will I tell him? Tell him in order to protect Oliver?

"Yeah." Oliver jams his hands in his back hip pockets. "I'm sorry."

I step forward, wrap my arms around his shoulders. My son. I need him as much as he needs me. Mike forms another wall of an embrace around the two of us. He claps Oliver on the back.

"Let's get this test over with."

MOTHER GLANCES AT her silver watch. There's a pinched worry line between her carefully waxed eyebrows. I know the look. She watches for the hearse out the open wooden slats that cover the windows of the dance hall.

"What's the plan, Mother?" My voice echoes off the rafters. Out the window I can see a family of tourists climbing out of their van and walking up to the Luckenbach store. Some bikers mill around in the shaded areas.

"They should—" Mother pauses and readjusts the level of her voice—"be here any minute."

"They?" I brace myself for more surprises.

"Mrs. Davidson?" a voice says behind us.

Mother turns. "Pastor Reese." Her voice is creamy. She

holds out her hands to a man who seems only a few years older than my son. He wears a Harley Davidson T-shirt, jeans, and black leather biker boots. "This is my daughter, Suzanne."

I shake his hand, notice the cross and rose tattoo on his forearm, and smile. I'm surprised Mother asked Pastor Reese to officiate at Dad's funeral. I thought she might go back to her Lutheran church in Fredericksburg. Of course, it doesn't matter since it's all fake.

"Oh, yes." Pastor Reese hooks a thumb through a belt loop on his jeans. "I saw you yesterday during the service. It was more crowded than usual because of the earthquake. Nothing like an act of God to roust folks out of bed on a Sunday morning. I'm so sorry for your loss."

I want to crawl under the nearest bench. I'm glad Oliver isn't here. What is this whole episode teaching him? Is it scarring him for life? Teaching him to lie? We've always put such importance on speaking the truth in our home, and now here we are, caught in a tangled web of lies. This doesn't even count as *stretching* the truth; Mother snapped the truth as easily as a rubber band. Then again, Oliver may already have learned to lie from me. What if he's lying to us now about the marijuana? What then? Is that the legacy I have given my child? My own hypocrisy handed down from generation to generation?

"Her husband and son," Mother's frown deepens, "aren't here right now. They'll be here later. Won't they, Suzanne?"

"Yes, Mother." I notice she doesn't mention where Mike and Oliver had to go. I don't either. Even the silence feels like another lie.

"The funeral home promised they'd have Archie's body here by noon." Mother takes charge like a commander of an army told to march without rhyme or reason. I can almost hear her voice in my head: *Be sure and lie convincingly to the preacher.* I glance out the window, past the canopy of leaves to the blue sky. No rain clouds. But that doesn't mean God isn't going to zap us with lightning.

"Can I call the funeral home for you?" Pastor Reese pulls a cell phone from his back pocket.

"Oh, my, no. They'll be here. I paid good money for them to be here, and they will."

I raise my eyebrows, but Mother ignores me.

"I am sorry for your loss, Mrs. Davidson." Pastor Reese's eyes slant downward in a sympathetic expression.

"Thank you." Mother clasps her hands primly at her waist.

Is there a special punishment for those who lie to a man of the cloth? Even if his cloth is leather?

"Here's the sheriff." Pastor Reese cranes his neck to look past Mother out the window. The official car executes an easy maneuver around the orange barricade that cordons off the crack in the ground where it stretches neatly across the unpaved parking lot, and rolls to a stop near the Luckenbach store. "Maybe he'll know where the hearse is."

"He's not needed." Mother sounds troubled. "Really, there's no need for the sheriff. It's not like there's been a wreck or anything. Well, not today anyway."

"We can make arrangements for the funeral while he's here."

"Arrangements?" I remember Drew had something he wanted to talk to me about. Does it concern funeral arrangements? Or something else? Suddenly my nerves jangle like I've had a triple latte from Starbucks.

"The sheriff's department will provide an escort for the procession going out to the cemetery, stopping traffic. Those kinds of things."

The pastor places a hand on Mother's shoulder. She stares at his hand until he slowly removes it. He clears his throat, rubs his thumb against his palm.

"Mrs. Davidson, we need to discuss the service when you have a moment."

"Of course. Maybe we can talk after the casket arrives. If you don't mind waiting until then."

"Not at all. Whatever's convenient for you." He squints, looking out the window again. "Oh, I was wrong. It's not the sheriff."

I try to ignore the fact that my stomach settles like it's been given a whopping dose of Pepto-Bismol. I look out and see Flipper, my father's best friend, step out of the squad car. He walks toward the church, stumbles over a tree root. It's been years since I've seen him. He looks older than I remember—more girth, less hair. When he steps inside the dance hall, he blinks as his eyes adjust.

"He here yet?"

"Not yet, Flipper." I extend a welcoming arm toward this man I've known my whole life. "Come on in and wait with us."

Grief etches deep lines across his face. The humor of the situation my mother has created comes crashing down as I see the ravaging effects of pain and loss. Of course, Flipper doesn't know my father is alive and well. He thinks his best friend is dead. And he's seen his ghost.

I move forward. "How are you, Flipper?"

"Suzie Q." His arms come around me, and he crushes me to his doughy chest. "You came."

"Yes, of course. It's all right." I pat his shoulder. The truth scratches its way up my throat. "It's going to be just fine."

Mother clears her throat, a clear reminder she's listening. But I don't care. I'm tired of this farce. It's a disgrace. When a man like Flipper has to suffer because of Mother's pride, then something must be done.

"Flipper, you must know—"

"How are you, Flipper?" Mother steps forward.

He sniffs and releases me, his hand lingering in mine for an extra moment. Then he walks toward Mother, almost tripping over my shoe. "Betty Lynne," he says, his voice coarse. But he can't talk. He engulfs Mother with his embrace, mussing Mother's dress and wrinkling her outfit. "It's just not fair."

Her nose squinches up, and she wiggles free. Does she feel guilty? From the way she readjusts her dress and pats her hair, it appears she feels no remorse for putting Flipper through such grief. She probably blames Daddy.

"Mother!" I'm unable to watch the poor man being tortured in such a way. "Tell him!"

"What's that?" Mother tilts her head as if listening to something other than me. She goes to the doorway, leans out, and listens as if she hears angel's wings or the devil's tail thrashing. "Do you hear that?"

"Tell me what?" Flipper rests his hands on the sides of his wide black belt.

"The casket should be here soon." Pastor Reese tries to fill in the blanks.

"Shh." Mother waves a hand to shush them. "Listen."

Far away a thrumming beat pulsates. I wonder if it's my own heartbeat, but it grows louder and louder, pulsing and throbbing.

"If that's one of those teens driving around with their radio too loud . . ." she says. "Disgusting music these days. Pastor—"

"Yes, ma'am?"

Then there's a loud honk, a crack like thunder, and a screech of brakes.

We crowd the doorway and stare at a black hearse that has crashed through the police barricade and hit the buckled rocks. It takes a moment, like an inhaled breath, for the situation to become clear. Then I take off running, and I'm not sure why. But the pastor is running beside me. Flipper is lumbering behind. Mother must be too because I can hear the click of her sling-back pumps against her heels.

I stop just short of the hearse. Tourists gather around and stare. Mandy, the gal that runs the bar, comes out. Rick, who watches the store on weekdays, cranes his head out the ever-open doorway. The hearse looks a good twenty years old, and the new dent in the bumper is not its only ding. The front side windows are down, and a steady, annoying musical beat rolls like a wave toward us.

I can barely hear myself think. "Mother?"

She steps beside me, along with Pastor Reese and Flipper. "This is not what I ordered. Who are you?" She has to shout to be heard. The driver doesn't seem to hear her though. His hearing must already be damaged beyond repair from the loud music. "It's a good thing Archie's dead and can't hear that infernal noise."

"He got a good enough jolt to bring him back to life, looks like," Flipper says, peering into the back of the hearse.

Lifting her chin a notch, Mother takes two strides toward the banged-up hearse. We have no choice but to follow. She bends down, peering in the windshield. "Excuse me." She taps on the half-rolled-down passenger window. "Excuse me! Can you turn that down? Or off?"

Suddenly the rap music stops. Silence throbs in my ears.

"Yeah?" a muffled voice from inside the hearse calls.

"Are you okay?" I look over Mother's shoulder at the driver. He resembles Alice Cooper with more makeup than I've worn cumulatively my whole life. His black hair is teased and sprayed into a wild array.

"Yeah." He twists his head from one to the other. "What happened, man?"

"You hit the road barrier. Didn't you see it?"

"I was looking around, reading the directions, making sure I was in the right place. This here Look-in-back?"

"You made it." Pastor Reese looks at the area with pride.

"Of all things," Mother huffs. "Did Cal Henry send you? I just can't believe this! This is not the hearse I agreed to bring my dearly departed husband to his final resting place."

"There was another funeral. We needed the other hearse for that service."

Mother's lips pinch tightly together.

Flipper walks around the back of the hearse, raps his knuckles on the roof. "Can you get out?"

"Yeah." Alice Cooper's twin alights from the hearse, unfolding his long, lean body. He's a walking cliché with black jeans, black shirt, tattoos, and piercings in his nose, eyebrow, and lip.

"I'm gonna have to write you up on this." Flipper's grief is replaced by an edge of irritation. "You went straight through a detour sign."

"Now, is that necessary?" Mother walks around the front of the hearse to defend her casket chauffeur. "I'll be happy to pay for it."

Flipper glowers at her. "He was recklessly driving a hearse with your husband's body inside."

"Yes, but after all, he's here. And isn't that what's important? It's not like he could hurt Archie or endanger him." She puts a hand on Flipper's arm. "Please. I just don't think I can take much more of all this."

I stare at her, wondering if she's totally lost it or ready for Hollywood. I'm not sure which prospect is more frightening.

"Well," Flipper seems to lose his starch, "I guess, if—"

"Good. Now, let's get Archie inside the dance hall."

"You think that's a good idea?" Flipper mops his damp brow with a handkerchief. "It's kind of hot today."

For a moment Mother looks as if she didn't consider that in her planning. "He's embalmed. It's not like he's going to start perspiring."

"Or stinking up the joint." The words slide out of the side of Pastor Reese's mouth.

Alice Cooper glances around. "You want it where?"

"I believe we'll put it center stage." Mother waves an arm toward the dance hall and the stage where so many performers have strutted their stuff. But they all pale next to Mother's current rendition of Lady Macbeth. Of course, guilt eventually overwhelmed Lady Macbeth. That seems unlikely with Mother.

"Pastor?" Mother crosses her arms over her chest, irritation lining each movement.

"Oh, um . . . yeah." He looks shell-shocked. "Yes, ma'am. Of course. Mandy and Rick said there aren't any festivities this week. Just outdoor concerts between now and the funeral. So Archie should be just fine. They lock up at night anyway."

"What funeral home are you with?" Flipper studies the outside of the hearse.

There's a brief pause when the painted face of Alice Cooper stares at the deputy as if puzzled by the question. "Boyle Brothers' Funeral Home."

Mother claps her hands together. "Why don't we all go on inside? You can take care of this, can't you?"

Alice Cooper scratches his head. His hair does not move. "I could use some help. It's kinda heavy."

"Sure, sure." Flipper stumbles forward. "I'll help. Might be able to take it around that back entrance." Sweat marks stain Flipper's uniform. "Where they bring in sound equipment. Might save a few feet of bumps and jostles."

Alice Cooper shrugs, his black T-shirt stretching over his thin frame, and gets back into the hearse.

"Wait!" Flipper holds out a traffic cop's hand. He rushes to the front of the hearse, bends low to check underneath the hearse. Finally he straightens. "Should be okay. Back up till you can turn around. Just move slowly. I reckon I should ride with you, show you how to get to the other side of the building."

"Sure, hop in."

"I don't think that's a good idea." Mother looks as close to panicking as I've ever seen her.

"Why not?" Flipper's brow folds into a frown.

"Well, because . . . because . . . I need you, Flipper. I'm feeling a bit shaky." She reaches out a suddenly trembling hand, and Flipper automatically steps toward her. "Suzanne!" She looks over her shoulder, as Flipper helps her out of the roadway and into the shade. "Will you help the driver, please?"

Does she mean pay him? Frowning I nod and climb into the hearse. There's a distinctive smell, kind of a sickly sweet odor, and I'm grateful the windows are down as he begins to back up.

"So, my mother hired you in Austin."

"Yeah."

"You work for the Boyle Brothers?"

"Not really."

"Is it a real funeral home?"

"Oh, sure! I know the owner. He asked me to drive this casket over here."

"I see. So there was another hearse that was supposed to be here today?"

"Yeah. But like I said, some guy popped off yesterday and the family wanted a quick funeral."

"Is this your own hearse then?"

"Yeah. I got it from my . . . from Boyle Brothers' when they got their fancy new one."

"I see." I glance back at the rear area where the casket

lies. Along the edges I see cords and electronic doodads. "Do you have a band or something?"

"How'd you know?"

"Good guess. Did anyone tell you the story here?"

"Nope." He doesn't seem the type to ask.

"Okay, well, we appreciate your help. And discretion."

"What do you mean?"

"Nothing." I decide not to explain it to him. If he blunders things, then that ends the farce. All the better.

I point him back onto the highway, then down the other entrance. It's easy to miss. Eager to get out of the hearse, and well aware of an empty casket behind me, I step out as soon as Alice Cooper comes to a complete stop.

"What's your name?"

"Bennie Boyle."

"Well, thanks, Bennie." I note the last name.

"Hey, what about payment?"

"I believe my mother is handling that. You'll have to speak to her." I close the car door.

Already Flipper is at the back, opening the rear door. Inside a gleaming champagne-colored casket waits. I feel a catch in my throat and force myself to remember that my father is not lying in the casket. He's not dead. Then Flipper blows his nose and snuffles into his handkerchief. I pat him on the back. I promise myself that as soon as I can get him alone, I'm going to tell him the truth. I don't care what Mother says. This is beyond cruel.

"Should we look inside, make sure Archie's okay?" Flipper's features wilt with misery.

Okay? He's supposed to be dead. That's as un-okay as I can imagine. But I touch Flipper's hand for reassurance. "He's all right."

"He got a pretty good jolt back there."

"I'm sure he's fine." I bite the word for emphasis, trying to send a subliminal message to my father's dear friend.

Pastor Reese steps forward. "Where's the lift?"

"The what?" Something clicks against Bennie's teeth each time he speaks, and I catch myself staring at the black lipstick outlining his thin lips. "I didn't catch a lift. I—" A gleam of silver flashes against his tongue. He has another piercing.

"The lift," Pastor Reese speaks slowly, "is like a platform with wheels. It rolls the casket, lifts it up and down. The funeral home usually brings one. It's standard procedure."

There is nothing standard about this.

The young kid shrugs a thin shoulder. "Don't have one. We just picked it up. Shoved it in the back there. Might be in the good hearse."

Flipper flinches. "That's highly irregular." He leans toward Mother. "What funeral home did you use?"

"I'm sure they're doing the best they can." Mother forces the corners of her mouth upward. "Now, let's get Archie unloaded. It's hot out here."

"I'm sure it's not that heavy," I offer. I don't add, *because it's empty!*

"I'll help." Flipper sniffs. "Wouldn't want Archie tipped over or nothing."

Mother has the look that says she'd dump Daddy in South Grape Creek if she could. "We'll wait for you inside."

She holds out her hand to me, wanting a partner in her crime. I am reluctant to participate in this charade any longer. I want out. But as in the old westerns that Oliver used to watch on Saturday afternoons, once you've hooked up with the outlaws, there ain't no goin' back.

"Suzanne?"

I move toward her but don't take her hand, then follow her into the dance hall like I'm walking to the gallows.

"I should have had him cremated," Mother whispers, "but I wasn't thinking clearly at the time."

And she is now?

SUNLIGHT SLICES THROUGH the open windows along the dance hall. The air is hot and heavy like a wet blanket. Mother walks briskly, her heels snapping and clacking against the hardwood dance floor.

I hear my name called from outside and turn.

Mike waves from the footbridge that goes over the South Grape Creek. He's wearing jeans and boots. And a cowboy hat. Not his usual style. He jogs up to the dance hall and through the doorway.

Oliver is a close second. He's wearing a do-rag.

What exactly happened on their trip to the clinic?

"What's with this?" I touch my foot to Mike's pointed-toe snakeskin boot.

"Want to look like a native."

"Dad got scalped." Oliver flops down on a bench.

"You too." Mike puts a hand on his son's red-bandannaed head.

Oliver's hair is shorter, but it was short to begin with. I lift the cowboy hat off Mike's head and gasp. His hair, longer than most men wear these days, is . . . gone! In its place is a field of stubble.

"What happened?"

"Horrible, right?"

"N—no. Really." I touch the chopped hair at his nape. I used to be able to run my fingers through it. It used to touch his collar. Now my nails simply slide along his scalp like a bare foot through cut grass. I lean forward and kiss him. There's no way to make him unattractive, but I suddenly miss the old Mike. "It's okay."

"You love me for my brains anyway."

"Right."

"The barber in Stonewall only knows one style." Oliver props his feet up on the seat in front of us.

"Short."

Mother gives us the "eye" and walks ahead of us, straight to the front of the stage. She looks at the floor as if a chair will miraculously appear for her. The queen needs a throne.

"Oliver." Mike prods our son's leg with the toe of his boot.

My son jumps up and drags a bench up to the front and positions it behind his grandmother. Primly she sits down on it and pats the wood for Oliver to join her. She looks closer at the rag on Oliver's head. I can't hear what she says, but I imagine it's not complimentary.

The side door to the dance hall, with a sign that reads "band only," opens. Pastor Reese hurries toward Mother.

"We went by and saw Archie," Mike says in a low voice as we watch the casket approach the dance hall.

"Oh, good. What did he say?"

"Nothing much."

Oliver clears his throat and glances back at us. The tips of his ears are red.

"What is it? Did you get the test results back?"

There's a flash of something across his face. It disappears as soon as it appears. "No too soon."

I get the impression there's something they don't want to tell me, but I don't press. "This is really horrible, Mike. Flipper is all upset. Of course, he thinks this is all real. It's sick, and it's not right."

"Maybe if we figure out a way to keep your mother from losing face, then we could settle this."

"How are you going to do that? The obituary came out in the paper this morning. Everyone knows."

Mother sits proudly, stiff and straight, not looking back at us. Through the open doors Flipper leads the casket. It starts to bobble. Mike starts to rise, but Oliver is closer and to the door in a flash. He takes over the lead handle of the casket. Bennie brings up the rear. Flipper bounces around the edges of the casket. "Watch the step. Careful, careful." He gets in the way, blocking the doorway but finally moves. "Okay, slowly, slowly."

"Did the test go well?" I ask Mike.

"Wasn't much to it."

"So what's the result?"

"We won't know for a couple of days."

Mike's cell phone rings. He pulls it out of his pocket and checks the caller. "I'll call them back later."

"Who is it?"

"I better go help. They're struggling."

I sink onto the nearest bench and lean against the table, feeling the hard wood against my spine.

"Can we set it down a minute?" Oliver's voice is more of a grunt.

"No!" Flipper's face is mottled red and dripping sweat. "You can't just set your grandpa down on the floor. That's just not done."

"But my fingers are numb."

"Come on, come on. You're almost there."

Not quite. I mentally measure about ten more feet they have left to go. Then what? What exactly are they going to put the casket on? The drums? The footlights?

Mike must have realized the same thing. "Suzanne, where are we going to put this thing?"

"We need a table." I rush forward. "Help me."

Together we lift a heavy wooden picnic table from along the wall. One leg of the table drags along the floor. The heavy wood pinches into my fingers.

"We need a resurrection." My words come out as tiny huffs. "Some sort of miracle."

"Especially since he's been embalmed." Mike's gaze meets mine, humor sparking in the blue depths, but also I see the strain at the corners.

He climbs onto the stage first, and Pastor Reese helps him lift his end up onto the raised area where the famous and not-so-famous have sung their hearts out. They manage to avoid the lights and cords. The men carting the casket ease their load onto the wooden table. It hangs several inches over the edge of the clearly smaller table. The men carrying the casket are exhausted, their faces gleaming with sweat. White and black makeup drips off Bennie's.

"Pastor," I say to the biker-turned-preacher, "do you think there's a tablecloth or something we could put over the table, make it look nicer."

"Could be. I'll go look."

"You think it's strong enough to hold this much weight?"

"It'll be fine." Mike nudges the table with his thigh, straightening it.

Oliver flops onto the floor, his long legs stretched out before him, his do-rag slipping sideways, revealing more of the scalping he received. Mother walks off with Bennie, digging in her purse I assume for his payment. But my gaze lands on Flipper. He's standing beside the casket, his face a crumpled wad of misery. My heart breaks for him. I can't take it anymore, his thinking Daddy is dead. I step toward him. He'll understand. He'll keep our dirty family secret. Maybe he can talk to Daddy and help him reconcile with Mother.

But then Flipper's hand reaches for the lid, as if to open it. He slides a bolt to unlatch it.

Across the room Mother's eyes grow wide. She apparently sees what Flipper is about to do. Then she screams.

The sound ricochets off the wooden rafters and reverberates through the barn structure. Flipper jerks back. The lid bangs down hard. The casket wobbles on its precarious perch. It tilts, momentarily defying gravity, then flips over onto the floor. Upside down.

17

We all stare at the upside-down casket. Mother is the first to recover or come unglued. She shrieks and falls back onto her bench. Immediately Pastor Reese and Oliver rush to her side. But Mike and Flipper stand next to me, frozen in place. I kneel down beside the casket, rest a hand on its cool surface. I look up at the deputy, then Mike. I don't know what to do.

But Mike does. "Deputy, if you'd help Mrs. Davidson out of the dance hall. My son and I will take care of this."

"It's my fault." Flipper buffs his face with the palms of his hands as if trying to erase the sight from his eyes. "I should fix it. I should be the one."

He reaches out, but I put a hand on his arm. "It's okay." I stand and urge him toward Mother. "If you could help me with my mother, Mike can handle this."

"But—"

"I know you want to help. And probably the best way you can," I place an arm around the deputy's shoulder and

185

feel the heat that rolls off him, "is by looking after Daddy's widow."

That must strike a chord in him because he sucks in his gut and squares his shoulders. "I can do that."

"Good." Mike squeezes Flipper's shoulder. "Good." Then he calls Oliver over.

After everyone is ushered out of the dance hall, properly tending the widow's tender nerves, I head back inside to Mike and Oliver. After we close all the windows so no one can see us, they flip the casket over. With a few grunts, they move it to the table on the stage. I lift the lid of the casket. It is thankfully empty. Mike digs down to the foot where the pillow has slid and straightens it. When the lid is closed again, I make sure the latch is bolted.

Once that's completed, Oliver starts to laugh.

"I WANT THE best that can be ordered."

We're standing in the florist's shop on 2nd Avenue in Fredericksburg.

"Of course, Mrs. Davidson." Phyllis Mabry, the owner of Flowers by Phyllis, glances at me but keeps her focus on Mother. She has steel-gray eyes and hair to match.

"Mother," I multiply the cost of the flowers in my head, "this is really expensive."

"Flowers don't come cheap." Phyllis has red-painted lips so thin that the lipstick bleeds into the fine lines around her mouth. "A full closed-casket spray is gonna cost you. Simple as that."

"Only the best for your father." Mother ambles around the florist's shop. "Red is too cliché."

Mrs. Mabry nods as if taking mental notes. "I got carnations. That's what we see 'round here most. We can get them easy. They're economical. Won't cost as much as roses. We got red, yellow, white, and pink. A little baby's breath and some greenery. Don't you worry. It'll look nice. We'll do you right, Mrs. Davidson."

Mother wrinkles her nose at the mention of carnations. "I want roses."

"That'll cost more. Special order and all. And the funeral is when?"

"Thursday," I supply.

The woman scribbles it on her pad. "We might be able to get enough in by Wednesday."

"I'm not concerned with the cost," Mother says.

"Well, we aim to please. Let's see," the woman taps a finger to her pursed lips, "yellow is fairly traditional for a man."

"I've seen the color I want. It's silvery."

"Silver flowers?" Phyllis scratches her head with the end of her ballpoint pen. "I heard tell there's roses dipped in fourteen-carat gold, but I ain't never seen a casket spray done up that way. And it'd be real expensive."

"No, it's not silver. Sterling, I believe, is what they call it."

Phyllis shakes her head and her double chin waggles back and forth. "Never heard tell of that. Where'd you see it?"

"Probably Martha Stewart's magazine." My comment goes unnoticed.

"Well, might be hard to come by."

"Where's your ordering book?" Mother asks.

"Mother," I whisper, but she ignores me. When Phyllis goes to the back of the shop, I insist. "How are you going to pay for all this?"

"Your father will pay." She dips her chin low, lifting her eyebrows at the same time. "Believe me, he'll pay."

He already is. "But Mother—"

"He deserves the best," Mother says this loud enough for the florist to hear in the back room.

Phyllis reenters the showcase area carrying a big blue notebook. She flips through the pages. Her fingers are nimble but calloused and rough.

"I know you wouldn't argue with that, Suzanne." Mother pats my arm, playing the part of a grieving widow, except for her dry eyes. "This is hard on you. Why don't you just wait in the car?"

"I'm fine." I'm not going anywhere.

The florist glances up from her book, assesses me. I imagine she's thinking that I'm not upset enough by my father's supposed death. I'm more upset by my mother's careless spending of my father's hard-earned savings.

"But Mother, you'll soon be on a fixed income. You can't frivolously throw away money."

"Then you can pay for it." Mother one-ups me. "You've got a husband who is well off. I'm just a poor widow trying to—"

"Mother, I'm not paying for this extravagance!"

"Now, Mrs. Davidson." The florist takes Mother's arm and leads her away from me. She throws a disapproving glance over her shoulder as if to scold me for my callous attitude.

I turn and walk the other way, giving us both space. I've given up trying to make Mother see reason. She's determined to bleed my father dry, to make him pay for whatever transgression she believes he's committed. Maybe this will be incentive for Daddy to come back. And when her spending spree is over, when Daddy starts to run out of cash, maybe Mother will be more willing to forgive and forget. It's not a lot to base a marriage on, I'll grant you, but it's a start.

"Just look at these beautiful flowers that have already been ordered for your husband." Phyllis's words make my head jerk up. I stare at a row of daisies and carnations—

flowers our neighbors and friends have ordered on behalf of my father. My heart begins to hammer.

"These are all for me?" Mother touches a vase, pleased as punch at the generosity and concern from her friends. "I mean, for Archie? Well, well, now isn't that nice." She brushes a finger against a tender leaf. "This needs a ribbon, maybe some more greenery."

"They're not ready to go." Phyllis's flaccid features pull into a frown. "I should get them finished and over to the dance hall this afternoon." She glances at her watch as if wondering how much longer this is going to go on. But with Mother, one never knows.

Mother focuses on a particular arrangement. She reaches into the vase, plucks out a rose, then replaces it in a position more to her liking. I hate to admit it, but it does look better. Mother has a good eye. But not a sensitive heart. She rolls her wrist and points at one vase filled with carnations. "Could we do something else with this?"

"What did you have in mind?" Phyllis's brows scrunch downward.

"Anything but carnations."

"Mother!"

"The customer requested those flowers." Phyllis deflects Mother's accusation. "They paid for the arrangement already."

"How much more would it cost to switch to dendrobium orchids?"

Phyllis gives her head a slight shake. "I don't got any of those."

"Oh, well, what else do you have? Certainly the customer," Mother glances at the card and sniffs at the name scribbled on it, "didn't realize what these would look like. Well, Verna might have. Her tastes do run common. Maybe freesia would work better."

"I might have some of those."

"Do you expect more arrangements will be ordered?" Mother seems a bit more excited by the prospect than a widow should be.

"Oh, I expect more orders will be coming in once news spreads," Phyllis's tone is respectfully funereal. "Your husband was well liked."

Mother seems oblivious to the subtle insinuation that someone else might not be as well loved. It's interesting how death brings sorrow to some, profit to others, and glory to my mother.

"Yes, he was," I agree.

Mother gives me a sharp look.

I finger a note pinned to a ribbon. It reads, "The Davidson Family." I imagine words of sympathy scribbled or typed on the card inside. People spent money on these flowers and arrangements. They took the time to write a note. Maybe they even shed tears. All for Mother's charade. I feel as if my feet are mired in the muck of lies Mother has created. We just keep getting deeper and deeper, sinking lower and lower. Perhaps quicksand will soon pull us under altogether. I'm afraid by then it will be well deserved.

"I'll go call about those flowers." Phyllis gives a tired sigh. "Maybe a place in Austin can help me out. I'll see if I can get them here in time."

"Check on those orchids." Mother calls after her. "I'll pay the difference. No one ever has to know."

"Mother! What on earth are you doing? Your friends and neighbors have paid good money for these flowers. They don't have money to just throw away on some farce that you've concocted. This has gone too far!"

"Nonsense." She leans forward and sniffs at a beautiful red rose. "I just want the dance hall to look nice for your

father and the service. It's such a drab place, but it meant a lot
to your father. It will take a lot to make it look just right."

"This is crazy! You don't care that it meant a lot to Dad.
You want it nice for *you*." I look around at all the flowers
friends and neighbors have bought for Daddy's funeral. "Don't
you feel the least bit guilty?"

She stares at me with a face full of innocence. "For
what?"

"Mother, people think Daddy is dead. They're sending flowers out of sympathy and grief, not to satisfy your
whim."

"If we were divorcing, it'd be like a death. Only this way
I get the sympathy I deserve. And flowers. Aren't they beauti-
ful?" She acts like this is the role she was born to play—the
Widow Davidson. Then her gaze lands on the carnations.
"Well, not those." She turns her back on them like they're the
black sheep of the family.

"This is wrong, Mother. Wrong."

"If your father and I were getting divorced, these so-called
friends would gossip about it and do nothing. This is much
better, don't you think? What sympathy would I get then?
Nothing but 'Ain't it a shame her husband walked out on her,'
or 'She deserved everything she's gettin'.'"

"Mother, you don't know that. Your friends would
encourage you. They wouldn't just talk behind your back."

Mother lifts her nose in the air, then leans forward to
sniff a white and pink lily. "I deserve this. And more."

I take a step back, imagine lightning streaking through
the window to strike my mother dead. My gaze lingers on
the sky outside, but not a single cloud floats into view. The
drought continues to take its toll. The sky's pale blue hue is
bleached almost white from heat.

"What if your friends and family find out this is all
make-believe?"

Mother gives a very unladylike snort. "They won't."

"But Daddy has lots of friends here, Mother. It isn't reasonable to expect he'll never talk to them again."

"He was willing to give them up for—" She clamps her mouth closed. "Well, it was his choice."

"For what?"

She squares her shoulders, her face looking red as a tulip. "For his own selfish reasons."

"Excuse me?" Phyllis says, coming back into the front room. "Am I interrupting something?"

"Yes," I say at the same time Mother says, "No."

"Those flowers can be here by Wednesday. Don't worry about nothin'. I'll take good care of you. Now, I'm short on help and I have a stack of orders waiting."

Mother wins. "Well, that's fine. That's plenty of time."

"Did you know, Mrs. Davidson, that those flowers you want are really a pale lilac color?"

"I believe I recall that, now that you mention it."

"You're getting lilac roses for my father's casket?"

"Sterling," Phyllis corrects.

"Mother! Daddy will—"

"—would—" She arcs an eyebrow.

"Puke."

"Well, he's not here to make this decision. I like Sterling. They'll go beautifully with the freesia and orchids."

MIKE SAUNTERS IN Mother's house, tosses his cowboy hat in the chair and flops on the couch beside me. I do a double take because I barely recognize him without his hair.

"Where've you been?" I ask.

"Had an errand."

His vagueness makes me slant my gaze toward him. "Calling on barbers to see if they do extensions?"

He grins and rubs the top of his not-quite-shaved head. "I kind of like it. May keep it this way. How'd the florist go?"

Mike may be an attorney, but he has never been the clean-cut type. In California he can get away with it. I find this new conservative look a bit unsettling. Maybe he's going through a midlife crisis. If so, then what is Mother going through at sixty. Or is sixty the new midlife? In Daddy's case, Mother seems to think dead is the new sixty.

"Mother's enjoying this charade far too much to ever want Daddy back."

He tugs his boots off and tosses them on the floor. "These boots sure are comfortable. I may start wearing them full time."

"Where did you get them? Fredericksburg?"

"No, in Luckenbach."

I start to laugh.

"What's so funny?"

"Those are gently-used boots, Mike."

"All broken in." He grins, nonplussed. "Guess they gave some other fellow blisters." He props his socked feet on the coffee table. The rubbed places have turned a burnt-orange color.

I place my feet next to his. If Mother were in the den, I wouldn't dare. But she's in the kitchen, putting on a pot of coffee, sorting through all the food that has been brought, throwing away anything she deems distasteful and writing her thank-you notes. "I have to stay on top of these things," she told me earlier.

"How's Daddy?"

"How'd you know I spoke to him?"

"I thought maybe that was your errand."

"We went to the Chester Nimitz museum."

"What if someone saw you together?"

193

"Tourists only."

"How is he?"

"Not having much fun. He ran into Kay Walker this morning and was met with a high-pitched scream and hysterics."

I sigh and roll my eyes. "More ghost stories will be popping up."

Mike nods. "Thing is, he refuses to stay in his hotel room. So when he runs into someone he knows, he tries to calm them down. Which only makes it worse. He's decided he's not leaving Luckenbach. But he doesn't seem interested in coming back to your mom either. He's enjoying his freedom."

"Just like you wanted." Resentment hardens my tone.

"I didn't cause this situation, Suz."

"I know that. But you're eager for my dad to spread his wings."

"I didn't say that. I just said it wasn't the worst thing ever. Either way, it's not our decision. We can't force them apart or together. You can't control this situation."

"I'm not trying to."

He stares at me.

"Okay, so I am." Uncomfortable staring at myself and seeing my mother's reflection, I huff out a breath. "So what will happen when the powder keg blows?"

"I hope we'll be out of the way. Otherwise, it's stop, drop, and roll."

We sit in silence, our hands clasped together, although I sense a resistance in me, a stiffness toward Mike.

"We need to wash your jeans." I place a hand on the dark blue material covering his thigh. "Looks too new to be real. But at least they're new."

He grins. "So you want new boots but faded jeans? Texas is like a foreign country."

I laugh. "If you want to look like a real cowboy, then they need to look like they've had cow stuff on them."

"Cow stuff?" He smiles, eliciting one from me.

"You know." I elbow him in the side. "Where's Oliver?"

"You didn't see him when you got back?"

I shake my head.

"I put him to work cleaning out your parents' garage."

"You didn't take him with you on your errand?"

"No, your mom complained about the mess your father always leaves—excuse me, *left*—out there in the garage. I figured it was good penance for getting in trouble the other night."

"We don't know that he did anything wrong."

"He admitted he shouldn't have gone off with that kid. Whether he smoked pot or not, he made a bad decision."

"What's going to happen with all that?" I ask, but I'm afraid to know. Suddenly I feel cold from the inside out, as if my blood has stopped pumping.

Mike puts an arm around my shoulders, but it's not comforting; it's simply a reminder of my own betrayal.

"He's a good kid. But even good kids make mistakes. We all do."

I feel the weight of his words in my stomach. I nod and wonder what Drew thinks of my family. He's the only other person who knows of my mistake. But he only knows part. Okay, Josie guessed, but she hasn't mentioned it again. I pray she doesn't. Pray Drew doesn't start thinking, questioning, wondering. Fear makes my insides shift. If there was one person I never wanted my son to run into it was Drew Waring. I'll be able to breathe easier when we leave Texas.

"In the meantime . . ."

"Your parents. Think we could put them both in a psych ward, let them duke it out there in a padded cell?"

"Maybe we could sell tickets."

He rubs his socked foot against mine. "There you go."

"We could use the money to pay back all their friends who bought flowers for the funeral."

"I've been thinking," his tone is serious, "there was a story that came out a year or so ago in the news where two girls were in a car crash. One was killed, the other injured. Except they mixed up the girls, due to the extent of their injuries. A few weeks after the funeral, one girl's family was told their daughter was alive, and the other family that had been at that girl's bedside found out their daughter was really dead."

"That really happened? How sad."

"Yeah, but see how we could say something like that happened with your dad? We could say he was driving with someone else in his truck. Maybe that person was driving for some reason, because your dad was ill, then the semi hit them. The driver was killed and your father has been in the hospital all this time recovering. Unbeknownst to us."

"You have a devious mind, Mike Mullins."

He grins. "I'm an attorney."

"So is what Mom doing illegal?"

"So far, I don't think so. She's not transporting a dead body illegally, and she hasn't signed any paperwork declaring him dead. But the potential is there."

"The potential for what?" Mother carries in a tray of coffee cups.

I immediately pull my feet off the coffee table. Mike doesn't move. Of course, Mother would never scold him. But she wouldn't hesitate to show her displeasure with me.

"Potential for getting arrested." I remove a pile of magazines from the corner of the table.

"Oh, no," Mother sets the tray on the far end of the coffee table, away from the place I've cleared, "Oliver didn't do something else did he?"

"No." My jaw tenses as I set the stack of magazines back in their place.

"Your father then?" She pours coffee out of the sterling silver carafe and into a china cup. "Sugar, Mike?"

"No, thanks."

"You, Mother. Mike is concerned that you might do something illegal with this charade of yours. The sheriff was asking questions just last night."

"That's nonsense. I haven't—"

"Not yet." Mike's voice holds an ominous tone. "But what are you going to do when you're asked to show Archie's death certificate?"

"Why would I do that?"

"Oh, I don't know. Taxes maybe. To claim veteran's widow benefits. Social Security. To have him taken off your checking account." He takes the cup from her and sips the hot black coffee. "There are a thousand reasons."

"Those are good ideas." Mother doesn't understand his sarcasm. "But I'm sure all those decisions are weeks away. I'll figure out something before then."

He sighs. "Look, Mrs. Davidson—"

"I know you're a terrific attorney, Mike. But the system is set up to catch someone committing murder. Not burying a fake person. So," she pats his arm, "don't you worry so much. Suzanne, sugar? Cream?"

I shake my head. Her logic frightens and, at the same time, exhausts me. I no longer know what to say. Neither, apparently, does Mike.

With a slight, indifferent shrug, she places a cup on a saucer and hands it to me. "I appreciate your expertise, Mike, but I've looked into this. I haven't done anything illegal."

"Mother, we're trying to figure out a way for you and Daddy to resolve this spat."

"It is not a spat." Mother pours another cup. "It's irreconcilable differences." She smiles proudly. "How's that for a lawyerly phrase?"

"What if Daddy doesn't want to leave Luckenbach?"

"He doesn't have a choice now. He left. He has to go." She raises her hand to her cheek. "Oh, dear, I don't have any of that fake sugar stuff. Is that what you use in your coffee?"

"No, Mother." I set the coffee on the table. I didn't want any to begin with. It's too hot to drink coffee. "Mother, Mike had an idea."

She looks toward my husband expectantly.

He almost chokes on his coffee, sputters, and places his saucer next to mine on the coffee table, united. "We could make an announcement that Archie didn't die. That the paramedics made a mistake."

"He's been embalmed." Mother doesn't blink an eye. "Too late for that kind of mistake."

Where I would probably roll my eyes and give up, Mike sets his jaw with determination. "We could say there were two men in the car at the time of the accident and the paramedics mixed up the bodies. One man died, Archie lived. But he's been unconscious and couldn't identify himself. They assumed since he wasn't driving that he wasn't the owner of the truck. Then Archie could come back, and everything could go back to normal."

Normal is a relative term. My family is anything but.

Mother sips her coffee slowly, thoughtfully. "Who was the other man?"

Mike shakes his head as if it's unimportant. "Could be anyone. Another salesman. A friend. An old high school buddy."

Mother's frown worries me. "Does it matter?" I say.

"Not that I want your father to be alive. But I was just thinking . . ." She taps the side of her saucer with the tip of her carefully rounded nail. "If Archie was having an affair with this gentleman, you know," she lowers her voice, "a homosexual thing, then that would perfectly explain a divorce."

"Mother, you can't make Daddy out to be gay!"

"Why not?"

"Because it's untrue!" Not that *that* has stopped her to this point.

"Oh, you're probably right." Her lower lip protrudes in a slight pout as she contemplates our suggestion. "Everyone would think I wasn't woman enough to hold onto my man." She shakes her head and smiles. "No, no, it's best if Archie stays dead."

18

You should know something."
    Mother's voice is startling first thing Tuesday morning. My brain isn't awake yet and I'm not sure I'm ready for any more revelations. Slowly I sink into the chair at the kitchen table. Mother pours a cup of fresh squeezed orange juice and places the glass in front of me. She sits in the adjacent seat, her back ramrod straight.

"Brace yourself."

"Okay." I blink, my eyes grainy.

"There's a rumor going around about Mike."

I frown, then try for humor to throw Mother off track. "Another rumor?" A wistful smile plays about my lips as I think of him in the bedroom getting dressed in his newly washed and dried jeans. It's an image that makes me want to laugh. "He's not dead too, is he?"

"Not yet."

My eyes open more fully, then narrow suspiciously. "What do you mean by that?"

Mother puts a hand on my arm as if to hold me in place, in case I jump up to grab a butcher knife or start to keel over. But I'm not like her. Or am I?

"It's about Mike *and* Josie."

My frown deepens. Then I laugh. "Mother, enough with the dramatics."

"I'm telling you," her lips pinch together like the edge of a pie crust, "that Josie is after your husband. And she's just the type of woman who can lead him astray."

"How do you know that?"

"Because I know the men she's lured away from their wives, even if temporarily. And I saw her eyein' your husband right here in this very kitchen."

"She was eyeing my son. But that doesn't mean anything. Josie eyes everyone. She's very observant. She's a people watcher."

"Uh-huh." Her utterance should mean agreement yet is anything but. Mother leans back and crosses her arms over her stomach. She raises one well-shaped eyebrow at me as if she holds some trump card. "Who do you think was seen coming out of the Old Hockheim Inn yesterday afternoon?"

"Mom, that's where Dad is—"

"And *with* whom?" She has a look of triumph on her face, as if she's suddenly convinced me my husband is having an affair. But this will take more than circumstantial evidence.

"So what if Mike was coming out of the hotel?" I toss back at her. "He was there to see Dad. That's where—"

"*With*," she emphasizes the word as if she sampled a stew and realized it needed cayenne pepper to give it a kick, "Josie."

"Maybe Josie was there to see Dad. Maybe she's after *your* husband." The thought is unsettling, but better my dad than my husband.

Mother's mouth opens, then shuts. She stares at me a

moment. "No." She shakes her head like she has a tremor that continues. "She's not his type."

"And she is Mike's?" Her logic makes no sense. I sip my orange juice and catch a seed against my tongue. I tuck away a tiny question to ask Mike, but I'm not worried. I know my husband. Josie is the only factor in this equation that is unknown and creates a problem.

I notice that above Mother's head the crack in the ceiling is growing longer. It's almost to the light fixture and seems to be splitting the room in half.

Mother leans forward, resting her elbow on the table and whispers in a conspiratorial tone, "Wanna have a double funeral?"

"LET'S GO FOR a drive."

Mike offers me his hand. After a hearty breakfast of egg casserole some neighbor brought over and Mother's homemade biscuits, along with peach preserves she recently canned, I realize my two men may have a tough time going back to egg-white omelets and fruit when we return home to California.

"Everything okay?" I ask.

His gently used boots are back on his feet, his button-down tucked in his slightly faded jeans. He even has a belt buckle as big as Texas. I'm beginning to wonder what's happened to my husband.

"I need out of this house." He takes my hand and leads me toward the rental car. I'm all for getting away from my lunatic mother.

We check on Oliver, who's out in the garage sweating and rearranging Daddy's tools. He's covered in dust and filth, sweeping out the garage with an old broom. There is definitely an improvement. The tools are lined up neatly in rows or hanging from a peg board. Oliver has inherited Mother's organizational skills.

Mother has tried for years to organize my father. She manages within the confines of the house, but she gave up long ago on his personal work space in the garage. She chooses not to acknowledge it, ignoring it the way she ignored her own mother's housekeeping abilities. When I was a little girl, we would visit Mother's mother, my granny. Mother would say as we walked up the swayed porch steps, "Don't touch anything."

Mother would sit on the edge of Granny's couch, her hands primly placed in her lap. I would sit beside her, taking in the accumulation of junk covering every square inch of the room. As Granny grew older and more feeble, needing more help, Mother happily took charge. The first thing she did was clean that house from top to bottom, scrubbing each counter and surface within an inch of its life.

"How's it going?" Mike studies his son's work.

"All right." Oliver's smile is a dazzling white against his dirt-streaked face. "Mom, I saw your neighbor over there. The one Grandma called the police about."

I glance over at Ned Peavy's trailer. There he is, sitting in his rocker, feet propped up on a makeshift porch railing that is warped from heat and rain. From what I can see, he is wearing no clothes. But then the porch railing is thankfully in the way. No fly swatter in sight either.

Not noticing her naked neighbor across the road, Mother brings her grandson a big pitcher of ice-cold lemonade. "If I'd known you were all out here, I would have brought more glasses."

"We're going for a drive." Mike tugs me toward the car.

"Oliver," I make eye contact with my son, giving weight to my words, "keep an eye on things." Meaning Mother.

He winks with understanding. I hope he can keep his

grandmother from doing anything else outrageous. I can't imagine what that might be, but I don't want to imagine beyond this current fiasco.

"We'll be back in—"

"A while," Mike finishes for me. He opens the passenger door of the rental car, and I climb in. The heat is oppressive until the air conditioning kicks in and blasts cold air at my face. I adjust the vent.

"So what's going on?" I fasten the seat belt across my lap.

"Nothing."

"Just getting tired of Mother?" I can't blame him for that.

"Who wouldn't?"

I laugh, trying to lighten the mood which seems dark. He's always been so patient with her. Sometimes when I complain about her, he says, "At least she loves you." Meaning his mother didn't. And I know this to be true. Mike's mother abandoned him. It's like never watering a plant: The ground grows hard and cracks, the leaves turn brown and crunchy, and eventually the plant dies. But Mother's love is like over watering a plant: The roots become waterlogged, and the plant drowns from too much care.

Mother has showered my husband with love, sending him tins of cookies over the years, doting on him when she visits California, treating him like an invalid who's unable to fetch even a glass of water for himself. And he basked in the attention like a little boy soaking up the nourishment. The first time I watched her in action I was appalled. But when I saw how Mike enjoyed the attention, I incorporated some of her tactics into our daily life, making him coffee, taking him a cup while he showered each morning. I have to admit, Mother might have been right about that one thing.

"So where are we going?" I smile and reach for his hand. "The Old Hockheim Inn?"

His grin is only lukewarm. "Not now."

Something inside me pinches. Mother's words come back to me. *Who do you think was seen coming out of the Old Hockheim Inn yesterday afternoon?* I push the thought away.

"I know this is difficult dealing with Mother. If you want, you and Oliver could go home." Which might be the best idea, but I refuse to admit that I'm looking to put Mike out of Josie's reach. Or protect Oliver from being unveiled as the sheriff's son. "I'll do my best with the situation here and try to help pick up the pieces when everything blows up."

"And it will." Mike pulls his hand away from mine and grips the steering wheel with both hands. He looks like a man on a mission. A man with something on his mind. "We can't leave anyway. Not with Oliver. He's stuck here until we get the test results back."

We skim down the highway, then turn onto a back road. It's the one Josie took the other night. "Are we going to Makeout Flats?"

"What's that?"

"Where kids used to park." I try to scoot closer to him but am restrained by my seat belt.

His mouth remains straight. "I thought we'd take a look at that split in the ground. Everyone is talking about it. It's a big tourist attraction these days."

I've seen it. But I keep that to myself.

"It was in the paper this weekend. Your mother isn't the only thing making headlines."

"You think *this* charade could hit the paper?"

The car jounces over a rut, and I grab the side door.

"Your mother's antics could be a movie-of-the-week."

I would laugh if it weren't so real. "Why can't Mother understand that she can not pull this off?"

"She sees what she wants to see."

"I guess you're right. She's managed to accomplish everything else she's put her mind to. Why not this?"

"Exactly."

He slows the car. Ahead are warning signs posted by the sheriff's department. Several yards away a trailer is parked beside the giant crack.

"Look at that!" Mike looks out the window. He turns and drives north, following the posted warning signs. "Is this where you were the other night?"

"Maybe. Looks different in the light." The chasm looks more alarming. "I don't see Josie's car. They must have pulled it out."

I realize then she didn't update me. But then I didn't ask.

"I wonder if there's much damage to her car, if it can be driven." My motives are clear to me, at least, but Mike doesn't seem to be paying attention. It's a trick Mother would try, and it turns my stomach. I try a different track. "But then Josie doesn't tell me everything anymore. Not like she used to. Friendships . . . relationships change." I glance sideways at Mike.

He has turned the car toward the rift and parked. He stares straight ahead. "The paper said it goes north for a mile. Really tore up a pasture, cracked the foundation of several houses, popped the rails on the railroad track."

"Amazing how one crack in the surface can cause so much damage," I muse, more to myself than Mike.

"Yeah."

I can't get over the fact that something is wrong, something is bothering Mike. I know from experience that he needs space to process what's bothering him before he can share it. So I wait.

For a long while we stare out the windshield at the jagged break in the earth's crust. The dirt and rocks are a rusty brown and pale limestone. I can't help thinking of the splits in my own life, cracks and fissures created by my own mistakes. I've tried to patch them. But have I? Do they remain buried deep, unstable, ready to shake my foundation and split my life wide open?

"Suzanne," his voice takes on a formal tone, "there's something we need to talk about."

I twist my fingers in my lap, brace myself. Are the rumors true? Does Mike suddenly have something to confess? No, I can't believe that. My own guilt swells up inside me. It has to be about Drew. Mike knows we dated back in high school. He just doesn't know what else. Did Josie say something? Did he notice the resemblance in Oliver and Drew, which seems so obvious now that I've seen them together. I realize I'm still holding onto the door handle, as if bracing for my own personal earthquake.

"Okay."

Mike fists the steering wheel, leans forward and curses.

"Mike?"

He's silent for a long moment.

"Are you okay?"

I reach out toward him but he looks stiff, like he doesn't want to be touched. But I do. I need the warmth of his touch to reassure me. I can feel heat coming off him in waves. I need to be held, need Mike's arms around me, to feel his strength, the security of his embrace, and at this moment I fear I will never feel that again.

"What's wrong?"

My heart pounds in my chest. *Please God, don't let Josie have talked to him, whispered her suspicions.* Is that what she was doing at the dance hall? At the hotel?

"Mike?"

"Okay, here it is." He doesn't look at me. He rubs a hand over his now nearly bald head as he used to do. Of course, he used to leave tufts standing on end. Not now. "Your mother told me there are some rumors going around."

"Rumors?" My voice is a hoarse whisper. "You don't hold stock in rumors now, do you?"

"No. But you might. So I wanted to tell you first. Before you heard . . . well, before you thought or questioned or . . ."

"Is this about you and Josie at the Old Hockheim Inn?" My voice trembles just slightly.

"You know?"

"Mother mentioned something to me."

Mike curses again, looks away. Is it guilt or anger? I can't read him. Whatever it is, it seems to be an overreaction to something minor. I'm not sure why he's even mentioning something. He is not one to give credence to rumors. When rumors reach me in our circle of friends, I'll ask Mike, "Did you hear that Travis and Michaela broke up?" He usually can't remember, doesn't care. So why now the angst over a rumor?

"What's wrong?"

"It's true."

My heart stops.

"I was there with her at the Old Hockheim Inn."

I catch a breath as if it could be my last. I stare at my husband, try to replay his words. My chest hurts. Feels like something has rammed into it.

"What?"

"Josie was—"

My heartbeat fills my ears. A trembling starts deep inside and spreads outward. Suddenly I'm outside the car. And I don't even remember opening the door or getting out. I'm walking away from the car toward the rift in the ground.

"Suzanne!"

I stop. I'm being ridiculous. I'm reacting like my mother. I pull in deep, calming breaths, then turn to face him as he approaches.

"It's not what you think."

"Did you sleep with her?" I figure that's the best place to start.

"No." He rakes his fingers through his hair. His short hair. It's an old habit. I realize that he didn't wear his cowboy hat today. "Of course not."

Relief washes over me. I start to laugh at my reaction, but Mike's seriousness quells it. I study him for a moment, the tense lines around his mouth, his narrowed eyes. Could it be about Oliver then? The truth pushes up into my throat. Should I tell him? But how? After all this time? I didn't really know the truth until I saw Drew again. And what would the truth solve now? Only rip us apart as a family.

"What is it? Why were you there with Josie?"

"She . . . I . . . well," He jams his hands in his jean pockets and hunches his shoulders forward.

"Was my father there too?"

"No."

"Just you and Josie?"

"Yes."

The sun is hot and I can feel it along my scalp. "Did she tell you something?"

His mouth twists as if he struggles with how to ask me.

I reach toward him, want to hold onto him. "You can tell me."

"Thing is, Suz, I can't. I promised. You've got to trust me with this."

His words seem broken, like slivers of glass embedded in my flesh. What is he talking about? It doesn't sound like this is about Oliver or Drew. This is about Josie. And him. Something he knows. A secret maybe?

Josie's words come back to me about how she dated a man old enough to be her father. Did she mean *my* father? No. I can't believe that about my father. Maybe Josie wanted to date my father. Maybe. But even that is a stretch for my imagination. My father wouldn't fool around with another woman.

"So what is it? What is the big secret?"

He doesn't answer.

I know if he promised not to tell me something, his honor will hold him to it. Frustrated, I say, "Mike, just tell me. I won't freak out. I won't tell Mother. I won't be mad. But I have to know what she's telling you." The words slip out of my own mouth before I can catch them. I try to cover them by saying, "I have to know that nothing is going on between you two."

"Do you trust me?"

My throat swells. I swallow my confession, my own guilt choking me. Shamed, I look away. I realize it's my own sin, my own inadequacies and weakness that makes me doubt.

"Can you, Suz?"

Silence throbs between us. My mind is numb, unable to think. My heart feels like this dry, broken ground, with its large, jagged crack. The doubts, the lies, they're all my fault. But I can't explain this to Mike.

I blink at him. Then again. His image blurs. Acidic tears burn my eyes, scald my cheeks.

"Yes."

He reaches for me, but I turn away. Before I realize what has happened, I'm behind the wheel and spinning the car around, leaving Mike standing by the crack in the dust. I don't know where I'm going. I don't know what I'm running from.

Yes, I do. I'm running from myself.

From the truth that stands between us.

19

I don't know how long I sit in the car, staring out the bug-smeared window at the hilly landscape. Tears come and go like a water faucet turning on and off. It's not Mike. It's me. It's not Josie or this weekend, this funeral or my parents. It's my past. I wish I knew how to fix things, how to rid myself of this guilt, these lies.

My thoughts keep shifting, an unstable foundation to my actions and reactions. Once when I was a child, my father found a snake in the garage. When he tried to kill it, the snake squirmed under the car, whipping first one way then the other. My thoughts feel like that now, burrowing into a tiny opening, winding inward, lurking in deep caverns, disappearing.

Would I even recognize the truth if I found it? I've hidden it for so long, I might not know it anymore.

I know how these things can happen. I know how the pressures and fears and needs blind and destroy. And in a hot, flashing moment you reach out. And regret it for the rest of your life. I know how those tiny moments, those decisions, those rationalizations occur. And I know about not being able to find the words to explain, to tell the truth. Sometimes it's easier to live with a lie.

Another thought rocks me. That's how it is with Mother. She'd rather live with a lie than admit the truth that her marriage died, that Daddy wanted someone else. Maybe our motivations are different. Maybe the lies are poles apart. But the heart of our difficulties is the same.

Mother isn't the first person to have difficulties in her marriage. When Mike and I couldn't get pregnant, we struggled. We suffered the humiliation and discomfort of medical tests. Our lovemaking was reduced to temperature readings and performing on demand. Then the battles began.

"Mike," I remember saying, calling to him, from the bedroom, "guess what?" I tried to make my tone playful, but I couldn't hide the desperation, the fear, the urgency.

He didn't answer. So I went to the den and found him studying some legal brief. He rubbed his tired eyes. It was late, past time for bed. I felt my internal clock ticking away.

"Mike," I tried again, "wanna take a recess?"

"I can't now, Suz."

"But—"

"I have to be in court tomorrow."

"But—"

"This is important. This is my job."

"I thought this was important to you too."

Anger rose inside me like the tide, slow but undeniable. I couldn't help it when my temperature changed, when my ovary decided to release its egg. *This* was the opportune moment. If we didn't make love now right now, it would be too late and we would have to wait another month. Another thirty days. Another seven hundred and twenty hours. How much longer would we have to wait? Would I have to wait?

"Mike—"

"Suzanne, I can't. I'm busy. I have to finish this."

It wasn't one argument. Or two. It was month after month. Mike's temper grew shorter, and so did mine. He started avoiding me, coming to bed later. Working late at the office, getting up earlier. I would go to bed with his side of the bed empty. I'd awaken with the sheets rumpled but cool to the touch. I couldn't think of anything but cribs and yellow blankets as soft as the downy head of a baby. During the day I would go to baby stores, touch the clothes, look at the stuffed animals. Inevitably some woman would walk in pushing a stroller and I'd find myself following after them like an obsessed fan. When Mike and I would go out to eat, I would see a couple with a baby or a young child. Mike would be talking about some case, but I wouldn't be able to stop staring at the baby, wondering if our baby would look as cute gnawing on a French fry.

"Suz? Are you listening to me?"

"Huh? Yes, of course."

But I wasn't. I couldn't.

My obsession drove Mike further into his work.

Then came the last straw.

"We haven't made love in two months!" I accused him. "You said you wanted a baby." He was letting me down. Abandoning me. The way it seemed God had. I had prayed for a baby. I'd even fasted a time or two. But nothing. No answer. No baby. "You said—"

"Yes, I want a baby! But I'm not obsessed with it. You are!"

He shoved his papers into his briefcase.

"What are you doing?"

He stalked out of the room and into our bedroom. I followed after him, hopeful he was going to make love to me even though he was angry. But when I reached the bedroom, there was a suitcase on the bed and he was tossing in clothes, his toothbrush, socks, underwear.

Cold sunk into my bones and I began to shiver. "What are you doing?"

"I can't deal with this anymore."

"But—"

"You don't want me, Suzanne. You want a baby, not a husband. This is all you think about!" He grabbed a box of pregnancy tests from the cabinet in the bathroom and threw it across the room. The box smashed against the wall, and plastic containers clattered to the floor.

Then he left.

I cleaned up the mess. One pregnancy test after another. I curled up in the chair next to the bed. And I cried.

I don't even remember how many days went by. One. Two. Maybe three or four. I would wake up, wander through the rest of the house. Sit in the nursery that I had decorated only in my mind. Restless, I moved to another room, then another. Sometimes I would sit and stare off at nothing, just the stucco wall, trying to find a pattern, an answer. I laid on the cold tile floor in the kitchen. I tried to pray, but the words wouldn't come.

I went to the phone. I didn't know who to call. I tried Mike's office, but he was in a meeting. Or in court. Or on the phone. He simply wasn't taking my calls or calling me back.

Never had I felt so alone, so lost.

Who could I call? Mother? And hear her condemnation? She would say it was my fault. I thought of friend after friend but then discarded each name. How could I tell them what I'd done, how I had pushed Mike away, how he'd rejected me?

When I finally stepped out of the house, the sun was blinding in its brilliance, stinging my eyes. I recoiled, my thoughts too dark. And I retreated into myself, into the house.

When the phone rang, I prayed it was Mike.

The voice was familiar. It touched a chord in me. I reached out for help.

Drew was in California. He wanted to see me. He's an old friend, I told myself. Maybe he's getting his life back on track. Maybe he needs me. Mike certainly didn't. And I needed to be needed. I needed something familiar. Something from home. Something or someone to make me feel secure and comforted and loved.

I didn't want to face the truth, that my own harping, my own obsession, had killed my marriage. I had turned into my mother. I simply wanted to forget the pain. I didn't want to think about whether my marriage was ending. I didn't want to think at all.

So I agreed to meet Drew at a park. He still rode a motorcycle. He still was handsome in that reckless way of his. A maverick. A loner.

We talked, then went to a restaurant for lunch. We wandered along the Imperial Beach Pier, reconnecting. He made an offhanded joke, and for the first time in days or weeks or months I laughed and began to relax.

Dinner followed. And more talking. We talked about old times. We talked about our lives, what was happening, or not happening. That is, Drew talked. I asked questions. I didn't want to talk about me. I didn't want to talk about my marriage or Mike or how I had failed.

Drew had been riding around the country, trying to find himself. I was trying to find myself too. And the spark of a flame we had once felt for each other ignited. We went to his hotel room. To talk. Only to talk. Or so we said. We didn't want to break the connection that had been tenuously restrung between us.

Maybe if I had driven my own car to the hotel, maybe if I hadn't wrapped my arms around him and ridden on the back of his motorcycle like old times . . . maybe things would have ended differently.

Sometime late in the night or early in the morning we kissed. For a moment it was like we were eighteen again. And then Drew was brushing a strand of hair off my face, caressing me, trying to see what I was thinking, peering into my very soul. I curled on my side and pretended to sleep. I wasn't even sure how we had moved from 'How are you?' to the bedroom.

What had happened? What had I done?

Guilt splashed over me like a massive, unforgiving wave of self-recrimination. I floundered in regret and self-flagellation. I couldn't talk. I couldn't move. I didn't know what to say to Drew. I lay in his bed, berating myself. He called my name in sleep, but I couldn't answer. I was sick inside with grief. Inside I was curling up into a ball, tighter and tighter, withdrawing from myself and the pain I had self-inflicted.

Finally I left. I took a cab to my car, then drove home. I laid face down on my own bed and wept. With my arms out wide, great wracking sobs shaking my body, I begged God for forgiveness.

I didn't love Drew. I didn't want my past. Or even some future I had dreamed up of a perfect Gerber baby, a perfect family that didn't exist.

I loved Mike, wanted him.

A couple of days later, miraculously, Mike returned. He was remorseful. He regretted leaving. He asked for my forgiveness. How could I not forgive him when my own mistakes were so much worse? Yet how could I tell him what I had done?

I didn't know what to do with the guilt. The all-consuming guilt.

I still don't.

I've prayed. Every time I go to church, every week, every day, I pray. Flat on my face. Staring up at a cloudless sky. Curled into a ball. But the guilt, the shame won't evaporate, even in this desert heat . . .

Mike!

He's not an afterthought. But once I get my thoughts off myself, I realize I have left my husband in the middle of nowhere. Alone. Defenseless.

I don't know what I was thinking. I wasn't. I was reacting. Just like Mother.

Guilt and recriminations are swift and succinct. Once again I give myself a quick mental kick in the backside. I turn the key to start the ignition and hear the motor grind. The car has been running all this time. I throw it in gear and drive back to find him.

But he's nowhere in sight. Either he's fallen into the crevice, which I seriously doubt, or he has caught a ride with someone from among the steady parade of sightseers. I figure the latter. I try to call his cell phone but can't get a signal. So I decide to go back to Mother's. Maybe I'll come upon him on the way, or maybe he's there already.

A few minutes later I pull into Mother's driveway, park the car, my hand still on the gear shift when I see another car, a white Cadillac, in the drive. Another friend or neighbor bringing an apple pie or tuna casserole, I suspect. Or maybe someone picked Mike up and brought him here. I draw a slow, heavy breath, like lifting weights, then release it. I don't feel ready to see Mother, friends, or old acquaintances. But I don't have much of a choice.

A quick glance in the rearview mirror shows mascara pooled under my eyes. I swipe at it with a tissue. What does it matter? Everyone thinks my father is dead. It makes perfect sense for me to have been crying. No one will question that. Except Mother. And Mike.

That's when I see Mother. She's standing on the porch, talking to some man. No, not talking. I lean forward to peer through the dusty windshield. But the picture is clearer than a motion picture on a big theater screen.

Mother is kissing him! The man's arms are around her, their mouths joined. And the man is *not* my father. My jaw drops as the shock sets in.

When the man pulls back, Mother releases her arm into a full-swing slap, right across the man's face. As if the blow were meant to galvanize me, I leap from the car.

"Mother!"

What is going on? Who is this man who's trying to take advantage of a recent widow. But Mother and the man in question don't seem to hear me. They are talking in hushed tones. It's not until I mount the steps, my breath coming in huffs, that I hear, "This is not the time, Cal. I told you a long time ago—"

Mother stops talking, turns to look at me. A flicker of irritation tightens her features, then miraculously disappears. "Back so soon?" She pats her hair, her hand fluttering from temple to throat. All she needs is a cigarette to complete the sultry pose.

"Yes." I walk toward them, staring at the man. He's tall, thick through the chest, bald on top. But he sports a mustache, gray yet tidy. He's wearing a baby-blue suit, white shirt, and bolo tie. Could this man be the reason Mother is in a hurry to bury Daddy? Or maybe why she doesn't want Dad to come back?

"Where's Mike?" she asks.

"He's not here? I should—" I gesture toward the car, know I should go find my husband.

"Cal Henry Boyle." The man who was kissing my mother sticks out a hand toward me.

"Oh, uh, hello." I shake his hand. "I'm Suzanne. Betty Lynne's daughter."

"Nice to know you."

"Mother? Are you okay here?"

"It's nice to meet you," he insists.

I glance at Mother, who looks like her dress shrunk a couple of sizes in the wash. She tugs on her sleeves, her skirt. But she's not explaining who this man is. I don't remember a neighbor or friend or distant cousin by the name of Cal Henry Boyle.

Footsteps behind me approach. Oliver walks up, grimy as an earthworm.

"Mr. Boyle," I say, lingering over his last name as it begins to ring some distant bell in my head, "this is my son, Oliver."

"We met already. I'm going in and shower."

"All right." I motion toward the door. "Shall we all go in? It's hot out today."

"That's not a good idea," Mother says as if she's overcome her momentary bewilderment. Is she trying to get rid of the man she slapped? Was he getting fresh? Or did I interrupt a lovers' spat?

"But Mother—"

"Cal Henry was just leaving." She takes his arm, pulls him down the porch toward the steps.

"I wouldn't mind sittin' a spell," he says over his shoulder at me as he grabs his hat off the porch railing.

But Mother's not having it. She is determined as she manhandles this man.

"Did you come over because of my daddy?" I ask, trying to figure out who he is.

"In a way." He stands at the end of the porch on the top step, his hands on the brim of his Stetson. "I've known your momma a long while. We go way back. Way back. Don't we, Betty Lynne?"

"I'm going to send you way back if you don't go on home and forget this nonsense," she snaps.

It strikes me as funny suddenly to see my mother flustered and out of control. Maybe she needs to experience what it would be like to have suitors coming to call if she really were a widow or divorced. Maybe this new development will be good. Obviously my mother can defend her own honor.

"But, Mother, this gentleman wants to stay and visit."

"No, he doesn't." She turns him toward his fancy white Cadillac and gives a push in that direction.

His boots do a quick two-step down the back steps and land in a puffy cloud of dirt. The man stumbles forward another step or two, then turns back, settling his hat on his head. "We was—"

"We dated. All right?" Mother says. "That's all." She marches along the porch toward me. "And the moment he finds out I'm a widow woman, he comes sniffin' around. But—"

"So you're from Marble Falls?" I ask. It's the town where Mother was raised.

"Originally, yes, ma'am. Live in Austin now." He nods and smiles. He has kind eyes and a firm jaw. "To be honest, Miss Suzanne, your mother and I have been mighty close. We was actually—"

"Cal Henry!" Mother interrupts. She is standing at the back door behind me. "That's enough now."

"Cal Henry Boyle," I say, as if testing a new coffee, deciding whether or like the bite, the roast. Then the name settles into place. "You're the own—"

"We was married," he blurts out.

I blink as if I misunderstood what he said. "Excuse me? Y–you, were what?"

"Married. Long time ago."

"Married?" I repeat, dumbfounded, the word not quite making sense, scattering my thoughts like dandelion fluff on the wind. "To my mother?" Slowly, I turn around and look at her. "Mother? Is this true?"

She looks pale enough to hang around my father, the local ghost. Immediately I know this man is telling the truth. But apparently there's a lot more to this story.

"Oh, this is ridiculous," Mother says. She walks into the house, bangs the door shut behind her.

I meet Mr. Boyle's gaze. He stares at me, whisks his hat off his head once more, looking kind yet determined. "Guess this wasn't the best idea. I might've spooked Betty Lynne. She always did like to feel in control." He takes a small step toward me as if in confidence. "I might've overplayed my hand."

I don't have an answer for him.

"I saw the obituary in the paper this morning."

"Oh?"

"Did you help write it?"

"Yes."

"You all did a fine job. And I should know. I read the obits every day. I've probably read a million obits in my time."

"I see." I snap my fingers. "Boyle Brothers Funeral Home. You own it, right?"

He nods, grins.

"So you sent the hearse, the driver."

He ducks his head. "Betty Lynne was really perturbed about that, I can tell you."

"It was kind of an old model."

"It's my son's. We had a last-minute funeral. And I had to use the good hearse for a customer. I thought Betty Lynne would understand."

"Mother likes things a particular way."

"Don't I know it." He rubs the back of his neck.

"So Bennie is your son?"

He nods. "Yep, that's him. When I bought the new hearse, I gave him the old one. It was big enough to haul his band's equipment around in." He looks off toward the windmill that is silent and still today since there isn't even the hope of a breeze. "Maybe I should've waited till after the funeral to come see her. Maybe next week some time. But . . ." He turns his hat around in his hands. "I've been waiting a long time to win Betty Lynne back. And I just couldn't wait any longer."

"I see." I can see a lot of things happening here, mostly Mother working and manipulating more people. Sweat is beginning to pop out on his forehead. What did Mother promise him for the use of his hearse?

"Would you care to come in, Mr. Boyle? Cool off under the air conditioner? Have some iced tea?"

20

Drew

A lone figure walking along the roadway snagged Drew's attention. He slowed the SUV, flipped the switch for the lights, and rolled up beside the pedestrian. Lowering his window, he recognized Mike Mullins, saw the sweat running down the edge of his face.

"Out for a noonday stroll?"

Mike stepped toward the SUV. "Might say that."

"Have car trouble?"

"Something like that."

"Get in." Drew tipped his head toward the empty passenger seat. "I'll give you a lift."

"Thanks."

Drew glanced over at Suzanne's husband, noticed the haircut and hid a smirk. Obviously he'd been to see R. J., the barber in Stonewall who knew only one haircut. "How long are you planning on being in town?"

"Long as it takes."

"Nice boots. New?"

"Not according to Suzanne. Thought I'd try to fit in with the natives."

Drew pulled back onto the highway. "The funeral is Thursday, right?"

Mike nodded.

"He was a good man."

"Yes." The attorney didn't elaborate.

Drew considered asking more about Suzanne's father but resisted. For the moment. It was always about timing. He tapped the steering wheel with his index finger. Silence grew in the car like rumors in a small town.

Curious about the man Suzanne chose to marry, Drew wondered what their marriage was like now. Almost twenty years ago, there had been problems. But maybe they had moved past all that. Suzanne seemed happy. Stressed maybe. But an earthquake and a funeral could do that to a person.

"How's your son doing?"

"I've got him doing some manual labor."

"That'll build character." He wished his father had taken the time to mold his own character. But he had been too busy trying to earn enough money to put food on the table or too tired at the end of the day. He was a single dad, and that wasn't easy. Drew had heard folks say it took a town or a community to raise a kid. But in his case, no one had taken the time to see beneath the hard edge, the self-defense, the anger, and the occasional spot of trouble he had got himself into.

Only Suzanne had.

Guilt ate silently away at him. He never should have called Suzanne in California. He had known she was married. But she hadn't acted too married, which had secretly made him glad. Still, he knew it shouldn't have happened between them. He shouldn't have . . . well, leaving California was the best thing he'd ever done.

He'd had to face himself then. And it hadn't been pretty.

"Mind if we take a quick detour?"

Mike rubbed his palm over the top of his boot. "Not at all. I've been on a few ride-arounds with friends who are cops in San Diego. Police work is fascinating."

"This won't be."

"Have the test results come in yet?" Mike studied the computer built into the dashboard.

"Should be today or tomorrow."

"I know you think I'd rather you drop the charges, but that's not true."

Drew glanced again at Mike, then forced himself to watch the highway.

Mike rubbed his palms against his thighs. "I'd rather him get in trouble now if it will keep him from getting into worse trouble later."

"Sounds like you're a good dad."

Mike shrugged. "I don't know about that. I try. Oliver's a good kid."

"Seems so."

"I didn't have a dad. Didn't have anyone. I got away with a lot."

"You love your son. That's more than some kids get. Has Archie Davidson been like a father to you?"

"In some ways, maybe." He knocked out a rhythm with this thumb against his jean-clad knee. "We haven't been around him much. But he accepted me right away, and that meant a lot."

"Sure."

"I've always believed family was important. Probably because I didn't have one."

"Heard some strange stories about ol' Archie this week."

Drew let the words hang out there like a lure lying upon the water, a speared worm wriggling to attract a big mouth bass.

"You mean all the ghost stories?"

"Partly."

"You don't believe in ghosts now, do you, Sheriff?"

Drew laughed and met Mike's curious gaze without trace of a smile.

"Not at all."

Mike Mullins was no big mouth bass. He didn't seem spooked. What was Mike Mullins hiding? What was he not saying?

Drew pulled into a gas station, just off the highway, and filled up the gas tank. A few minutes later, carrying a couple of water bottles back to the car, he handed one to Mike.

"Thanks."

"Don't know what's gotten into folks." Drew shook his head. "Maybe it's the earthquake. Or whatever caused that crack. Even my deputy . . . It's all peculiar."

Mike glanced out the passenger window. "Death can scare people into thinking or seeing all sorts of things."

"Uncertainty. Yep, that's frightening to a lot of folks."

He was just turning into Suzanne's parents' driveway when the speakers on the radio crackled. "Sheriff?"

Drew reached for the receiver. "What is it, Martha?"

"You better get on over to the Luckenbach dance hall."

"Tourists," Drew offered as explanation to Mike. "Often cause trouble. They have a tendency to cut up when they're away from home." He clicked the voice button and said to the dispatcher, "What's the problem?"

"Mrs. Hoover's over there. She's downright hysterical."

Over Archie? A frown pinched into the beginning of a headache. "Where's Flipper? Can't he handle it?"

"He's not on duty."

There were other deputies, but none knew the drill quite as well. Most were young, inexperienced. Mrs. Hoover was too much for a wet-behind-the-ears deputy. "Okay, I'll head on over. I'm not far." Drew braked.

Mike opened the door, put a foot on the gravel drive. "Thanks for the lift."

"What should I tell Brother Reese to do?" Martha's voice came from the speakers again.

Drew sighed, knowing his quiet afternoon was a lost dream. "About what?"

"About the dead body?"

His gaze locked onto the radio as if he'd misunderstood. "Come again?"

Mike stayed in the SUV and listened.

"Mrs. Hoover found a dead body in Archie Davidson's casket."

"If I'm not mistaken, Martha, there should be a dead body in the casket."

He used his peripheral vision to watch Mike's reaction.

"It ain't Archie Davidson in there."

21

Suzanne

Why hasn't Mike made his way back to Mother's yet? I decide to go in search of him, but before I can explain to Mother and Mr. Boyle, the door bursts open behind me and Mike is there.

Relief pours over me. I rush toward him, put my arms around his waist. "I'm sorry," I whisper against his chest.

He kisses the top of my head. "Come on. There's a problem at the dance hall." He leaves the door behind him wide open, a no-no in Mother's house. "Sheriff's waiting."

Mother is pouring tea into her fancy teacups. She's regained her composure and cares enough about what Mr. Boyle thinks not to use Dad's bass fishing coffee cup to serve her gentleman caller. Her ex-husband.

Mike's gaze lands on Mr. Boyle who is sitting at the kitchen table. "Oh, hello," he says, giving a nod toward the older gentleman. "I'm Mike Mullins."

"Nice to know you. Cal Henry Boyle."

If I'd had time to process this latest wave of chaos, I might be worried how awkward it will be with Mike, or how disconcerting it is to learn my mother was married before, or that her ex-husband provided the rent-a-hearse service to haul her current husband's empty casket. But immediate trouble has a way of taking precedence. I can see trouble written all over Mike's anxious features. Trouble with a capital T and that rhymes with D, which probably stands for Daddy. After all, what else could be causing trouble at the dance hall but Dad's casket? Or the arrival of the corpse?

I grab my purse. "Does Mother need to come?"

"Might be best if she didn't."

"What do you mean by that?" Mother sets the teapot on the table and props her hands on her hips. "If it concerns your father, then I'm coming."

"Mother, tell Oliver we'll be back."

"But what about tea?" Mother holds an empty cup and saucer.

I'm not sure it's the best idea to leave Mother alone with a suitor, an ex husband. But at least Oliver is there to chaperone.

Then I see the sheriff's waiting SUV. Suddenly, my feet drag the ground.

"Is that how you got home?"

"Yeah." Mike's tugging on my arm so I'll walk faster.

"I'm sorry I left you." Reluctant to see Drew, to get into the sheriff's car again, I stop only a couple feet away from the SUV.

"Suzanne," Mike puts a hand at my elbow, "I'm fine. I'm a big boy."

"But—"

Then Mike explains the emergency at the dance hall.

One minute later lights flash and sirens blare.

"Mrs. Hoover was snooping around." Drew's features pull downward into a professional frown.

"Sounds like her." I make a grab for the door handle and remember to fasten my seat belt when I almost slide across the bench seat.

"Whose body could be in the casket?" The sheriff's question sounds rhetorical. The obvious answer is my father, but I know he's not there and that's not the question.

"I don't understand the fuss." I try to put a calm face on this situation. "Isn't there supposed to be a body there?" I say, as if it needs an explanation. Maybe it does. I'm starting to get confused myself. Isn't that a good enough reason not to lie? Because in keeping track of all the stories, all the threads become like a spider's sticky silk, jutting first this way then that and eventually trapping you in your own lies.

What if there is a body in the casket? What if Daddy's body is in the casket? The thought panics me. But then Mrs. Hoover wouldn't have run screaming; she would have expected to see Daddy's body. Still, I reach for my cell phone to call Daddy and make sure he's all right.

"If your father isn't there and another body is, then that makes two mysteries." Drew glances in the rearview mirror at me, his blue eyes steady even as the SUV weaves and bumps along the road. "Two crimes." The ominous tone of his voice sends chills down my spine.

"Who are you calling?" Mike cranes his neck to look back at me.

I lean way back in the seat to make the call as inconspicuous as possible. "Uh, Oliver. I forgot to tell him we were leaving."

"Hello?" Daddy's voice booms in my ear.

"Hi." I refrain from saying his name. "Are you okay?"

"Yes. You?"

"Oh sure. I just wanted to let you know where we are."

"Okay." Dad doesn't sound particularly thrilled to hear from me. "Where are you?"

"On our way to the dance hall. We'll be back at the house in a little bit."

"Okay. There some reason you want me to know this?"

"Just in case you missed us."

"I'm not coming to the house, Sugar Beet."

"I know." There's a pause. I sense the sheriff and my husband listening from the front seat. "Okay, well, that's all."

"Okay."

I click off the phone. Mike winks at me. He understands. I breathe a little easier knowing my father is okay. But my heart still hammers away at the possibility that someone else may not be.

"Who was that at the house?" Mike's question startles me.

I shove the cell phone back in my purse. The SUV bounces and my knees knock the metal cage. "You won't believe it."

"Try me."

"Cal Henry Boyle."

"That's what he said. But who's that?"

"Mother's ex-husband."

He looks at me then. So does Drew. The SUV veers out of its lane and the sheriff jerks his attention back to the roadway. But Mike still stares at me. "You're kidding, right?"

"He . . . uh . . ." I decide to edit the real story into a bite-size chunk that's consumable for all in the SUV. "He read Daddy's obituary in the paper this morning. Apparently it was in the San Marcos and Austin papers as well. He thought he'd come over and check out the new widow. Seems he's been harboring a love for Mother all these years."

"She was married to someone else? Did you know that?"

"Nope. I'm not sure anyone did."

"So if she was divorced before, then why all the fuss . . ." Mike's brow furrows and I understand his unspoken question. Why is Mother putting up such a stink about another divorce?

"Well, they weren't actually divorced." It's not easy sorting the facts as Mother explained them to me while she boiled water for tea. "Their marriage was annulled. Her parents insisted on it. You see, Cal Henry wasn't of age. It caused quite a stir in their little town. Very embarrassing for Mother and her parents. No decent girl would chase after a younger man. And a seventeen-year-old boy can't earn enough money to support a wife. Of course, Mother was only a year older, but you know how rumors exaggerate the truth, make things out to be much worse than they are. So to save face, Mother was shipped off to Killeen to stay with relatives."

"Very controlling of her parents." Mike's tone is pencil thin but heavy as lead.

I begin to wonder if the need for control is a genetic trait handed down from generation to generation, from mother to daughter. So Mother's parents controlled her life with an iron hand, and she controlled mine. Or tried to. Do I now exhibit the same controlling behavior? Have I inherited Mother's ways? Buck teeth would have been preferable.

Drew turns the SUV on the highway that runs past Luckenbach. "What about your dad?"

"That's where she met dad. He was stationed in Killeen. He'd joined the army. Mother fell in love, and that was that. Poor Cal Henry was left behind."

The SUV slows and I brace a hand against the metal cage. The tires screech as Drew pulls to a stop in the community parking lot near the dance hall. It's a slow day in Luckenbach, but a few tourists wander around among the roosters and chickens. Drew's out of the car before I can dislodge myself.

"Let's go," he says, "and see if I've got a murder investigation on my hands."

I mentally note that Mother would be his number-one suspect. And Mike and I would be accessories.

MRS. HOOVER'S SNUFFLED tears echo in the rafters of the dance hall. A couple of the windows have been propped open for air circulation. Through the open doorway, I see the casket. It's still on the table up on the stage where we placed it earlier. There wasn't a dead body when it flipped over or when it crashed in the hearse, so if there is one now then it's what you might call fresh. I cringe at the thought.

Drew walks right past everyone lingering outside the doorway—Pastor Reese, Mrs. Hoover, the bartender and store manager, and a few tourists who no doubt heard the commotion. Mike and I follow, giving nods of greeting.

Acting as Drew's deputy, my husband pauses and waves everyone back. "Let's vacate the dance hall."

When the door is closed, Pastor Reese joins us in front of the casket. Sprays of flowers and potted plants have been delivered, filling the hall with a sweet aroma. But lurking just outside is a horrible stench of deceit.

"Did you want to talk to Mrs. Hoover?" Pastor Reese jams his hands in his front jean pockets.

"Not now." Drew climbs up on the stage.

"But she's waiting."

Drew doesn't answer.

"She just went berserk." The pastor points at Mrs. Hoover with his thumb. "Started screeching there was a dead body in there. Of course there is. I don't know what else she expected to find in a casket. But she said it was the wrong body. So we called the sheriff's office. You think the funeral home made some kind of mistake? I've heard of things like that happenin'."

Pastor Reese looks toward Mike. "But wait a minute. That can't be. When the casket flipped over the other day, and you righted it, Mr. Mullins. Was the right body in there?"

Mike gives the question some thought. Drew is watching him. I feel sweat run down along my spine.

Slowly, confidently, Mike says, "Everything was as it should be."

"Well then, that's good. We've locked the place every night. Didn't want no vandals." Pastor Reese shakes his head. "Just don't see how something like that could happen. It'll be terrible if Mrs. Davidson finds out."

Drew steps up on the stage, carefully examining the area around the casket. "The casket was closed then since it arrived?"

We all stand there staring at the casket as if it were a zoo exhibit.

"Mrs. Hoover was snooping around," Brother Reese confides in a low voice, "wanting to get a peek at Archie. Mrs. Davidson insisted it be a closed-casket funeral, which was understandable with the blunt trauma her husband took. But you know Mrs. Hoover."

"So is there a body?"

"I don't know." Pastor Reese's brow lifts toward his do-rag. "I didn't look. Apparently, Mrs. Hoover slammed it down and ran."

"You might want to stand over there." Drew tilts his head toward a table and bench that are far enough away not to offer a direct view of the insides of the casket.

My heart hammers, and I grip Mike's arm. Did Mother go over the edge? If she did, then I'm responsible too. After all, I didn't do anything to stop her. And I've been thinking she's only delusional. More like diabolical.

"Maybe we should talk to Mrs. Hoover first," I say, stalling, knowing we could find only an empty tomb, so to speak, and then there will be a lot of explaining to do. Or what if there is a body? A real body? This one wouldn't have the luxury of being embalmed. This, I remind myself, isn't some television episode. This is real. With real blood. Real murder. Real death.

Drew stops before his hand touches the casket. He looks at me. "I don't deal with hysterical females."

"But Mrs. Hoover might be able to tell us more."

"This will tell us all we need to know." He reaches out to lift the casket, looks back at me. "You're not going to start screaming, are you? If so . . ." He tilts his head, indicating Mike should escort me out.

My spine stiffens, as does my resolve. "I'm fine."

Mike grins at me, reminding me with his jeans and boots and shaved head of Butch Cassidy and his cavalier attitude.

Drew turns back to the coffin, and the muscles along his shoulders bunch as he checks the bolt. "Unlocked." He pulls a handkerchief out of his pocket.

"*You're* not going to scream?" My voice causes Drew's hand to pause midair. "Are you?"

He ignores me. But Mike whispers, "Watch out."

"I'll go check on Mrs. Hoover." Pastor Reese walks hurriedly toward the entrance door, leaving only the three of us. A moment later we hear the *th-thunk* of the doors closing.

Drew uses the handkerchief so that his hands don't actually come in contact with the casket. "Fingerprints," he explains.

He doesn't want to destroy evidence. For a trial. Our trial? Or Mother's? For fraud and libel? Or murder?

Drew pushes the lid of the casket upward. Even from a few feet away, I can see there's a body, a pale profile with a waxy-looking nose. My knees weaken, and I plop down onto the nearest bench.

"What has Mother done?" I whisper.

Mike puts a hand on my shoulder. I'm not sure if it's to comfort or to silence me before I incriminate my own mother.

Then it sounds like Drew is laughing. My head jerks up. A rumbling sound drifts toward us. I realize it's not Drew but the body.

Standing I step forward with Mike. Inside the satin-lined casket, my father's best friend, Flipper, lies there, eyes closed, hands clasped upon his chest, mouth open. He snores almost as loud as my father does.

"Oh, poor Flipper." I reach out and touch his very warm arm.

"He's been upset about your father. Started drinking again." Drew extracts an empty bottle from beside the very live corpse.

"You can't blame him," I say. But I can blame my mother for this.

"I don't plan on it. But—" he looks like he intends to blame someone—"this explains the body. It doesn't explain the missing one." Then he looks right at me. "And I know your father is not dead."

Mike is nonplussed. "Do a search online?"

"I saw Archie's truck parked at the Old Hockheim Inn. I called over to Austin PD to check on Mrs. D's story. There was no reported wreck. No body to transport. So I figure these ghost stories are really Archie, walking and talking to his neighbors. Except they think he's dead. That about right?"

"About sums it up." Mike shrugs.

"You want to explain?" Drew glances from Mike to me, while leaning an elbow on the open casket.

"Mother."

Drew's eyebrows lift.

"Daddy left her. She decided she liked the idea of being a widow, not a divorcee."

"I see. So you've been harboring this information. Protecting your mother?"

"And Daddy too. Trying to get them back together. Without embarrassing them or . . ." It seems impossible to explain. "What are you going to do about this? About Mrs. Hoover?"

"MRS. HOOVER?" THE sheriff startles her.

She looks up from her soggy handkerchief, her eyes rimmed in red, her lipstick smeared. She's sitting at a picnic table under the shade of a large oak. "Was he d–dead?"

Mike and I stand just off to the side. Far enough not to intrude. Or laugh. But close enough to hear everything.

"No." Drew kneels down next to her.

"So where is Archie's body?" Her question sounds more like that of a reporter than a hysterical witness.

"Don't you worry about that." He touches her elbow, helps her stand, and starts moving her toward the parking lot. "Now I want you to go on home. Don't worry about anything here. I'm not going to file charges against you."

"What?" She stops dead in her tracks, sways slightly. A rooster crows nearby. "Me? What on earth for?"

"Like I said, I don't plan on filing any charges. That is, if you do as I say and go on home."

Lickety-split, Mrs. Hoover scuttles away before we can say good-bye.

"That'll give her something else to think about for a few minutes." Drew winks at us both. "Now," he rests his palm against the handle of his revolver, "I'd like you and the delinquents responsible for this mess in my office in one hour."

He glances over at Pastor Reese. "You too, Reverend. We can use your help. Let's get this cleared up."

"I don't think Mother will be willing—"

"I'm not sure I understand what's going on." Pastor Reese scratches his head.

"Get them to my office," Drew interrupts, his expression stern. He glances at his watch. "Be there by four o'clock, or I'll arrest them both."

With the pastor handy, I suppose we can either remarry them or bury them both.

22

We stand on the front porch of my mother's house. Mr. Boyle's Cadillac is still parked out front. Drew's SUV rumbles back down the driveway. I have to go inside and convince Mother to go with me to discuss this situation with the authorities.

"I'll see you at the sheriff's office." I reach for the door.

Mike puts his hand on my arm. I look at his fingers circling my wrist, holding me. Then my gaze travels to his face. I read regret and pain.

"Are you okay?" he asks.

Words collide in my throat. "Yes."

"I'm sorry about all this."

"It's not your fault. Mother—"

"Not that."

"Oh." I don't know what to say. "It was really my fault."

"We need to talk some more."

"Are you ready to tell me what Josie said? Or why you were in a hotel room with her?"

"As soon as possible." He rubs the palms of his hands against my arms as if trying to warm me. Smiling that smile that has always worked its charms on me, he says, "You're not planning something like your mother, are you?"

"You mean to kill you off?" I attempt a laugh but can't quite. None of this is funny. "No. I wouldn't do that. Don't you trust me?"

"Yes, I do. Do you know that I would never—"

I put my finger to his lips. I can't bear to hear him say it. Reluctantly I pull my hand back. Feel his touch, insistent, on my arm still. I glance down. His fingers are tan and strong, and my flesh looks weak. I wish for the security of his arms to hold me together, yet I'm not sure his embrace offers security anymore. This isn't about his fidelity; it's about mine. But I can't explain that to him.

Slowly I push beyond his touch, move forward, opening the door and entering Mother's house. My legs feel wobbly.

"MOTHER," I FOLD a black-and-white-checked dish towel and lay it on her counter in the kitchen. "You have to go."

"I do not." She starts another pot of coffee. "Cal Henry, would you like some coffee cake? It's not my recipe, but it's not bad."

Mr. Boyle seems to have become a permanent fixture in my mother's kitchen. I regret asking him inside, like one of the three little pigs opening the door to the big bad wolf. Although Cal Henry doesn't look big or bad. Still, he could gobble what's left of my hope for getting Mother and Daddy back together.

"I believe," Cal Henry rubs at his top lip, "I would like something sweet."

I ignore him. Ignore this little domestic scene. Which is all wrong. "Mother, the sheriff ordered it."

"I do so like feeding a man." Mother takes three dessert plates out of her cupboard. "Don't you, dear? There's something very natural about it. I've missed it." She acts like Daddy has been gone a century. With knife in hand, she approaches the cake cover and, in the same tone as if we're discussing whether we prefer tea or coffee, she says, "I don't care if the pope orders it. I'm not going. And that's final." With cake cover raised, she pauses. "Would you care for a little chocolate sauce on top?"

"No, thanks, Betty Lynne." His eyes practically shine when he looks at her. "Think that would be too rich."

"You're probably right."

"Mother, the sheriff will arrest you."

"Oh, he will not. For goodness' sake!" She looks over at Mr. Boyle. "The sheriff is Suzanne's old boyfriend. Never did like him. Trouble from day one. I should have done the same thing my parents did and shipped Suzanne off sooner, before she formed such an attachment to him." She waves the knife in my direction. "You watch yourself with him, missy."

"Mother, I'm not interested in him. And he's not interested in me. He's interested in getting this . . ." I don't know a better word for it, "*thing* over with. And getting life in Gillespie County back to normal." As normal as it can be. I purposefully don't look out the window toward Ned Peavy's trailer. "You don't want to end up in jail, do you?"

"For what?"

I don't have an answer. "He doesn't have to have a reason."

"He can't just go around arresting people for no reason."

"For fraud." I throw that out for starters.

"Fraud?"

"Yes. And libel. You're slandering Daddy when you say he's dead. You're also disturbing the peace."

"I suppose you're going to tell me the trouble in the Middle East is my fault too?"

When I was a teenager, Mother would not have allowed us to air our so-called dirty laundry in front of others, like Mr. Boyle. But frankly, neither of us seems to care today. And Cal Henry, a smile lurking about his thin lips, seems amused by it all.

"Mother, this charade has to end. Are you seriously going to pretend that Daddy is dead forever? That you're a widow. And then go gallivanting around," I cringe at my word choice and realize I've been in Luckenbach too long, "with this . . . this . . . suitor?"

Mother cuts a slice of a buttery coffee cake and hands me a plate, with napkin underneath and fork lying alongside the cake. All so proper.

"I don't want cake, Mother. I want you to be reasonable."

"That's not for you, Suzanne. It's for Mr. Boyle."

With a heavy sigh, I pass the cake to my mother's ex.

"For your information, I am being reasonable." Mother continues slicing cake. "Everyone else seems to be upset. But I'm not. I'm perfectly fine."

Obviously everyone else being upset doesn't bother her. "Please, Mother, just go talk to Daddy."

"I will not." Her tone is that of a petulant child.

"You have to face Archie sometime." Cal Henry wedges his fork into the cake.

I stare at him for a moment. "You know about this whole charade and you don't care?"

"I love Betty Lynne. Always have. I'll take her anyway I can get her."

Good luck is what I want to say but refrain.

"I don't know why I have to face Archie at all," Mother counters. "His attorney, my attorney—they can take care of things without us getting in the middle of it."

I take the knife away from Mother and cut myself a piece. Mother holds the plate for me. Silver fork in hand, I shove a bite into my mouth and chew before I realize I'm not hungry. Pushing away the cake, I say, "So you're going to divorce Daddy and take up with this man?" I wave toward Mr. Boyle. "Are you still in love with him?" Are her fears about Drew and me based on her own feelings? Feelings for a man other than her husband? "Have you been in love with him all these years?"

She covers the cake and wipes the knife on a paper towel. But she doesn't answer me.

"Is that why you decided to kill Daddy off? Pretend he's dead? So you could call Cal Henry for help, use his hearse? Is that why you're so unforgiving of Daddy? Because you want another man?"

Mother props a fist on her hip. "Now, Suzanne, that is so melodramatic."

"Mother." My voice has that commanding tone I hold in reserve for Oliver when he's pushed me beyond my limits. "You will get in the car and go see Daddy. Right now." She opens her mouth with another protest, but I don't give her the chance. I have no choice either. "Or I will march down to the newspaper office in Fredericksburg and tell them my version of this story. You will be the laughing stock of Gillespie County."

"You wouldn't dare."

I cross my arms over my chest. "Try me."

Mother's mouth thins into a straight line. She glares at me, but I remain firm. I have had it with the lies, the deceit, the trickery. Too many people have been hurt. Finally she stands, picks up her purse, and says, "All right. Let's get this over with. I have a funeral to arrange."

She opens the back door but stops. "I'm not going to speak to him."

"Fine."

"Just so you know."

"Okay."

Then she looks over her shoulder at Mr. Boyle. "Cal Henry," her voice softens to room-temperature butter, "aren't you coming?"

The light above the kitchen table flickers and goes out. Cal Henry walks over and studies the crack along the ceiling that has continued on its path bisecting the kitchen. "Betty Lynne, looks like you got yourself a foundation problem. It might be affecting your electricity."

"What on earth? What would cause that?"

"The ground's been shifting with the drought. That crack that opened up not far from here might be causing this."

"Well, I'll be."

AFTER CAL HENRY cuts the electricity to make sure the house doesn't burn down while we're gone, we drive over to the sheriff's office. The blinds are drawn for privacy. I bring Mother in through the front and leave Mike a message on his cell phone to bring Daddy in through the back so he won't be seen. All we need now is another ghost sighting. Drew sits at his desk, looks up when I knock on the door frame and motions us inside. He doesn't smile.

There's something in the way his hair curls over his forehead that reminds me of Oliver. It hurts to look at his face, to see my son there . . . to know my sins. But my love for my son is pitted against my guilt. My throat feels parched.

Several chairs have been placed in a semicircle around Drew's desk. Which, I notice has a chunk missing from the corner. I can see papers and folders lined up inside the cabinet.

"Mrs. Davidson," he says, "why don't you have a seat?"

Mother glances at her watch. "I hope this won't take long, Sheriff."

"All depends."

"On what?" She sits on the edge of the wooden chair, her purse perched on her lap.

"On you."

"I don't know what you mean by that. If it was up to me, we wouldn't be having this meeting in the first place."

But Drew's not listening. His focus has shifted to Cal Henry who stands back at the entrance. "What can I do for you?"

"Oh," Mother rolls her wrist by way of introduction, "he's with me."

Drew's gaze flicks to me, then back to Cal Henry. "This is not a good idea. This should be a private family—"

"He stays." Mother pats the seat next to her. "Or I leave." Cal Henry dutifully sits down beside her. "What on earth happened to your desk . . . your window, Sheriff? You didn't get careless with a gun, did you? Why this is a disgrace for the sheriff's office."

I notice along the window there's a large chunk out of the windowsill.

Drew grins. "A small incident with a prisoner who decided to escape."

Mother's forehead wrinkles.

"Suzanne." Drew pulls his chair around the side of the desk and places it next to Cal Henry. I sit on the outskirts of the semicircle, wishing I was sitting back at home, outside the confines of this whole charade.

"Suzanne," Mother shifts her gaze from Drew to me. A frown puckers her brow and she licks her lips. "Why don't you wait for me in the car?"

I hesitate. I'd rather not see my parents' marriage unravel before my eyes. I don't want to hear the petty details of he said/she said. But then again, I don't want my mother to actually kill my father either.

"Your husband called, Suzanne." Drew fiddles with a pen on his desk. "Your father is concerned about his safety." His gaze settles on Mother. "Can I see your handbag?"

"What? What for?"

"To check for weapons."

"Oh, goodness gracious. I am not going to shoot Archie."

Drew holds out a hand, palm up.

Mother glares at him. But Drew has perfected the art. Being a sheriff, I'm sure he's had to stare down speeders, thieves, and crooks of all varieties. Mother crosses her arms, pressing her purse close to her chest. Drew doesn't relent. His gaze remains steady, uncompromising. Finally she huffs out a hot breath, stands and hands him her purse. "Don't mess anything up in there."

"No, ma'am." He pops the metal clasp and peers inside. With one finger, he pushes something aside, then closes it and hands it back to Mother.

"You're not going to frisk me too, are you?" Her tone is sassy.

"It crossed my mind. All depends on if you give me reason."

Mother clamps her lips tightly closed and sits back in her chair.

"Please cooperate," I whisper.

"I'm not going to bite your father. Or try to escape." She looks down her pert, non-threatening nose at the sheriff. "But I do want it known I'm here against my will."

"Duly noted, Mrs. D."

"Is this the right place?" Pastor Reese stands in the doorway, looking more like a prisoner than a preacher.

"Sure thing, come on in." Drew ushers in the preacher and has him sit in a vacant chair beside Mother, right in the middle. The other two chairs are for my father and Mike. "The rest of the party will be here soon."

"Good afternoon, Mrs. Davidson," the pastor says.

She gives him a polite but cool nod.

He shifts in his seat, looks around, checks the clock on the wall. "We, uh, still need to discuss the funeral when you have time."

"Now's as good a time as any. I've given it a lot of thought. Of course, I want the funeral to be respectful and heartfelt."

That word almost makes me choke.

She frowns at me, then offers a smile to Pastor Reese. "I suppose we should have the Twenty-third Psalm read."

Drew stares at Mother with a combination of incredulity and something close to mild respect. Anybody with that much gall demands admiration or at least close inspection.

"It's become a standard." Pastor Reese nods. "Did you want any hymns sung?"

"Of course. We can have the mourners sing 'Amazing Grace.' I've already asked Josie Bullard to sing 'It Is Well.'"

"You have?" Given Mother's disdain for my friend, not to mention the rumors about Josie and my husband, her choice seems tasteless.

"She may be a slut," Mother straightens her skirt, making a crease lay flat along her thigh, "but she has the best voice in town."

"Mother!"

"It's true. Now I was thinking—"

"Mother," I interrupt, look to Drew for help, but he seems content to watch the proceedings, "don't you think this is all a little premature. Considering what we're here for."

"This has to be discussed." Mother dismisses me and focuses on the preacher. "You heard Pastor Reese. He wants to be prepared."

"Doesn't he know?" I tilt my head toward the preacher.

The sheriff shrugs, making his starched shirt bunch momentarily along his shoulders.

"Know what?" Pastor Reese's eyes narrow.

A scuffling at the door distracts us.

"Hurry!" Mike waves to someone we can't see.

Then my father steps into the room and Mike jerks the door shut behind him. Pastor Reese gasps.

"Sorry we're late," Mike apologizes.

"It's all right." Drew claps the preacher on the back. "I should have told you, but I couldn't risk you telling anyone else. Not until this matter has been settled. As you can see, Archie Davidson is alive and well."

"Alive maybe," Daddy says.

"But most decidedly not well," Mother finishes.

23

ᘛᘚ

Pastor Reese clears his throat after Drew explains the purpose of this meeting. Looking pale as a corpse himself—which is supposed to be my father's role, but Daddy's actually looking ruddy-faced and embarrassed— the preacher fidgets and takes off his leather jacket. Mother seems annoyed, her arms crossed over her chest. I sit one seat over from Mother, beside Cal Henry who's placed a possessive arm along the back of Mother's chair. Mike sits on the other side of Daddy's designated seat. Our gazes meet briefly. He doesn't look as worried as I feel. Drew sits on his desk, presiding over the whole mishmash.

"This is kinda odd," the biker-turned-pastor rubs his arm, making his muscles bulge, his tattoo flex, "giving marriage counseling to a widow."

No one laughs at his attempt at humor.

"What are you going to do about Flipper?" Daddy's face is a map of concern. He still stands in front of the sheriff's desk. "I didn't know he thought I was dead. If I'd known, I would have called him first thing. I didn't want him grieving for me."

"Don't worry about Flipper." Drew points him toward his seat. "I'll tell him the truth. Soon as he wakes up."

"He's not going to get in trouble for drinking, is he?" Daddy presses.

"No. He wasn't on duty. And if anything, he's been provoked." The sheriff looks straight at Mother.

"You cannot blame me for someone else's drinking problem. Next thing you know, you'll be blaming me for global warming."

"Betty Lynne," Daddy turns on her, "you could drive any man—"

"Now, Archie." Mike stands, puts a hand on my father's shoulder and pulls him toward his seat. "We're here for a peace treaty, not to hurl insults."

"Who's that?" Daddy gives a nod in Cal Henry's direction.

"He's with me." Mother purses her lips.

"Is he your attorney or something? Well, I got my own attorney right here." Daddy claps a hand on Mike's back.

"Wait a minute," Mike protests. "I'm not here in the capacity of—"

"No, this is not my attorney," Mother cuts him off. "I don't have one. Yet."

"Then who the—"

"Cal Henry Boyle." Cal Henry rises and sticks out his hand.

"Archie Davidson." Daddy stands. They shake hands like they're standing outside the post office, passing the time of day.

"Nice to know you." Cal Henry smiles the smile of a car salesman.

"I still don't know who you are." It takes all the muscles in Daddy's face to form such a scowl.

"I'm Betty Lynne's ex," Cal Henry explains. "Soon to be—"

Daddy takes a step back as if knocked square in the jaw. "Ex-what?"

"Ex-husband."

Daddy starts to sit down, as if his knees gave way, but stops and stands back up. His long, narrow face grows longer with disbelief.

"Well, that's not exactly true," Mother stands. She puts a hand on her husband's chest as if holding him back from attacking Cal Henry and explains. "Our marriage, such as it was, was annulled. So legally we were never really husband and wife."

"When did this happen?"

"A few months before I met you."

"But you never said nothing."

"Well, there wasn't any need to. It would have just got you all riled up. See! No point in that." With her fingertips, she gives a slight push, but Daddy doesn't budge. "Now just sit back down, Archie."

The sheriff stands, stepping between the two men, and encourages everyone to take their seats. "We're getting off track here. What's in the past isn't relevant. The immediate problem is this funeral scheduled. Since there's not a corpse, we can just call off the funeral."

"Now, Sheriff—" Mother stands toe to toe with him.

"Right now," Drew finishes, not intimidated as others might be. "Only two ways I can see this ending. One with a happily-ever–after, and the other with divorce proceedings. But the first thing that has to be done is to explain what's happened so everyone knows the truth. If Mrs. Davidson wants to save face, fine. But it's my job to make sure Mr. Davidson don't get buried." Drew looks about as uncomfortable as a lone dog caught on the highway in heavy traffic.

Pastor Reese coughs, rolls his shoulder, and pops his elbow like he's ready to step into the ring. "Yes, well, now, Mrs. Davidson, why'd you make up this story in the first place? Why would you pretend that Archie was dead?"

"I believe that's a personal matter."

"I left." Daddy meets Pastor Reese's gaze steadily. "I'm not saying it was right or nothin'. But I did. And it ticked her off."

"Set her off is more like it," Drew mumbles loud enough for me to hear.

"Did you have a fight?"

"No, we did not." Mother's lips are puckered so tight it looks like she's about to whistle.

"To be honest, pastor," Daddy leans toward him confidentially, "I—"

"Archie Davidson," Mother claps her hands, reminding me of her docudrama on Daddy's death, "if you say one more word . . ."

"I'm just trying to be honest here, Betty Lynne."

Honesty is not what Mother is looking for.

"This is a private matter. I will not air our dirty laundry for everyone to see and smell."

"I told her I wanted out. I wanted my freedom. After forty years of dealing with—"

"And you wanted my blessing?"

I wait, hoping Mike will say something. He can sway a jury with the quirk of an eyebrow; surely, he can say something to persuade Mother and Daddy. But he remains quiet. Maybe Pastor Reese will interject some Scripture, something convicting. But my parents exchange words like an angry racquetball match, with the verbal assaults coming fast and furious. The rest of us try to stay out of their trajectory.

"Why would I want your blessing?" Daddy argues. "I wanted a divorce. You're the one that went berserk and—"

"How did you expect me to react? One minute we're having dessert and coffee . . ." She pauses and looks at me imploringly. "I made your father's favorite banana cream pie." She looks from Drew to Pastor Reese, seeking a sympathetic listener. "Have you had my banana cream pie?"

"Of course. Who hasn't? You brought it to the Easter picnic."

But Drew shakes his head. "Must've missed that."

"Well, trust me, it's the best. It's not easy getting the meringue just right. And what's the thanks I get for all that trouble? 'Thanks, I'd like a divorce.' How would you react, Pastor Reese?"

He stammers.

"Exactly!" Mother squeezes his forearm as if thanking him for his support. "That's just how I felt. Stunned. Shocked. Why, Archie was the one that suggested I kill him!"

"I did not!" Daddy throws up his hands. "You are crazy!"

"I asked you what exactly I was supposed to do. Your bag was packed like you were leaving on your honeymoon. Did you pack it while I was making your favorite chicken-fried steak dinner?"

Dad looks down sheepishly.

"You said you didn't care what I did. That I could say you was dead for all you cared. And after you walked out the door, I decided I couldn't see myself as a divorcee. I deserved respect for all the years I gave you. My best years. I was not going to be scorned or pitied. And so the only reasonable course of action was for me to become a widow. A widow gains respect and even admiration. A divorce . . . that means failure. Like *I* did something wrong. And I didn't. And so, as you can see, Sheriff, Pastor Reese, Mike . . ." She's gathering her troops. "I was forced to kill my husband."

I'll bet that is the oddest confession Drew's ever heard. He looks speechless, as if he doesn't know what to do now.

"Of course, I understand," the pastor says, "I'm sure it was shocking." He looks down his sharply pointed nose at my father.

"Pastor," there's a note of warning in the sheriff's tone.

"How can you blame her?" Pastor Reese crosses his arms over his chest. He looks like a biker version of the Archangel Michael, sent to avenge some wrong. "She was under extreme stress. She devoted her life to this man. And he betrayed her trust."

"We're not here to take sides," Drew says. "We're here to come up with a solution. If you want a divorce, fine. But this mock funeral cannot proceed. And I won't have a ghost running around town scaring citizens. Jeremy Parsons almost ran his truck into the postman yesterday evening when he saw you, Archie."

"Then Archie will have to leave town." Mother sits down, crosses her ankles and clasps her hands in her lap. "You said you were going to live in Oklahoma or New Mexico. So do that, Archie. Move to Santa Fe."

She opens her purse, pulls out a handkerchief she has embroidered with snapdragons. She dabs the side of her face and neck, then places the wispy cloth back in her purse and snaps the clasp closed. "If you can forget that trip we took there. Remember our twenty-fifth anniversary? Do you? Do you remember that little bed and breakfast where we stayed? They put chocolates on our pillows every night. And they made the most sumptuous waffles for breakfast. What was that beautiful purple plant growing outside our bedroom window?"

"Lavender." Dad's tone has an edge to it.

"Do you remember that spa we went to, Archie? Where we had our own private Jacuzzi?"

He nods, his throat working up and down.

Mother is quiet for a moment as if lost in memories. I remember Mother occasionally doing something crazy like tossing Daddy's clothes out the bedroom window or chasing down some phantom woman she thought Daddy was seeing. But I remember happy times too. Mother's laughter. Daddy dancing her around the living room when he received a fat bonus at work. The two of them cuddling on the couch. Were the smiles and merriment only a façade?

No relationship is perfect. It's a dance. Sometimes one partner makes a misstep and crunches the other partner's toes. But that doesn't mean the dance ends. There are dips and turns. As the old song goes, one step forward, two steps back.

I look to my father, wish he would make a move toward Mother. This could all end with a reaching out, clasping hands, and a little forgiveness. Or a lot. Hope inside me flickers when I see a wistful gleam in his eyes, as if he's remembering too and feeling a tug on his heart.

Then Mother jerks her chin. "So fine, go there. Live in Santa Fe. It's as simple as that."

The softness in his eyes hardens. "I'm not leaving." He sits down, arms crossed, mouth firm. I've seen that look before, not often, but enough to know he's not budging. "Everybody I know is here. This is where I was born and where I'll die."

"Exactly." A smug smile spreads across Mother's face. "And the casket is all ready. Make yourself comfortable."

I look to Mike. He shrugs, then leans forward, bracing his elbows on his knees. "Look, we can easily come up with an explanation that will help Mrs. Davidson save face. But we need to agree—"

"I do not need to save face. I am fine. My reaction is perfectly reasonable. It's Archie who has been making a spectacle of himself."

"And what about this man here?" Daddy bellows. "Why I'm not even six feet under and already you've got a man you're leaning on. I see his arm around you there. Around *my* wife." Cal Henry has the good manners to redden. But he leaves his arm where it is on the back of Mother's chair.

Suddenly Daddy stands, leaning forward, his face reddened with emotion. "You don't know, mister, what you're getting yourself in for. Believe you me, you better run for the hills. You don't want to tangle with Betty Lynne Davidson. Oh, things might be lovey-dovey now. But there's an end to that. You only experienced the honeymoon. But it don't last. I spent forty years with her. I know. Soon she'll be harping at you to pick up your socks, take out the trash, call before you get home, call when you leave. Do this, don't do that. And you'll never keep all the rules straight."

Pastor Reese holds up his hand. "It's reasonable for Mrs. Davidson to want a public apology. Archie, would you be willing?"

"For what? I didn't *do* anything."

"Didn't do anything?" Mother stands, turns on her heel, then whips back around. "Archie Davidson, I . . ." For the first time, Mother seems speechless. She slaps her purse against her leg. "If we're finished here, Sheriff, I have a funeral to attend to."

"THAT'S NOT WHAT I would call a successful negotiation." I stare out the window of the sheriff's office. Mother leaves in Cal Henry's Cadillac, with her new beau and ex-husband driving. Daddy already left with Mike. They headed in opposite directions, of course. So for at least the next few minutes I don't worry that Mother's going to corner Daddy in an alley.

"No one pulled a gun at least." Drew leans back in his chair and clunks his boots on the corner of his desk.

I turn and meet Pastor Reese's blank stare. He sits in front of the sheriff's desk as if he's strapped into his chair with a seat belt. He scratches his head, making his do-rag slip sideways.

"Was this kind of situation discussed in your seminary class Dealing with Difficult Congregational Members 101?"

A wisp of a smile touches his lips, then he shakes his head. He crosses his arms over his chest, and the cross-and-rose tattoo on his forearm twitches as his muscles tense.

"What do you recommend we do?"

"I could talk to them." Pastor Reese rubs his hands down his jean-clad thighs. He stretches out his legs, sticks out his square-toed black leather boots. "Separately, of course. But I'm not sure that's going to do much good either. Your mother is hurt. Angered by your father's betrayal. Your father's a bit shocked. Learning your mother was married before . . . well, that's a lot to swallow in one day."

"But not telling someone isn't the same as lying, is it?" I'm not exactly asking on my parents' behalf.

"If it has bearing on the relationship, then it should be discussed. Not fair otherwise."

That is not the answer I want to hear. But he's not my pastor. Maybe he didn't even go to a real seminary.

"You see," Pastor Reese folds his hands together over his belt buckle (or where a belt buckle would go if he wore one), "something made your mother and Mr. Boyle get an annulment. And I'd bet that same emotional stumbling block is what's affecting your mother today. But something made your father want to leave. The reason don't matter as much as the fact. What does matter is that something was missing in your parents' relationship. Now if we could find that, then maybe we could get them back together."

"You think that's possible?"

"All things are possible."

"I don't see that happening." Drew clasps his hands behind his head.

"They still care about each other," Pastor Reese argues. "Did you see jealousy spring up in Archie when he found out who Cal Henry was? He cares. But it takes more than caring to make a relationship work."

"He was just being territorial." Drew's cynicism reflects my own. I wonder what makes him that way. Was it our relationship? Or others along the way?

But I don't have a right to be cynical, despite the years of watching Mother and Daddy. My marriage survived, not because of me or Mike but because of God. If our relationship can survive what I did, then anything is possible. Hope begins to find its spring inside me.

"Did you see them remembering that trip to Santa Fe?"

"Oh, yeah." Pastor Reese touches my hand, gives my fingers a squeeze of encouragement. "They were remembering, all right. I'll be thinking on this. You call me if I can help." He stands and shakes the sheriff's hand, then turns to go but stops at the door to Drew's office. "What should we do with the casket?"

"Leave it where it is." I grab my purse, eager to follow the preacher out of Drew's presence. I wonder if the reason my marriage survived is because I kept a crucial part secret. If I'd been honest with Mike, if I'd told him about Drew, the relationship might have collapsed. Suddenly my optimism implodes. "We might need it yet."

24

Tuesday afternoon Oliver and I head to the local Wal-Mart in Fredericksburg to stock up on milk and eggs and other staples. He's been wanting some sodas too.

"What else sounds good?" I push the cart, trying not to notice the grungy gray splotches along the handles. My son has worked hard today, not only cleaning out my parents' garage but also mowing the yard. I remember when he was young enough to sit in the cart, facing me, kicking his little legs and smiling. Sometimes it's hard to believe he's almost a man.

"I'm tired of the stuff Grandma makes. Couldn't we just have plain ol' hotdogs?"

"Your grandmother would keel over from the shock."

Oliver grins. "But it might be fun to watch her choke down a hotdog. Besides, if she made me eat that spinach thing, she can eat a hotdog for me."

Only for Oliver. Or Mike. Mother would do most anything to please them.

"I suppose we could tell her the hotdogs are kosher."

"Organic."

He grabs a couple of packages and tosses them into the cart.

"Mom?"

"Yeah?" I redirect the cart toward the bread aisle.

"Why's your mom so . . . ?"

"Weird?"

"Stiff. Crazy. Whacked out. I mean, to be doing this funeral—"

I place a hand on his arm and glance around us to make sure no one overhears. Instantly I regret stopping him, putting what others might think ahead of speaking the truth. What am I teaching my son? What weird traits or habits am I passing down to him? "Oh, Oliver, I don't really know. It's hard to know what's in someone else's heart."

He grabs a package, squeezes the buns through the plastic covering, and puts it back on the shelf. He scans the shelves, then notices the bags along the bottom are orange. Just like I would, he takes the whole-wheat buns. Eating healthy is not a bad habit for me to have taught him. Is it? A mother should teach her child important things like hygiene and nutrition. But I'm suddenly feeling paranoid and vulnerable about my parenting skills or lack thereof.

"Her father, my grandfather, was a perfectionist too. Wore my grandmother out trying to please him. He couldn't delegate. No one else could hold to his standards or live up to his expectations. When he died, my grandmother became a total slob. Her house was a junkyard. It drove my mother crazy. She couldn't stand it."

"If Grandma inherited her father's—"

"Or learned it."

"—then how come you're not that way?"

"A compliment!" I hug him around his broadening shoulders. But guilt is a powerful force. "In some ways I am though. And I'm sorry about that. I hope I haven't warped you too much. I saw the damage perfectionism caused. It stripped my family of any joy. It beat my father down." I point us in the direction of the condiments, knowing my mother doesn't have yellow mustard in her pantry. And you can't have hotdogs with Gulden's.

"Was it hard on you too?"

"Absolutely." I grab a bottle of ketchup because I know Oliver likes it on his hotdogs. "Unfortunately I'm more like her than I realized." Voicing my uncertainty feels like I walked out of the bathroom trailing toilet paper from my heel.

"You're not like her, Mom. Believe me, you're nothing like her." His intonation makes me smile. "So how'd you end up not warped?"

"God changed my heart. Otherwise, I might be a lot more like your grandmother." But I don't tell him that in many ways I'm worse. So much worse.

Oliver nods sagely. He's been raised in the church and understands spiritual matters. "Does she not know Jesus then?"

"Oh, she knows. But sometimes head knowledge doesn't always translate to heart knowledge. Do you know what I mean?"

"I see that in a lot of kids at church. Not that I'm perfect but—"

"You're right." I reach up and ruffle his hair, which doesn't ruffle as it's now too short. "You're not. But nobody is." Especially me. "Do you think you could forgive me if I did something . . ." My throat starts to close with emotions. "Something that changed everything?"

"Sure," he says without hesitation, "you're my mom. I may not show it all the time, but I love you."

I hug him, sniff away the tears that threaten. If only I could believe that. If only I could believe that my husband would forgive me too, that my sin was forgivable to those I love. If only I could believe that telling the truth wouldn't jeopardize my marriage, my family, my life.

Oliver takes the cart from me and pushes it down the aisle.

"What are you looking for?"

"Chili. I want a chili dog."

"That's over near the beans probably."

So we turn the cart around and head back the other way. Mother's going to love this meal. Not. But maybe it'll be good for her. Maybe she needs to loosen up her standards. That is, if she wants Daddy back.

At the end of the aisle, we turn left. Oliver pulls up short to avoid running into another cart.

"Suzanne!" Estelle Rodriguez and two of her children . . . no, three—another zooms around the corner—stop beside our cart. "How are you? I've been meaning to come by."

"It's good to see you again."

"I saw your father's obituary in the paper. It was very nice. Is everything going well with the funeral arrangements?"

"I suppose."

"Do you need some help? I could get my husband to watch the kids tonight and . . ." She looks around, grabs the side of the cart. "Esteban?"

"Over there." Oliver indicates the cookie aisle.

"Oh, dear. I better . . ."

I give her an understanding nod. "I'll see you later."

Estelle's soft face pinches with concern or regret.

"It's okay," I say. "You're busy. Don't worry."

Then she moves on, chasing down her son.

Oliver pushes our cart forward, and we go in search of chili.

"She was my friend in high school," I explain to Oliver. "We took English together and loved talking about books like *To Kill A Mockingbird*."

"You were friends with Josie too?" He slows the cart and peruses the jars of pickles.

"I had very eclectic friends." I take a jar of Mrs. Fanning's butter pickles, which I haven't seen outside of Texas, and put it in the cart.

"She doesn't seem your type."

"We had our difficulties in high school. But she has a good heart. Like Slater." He was the kid that Oliver got in trouble with last year.

"We're still friends," he shrugs one shoulder more as a reflex, "sort of."

"Exactly. Sometimes we don't always understand our friends. Sometimes we see them doing destructive things. But we still have to love them."

"Grandma keeps saying a man is known by the friends he keeps. But didn't Jesus hang with sinners?"

I put a hand on his shoulder. Pride fills my heart. "You're right, he did. But his friends didn't change him. He changed his friends. Not many of us are capable of that kind of strength. That's why you had to put some distance between you and Luke."

"So he wouldn't drag me down with him."

I slide my arm around his shoulders, his very broad swimmer's shoulders. "How'd you get to be so wise?"

He shrugs, looks down at the cart, but I see the hint of a smile curling the corner of his mouth.

"Did you hit it off with my friend, Josie? I saw her talking to you the other night at the party. She wasn't boring you with tales of my childhood, was she?" I'm hoping she wasn't coming on to him.

"Not really." He looks away, avoids my question. "Dills for Dad?"

I refrain from asking more directly what Josie wanted. But I decide to keep an eye on her just in case she has her eye on my son. Or my husband. "Of course."

He picks out a jar, and we move on past cans of tomatoes, stewed, pasted, and sauced. Then the pasta sauce. Paul Newman's Sockarooni sauce has made it to Texas too. Finally we reach the chili. I'm surprised to find a vegetarian organic variety in this neck of the woods.

"Why are Grandma and Josie so worried about you seeing the sheriff?"

I knock a can off the shelf, and it rolls along the linoleum. "Josie's worried about me seeing the sheriff?"

"Yeah." He picks it up, places it in the cart, then adds another. "She said y'all used to date. Grandma doesn't trust him either, does she?"

My throat tightens again. It's one way I know I've been different in parenting. Oliver made a mistake with his friend Luke. I could have hounded him about it, but I didn't. I chose to trust him again. And this incident here with that local boy . . . well, I'm choosing to believe what my son says. My mother wouldn't. "It's not the sheriff as much as it is me. She doesn't trust me."

"Why? Did you do something bad? With him?" My son stares at me. "Get in trouble?"

My thoughts scramble and I try to scrape them together, figure out how to respond. I don't want to hide anything from him. I want to be honest. But how? Very cautiously, I move forward. "We dated. Way back in high school. Grandma didn't approve."

I think back to the girl Oliver liked last summer. She wore skimpy Britney Spears-type clothing, and I instantly disliked her. But I tried not to say anything. I wanted Oliver to come to that conclusion on his own. And he did eventually when he caught her flirting with some other guy. A painful but good lesson for a boy.

"Mother thought Drew was bad news. Bad for me."

"Did she approve of Dad?"

"Oh, yes. He was a year away from getting his law degree, which was perfect. Her dream son-in-law. But she didn't know his story or she would have had more reservations."

"What do you mean?"

"You know that your father . . . that his parents abandoned him. It wasn't until our wedding that Mother learned he was raised in an orphanage."

"How could she not know?"

"She never asked. She saw what she wanted to see: a law student with a promising career and a secure future."

"What did she say when she found out?"

"At first she was upset. But then she turned it into a positive. Your grandmother is the best at rationalization. She decided your dad was even better than she thought. He'd pulled himself up by his bootstraps. He had to be the smartest boy to beat the odds, go to school, get his law degree."

"But what about Sheriff Waring? He's a good guy." Oliver clears his throat. "At least he seems like it."

I catalog all the groceries in our cart, try to think of anything we might be missing. "Is this all we need?"

"Chips."

"Okay." We head off in the direction of snack foods. I'm ready for this discussion to be over, but I sense it's not.

"So did the sheriff end up being trouble like your mom thought?"

"He's a decent man. Nice and kind. We cared a lot about each other at one time. But we don't have those feelings anymore. Kind of like that girl you were gaga over in kinder-garten. Remember her? Kelly?"

Oliver's face reddens and he ducks his head.

"Do you still love her?"

"No. She's—"

"Exactly. But you care about her. You wouldn't want anything bad to happen to her, would you?"

"Of course not."

"And that's how it is with Drew . . . the sheriff."

I watch my son as he scans the chip aisle. His profile is exactly like Drew's. How did I not see it before? Maybe I chose not to see the similarities, just as I've chosen not to see the simi-larities between my mother and me. Oliver's eyes, hair, even his economy of motion reminds me of his biological father. Oh, Mike is there too. You can't be near someone your whole life without bits and pieces of their personality rubbing off on you.

Going to England one summer in college, I looked up my father's family who came from Yorkshire. I only found tombstones in an ancient churchyard, but I took rubbings and brought them home. Mother didn't want them, so I framed them and hung them in my dining room. The dark charcoal shows the names and dates and makes me think of how our lives rub against others, and we take on others' qualities just as they take on part of us.

Mike's words and actions have placed a permanent fingerprint on our son's heart. Maybe Oliver is a compilation of the best of both men.

"Did you sleep with him?"

I turn the cart too sharply and hit the corner of an aisle, crunching a bag of chips. Nothing like a direct question from my teenage son. Hard to dodge.

"The sheriff?"

My mother would avoid the question or say it isn't any of my business. But that's not the type of relationship

I have with Oliver. So I take a slow, deep breath and pray for guidance. "Do you remember how I told you when I was saved?"

He nods. I've told him the story many times. "On the beach."

"Yes. I was in college."

"So you did sleep with him?"

I don't want him to think he has a free rein to sleep with girls. Both Mike and I have talked to him about sex and its consequences. "I made a lot of mistakes in high school," I say. "In college. And after. Even now. I'm not perfect." Which my mother likes to point out. "None of us are, I suppose. That's the whole point of grace, right?"

"Yeah."

"Have you made mistakes you regretted?"

"The other night."

I place my hand on his arm. "Mistakes happen. We can either dwell on them or move on and try not to make them again. Right?"

"Can you forgive me?" Oliver asks.

Tears fill my eyes. "Of course."

"Even if you're not sure whether I did it or not."

I clasp him to me, wrap my arms around his broad shoulders. "I love you, Oliver. Always."

I HELP MOTHER in the kitchen as she goes through the leftovers from what friends have brought. She tosses out what she doesn't deem edible or salvageable. Cal Henry is in the attic working on the electrical wiring above the kitchen. Oliver is outside finishing up in the garage, and Mike hasn't returned from Daddy's hotel yet.

"You don't want to eat one of Mamie Reynold's casseroles. Trust me." In the trash it goes. She glances up at the ceiling, at the *thump, thump, thump* of Mr. Boyle's footsteps overhead. "Hamburger Helper!" Mother wrinkles up her nose as she sniffs some tin-foiled concoction. "Can you believe someone would—"

"Mother! These friends took the time to make something nice for you. They spent their hard-earned—"

"Oh, please. Somebody stopped at Wal-Mart on the way over." It disappears into the bulging trash. "One thing has surprised me in all of this."

"What's that?"

"Hazel. I haven't seen hide nor hair of her this entire week. Why, when her husband died, I was right there beside her, helping her. And she's practically left town."

"Maybe it brings up memories that are difficult for her, Mother."

"Well, maybe." She pinches her lips together. Then she opens a container. The bottom is stained orange from marinara sauce. "Oliver had spaghetti for a snack and stuck the empty container back in the refrigerator." She rinses it in the sink. "And the rest of the coconut cake." She lifts the cake lid—there's only tiny flakes left on the platter. "Too bad. Hazel's cake was good." She pinches coconut between her fingers and slips it into her mouth. "It's her best recipe. But she won't give out the secret. I think it's a liqueur."

The lights go out again. I glance up at the ceiling, wonder what we'll do if Mr. Boyle electrocutes himself.

"Cal Henry!" Mother calls.

"I'm okay!" his muffled response filters through the plaster.

After Mother has emptied containers, and I've washed and dried them, she decides to make her famous chicken tetrazzini for dinner, not bothering to consider Oliver's request for hotdogs. Mother's tetrazzini is the best. I've tried to make it, but it came out watery. While I'm chopping onions, my eyes beginning to burn, there's a knock on the back door.

Mother grimaces but wipes her hands on a dish towel. "Who could it be now? I never thought I'd say this, but I'm tired of people bringing over pathetic offerings to compensate my grief. I mean, really, who thinks a chicken pot pie is going to make a grieving widow feel any better?"

"You did, when you took Mandy Porter blueberry muffins when her mother died."

"They were homemade. From scratch." She opens the door and is full of smiles and happy greetings. Her reaction to our visitor is imperceptible to others, just a slight stiffening of her already-straight spine. She takes a step back, opening the door wider. "Come on in."

"Is Suzanne here? I don't want to intrude."

I recognize my high school friend's voice and quickly wash my hands of onion juice.

"Yes, of course."

Estelle Ramirez walks in carrying a Bundt cake. "I thought I'd bring you a little something. What with all the company you've been having."

"How thoughtful of you." Mother takes it from her and sets in on the kitchen table. Behind Estelle's back Mother mouths, *Betty Crocker.*

I ignore her. Estelle has her hands full with so many young children. What does Mother expect, an old family recipe? The fact Estelle was able to bake anything probably took extreme effort on her part. I give her a quick hug. "I'm glad you came by."

"I felt bad about the grocery store."

"Oh, don't worry. I've had a little one that I've had to chase before."

"I'm sure it's been busy around here." She looks at the obituary that was cut out of the paper and taped to the refrigerator. "What with all the preparations."

"Where are all your children?" Mother peeks outside the door before she shuts it completely.

"Naldo has them."

Folding the dish towel, I lay it on the counter. "Why don't we go sit down in the den so we can visit? Mother, the onions are all cut."

The lights come on, and Estelle's brown eyes widen. "I didn't stop by at a bad time, did I?"

"Not at all. Mother's having electrical problems."

She stares at the crack along the ceiling. "The earthquake affected a lot of homes. We've had splits in the concrete on our patio. Naldo's worried it might affect the foundation."

"It could." Mother pulls out a frying pan. "No telling what damage it's caused. I need to call the insurance company."

Not wanting to get into all the damage this week is causing in so many other areas, I usher Estelle into the den. "Mother's making chicken tetrazzini. I hope I don't smell like onions."

"You're fine. You look great."

I lead her past the dining room and into the den where her daughters danced and twirled the other night.

"Your mother's a fabulous cook. I've had her tetrazzini."

"It's the best." No one would dare refute that.

"She's good at everything, it seems." Estelle looks around at the beautifully decorated den with its matching sofa and love seat. The colors are tasteful but striking, comfortable and warm, but not homey. There's something stiff and reserved about the furniture. Mother has poured over all the latest home decor magazines. She knows every trend and trick, and she has impeccable taste. But even though every-thing coordinates perfectly, something seems to be missing.

"Definitely." I sit on one end of the sofa and pat the cushion beside me.

"That's a lot to live up to." She tugs on her pants' leg. "At least I don't have to worry about my kids feeling inadequate. They won't have some image to live up to. Whatever they do will be better than what I've done."

"Nonsense. I'm sure you're a very good mother. Parenting is more than keeping a neat home and making the perfect tetrazzini."

"You're probably right."

"I don't let Mother's perfectionism affect me." I straighten my skirt. "I've learned we're all in different seasons of our lives." Then I realize how I do, in fact, compare my meager hostess abilities to Mother's. "Would you like something to drink? Coffee? Tea? Maybe a soda?"

"I'm fine. It's nice just to sit here for a minute without someone tugging at me or needing something."

Smiling, I settle back into the couch. It feels like when we were in high school. Estelle would come over and we'd sit cross-legged on my bed. We would study for a while, then talk about boys or an upcoming party.

"When Oliver was a baby," I say, "and I was totally overwhelmed with taking care of him. I didn't even manage a shower every day, but I remembered how my mother was always dressed and ready for Daddy to come home from work. How she made sure she freshened her lipstick and touched up her makeup, even putting on perfume." I roll my eyes. "It was like living with June Cleaver."

Estelle laughs.

"Please don't tell me you manage that way when you have more children than mother and me put together."

She keeps smiling. "No way. There are *weeks* I don't get a shower. Most mothers experience that. If they're honest."

"I like to imagine it was the same for Mother when I was a baby. And if it wasn't . . . well, I don't need to know that. No one is perfect. So don't let Mother fool you."

"Well, you're the one that seems perfect to me." She gestures toward me. "You have beautiful clothes. Your makeup always looks perfect. And your hair . . ."

"Tell me I'm not a chip off the old block." I laugh uneasily. Mother is the last person I want to emulate. "Well, I'm not perfect. Not by a long shot."

Estelle nods, as if she's absorbing my words but not quite believing them. She picks at a dry spot of food on her shirt. I want to hug her, but I resist. It feels as if my sins might rub off on her. And she looks so innocent. So sweet.

"I'm sorry about your father, Suzanne. I really am."

Inside I cringe and I want to tell her the truth. "It's okay, really."

"It is?"

"Well, you know, I'm fine. Mother's fine."

"She seems to be handling all this beautifully."

"Of course." She's the master orchestra leader.

"I saw your son outside. He's so handsome."

"Thank you."

"Do you think he looks more like you or his father?"

I've heard that question a thousand times from friends over the years; it's harmless but unsettling. "I don't know." I glance toward a portrait of Oliver when he was two, barefoot and chunky, with a wide, dimpled grin. Those days were so much simpler then. "How many children do you have now?"

"Five." Estelle settles a pillow on her lap, toying with the corners.

"You are busy. And to think you took the time to make

a cake." Guilt twists inside me. All of this care and concern for nothing.

"They're good kids. Most of the time."

"Naldo must be a good father to keep them for you."

"He's the best. I'm very blessed." From her smile I know it's true. "All the kids look like him, but that's a good thing. He's very handsome. Your husband is handsome too. And kind."

"To put up with my mother, he'd have to be!" I laugh.

"Naldo ran into him at the barber's the other day. Asked him for some business advice. You know, legal stuff. And your husband was so kind to help. Free of charge. I'm surprised there's not a line outside the door. He must be making house calls."

I frown. "What do you mean?"

"Oh, I saw him going into Josie's house. It's on the way from my house to your mother's. He should open an office here. I bet he'd have enough business to keep him busy for years to come."

I don't respond. Moving back so close to my parents is not an option. Especially with Drew living here.

"Do you remember dreaming as teenagers that we'd meet some fabulous man, handsome and rich and, well," she sighs, "to think our dreams have come true. Mostly true. Mine's not rich, but I couldn't ask for a better husband than Naldo. I've had friends who've worried if their husbands are faithful. You know, are their hunting trips for quail or something else? But Naldo isn't like that. He's faithful. Did I say something wrong?"

"What?" I give myself a shake. I'm not sure what she said after the part where she saw Mike going into Josie's house.

The lights flicker, brighten, then extinguish themselves. From the kitchen Mother hollers up at Cal Henry. A moment later the lights return.

Despite the distractions Estelle's focus is on me, her gaze steady. She places a hand on my arm. "Is something wrong?"

I know she's not referring to the lights. My smile feels forced, as forced as the electricity that provides counterfeit light. "No, not at all."

"I shouldn't have talked so much about husbands and fathers. I'm sorry. And you're grieving the loss of your own. Please forgive me." Her eyes are wide, the brown deep and earnest.

"There's nothing to forgive."

25

It's not until after we sit in front of the television watching *Super Nanny*, Mother's favorite show, that I decide to turn in. I'm exhausted, weighted down with stress and anxiety. Mother agrees and goes to her own room, saying she's going to work on the eulogy for Daddy. I don't offer to help. She is on her own now. With a brief brush of my hand against Oliver's thick but short hair, I whisper good night as he switches the channel to ESPN. Mike follows me to the guest room.

In silence we turn toward our own suitcases set up in opposite corners of the room. There's an awkwardness between us that is my fault. I wait until he goes down the hall to brush his teeth, then I slip off my clothes and pull on my nightgown and robe.

I wonder how will we survive this latest crisis. How can I step over that invisible line and believe him? He's never given me any reason to doubt before now. He's always been faithful. Steady and solid. I know my doubt protrudes from my own sins, my own failings. Should I confess, prove to him there is no reason for him to trust me?

Confused, my life feeling like a world-class roller coaster, I sit on the edge of the bed. I know I have a choice to make. I can focus on my own sin, which makes me doubt Mike. Or I can choose to trust him.

When Mike returns, he folds his clothes on top of his suitcase. Without a word we move through our routine. It's a dance of sorts, each of us anticipating, aware of the other's movements. Yet not touching.

I take my turn in the bathroom, lingering longer than necessary, studying my face in the mirror as I apply moisturizer. Dark shadows have formed circles under my eyes. This week has added years to my face.

I decide to run a quick bath, hoping it will help me relax. As the water pours into the tub, I secure my hair on top of my head. At first the water is too hot, but as it cools and my skin adjusts, I lean back against an air pillow Mother keeps under the sink. I close my eyes, try to let my mind go blank, but instead up pops an image of Josie running her hand along Mike's shoulders in a flirtatious way.

My eyes open. I sink farther down into the water without getting my hair wet. I want to hide. Could I be as devious as Mother? Do I have that potential? Could I concoct an elaborate plan to save my dignity, my pride? Could I be angry enough to kill my own husband, figuratively as Mother has done?

I know what it feels like to be abandoned, to be left, lost and alone. Sympathy wells up inside me. I hurt for my mother. To be rejected by the man you love is painful beyond measure. Did she suspect before Daddy told her? Did she have doubts? Were there signs? There were signs in my own marriage. I pushed him away. I wasn't surprised when he retaliated with angry words and left. But was Mother blindsided?

My mother doesn't usually elicit sympathy. She's not the victim type. She's strong, demanding, forceful, irritating. Yet she's a woman. And somewhere, deep below the flawless facade she's created, beats a woman's heart. She gave herself, the best way she knew how, to her husband for more than forty years. She cleaned up after him, washed his clothes, cooked for him, laid in his bed at night, gave him a child. Loved him. Her love wasn't perfect, but then whose is? It was all she had, all she knew.

I wrap my arms around my bent knees, lay my cheek on top. I consider my own marriage, my own inadequacies as a wife and mother. Yet I've loved Mike. I've supported him. I've done so many things for him, for our family. Withholding truth has been a part of that protection. But the cost keeps adding up. Tears leak out of my eyes and run into the water. Because I failed him. Betrayed him. And it was a mistake. In reaching out for comfort and security from Drew, I put everything at risk.

I fear what might happen if Mike finds out. I never want him to feel the way I'm feeling now, betrayed, bereaved, bludgeoned by doubts. All we've worked for—our family, our home, our marriage—could so easily be destroyed. Because of my own foolishness.

THE ROOM IS dark when I climb into bed. I can see the bump of Mike's shoulder. I consider reaching out, touching him, trying to bridge this space between us. But I don't know what to say. I long for the comfort of his arms, yet those same arms make me ask too many questions, while at the same time withholding information from him. I turn away, pull the covers up, and lay on my side. I hear his steady breathing and assume he's asleep. But then a hand touches my shoulder.

"I thought you were asleep."

"I was waiting for you." His voice is deep and rumbling.

Guilt once more churns inside me. His thumb begins to knead the tight muscles along my neck. A part of me needs him, needs this, and wants to lean into him. Yet another part of me is afraid to need him too much for fear I could lose him if he were to learn the truth.

"You okay?" he asks.

"Sure."

"You're tense."

Of course. Now he uses two hands. His fingers knead and press along my tight muscles. In the quiet of our room, we're alone together for the first time all day. "How was Dad?"

"Tired of being dead. Open to any ideas."

"What if Mother won't change, won't bend?"

"Then we might have to accept the idea that they'll get divorced."

"No." My tone is harsh, desperate.

"Suzanne, you've got to accept it's a real possibility. You're not five. You'll be okay. They'll be okay. Maybe better."

"How can you say that?"

"Look, I love your folks. But they're not happy. I'm not the one to say what they should or shouldn't do. It's their decision. Their lives. Right?"

I sigh, roll onto my back with a huff. Mike is silent for a long time, but I can feel his gaze as firmly as his caress.

"Are you still angry because of those rumors?"

"No. Not really. I—"

"You're not going to get a wild hair and go off the deep end like your mother, are you? Should I hide any guns or knives?"

"Mother killed Daddy with her tongue."

"It's sharper than a two-edged sword. But she also used the pen."

"The obituary," I whisper. "It's mightier than the sword."

"You didn't answer my question."

"Of course I wouldn't pull a stunt like Mother." But my ability to react like my mother is unsettling to me. She would think the worst. She would run off and leave Daddy stranded in the middle of nowhere, just as I did to Mike. "I'm sorry," I say, "for all of this. For running off this afternoon. For doubting, fearing—"

"You don't have anything to be sorry about."

"Oh, yes, I do."

He wraps his arms around me, and I hold onto him like I'm clinging to the edge of a cliff. "Do you trust me?"

"Yes." But belief in Mike only points out the disbelief in myself.

I'M UP EARLY. I'm not sure I slept much. Long before the alarm ever thinks of buzzing, I creep out of bed, tug on a pair of shorts and top, slip on sandals, and sneak out the back door. Outside it's cooler than I imagined and chill bumps cover my bare skin. Dark as how I feel inside, it's not quite night and not quite day yet. A thick fog hovers over the ground, thickening around the trunks of the peach trees.

It only takes me ten minutes to reach my destination. Josie's house is more of a cottage, small and dainty, with peach trim and a front door of etched glass in a large oval shape. Spotting her car in the port alongside the house, I climb the steps and hope she doesn't have company. At least I know it's not Oliver, who was sleeping on the couch when I left. Or Mike, who was snoring in bed. Before I can rethink the decision I made sometime between the hours of two and three, I ring the bell, then ring it again when no one answers.

Finally, a faint glow of light appears, and a fuzzy shape approaches the front door. The bulb above my shoulder splashes the porch in light and makes me squint.

"Who is it?"

"It's me. Suzanne."

The bolt clicks and the door opens. Josie is wearing flannel PJs with snow bunnies all over them. Her hair is wilder than usual, pressed flat on one side of her head. Remnants of mascara and liner circle her eyes. "Come on in."

"I'm sorry it's so early."

She turns her back on me, wanders down a hallway and waves for me to follow. "You want coffee?"

"No, that's okay." She doesn't seem to mind the early morning hour or the unexpected company. Maybe she's used to visitors at all hours. Maybe she's simply more laid back than I am.

She pulls open the fridge, offers me one of those energy drinks, but I shake my head. She pops the tab and takes a long pull. "For when you don't have time to percolate."

I smile, then remember why I'm here. "Look, Josie, I'm sorry to disturb you but—"

"I know what this is about. I expected it."

"You expected me to come?"

"Sure. What wife wouldn't?"

I blink. Scuffing her bare feet across the wood floor, she settles at the kitchen table. It's a white wicker table with a glass top and dainty chairs that remind me of an ice cream parlor.

"So you . . ." I'm at a loss for words. All the things I thought about saying collide like a ten-car pileup in my brain. "You and . . . well, Mike . . ."

"Sit down, Suz. Take a load off."

I remain standing. "This won't take long. Are you after my husband? Or is it my son?"

Her laughter rankles me. "That's ridiculous."

"Why? I know you. You've told me you date men who are married, men who are old enough to be your father and young enough to be your son. So is it my dad? My husband? My son?" I realize then all three are contenders and none would please me. I feel my fists clenching.

"Oh, Suzanne, sit down. I'm not after anyone." She slurps down more of her energy drink. Already she seems wide awake. "But I can see you don't believe me. You know, Suz, maybe you should pay less attention to your paranoia and more attention to how you've become just like your mother."

Her words slap me. My face feels like it's on fire. "How can you say that to me?"

"Because it's the truth. You are just as controlling as she is."

"How? What am I doing? Trying to keep my marriage together? Trying to protect my son?"

"You're trying to get your parents back together. Most people would just accept that their folks were divorcing. But not you."

"What's wrong with that? Oh, yes, I remember. You don't believe in marriage anymore. But some of us do." I flatten my hand against my chest. "Why shouldn't I want my parents to stay married?"

"Because it's not really about them, is it?" She leans back, props one foot on the other knee. "Isn't it more that you don't want your life to be changed? Or disrupted."

"That's not true. I want them to be happy."

"And were they? Really? You can stand there and tell me your father was a happy man for the last forty years?"

My thoughts scatter like a flock of birds startled, wings flapping, beaks squawking. Bits of arguments surface and are overtaken by more. By truth.

"That's what I thought." Her hand cups the energy drink, turning it around and around. "Your father hasn't been happy. And now he has a chance for happiness."

I shake my head. "But divorce is wrong."

"Maybe. Maybe not. Maybe it's correcting a mistake that he made forty years ago. Maybe there's no fixing some relationships. Would you tell a woman married to a man who beats her that she has to stay, has to take it?"

"No. But—"

"What about a woman married to an alcoholic? Should she stay? What if the man doesn't want to change? What if a man is married to a woman who cheats on him?"

That barb is a little too close for comfort.

"And she doesn't want to change. Or she can't help herself."

I swallow hard.

"So where is that fuzzy line that determines what's right and wrong? Your father has kowtowed to your mother for forty years. What if he couldn't take it anymore? What if he just said, 'Enough'? Is that wrong? What if he's tried to get your mom to loosen up but she resists? I don't know the answers here. But I can't point my finger and say that's wrong. Can you? Isn't that between him and God? And if it is wrong, is it the worst sin imaginable? I don't think so. So, tell me, is it that you're really so devastated that your parents aren't together? Or is it that you don't want things to change? Don't you just want everything to go back to normal so you can go home, go back to your own life?"

Her words cut me deep. I want to argue, but the arguments die on my tongue. "Am I that selfish?"

"No," her voice is tender, "I didn't say selfish. I think it's fear."

My eyes ache with the pressure of hot tears.

"And it's fear that keeps your mother controlling and

manipulating. I'm not saying she's the worst woman in the world. She has a caring heart when she allows anyone to see it. But she's so scared, so fearful of what, I don't know. Why do you think she's doing this whole bury-the-husband thing? She's scared. Scared to be abandoned. Scared of not being loved. Scared of being alone."

Her words resonate deep inside me. It's fear. Fear of my own. Fear that has turned me into my own mother.

MOTHER IS AWAKE when I return home. She's already in the kitchen when I walk in the back door. She looks startled, surprised to see me. "Where have you been?"

"Is Mike still asleep?"

"Far as I know. But then I thought you were too."

"Oliver?"

"On the couch. What's wrong?" Mother's hand pauses as she is sharpening a paring knife. A bowl of fresh-picked peaches sits on the counter. "Is everything okay with you and Mike?"

I contemplate making a U-turn. I'm not ready for any more confrontations this morning.

"You're not getting a divorce, are you?"

I open the fridge and search behind leftovers for the cream. "No, Mother. We're fine."

Fine. At least I hope so. Once I left Josie's, I realized she never answered my question about whether she was after my husband, father, or son. She changed the subject.

"I thought you drank your coffee black." Mother watches me pour cream into my mug of coffee.

"I forgot." I put the cream back in the refrigerator and slurp coffee, obviously needing it more than I thought. The coffee is hot and perfect.

"If everything is fine, then why aren't you having sex?"

I almost spew out a mouthful of coffee. I choke down a swallow. "What?" I sputter. "Mother!"

"You've been here how many nights now and nothing—"

"Who are you? Mrs. Hoover? One day you're telling me my husband is cheating on me with my high school friend. And the next day—"

"These walls are very thin, Suzanne. Your father was cheap when he built this house. About those rumors . . . well, you should just be careful. Not give Mike such a free rein. And keep your eye on Josie. I'm not saying anything has happened there, but you can't be too careful. As a wife, you have to take precautions against these things."

"And having sex with my husband will do that?"

"Well, that's often where the troubles start." She begins peeling the skin off a peach, her knife precise, the peach skin curling and falling into the sink.

I blink, sip more coffee, feel my synapses spring to life, but I want to crawl back in bed and pull the pillow over my head. "What are you talking about?"

"For us, well, when your father and I stopped having sex . . ."

The nearest chair catches me as I fold into it, my legs feeling suddenly weak. There's not enough coffee in the world, not even French-pressed, to prepare me for this conversation. "Uh, Mother—"

"Don't look at me that way. It wasn't my fault. I was willing. I even missed it. But your father . . . well, he started having headaches, or he was stressed about work, or . . ."

Tired from being bullied. But I never utter the harsh words. I just stare at Mother. I know the toll it takes on her to make such a personal confession. A flash of white outside the window catches my eye. I glance out the window and see Cal Henry's Cadillac pulling up the drive.

"Your boyfriend is here."

Mother follows my gaze. Her lips tighten. She quickly finishes slicing the peach, letting the slices slide into a serving bowl, then rinses her hands under the faucet.

"What are you going to do about him?"

She wipes her hands on a towel. "I don't know yet."

"You're not seriously thinking of marrying him, are you?" At her blank expression, I protest, "Mother! You're married."

"Oh, pish-posh." She waves her hand as if dismissing my arguments. "Anyway, it's neither here nor there now. Doesn't matter anymore. What concerns me is you and Mike."

An exasperated sigh escapes me. "We're fine. We've been here three nights, Mother. The conditions here are not the most romantic."

"I'm simply saying a virile man like Mike might not be looking, but if his needs aren't met, then when some floozy like Josie comes along he's ripe for the picking." Mother cups a peach in the palm of her hand and smells it. She then begins to peel the skin off it.

I already have a truckload of my own guilt, but now, thanks to my mother, I can add a few more shovelfuls onto that. So if Mike is fooling around with Josie—and I'm not saying I believe that—then part of the guilt is mine. This is the gospel according to my mother. Which then demands the question in reverse: Does Mike carry part of the blame for my sin? After all, he was the one who walked out, leaving me vulnerable and scared. I didn't know if he would ever come back or not. I've never contemplated this possibility. Quite frankly it leaves a bitter taste in my mouth. I refuse to blame Mike for my own mistakes.

But then I realize Mother is actually admitting she played a part in Daddy leaving her. It's the first chink in her armor I've ever detected. Truly, it's a first of historical proportions.

Mother glances out the window toward Cal Henry's car. He hasn't emerged yet. Unfortunately that leaves us another minute or two to talk. Her brow pinches into a frown. "I was right. It is bad between you two. That's what I was afraid of."

"No, Mother. What's awful is that you would blame me. It's my fault if Mike looks at another woman. Because I'm not pretty enough or entertaining enough or satisfying him in bed—"

"Uh," a male voice makes us both turn. I stare at my sleepy-eyed husband. He rubs his spiky hair. "Just needed a cup before my shower."

"Let me get that for you." Mother stands, nudges me in the back as if to say, *This is your job*. But he's already pouring himself a mug. "Would you like some cream?" She hovers about his elbow. "Sugar?"

"Black's fine." He lifts the mug in a half-hearted salute. "Ladies." He eyes me, then heads down the hallway toward the shower.

Mother pulls a carton of eggs out of the fridge, along with a plastic container of bacon. "I never said you weren't pretty enough. Or smart enough. Or anything of the sort." She looks out the window again as if to check how much time she has before Cal Henry interrupts us. She cracks an egg on the side of a ceramic bowl. "But everybody has to work at it. You're not eighteen anymore. Young women are your competition. That is, if you want to keep your husband."

"You've always made me think I wasn't good enough, Mother."

"Nonsense. You were. Are. Who else in this neck of the woods could have snagged a man like Mike? Estelle?" The bridge of her nose crinkles. "Not likely. She was pretty enough once, but she has really let herself go."

"She's had five babies."

"Exactly."

"No one can remain a size two, Mother."

"Not if they keep having babies. And wearing clothes with spit-up all over them. And your friend, Josie—" she snorts—"she wouldn't have made it into a school like UCLA. Oh, she might attract a man's interest for a short period of time, but she can't keep one."

"Mother—"

"Why, with her, shall we say, loose morals, she would have lost a man like Mike long ago. A man likes to know he's the only man in your life. That you belong to him."

"Is that why you never told Daddy you were married before?"

She pauses for only a second, but it's enough to tell me I hit close to home.

"Oh, it didn't matter. Not in the least. Besides, it wasn't a marriage; it was insanity. And it was all annulled."

"Like it never happened. Right?"

"Exactly."

"But it did happen, Mother. You can't just erase something because it's offensive to you. Life isn't a counter that Clorox bleach can clean."

"I never said—"

"But that's how you act!" I interrupt. It's not often someone, especially me, can get away with such a thing. I rush forward before she can stop me, before I can stop myself. "You don't like what Daddy does, so you kill him off. You don't like the fact that you got carried away in the heat of the moment and married a man, so you pretend it never happened. You have to maintain control. Always. Well, you can't always be in control, Mother! Of your emotions. Or of things that happen to you."

My own words strike me. Isn't that what I've done? Tried to pretend that the night with Drew didn't produce a child? Josie's words echo deep inside.

Mother opens her mouth to remark, then closes it. Stunned that I've managed to silence her, I am caught off guard. My words have made me vulnerable to the truth as well.

"You're right," she finally manages. "There are some things you can never erase. No matter how hard you try." Her gaze is cold and hard as ice. "Now Cal Henry," she says slowly, as if tasting the name after so many years, "was not the man for me. It was a bit of a lark. Just like that old boyfriend of yours, Drew Waring. He never aspired to anything. He would have made you miserable. The fact that Cal Henry did as well as he has done is a surprise." She whisks the eggs into a yellow froth. "But you're wrong. You are always responsible for your actions. Always."

I sigh. Once again she has twisted my words. She misses my point but manages to skewer me with hers. She'll never understand. I set aside my coffee, turn away from her, and busy myself opening the bacon package. Carefully I lay slices in the pan. Each long, even slice reminds me of our lives laid out side by side.

"Maintenance," she goes on. "That's all I'm saying. It's the key to a long, healthy marriage."

Out the window I see Cal Henry still sitting in his car. What is he doing? Why isn't he coming in? "So what did you do wrong in your marriage?" I say, angry and irritated. A tiny voice in my head says, *Honor*. So I add, "I'm just trying to learn from your mistakes."

Mother pulls out the toaster and places two slices of bread in the slits. "I'm sure I did many things wrong, if you want to know the truth. You think I can't own up to my own mistakes? Well, I can. Would a face-lift have kept your father interested? The Karma Suntra?"

My mouth drops open, then curves with a smile at her mispronunciation.

"I should have insisted that your father perform his duty."

"That would have gotten Daddy in the mood, I'm sure."

"Men don't need candles and music, Suzanne." She looks at me as if I'm too naive and stupid for words. This conversation comes about twenty years too late. Too bad Mother wasn't as forthcoming with information when I was a teen. She never even liked me to use the word *period* and was furious when I asked Daddy to buy me tampons when I was in high school.

"This is all I'm going to say on the matter, Suzanne. Mike is your husband. But if you let him get away, if you allow a woman like Josie to steal him right out from under your nose, you'll regret it." Her mouth tightens. Does she regret letting Daddy get away? Doesn't she realize she could have him back? Only her pride stands in the way.

"Okay, one more thing."

Cringing, I bite my lip and reach for another slice of bacon.

"I know you've *known* Drew Waring. Since high school, I mean. In the biblical sense."

My hand falters. My soul cringes. I refuse to look in her direction.

She grabs my elbow, pinches hard till I look at her. "I'm warning you, Suzanne, you will lose Mike. And it will be the worst thing imaginable. You don't think it's obvious who your son looks like?"

I suck in a quick breath.

"You'll realize soon enough your mother knew a thing or two. I must say my disappointment runs deep, Suzanne. Deep. So don't lecture me about my marriage any longer. You haven't had a perfect track record yourself."

A knock at the back door announces Cal Henry's arrival.

"I'll let him in."

Her tone floats over me as I sink deeper and deeper into the mire I've created.

26

I sit on the back porch, unaware how long I've been here. I stare off at the prairie dog mounds. Occasionally I see a little brown furry critter dart out of a burrow and zip along the terrain. They look playful and cute as they scamper this way and that. Life, an observer might think, is fun and games for prairie dogs, but they would be wrong. The cuteness is a lie, a façade. Prairie dogs scurry back and forth because they're hiding from predators who would eat them for lunch.

My thoughts scamper and scurry in their own directions. They burrow into the certainty that my mother is a liar. Everything she says. Before this weekend I often laughed off Mother's tendency to exaggerate. If she had to chop ten carrots, it became a hundred. If she took food to an ailing friend once, the story became ten times. If someone, especially my father, acted foolishly, she'd say, "No one has ever acted like such a doofus." Harmless exaggerations, really. But are they so benign? The odd thing is, she's known throughout the area for this trait, and yet everyone seems to have bought into her lie about my father's death.

And now I learn that she's been covering up things in her past. Like a marriage. An annulment. And what she believes about me. It's just another form of control. These cover-ups are starting to look little prairie dog mounds of dirt.

I remember running through the fields as a little girl. Suddenly, the ground I thought was there wasn't. My foot went right through a prairie dog tunnel, twisting my ankle. Prairie dog mounds of lies leave the ground uneven, unsafe. Has my own lie, which is far worse than any my mother concocted, left my marriage on unstable ground?

While Mother lectured me about saving my marriage, exaggerating that I was about to lose Mike because we hadn't had sex while we were sleeping in her house, I knew her concern was not that marriage is a sacred thing. She simply doesn't want me to lose Mike who makes a "gazillion dollars." But all the money in the world can't compensate for a satisfying, trusting marriage.

"He's the catch of the century," she said when we got married. No one believed her, but everyone smiled and went along with it. The proud mother of the bride. Or should I say, the proud mother-in-law of the groom who had a brand-new law degree.

Now she tells everyone at the Dippity Do how he handles case after case and rakes in the dough. She rhapsodizes about our house overlooking the Pacific Ocean. Now I realize why she hasn't been keen on us coming home: She knew my secret. *Knew it!* Knew my son wasn't Mike's. And she didn't want anyone else to know. It's why there are no pictures of Oliver over the age of five in the house. She didn't want anyone else to notice the resemblance between her grandson and the local sheriff.

"Mom?" Oliver steps outside. His face is creased from the sofa pillow.

"Morning." I pat the swing. "Did you sleep well?"

"Okay." He grunts as he settles next to me. "That guy's in the kitchen with Grandma."

"Cal Henry. Yes, I know." I draw a slow breath and release it like I might be able to see it. But the day is already warm.

"We're supposed to call the sheriff's office today."

"I know." I rub his shoulder. "It's going to be okay."

"How do you know? What if the test *is* positive?"

"I don't know what will happen. But I do know we'll stick together. No matter what. Your father and I are here with you." I look him in the eye trying to make him understand the love we have for him. If the result is positive and Oliver is charged, I don't know what I'll do. Will I stand back, let the chips fall as they may? Or will I step in, try to fix things? "Do you want me to call the sheriff for you?"

"No. I'll do it. Or maybe I'll go see him myself."

"You know I'll protect you. I won't let anything—"

"You can't do anything to stop this, Mom."

"I can—"

"What are you going to do? Call your ex-boyfriend?" His tone dips into that teen range that sets my nerves on edge. But I know it's simply fear speaking. It's fear making me want to protect him.

"That's enough!" I put a hand on his arm. "It's my job to protect you."

"But you can't, Mom. You can't. I don't want you to do anything." He pushes away from the swing, walks several feet away. Then he turns back. "Don't do anything."

I watch him walk to the end of the porch and down the steps. I slow my respiration one breath at a time, adjusting it like a metronome. I always prided myself that I hadn't become my own mother. I wasn't obsessed with furniture or redecorating or creating the perfect pot roast. I didn't exaggerate. I didn't look down my nose at others. I tried to love, encourage, and nurture my son to the best of my ability.

But it hits me just the same. My mother is a world-class liar, and this funeral is her curtain call. Oh, how pride can lead to a downfall though. And I'm falling, falling, falling fast.

Because I too, am a liar.

I haven't changed my story. I don't concoct wild fabrications or fantasies as Mother has. My lie is one of omission. I left out something fairly important. Not that my hair is not really blonde or that I've had my teeth whitened. Or like my friend Cindy who had breast implants. Those things would never be talked about but would be fairly obvious to the casual observer.

No, I've been lying to myself. To Mike. To our son.

My whole life is a lie. Everything I stand for. My friends think I'm a strong Christian, going to church, running charity drives, even going on mission trips. But it is all a façade hiding my sin deep down inside. The outward appearance doesn't make me clean or pure or safe or nice. It simply makes me a liar.

27

Drew

Drew couldn't have been more surprised when the kid walked into his office than if he'd come in doing a handstand.

"This okay?" Oliver asked, his dark eyes intense. "Me coming here?"

"Always better of your own volition. I was just about to call your grandmother's place."

The kid hesitated, then moved into the office. He didn't smile.

"Have a seat." Drew closed the folder he'd been working on. "What can I do for you?"

The teen shrugged one shoulder, more an uncomfortable tick than an answer. He slunk into the chair facing the desk. "What happened to your desk there?"

"Got shot."

"Did it try to get away?" Oliver said, humor loosening his stiffness.

"A snake actually."

Oliver's eyes widened.

"My deputy shot the desk, missed the snake."

The kid cracked a smile at that. It was only the second time Drew had seen him smile. He seemed the serious sort. But Drew wasn't sure if that meant he was studious or simply disturbed.

"What happened to the snake?"

"I killed it." Drew tilted his head toward the windowsill where the chunk of wood was missing.

"You get snakes in here often?"

Drew shrugged. "It's a jail."

Oliver laughed outright then. He leaned back in his chair, more relaxed than when he first came into the office. "I was wondering if you were going to file charges against me or what?"

"Or what?" Drew smiled this time. "We don't use the stockades anymore."

Oliver didn't laugh. "Did the test results come back?"

Drew leaned his elbows on the desk, met the kid's direct stare. "You staying clean?"

"Yes, sir." Then that half, sly smile emerged again. "My dad's got me cleaning out my grandpa's tool shed and garage. So maybe clean isn't the right word."

Hard work was something Drew would have done to his own son. If he had one, and if he been caught doing something against the law. "I've seen Archie's tool shed. You got your work cut out for you. Do you think your grandpa will come home eventually?"

"If Grandma will let him."

"She can't keep him out. It's his house. His right."

"You know my grandmother, right?"

Drew laughed. "Yeah, I do."

The kid rubbed the palm of his hand with his other thumb. "What about the test?"

Drew leaned back, and his chair squeaked. He gave the kid a moment to sweat, but he didn't seem nervous. "Looks like you told the truth. Or maybe you got lucky this time. But the test showed you weren't smoking."

"What about the others?" Oliver asked. No slump of relief. No smile that he'd gotten away with it. Just a simple question about those who got caught with him.

"I can't discuss pending cases."

He nodded. "Can't you let Rick go. Just this once?"

"What do you care about Rick Parker?" Drew countered. "You just met him. You haven't seen him since Sunday night, have you?"

"No, sir. I just . . ." He shrugged, more awkward than evasion.

"You feeling guilty for getting off?"

"Maybe."

"Don't. I don't like to see kids go to court, much less juvenile detention. But if that'll scare you straight, then I'd do it in a heartbeat. Look, Rick Parker . . . I've known him a long time. Know his family. This isn't the first time he's been in trouble. Not even the second. He's never taken my warnings seriously. Now, I hope he will. Understand?"

Oliver leaned forward, resting his elbows on his knees. He took a couple of deep breaths, his head down as if wrestling with more questions. Finally, he looked up. "Are you doing this because of my mom?"

That sucker punched Drew.

"Did she ask you to?" Oliver went on.

"No." He had asked himself the same question though. But without any evidence, other than being in the wrong place at the wrong time, the case was clear cut. He wouldn't show favoritism because of feelings he once had for the kid's mom. That was over. But he admired the kid, especially because it seemed Oliver didn't want favoritism either. A remarkable trait in anyone. Especially a boy trying to be a man.

"But you know her, right?"

"I do."

"You used to date her, didn't you?"

"That was a long time ago. We were young and stupid. That was before your daddy swept her off her feet." Drew didn't want the kid thinking anything.

Oliver kept on staring, as if he wasn't sure what to say or do, as if Drew hadn't answered the way he expected.

"Don't worry, kid. I'm not doing you or your momma any favors. If you even smell of pot or anything else illegal, you'll see the inside of my jail and then the courthouse so fast your head will be spinning. And our judge won't go easy on juveniles. No matter who their momma or daddy is." Drew didn't want the kid to think his famous attorney father could get him off either.

Oliver glanced at the windowsill again and nodded without trace of a smile.

Drew considered the impromptu meeting over. But the kid didn't seem to be in a hurry to leave. Needing to get back to work, Drew opened the file folder again. But Oliver didn't take the hint. So after a moment or two Drew slapped the folder closed. "How'd you get over here? Hitch a ride? Drive?"

If so, that would be illegal since the kid didn't have a driver's license yet.

"Walked."

"That's a ways. Come on, I'll take you to your grandma's." Drew reached for his hat and felt the kid's keen gaze watching him.

"Are you after my mother?"

The question stopped Drew in his tracks like a pulled gun. "What are you talking about?"

28

Suzanne

The back door opens. Mike peers inside the kitchen but doesn't step in. He looks from Mother, who is turning the bacon on the stove, to Cal Henry, who is drinking coffee at the kitchen table, then locks gazes with me.

"What's the matter?" I ask.

"Mike," Mother waves him inside, "you're just in time for breakfast."

"Suz," he ignores her and remains in the doorway, "hand me that apron over there."

I take Mother's apron off the peg on the wall and hand it to him. "What is—" The man—the naked man—standing behind Mike catches me off guard. "Oh, uh . . ."

Mike pushes the door open wider. "Come on in. It's okay."

The tall, gaunt man, with head down and eyes downcast, steps inside my parents' home. His bones push against his leathery, wrinkled skin. Mother's apron is now wrapped around his waist.

"Mr. Peavy," I say, catching Mike's imploring gaze, "of course, come on in. Welcome. It's been a long time since I've seen, um, since . . ." I scramble for more appropriate words. I can see a bit too much of Ned Peavy at the moment. Luckily Mother's apron hides most. In his hand he carries a faded yellow fly swatter.

"What in tarnation?" Mother asks, holding the tines of a fork upright like a pitchfork.

"Mother, Mr. Peavy's going to have breakfast with us." I feel Mike's hands on my shoulders as he kisses my neck from behind. "Mike, why don't you take Mr. Peavy back to Mother and Daddy's room. Find some of Daddy's clothes . . ."

He nods and leads Ned in the right direction. I turn in time—before I'm confronted with Mr. Peavy's back side—and watch Mother's consternation turn to downright shock. Her eyes widen, followed by her mouth pinching tight.

"Should I scramble some more eggs, Mother?"

"Cal?" Mother's voice trembles.

"Looks like that man could use a hot meal." Cal Henry folds the paper.

By the time we're all seated at the kitchen table, Ned Peavy, wearing Daddy's chambray shirt and jeans, Mother wearing a perturbed expression, Cal Henry has loaded his plate with toast, bacon, and eggs. Oliver still isn't back from his walk, but I'm not concerned. Not yet anyway. You might not be able to lead a teenage boy anywhere, but he will come when he's hungry. With Mike sitting next to me, I hear the crunch of gravel outside as a car pulls up the driveway. I recognize the sound of the squeaky door closing.

Mother freezes as she reaches to pass Mike the platter of buttered toast. "What on earth is *he* doing here?"

"I called him." Mike takes two slices of toast. "Asked him to come over. Ned's air conditioner is out. I thought Archie and I might figure out a way to fix it for him."

Mother's face is a collection of emotions, the lines expressing her irritation better than any words. It takes almost a full minute before her wrinkles smooth out and she appears at ease.

"How long you been having trouble with the air conditioner," Cal Henry asks around a mouthful of bacon.

"Two, three year. Maybe more."

"I bet I can help. Had experience working on my own."

Mother glances at Cal, then at Daddy walking in the back door. She sets the platter on the table with a *thunk* and slumps back in her chair in defeat.

29

❧

Drew

Wat are you talking about?" Drew asked Oliver again, a band of emotions tight about his chest.

"You've slept with my mom, right?" Oliver didn't flinch from his question. He threw it out there like a solid punch.

"Look, Oliver, that kind of thing is none of—"

"Don't tell me that!" There was a flicker of rage in the boys' eyes. "You've slept with her. I've seen you over at my grandma's house. Everybody's talking about how you brought my mom home late. Early in the morning before my dad and I arrived. And again this morning. She snuck out while everybody was sleeping. Was it to meet up with you?"

"I don't know what she was doing this morning, but she wasn't with me. Your mom and I—" He stopped and redirected his thoughts. "I brought her home Saturday night along with her girlfriend Josie. They were out and had an accident. The car couldn't be driven." To say the least. "So

I gave them a ride. It's part of my job. So there wasn't anything sordid about it."

"But you've dated my mom, right?"

"A long time ago. Long before you were born. Way back in high school." Drew didn't bother to mention the one time in California. It was inconsequential. And it wasn't actually a date.

"But—"

"Look, Oliver, I like your mom just fine. But I'm not in love with her." It was true. He was at one time. But not anymore.

He hadn't been with Suzanne since that crazy night in California. He remembered her tears. He had wanted to comfort her, but he knew that only her husband's arms could. He had made a serious error in judgment. Yes, he knew why he'd called her in the first place. Exactly what he wanted to happen had happened. Afterward he realized he had wanted more. More than a one-night stand. More than he had a right to. Because Suzanne's heart belonged to her husband. He tried to call her after she left. In fact, he had called her again and again. Then one night a man answered. Her husband. Drew had hung up and left town for good.

What year was that? He realized then it was about sixteen . . . or fifteen . . . years ago. Sixteen, had to be. But could it—

He gave the kid a hard, close inspection. The kid was fifteen. Drew could look up his birth date in half a second if he wanted. But he wasn't sure he wanted to probe this particular mystery any further.

30

Suzanne

G et in the car." Mother holds her purse over her arm.
Thinking she might be on the verge of running
away from the tangled web she's woven, I decide I better
go with her. Having a first and second husband working
together might be too much for any woman.

While the four men walk back over to Ned Peavy's to
work on his air conditioner, Mother and I get in my rental
car. Slowly, carefully, I buckle the seat belt. "Where are we
going?"

"I need panty hose."

I pull out onto the highway. Mother tells me to slow
down. "Mother, we'll get run over by an eighteen-wheeler
if I don't—"

Sudden flickering lights in my rearview mirror have
me braking instead of accelerating. Great. Now Mother will
have something else to berate me for. I should have expected
this. Frowning, I brake, pull to the shoulder of the road, and
stop. The SUV pulls behind me, lights still flashing. I watch

Drew walk toward my rental car, his pace slow, unhurried. I clutch the steering wheel, glance at the dashboard clock.

He bends down, peers in the window. "Ladies."

"Sheriff, I told Suzanne she was driving too fast. You know California drivers. You've heard how it is out there, with shootings and wrecks."

"Suzanne, could you step out of the vehicle?" He ignores Mother's ranting.

I scramble in my purse for my wallet. When I reach the back end of the car, I hold my driver's license out to him.

He doesn't take it. What's the protocol for this? "What's wrong?"

Drew's wearing sunglasses, and I can't look into his eyes to try and read what he's thinking or feeling. He stares down at the ground, then looks out at the highway and watches a semi rumble past. A truck hauling hay goes at a much slower pace. Then a herd of motorcycles zips along, heading toward Fredericksburg. Drew glances back over his shoulder, and my gaze follows. In the front seat of the SUV, there's a dark outline of a passenger. Oliver.

"I've got your son."

"The test results came back?" Panic inches along my spine. "Drew, I wish you would have called us first."

"That's not what this is about. The results are back. Your son is free and clear. He came into my office today to find out for himself." Drew shifts and the heavy thick leather of his gun belt creaks. "I was bringing him home when I saw you."

"Thanks." But I notice Oliver isn't getting out of the SUV. I don't know what else Drew could want him for.

Finally, he takes off his sunglasses and squints against the sun's rays. "Your son thinks I'm after you."

"What?"

"I set him straight on that. He's heard rumors that you and I were involved, and he put two and two together. I brought you home late that first night you were back. You snuck out of the house early this morning. He assumed it was to meet me."

"Rumors," I spit out the word. Remembering the rumor Mother told me about Mike, I glance behind me at Mother sitting in the passenger seat of the rental car. Her posture, as usual, is erect, a measuring stick of propriety. She's pulled the visor down and is watching us in the mirror. "Drew, I went to see Josie this morning. You can call her and ask her."

"It doesn't matter to me who you went to see. I told him it wasn't me. I'm *not* after you. You're married. I have someone else in my life."

"That's great, Drew, but . . ." I'm not sure what the point of all of this is. Why did he pull me over to tell me this?

"I don't want your son thinking anything improper is going on."

"I don't either." And I don't want him to know about our past either.

"But," he pauses. His solid, unwavering gaze makes my insides squirm. "I need to know something. I need to ask you . . ."

I remain silent and wait for him to finish.

"It never really occurred to me." He swallows, looks down. His hand rests on the butt of his gun. "I didn't pay much attention when I first met Oliver. But . . . well, when he came in my office, started talking about all this . . . it made me think about . . . us. I checked his birth date. And the timing would have been right. Or wrong. Whichever way you want to look at it."

I'm listening to his words. They strike against my eardrums and shatter into hard pellets that shoot through my mind, imbed in my soul. My heart begins pounding.

"Depending on your point of view." A car streaks past us. Drew follows it with his eyes, then his gaze reverts back to me.

I can't speak, can't respond.

"Is he . . ."

My head feels like it's swelling. My fear is realized and it pulses through me. I want to start walking and never stop. Maybe I could jump in the car and drive. Make a getaway. But I can't. This is what I haven't wanted to face. The same emotions coil inside me that once had me curling into a ball and sobbing on my bed.

"Is Oliver my son?"

31

Drew

Drew had made a fatal error. Knowing Suzanne's mother, he wouldn't be surprised if, mother-like-daughter, Suzanne jumped in her car and ran him down. What was he thinking asking such a thing? It was probably a foolish thought. Maybe he was a fool for seeing some part of himself in the kid.

Prepared for a verbal assault, maybe even a slap across the face, Drew wondered if it was too late to take back his reckless words. "Suzanne—"

She looked at him then. Tears ran down her face, washed over him with the truth, and suddenly he couldn't breathe. She turned away from him then. For a moment she leaned on the trunk of the car. Her shoulders shook as silent sobs destroyed her usual composure.

What had he uncovered? He wiped the sweat off his brow, cursed, then said a hasty prayer. He didn't want to see what was obvious. He wanted to take a step back into time, forget all this, walk away. But he couldn't. Still, he wasn't sure what to do. He glanced back at his SUV, then saw an eighteen-wheeler approaching. The wake of air nearly took his hat. Slowly he edged toward Suzanne like she was a wounded animal. He reached toward her, touched her shoulder.

"I–I never t–told." She shook her head as the words poured out. "I never wanted Mike to know. To suspect. To question. And he hasn't. He hasn't. I thought I was the only one who saw the resemblance. But then we came here. A–and first Josie noticed. Then my mother said she's known for a long time. Now . . . you." She covered her face with her hands. "All I ever wanted . . ."

All *she* had ever wanted? What about what he wanted? He had wanted Suzanne. A long time ago. It was a selfish kind of want. A selfish need. But he'd never wanted a kid. He would be a lousy parent. And the world didn't need another messed-up kid. But now . . . he had a son.

The thought astounded, overwhelmed, staggered him. A son.

But there was more to think about than what he wanted. So many lives were tangled up in this. So many could be strangled with the news. Most of all, Suzanne. She had been holding this in, hiding this for so long. For fifteen years.

"What?" Drew asked. "What did you want?"

"A family. A family like I never had." She looked at Drew with waterlogged eyes. "And now I've destroyed even that."

He didn't care if Oliver was watching from the SUV or Mrs. Davidson from the rental car. Gently he pulled Suzanne toward him, wrapped his arms around her and held her. Her body was stiff, unresponsive, as if she was steeling herself. She didn't belong to Drew. She never had. She needed someone else's arms, someone else's comfort. But would this revelation destroy her marriage?

Drew released a slow breath along with Suzanne.

Now what were they going to do?

32

Suzanne

S o what is it? What's wrong?" Mother asks when I finally climb back into the car.

"Nothing," I manage even though I feel like I'm chewing glass. I curl my fingers around the steering wheel, grip it hard, then I reach for the ignition. The engine squeals.

"The car's on, Suzanne."

I realize that. My nerves are shredded. "Okay. Okay." I'm talking to myself, not Mother. "It's okay."

"What did Drew say to you? Did Oliver's test come back?

I glance in the rearview mirror, watch Oliver walk toward my rental car.

"He's being arrested isn't he? He's going to jail. Well, I knew it. You are far too permissible with that boy. And now, this is going to ruin his life. Oh, boy, we're going to have to read about this in the paper and hear folks—"

"Enough!" I glare at her. "Stop it, Mother. This is not about you. And Oliver is innocent."

The back door of the rental car opens and Oliver slides inside.

"Well, where have you been?" Mother asks. "You missed breakfast."

"I'm not hungry."

"You sick?"

"No."

My gaze meets my son's in the rearview mirror. No words pass between us. His eyes are flat—not angry, not anything, just flat.

"Well, are we going? Or are we going to pick up anyone else on the road?"

I pull out onto the highway. A car whizzes past my left and makes me flinch. I inch the car over into the next lane, pull into the medium, and make a U-turn.

"Well, that will certainly get you a ticket."

I ignore her.

"Where are you going?" she continues. "The pharmacy is the other direction. I need panty hose."

I make the turns and am soon driving too quickly up the gravel drive toward Mother's house. "I'll go to the store for you, Mother."

"But you don't know what I want."

"Hose," I say, squeezing the steering wheel as if drawing strength from it. I'm well aware of Oliver's silence expanding in the back seat like a sponge filling with water. "Black, right?"

"Well," she huffs, her hand lingering on the door. "I don't want a reinforced toe."

"All right."

"Control top." She finally opens the door.

"Got it." My mind feels heavy, unable to process the last few minutes. I need to be alone. I need . . . I don't know what.

Mother slowly gets out of the car but then pauses again. "Size A, you know."

The back door opens, and Oliver steps out. I roll down the window, reach my arm out toward him. "Oliver."

He stops and looks at me. Just out of my reach. Have I lost him already?

"Are you okay?" I ask.

"Yeah."

"Do you want to go with me to the store?"

"No."

I swallow the emotions that are lodged in my throat.

"Okay. Can we talk later?"

He nods but doesn't say anything, just walks off toward the garage, taking my heart with him.

I KNOCK ON the door once.

"Who is it?"

"Suzanne." I hear the rattle of the chain, then the door opens. Without preamble, I walk into the hotel room. "Daddy, I need to talk."

"What is it, Sugar Beet?" He closes the door as I sit on the end of the bed.

"I've been driving around for hours, trying to think, trying to figure out what to do."

He drags a desk chair over and sits in front of me. He leans forward, his elbows resting on his knees, and takes my hands. "Suzy, your mother is not easy to—"

"It's not about Mother."

He studies me a moment, his pale brown eyes thoughtful. "What is it?"

The words stall, like a car engine on a frigid morning. "Did you figure out the problem with Mr. Peavy's air conditioner?"

"Sure. We got it runnin' again. Is that why you came here? To ask me about his air conditioner?"

I shake my head, weary of being afraid, of hiding the truth. "No, it's me. Something I've done. That I can't undo. And . . . and . . ." Tears swell in my throat. I take a shaky breath. "I don't know what to do."

He leans back, crosses his arms over his chest. The same posture on Mother would seem judgmental, but on Daddy I know it's his thinking position. I remember when Drew and I were caught on Makeout Flats and the sheriff brought me home. After Mother ranted and raved about my reputation and what a loser Drew was, Daddy simply leaned back, arms crossed, and watched me. "Suzy," he had said, "are you okay?" Later he asked, "What'd you learn?"

He hadn't blamed, hadn't accused. He had accepted. And I search his face for that love that I need now. It's there, etched in every crease, every line.

He doesn't prod either. He simply waits.

But I can't find the words to tell my father what I've done. Of how I've messed up not only my life but Mike's and Oliver's and Drew's. It's worse than any funeral Mother could arrange.

"Daddy, have you ever done something you were ashamed of? I mean, really ashamed of. And you had to keep it a secret. And yet you couldn't? And you knew when it came out that lives would be shattered?"

"You're living it right now." He runs his fingers through his thinning gray hair. He's not a particularly handsome man, but he used to be. What's been worn away has left not a hardness, not bitterness, but a kindness. "I shouldn't have ever started toying with the idea of—" He stops himself. "Here's the truth, Suzanne. I didn't want to tell you this." He huffs out a breath. "Truth is, I didn't want to see disappointment in your eyes. That might break me."

I reach for him, hold his hand. "What is it, Daddy?"

"I been studying . . . while I've been sitting around here the last few days. Lookin' at the good book. And I found a verse there that cut me to the core. I've been hiding this thing inside. Hiding the truth even from you."

"What is it, Daddy?"

"The good book says somewheres in Proverbs that if you cover up your sin, which is what I've surely been doin', then you can't win, can't *prosper*, I think is the word it uses. But if you confess, say it was wrong, wrong, wrong and walk away from it, well, then there's mercy. Do you believe that?"

"Yes."

He gives a nod, as if telling himself to go on. His mouth is in a tight line, a last resistance. Then he squeezes my fingers. "Sugar Beet, there is another woman."

His words knock the breath out of me. I feel my insides flinch. I try to school my reaction, to control it. "But Daddy—"

"Oh, I know." He pulls away, stands, and walks to the end of the bed. "I was a fool."

He shrugs as if uncomfortable.

I fight the tears that suddenly sting my eyes.

"Or I should say," he goes on, "I thought there was."

Confusion and disappointment churn inside me. Being married to an attorney, I know the statistics on divorce. I've seen our couple friends swap spouses so often it makes me dizzy. But if anyone is the least likely to fool around on his wife, it's Archie Davidson. Still, I know better than anyone how something foolish and stupid can happen in only a split second. I've heard a lot of excuses. "We grew apart." "He doesn't understand me." "I couldn't stop myself." I've even come up with a few of my own. "I wasn't thinking." "He left." "I needed someone." But, I have to admit, excuses don't excuse.

"What do you mean? You *thought* there was another woman?"

"Well, there was somebody I was interested in. She made me feel . . . well, different. Better. Like I wasn't always doing something wrong. Like maybe I was doing something right for once. I thought the feeling was mutual between us. You probably know me well enough to know I ain't the type to sleep around." His glance slips toward me then away, makes my own guilt more acute. "Don't look at me like that, Sugar Beet." He walks back to me, puts a hand on my shoulder. "I've always been faithful to your mother. Thought I was a good husband, you know?" His mouth twists.

"I know you have, Daddy." I pat his hand. I realize the toll his secret took on him and how hard it was to tell me. But do I have that kind of courage?

"But then I started talking to . . . well, it doesn't matter who."

A cold lump forms in my stomach. Was it Josie?

"I thought I'd leave your mother first and then be free to pursue . . . well, you know." He runs his hands along the edge of the bed and sits down in front of me again. "Thought I had it all figured out. Knowin' your mother, I figured it would be uncomfortable stayin' here. Her givin' us the evil eye, making things awkward. So I planned to take off with . . . this woman. We could settle someplace else. Oklahoma maybe. My territory runs into Oklahoma and New Mexico, so I could move anywhere. I thought Santa Fe might be nice."

I nod, realize my own infidelity wasn't as well thought out. But Daddy had planned it all. My stomach clenches with suppressed emotions.

"But I spooked the lady." He swears, which is a rarity. "She was interested, I'm sure of it." He slaps his hand on his thigh. His jowls turn a bright red, moving right up to his ears. In a softer voice, he adds, "But she didn't want me full-time."

"She liked you better when you were off-limits?"

"I been thinking about this and trying to figure out how I could be such a fool. I didn't feel loved by your mother. I took her criticism as rejection. And that left a hole in me, a vacancy. And I started searching for something, someone to fill it up." He rubs his jaw and his whiskers make a scraping sound against palm. "When you try to love someone, then get rejected . . . well, there's just almost nothing worse. I shouldn't have left your Mother, I know that now. I was wrong. I was searching in the wrong places. Now I've ruined everything. She feels rejected, and she's trying to fill up that hole that I left with flowers and sympathy. Look what problems I've caused."

Tears well up in me. I know the rejection. I felt it when Mike walked out of our home so many years ago. Leaving me. Rejecting me. Hurting me so deeply I couldn't breathe. I just wanted to be happy. I just wanted to be loved. And I know that's what my daddy was feeling. I reach forward, place a hand on his knee. "You just wanted to be happy."

"Oh, sure. Don't we all? But it's not always about us, is it? If I hadn't started seeing . . ." he clears his throat, "this other woman, then maybe I would have gone on thinking everything was just fine. She made me want more. More than I deserved. And I made a fool of myself."

"I know what that's like."

"Do you?" He tilts his head to study me. "Well, now I've made a real mess of things."

"But Mother—"

"This ain't her fault, Suzy. It's mine. And I take responsibility. Now she's fooling around with that old beau of hers."

"She's not fooling around, Daddy. I don't think—"

"Well, I didn't mean having sex. But seeing some other man by her side has reminded me of when I fell in love with your mother. And it's made me realize I do want her back.

I'm just not sure how to go about it." He leans forward, covers my hand with his. "But this isn't about me. This is about you. And your problem. So in answer to your question, yeah, I've done foolish things, things I'm ashamed of, things I wish I could undo. But I can't. And now I have to figure out how to make it all work."

"But . . ." I start then stop myself, unsure of my question, unsure of what to say.

"But?"

"What if you'd kept your love for this other woman secret?"

"Well, then I'd be a liar. To myself. To your mother. Speaking the truth is better than living with a lie. No matter what happens now, even if I've lost your mother and my family and everything. Because in speaking out, in a way it was crying out, it could pave the way to reconciliation. Or not. There are consequences, right? But God's merciful. I'm just not sure your mother is. But living the way we were living wasn't right." He touches a lock of my hair, rubs it between his fingers. "So how can I help you?"

"I don't think you can." Tears choke my words. I rub my hands along the tops of my thighs, wishing there was something to grab hold of, something to hold onto, but I feel my life slipping off the edge of a sharp cliff. "I've been covering up something too, Daddy. And I have to tell Mike. I have to own up to it. But I don't know how. And I don't know what he'll do."

"You have a good man there."

I nod, unable to speak.

"You should have seen him working with Ned Peavy. You know all your mother could see was some naked man swatting flies and ruining her view. But not Mike. He walked over there. Risked getting shot, I guess, because when you're dealing with someone like that, you just never know."

"At the least," I say, "he could have gotten swatted."

"Exactly. But he reached out to that poor old man. None of us knew his air conditioner was out. Mike's a good man."

I bow my head, feel in the fibers of my being the awfulness of what I've done. How will he ever forgive me? But now that Drew knows the truth, and Oliver, I don't have much of a choice but to tell Mike. But I also know inside my heart that it's the right thing to do.

"I don't think Mike will give me a funeral next week," I say, "but it could destroy my marriage. Break apart my family . . ."

My father's mouth thins then twists. "If you've been hiding something, hard as it might be, then you gotta face it. Hope for the best, Suzy. Pray for Mike. Pray he can forgive or forget or accept. But prepare yourself for the worst."

"I am, Daddy. I am."

"God will see you through this. No matter what happens."

My throat feels thick with emotions and I can only nod and hold onto my father's hand.

"Then just know that whatever happens, I love you. And I'm always here for you."

I lean forward, rest my head against his chest, feel his arms close about me. He smells of Chaps cologne and butterscotch candies. "That's good. Because if Mike kicks me out, then I guess I'll have to get a room next door to you here."

33

❧

"Does Dad know?" Oliver sits on the riding lawn mower. His legs are covered with bits of dirt and grass.

I came back to Mother's and found him doing more chores for Mother. Mike's rental car is gone. I don't know where he is or what he's doing. I lean against the wall of the garage, aching for my son who is fighting so many emotions as I'm fighting my own. Mike should have been the first to know, but Oliver's needs eclipse everything at this moment.

"I haven't told him yet." *Yet*. That word strikes fear into my heart. "But I will. Did you say anything?"

"No." He doesn't quite meet my gaze.

"But I will. I will, Oliver."

"So what will happen now?" He digs his thumbnail along the hem of his shorts.

"I don't know. What do you want to happen?"

He shrugs. "What does that matter?"

"It matters a lot, Oliver. This concerns you even more than the rest of us."

He gives a barely perceptible nod.

Feeling awkward and stiff legged, I walk toward him, kneel down beside him so I can look up into his face. I place a hand on his knee. "Oh, Oliver. I am so sorry. So, so sorry."

"If I wasn't here, you wouldn't be in this mess."

"No, that's not what I meant. I'm sorry that I lied to you, to your father, to Drew. I'm sorry about what I did. But at the same time, I'm not. Because if I hadn't . . . well, then you wouldn't be here. And I don't know what I'd do if I didn't have you in my life. You are my joy."

The muscles along the length of his throat contract. He swallows hard. "You don't blame me?"

"Blame you? Oh, sweetheart! This isn't your fault. I'm the one who . . . I did this. I–I—Can you forgive me?"

For a long moment he doesn't move or speak. Fear rattles my nerves.

"It's okay if you can't. I understand. I can't forgive myself either. But just know, Oliver, that I love you. And I'm here for you. And we're going to try to work this all out. Okay?"

His mouth pinches at the corners, making tiny dents in his cheeks. He nods, then he turns the ignition and takes off on the riding lawn mower to be alone.

THE SUN HAS long since begun its descent. It's the end of the day. Tomorrow will bring my father's funeral and all that entails. The horizon deepens to the color of a ripe peach. As the sun dips lower, the sky darkens to the shade of brand-new Levi's. I've been sitting out here on the porch since dinner. Mother fancified Oliver's hotdogs with side dishes and sprigs of parsley set around the serving platter. My mind is unable to clasp onto anything but what will happen next.

The back door opens, and Mike joins me on the porch.

He sits on the swing next to me and offers me a glass of iced tea. Fresh from his shower, he smells of Dove and Mother's Herbal Essence shampoo.

"Where's Oliver?" I ask.

"Watching ESPN and trying to explain hockey to your mother. He's been fairly quiet since he got the test results back. You think he's okay?"

"I don't know."

Mike puts an arm loosely behind my back. "Your mother seems chipper."

"Well, she is burying her husband tomorrow."

He grins briefly. "Look, Suzanne, I know something is wrong."

"Everything is wrong with this situation."

"You can't solve your parents' problems."

"This isn't about my parents." I place a hand on his thigh, need to feel his solidness before I rock his world with my confession. I wish we were home, someplace we could have total privacy. But I know this can't wait any longer.

"Is it about Josie?"

"No. Being home has brought up a lot of memories and emotions from long ago. A hard time for us. For you and me." I glance sideways at him, feel my heart pounding.

He stops the swing from idly rocking back and forth. "Is this about Drew Waring?"

My heart stops mid-beat, then races.

Mike stands suddenly. The swing rocks in an uneven way. I press my feet into the wood planks to right it.

"Let's not go back." He leans against the porch railing. "You can't drive a car by staring at the rearview mirror."

"But it's back there, Mike. It's following us like a big trailer. It's all my fault." I stand and walk over to him. We don't look at each other but out across the rocky terrain at the flames of sunset. Then I clasp his hand, his rough palm against mine, his fingers squeezing with an intensity I feel all the way down to my bones. "I'm sorry, Mike." My voice starts to break. "It was all my fault."

"No." He turns to face me, brushes the hair back from my face that the wind tossed sideways. "No, it wasn't."

"I wanted a baby so badly that I put that in front of everything else. It put pressure on you. On us. And then—"

He pulls me against his chest, holds me there, his arms around my shoulders. "I'm the one that left, Suz. I take responsibility for that. No one wanted us to be a family more than I did. And when I couldn't . . . when we couldn't . . ."

It occurs to me then that Mike isn't surprised Drew has something to do with that time period. He doesn't ask what I'm talking about. He doesn't wonder what a high school boyfriend has to do with the trouble between us. Maybe he thinks it's baggage I carried into our marriage. Maybe he thinks I still harbor a love for Drew after all these years.

"I don't love him now," I say, my words drifting toward the darkness.

He doesn't respond. But he doesn't push me away either.

"How did we make it?" I ask in wonderment, resting in the solidness of his embrace, praying it isn't the last time he holds me.

"God." Mike's answer is simple. "That's how I managed. It's as simple as that. God got me through it. He brought me back to you when I didn't have the courage. He helped me to see my mistakes, my failings. He helped me—" Once more he cuts off his words.

"Helped you do what?"

"It doesn't matter anymore. But if I had acted the way I wanted, then we wouldn't be here together."

"We have a strong marriage," I reassure him and me, bracing myself for the inevitable crack that is to come.

He nods, resting his cheek against the top of my head. "We've survived."

The conversation ebbs, and I contemplate letting it go. But something rises up in me, pushes me to confess what I never wanted Mike to know, what I tried to protect him from. Am I being masochistic, throwing everything at our marriage to see if it's strong enough to withstand another blow? After all, Drew isn't demanding visitation rights. Oliver is quiet but resolute. I don't know. Is it God urging me to clean the slate once and for all? Or do I simply want all our secrets out on the table where nothing else can shake us to the core again. The answer I had been searching for came to me when Daddy told me what he'd learned over the past few days. Hiding sin doesn't make it go away; it makes it seem bigger, more overwhelming than it is. Bringing it into the light, confessing it, well, it might not work out. It might ruin what's left of my life. But at least fear won't rule my life anymore.

"I'm proud of you, Suzanne." Mike's words surprise me, catch me off guard.

I pull away from him enough to look into his eyes. They're deep and soulful. "What do you mean?"

"With rumors going around, well, other wives might kick their husbands out of the house or at least out of the bedroom."

"Well, I considered that. But where would you go? The sofa is taken. To bunk with my dad at the Old Hockheim Inn?"

"I'm serious. I know God is sustaining you. And it's powerful . . . and convicting to watch."

I shake my head. "I'm not a saint, Mike."

"You are to me."

"I went to see Josie the other morning. I couldn't sleep. I couldn't rest. So I got up early before even Mother awoke and went to Josie's house. You know, she never even answered my charges. She never said she wasn't after you. But she spoke the truth to me. She helped me see that fear was running my life. Fear was making me run."

Guilt pushes me that extra inch, right out onto the rocky cliff where I stand teetering in the moment that could change everything. I release a shaky breath. "Mike," I manage, "I owe you an apology. I never thought you should know. I believed it would be easier if you didn't. I believed keeping it from you saved our marriage. Or I thought so at the time."

His brow crinkles into a frown. He searches my face, starts to say something but stops himself. "Then why tell me now?"

"I don't know. I think God wants me to." Tears tighten my voice. In my head I hear the words *liar, liar, liar* chanted over and over again. "I owe you an apology. I owe . . ." My words collapse under the strain. I'm trembling all over, shaking with fear and relief.

"No, you don't."

I step back, wonder if my legs will hold me, then clasp his hands between us. I look up into his face, brace for the reaction I know will come, the anger and disappointment and grief I deserve. "Yes, I do. I-I . . ." The words catch in my throat but I have to say them now. "When you left . . ." I fight the tears. "Sixteen years ago, I didn't know—" I stop myself. It wasn't his fault. I won't blame him now. "It was a long time ago. And I've never done anything like this before or since. Never wanted to."

"Suzanne—"

"—Mike—"

"Don't—"

"Hear me out, please."

He stops, waits.

I can't look at him. Shame pours over me. I stare down at the space between us, the dusty wooden planks, weathered and worn but sturdy and strong. I try to remember, try to forget. Maybe confessing will help block it out of my memory. But I know that's not true. I remember every time I look at my son. "I-I slept with another man. W-with Drew. While you and I were married. And I-I'm sorry. So sorry."

He takes me in his arms again, holds me when I can't speak anymore. I clasp my hands to his back, dare to hope, pray this won't destroy us. His chest presses against my face. His strength, his fierce hold on me frightens and comforts me at the same time. Then he pulls away. Through a haze of my own tears, I watch tears running down his face. His pained expression makes my insides ache. "I'm sorry, Mike. I'm so . . . so sorry."

His mouth pulls into a taut line. "I know, Suz. I know."

I can't speak for a long time as I watch his features change and alter like the expressive Texas sky. Shadows of night falling darken his face. He stares out at the prairie stretching outward like my sin that doesn't seem to have an end in sight. My throat constricts as I try to hold back the tears that won't stop. There's been a drought here in Gillespie County, just as I feel there has been a drought in my own soul. Now it seems the rain has come.

"Mike?" I whisper, my emotions choking the words into a strangled gasp. "I know it's a lot to ask. I know . . . you have every right to hate me. But do you think . . . can you ever forgive me?"

He's quiet for a long moment. I can hear my heart beating, ticking off each second. I watch the muscles along his jaw twitch and flex. Finally he looks at me, his eyes soft and dewy. "Oh, Suzanne," he cups my face, his thumb tracing my jawline, "I already did. Fifteen years ago."

34

W hat do you mean?" I ask Mike. "You've known?" My legs start shaking, and I start to sit where I stand. But Mike grasps my arms, moves me back a couple of steps to the porch swing. The edge pokes into the back of my thigh. "You've known since . . . but how?"

"When you got pregnant. I knew."

In a flash that night comes back to me. I remember sharing my joy, crying with relief when I told Mike that I was pregnant. He had hugged me, but he hadn't spoken, hadn't said much of anything for a few days. I hadn't paid attention. I was too excited and too focused on the changes occurring in my body. If I had thought about his reaction at all, I would have thought he was simply relieved.

He turns now and squints at the last remnants of the setting sun. "I did some research. Traced the phone calls to your old boyfriend. Drew Waring."

My stomach clenches. All this time, he knew. He knew. And he never said a word. Never railed at me. Never accused. Never threatened to divorce me.

He leans forward, resting his hands on the railing, his shoulders flexing beneath his shirt. His sleeves are rolled up, and I watch his muscles tightening as if he could break that wooden plank in half.

"So all this time," I say, my throat filled with tears, "our marriage has been a lie?"

He turns and looks at me. His features fierce. "No. A lie would have been if I didn't love you. Or if you didn't love me. What was there to say about this? You weren't going to leave to be with him."

"How do you know that?"

"Because I would have fought for you."

I realize then, he did fight. He fought his anger. His loathing. He even fought me.

"When?" I ask, my thoughts jumbled and unclear. "When did you manage to forgive me?"

He turns, sits on the railing, crosses his arms over his chest. The burnt-orange sun brightens his hair, makes the short strands shimmer silver and black, makes him look ten years older. "I thought about leaving. I did. I was angry. But more at myself. I knew it was my fault. Hey, I was the one who'd left. Just like my mother. I wondered what I would have done if she'd ever come back into my life. I knew I wouldn't be forgiving.

"And I didn't know if I could forgive you for a long time. But then one night . . . not long before Oliver was born, you were asleep. And you whispered my name. I knew then *I* was in your heart. Not Drew." His throat flexes, and he looks down. "I knew I couldn't ever leave."

Before I can blink or capture a coherent thought, I'm in his arms. I'm not sure who moved first. Or if we moved as one. Maybe that's how it's always been between us. I cling to him as if the world is shaking and he is the only solid, unshakeable presence.

Slowly Mike kneels before me, his arms around my waist, his face pressed against my belly. "Can you forgive me?"

"Oh, Mike, get up. There's nothing to forgive. This isn't your fault. It's mine."

"Do you know why I left?" he asks then.

"Because I was acting like my mother. Because I was demanding. Because I'd forgotten about our relationship and was focusing, obsessing about getting pregnant."

He shakes his head. "Because I found out I couldn't give you a baby."

My hand stills, then I sift my fingers through what's left of his hair. "When?"

"We had those tests, remember?"

I nod. His embrace loosens, and I back toward the swing for its support. Slowly Mike stands. "The doctor called me that Friday and told me the bad news. I couldn't give you what you most wanted. And you were ovulating and calling to me. And I couldn't breathe. So I left."

"Oh, Mike. I wish you'd told me. We could have—"

"My pride wouldn't let me. I was afraid you'd walk away from me."

He doesn't say the words but I know what he's thinking. He feared that I would leave him the way his mother had. In his eyes I see the little boy, his eyes fearful, blaming himself.

"Do you know where I went?"

I shake my head, unable to speak.

"I went searching for my mother. I thought if I could find her, if I could find out why she rejected me, then maybe I could . . . I don't know."

My heart thumps hard in my chest. "Did you find her?"

"I went back to that little amusement park where she abandoned me. I didn't even know it still existed. But it did. You know, I was eight."

I realize I'm holding my breath. Mike has never really talked about his mother abandoning him. Only the factual stuff, not the actual story.

"It was just us, my mom and me. I didn't have a dad. Which made other kids think I was weird. Mom was going to school some, working two jobs. We lived in a little apartment with one bedroom. My bed, really just a pallet of blankets, was in her closet."

He leans back against the slatted wood swing, his legs making it rock slowly, gently. "Every now and then, we saved up enough money to do something fun. So that Saturday we went to this amusement park. There were hotdogs, popcorn, and cotton candy. A short Ferris wheel with red and blue lights. They've replaced it with a bigger one now. But my favorite ride was the purple octopus with eight legs that twirled and spun around. I was laughing and dizzy as I stumbled off. I looked around for my mom. She was supposed to be right there waiting for me. But she wasn't.

"I waited a long time." He looks out at the darkening sky, the sun having disappeared below the horizon. His features look hard, not that of a little boy, but there's a softness in his gaze, a vulnerability. "Then I wandered over to the women's restroom, asked some old lady to go inside and call for my mother. "Nancy!" I could hear her voice bounce off the tiles and out the window high on the brick wall. But my mother wasn't there. And she didn't come back. A vendor gave me a hotdog for free. The guy running the octopus ride let me go round again, but it only made me feel like I was going to be sick. I wanted to get up high, try to see around the park, try to find my mom.

"By the time the park had closed, I was the only kid left. A guard came up to me, asked me a bunch of questions. I knew I was in trouble when he put me in a police cruiser. Some family took me in that first night. I laid on a cot with a thin blanket and started to cry." He stops speaking for a moment as if gathering his emotions back to himself.

"So going back to that park, I remembered all those feelings. And I realized that's exactly what I'd done to you. Something in me had made me run away. Just like something in my mother had made her give up and run off. And so I came home, determined to never run off again. I promised God I would not abandon you. No matter what. But that promise was put to the test."

"When I told you I was pregnant."

He nods, clasps his hands between his knees. "For a while, I thought that's what I deserved. But then I started to think of it as something healing. I could love this child, our child, like my own, the way no one had ever adopted or loved me."

"Oh, Mike." I put a hand on his shoulder, wanting to pull him toward me, to comfort him, love him.

But he shifts away, looks at me, his eyes dark. "And I was selfish. It was the only way I thought I would ever have a family. The family I never had."

I can taste the salt of my tears on my lips.

"That's when I found God. That's when he filled up all those spaces in my heart and showed me I wasn't alone. He'd been rejected too. His own people rejected him. Just like my own mother rejected me."

He reaches out, wipes the tears from my cheeks. I can see tears glistening on his lashes.

"I love you, Suzanne."

He kisses me, his mouth soft, tender. For a moment there's only us. And I know now that he does love me. More than I ever imagined.

35

Thursday, the day of the funeral, brings rain. Heavy rains. Rains like I haven't seen in a long time. Thunder rumbles. Lightning slashes across the sky. Mike and I stand on the back porch watching the gray, swollen clouds churning as we drink our coffee.

Last night, together, we spoke to Oliver, explained as best we could about the situation and his biological father. He nodded and listened. He seemed calm and composed. He hugged us both.

"Do you have any questions?" I asked, knowing we didn't have any answers. We weren't sure how all of this would shake out, if Drew would want to spend time with his son, if Oliver would agree, and how that would change our family. I suppose I was really asking if Oliver thought we had ruined his life.

He simply shook his head and said, "I understand."

"Do you think he's okay?" I ask Mike for maybe the thirty-seventh time.

"Seems to be doing remarkably well. I'll talk to him some more."

I sip my black coffee and shudder at a sudden flash of lightning.

Mike slips an arm around my shoulders. "He knows we love him. We'll just have to keep showing him."

Emotions tighten my throat and all I can do is lean my head against his shoulder. Like Mike said, I can't do anything about the past. Nor can I foresee problems which might occur. I can only live moment by moment and pray that God will give me the grace to get through each.

"What time do we have to be at the dance hall for the funeral?" Mike asks, pulling me back to this day and this crisis.

I look at my watch. "We need to start getting ready."

"The funeral is still on, huh?" Mike rubs his jaw. "Whoever said small towns were dull never visited Luckenbach."

"I thought I'd go over to Daddy's hotel and talk to him."

"Want me to go?"

"No, I need to talk to him alone."

"You'll take the body," he smiles, "to the church?"

I ball up my fist and punch him playfully on the shoulder.

His grin widens. "It's going to be interesting."

I frown. "I'm afraid it's going to make headlines."

"DADDY," I SAY when he opens the door, "we need to talk."

"Okay." He takes my dripping umbrella and sets it in the corner. The bed behind him is made. Mother's rule was whoever gets out of bed last has to make the bed. Dad typically made the bed, unless he was traveling. Seeing the green-and-orange paisley comforter tucked in neatly around the pillow makes my chest ache.

"Can you believe this rain? We haven't had a good rain in . . . well, I can't remember when." He offers me the chair and I sit at the desk, shifting to face him. "Have you had breakfast?"

"Yes. Have you?"

"I'm not hungry. What did your mother fix this morning?"

"Eggs Benedict."

"She is a good cook."

"Are you missing her?" I ask, hopeful.

"Some things." He sighs and sits on the edge of the bed. "Your mother . . . well, she's a good woman. She means well. She's been striving her whole life. It's wearying."

"I know."

"This whole thing got out of hand, didn't it?"

"Do you think you can forgive Mother?"

"Forgive her? What do you mean?"

"Can you forgive her for harping on you for years?"

"It's strange, Sugar Beet, but I miss her. I do. When I left, when I walked out, I never thought I'd miss her nagging. But I feel kind of lost without her. Like my right arm is missing."

"Daddy—"

"I don't feel like your Mother needs to apologize. She is the way she is. But I know what I've done wrong, and I have to apologize to her. If she'll hear me out. But your mother isn't one to forgive. When she gets mad, when she cuts someone off, that's the end. And it's all my fault. I don't have anyone to blame but myself."

"Maybe Mother needs to learn some about forgiveness. As I'm learning."

"It's not easy."

"No, it's not. But I suspect Mother misses you too."

"You do?"

"Sure. I mean, right now, she has Mike, Oliver, and me to razz."

"What about Cal Henry?"

"Oh, yeah. Him too." Although he hasn't made an appearance yet today. "But when that house is empty—"

"It'll finally be just the way she's wanted it for the last forty years: clean."

I reach out to my father, hold his hand. "I don't think so. Maybe all her cleaning, all her striving, all her nagging is her way of controlling life. It's a façade. It's not real. No one can really control their life. But there's some fear deep down inside her, something she's afraid of. But I don't know what it is. I'm not sure even Mother knows."

He rubs the back of his neck thoughtfully. "I hadn't thought of her that way. No one would imagine your mother being fearful. She's so formidable. But you might be right. You just might be right."

"What do you think she's afraid of, Daddy?"

"I don't know. But if she is afraid, I haven't done a very good job of making her feel secure over the years. Maybe your mother and I both need to change."

ACCORDION MUSIC SWELLS and pulses in a warbling antique voice. I've never heard "Precious Lord, Take My Hand" played with a lilting polka rhythm. A friend of Daddy's, Ralph Hall, who has played at the Luckenbach dance hall numerous times, sits beside the casket, cradling his beloved instrument. He softly taps his mud-covered boot in rhythm.

The flower arrangements, which sit along the base of the stage, are color coordinated the way Mother requested. I have to admit, Mother puts on a beautiful funeral. Even in a dance hall. The mood will be set with just the right selection of hymns. It doesn't hurt to have a mournful rain falling outside, though if Mother could have ordered sunshine, I'm sure she would have. Only a couple of the wooden windows have been propped open for air circulation.

We all look a little damp around the edges as the rain has continued all morning, making a mess of the unpaved parking lot. My hose are damp and my hem splattered with mud from my mad dash through the puddles outside. Mother too, looks a bit wilted, her black linen suit not nearly so crisp and starched as she would prefer.

Josie now stands at the front in a conservative dress that still accents her curves. She's warming up her voice, practicing "It Is Well" and testing the sound system. Her voice floats up toward the rafters as if on the wings of angels.

Mrs. Hoover approaches me. "Who's that sitting next to your mother?"

In the front row, directly facing the stage and the casket, Mother and her beau, Cal Henry, sit together. But explaining Cal Henry's presence is a bit difficult. "Oh, he's . . . uh . . . uh . . ."

"The funeral director?" she supplies.

"Sure." That works. "Yes, I mean."

Then the preacher steps through the side door. He's wearing his usual biker wear with do-rag and leather vest, jeans and black boots. He's our cue.

"Oh, Mrs. Hoover, we're going to open the casket for a few minutes and let my mother say good-bye."

The gleam in Mrs. Hoover's eye says it all. She wants to watch. She probably wants to make sure Archie is tucked inside nice and neat. She hasn't said a word about the incident where she discovered Flipper in the casket instead of Daddy. Maybe Drew's threat to arrest her was enough to curb that bit of curiosity. Or maybe she thinks she imagined it. Whatever she believes, I'm sure she would love to be able to report in the paper whether my father looked "natural" or "trauma-tized" by the car wreck. What she doesn't know is the reaction from Mother when Mike's plan swings into gear.

"In private," I add, turning her toward the doorway.

Mrs. Hoover forms an *Oh* with her mouth. "Well, I'll wait outside then, guard the doors so no one interferes."

"Thank you." I follow her to the steps. A few early birds waiting for the funeral hover outside the church. I gently close the main door and unlatch the windows. They're heavier than I realize and make a dull *thud* as wood thwacks wood.

Mike enters through the 'Band Only' door. The preacher bends down and says something to Ralph. The last notes of his accordion vibrate through the dance hall and fade. Then he and Josie leave.

Pastor Reese moves over toward the casket and lifts the top half, locking it into place. Even though I know it's empty, I still crane my neck to see the white satin inlay covering the resting place where, if my mother had her way, my father would be lying peacefully for all eternity.

I marvel how Mike is so different from my mother. Where Mike forgave me, my mother has wrought revenge. It's a startling contrast. At least Mother stopped short of actually killing Daddy. I've read in the newspaper of others who crossed that line. Not to excuse my mother's behavior, but I'd much rather be at a pretend funeral than a real one.

"Everything all right?" Mrs. Hoover's voice startles me.

"Mrs. Hoover!"

Mike turns and looks at us across the dance hall.

I put a hand on the older woman's arm, place myself between her and the casket which, thankfully, is at least thir-teen rows of seats away. "Let's go outside."

"Is your mother doing okay?"

"Oh, you know Mother." I push the door open.

"She needs to cry." Mrs. Hoover glances over her shoulder toward the casket.

"She will," I say. "Believe me, she will." I need something to distract her and get her away from the building. "Oh, look over there. Is that who I think it is?"

"Who?" Mrs. Hoover jerks around.

"Well, I can't be sure."

"Was it Willie Nelson?" Her beady eyes glitter with excitement. "I heard he might make an appearance."

"Well," I say, "he does know, or knew, Daddy."

Mrs. Hoover bustles across the parking lot toward the old shack that used to be the post office and is now a store for tourists. Oliver steps forward. He's drinking from a can of root beer. "I'll watch the door, Mom."

"Thanks." With a relieved smile, I go back inside the dance hall and see my father enter through the side door. Suddenly the dance hall is anything but quiet. My parents go at it like hockey players, bodies tilted toward each other, faces red and angry.

"You're just lookin' for an excuse to go back to that man!" Daddy points at Cal Henry.

"That's the most ridiculous thing I've ever heard of. I am not looking for a man. It's not my fault Cal Henry is here."

Actually, it is. But no one points this out. She did, after all, call him to borrow his hearse.

"Why," Mother continues, "I can't stop a man from doing what he's set on doing. Like I could have ever stopped you from traveling. Or made you do one thing you didn't want to do."

"You underestimate yourself, Betty Lynne." Daddy glares at Cal Henry. "Why don't you tell that man to go on home?"

"Why would I do that? He has every right to be here." She smiles in a simpering Scarlett O'Hara kind of way, as if she's dangling two men by a thread. What she doesn't seem to understand is that she could easily lose them both.

"See!" Daddy explodes. "See what you're doing there? Flirtin'! Flirtin' at my funeral."

With a huff, Mother simply turns away, her back rigid.

"You won't listen to reason!" Daddy's arms are stretched out wide. "I've apologized. What more do you want?"

"You said you were leaving town, Archie. You were leaving for good. So why don't you just go?"

"Because this is where I've lived most of my life. This is where I wanna live and—" He stops himself from going to that inevitable next line as Mother seems all too willing to make that a reality.

"Now that your girlfriend doesn't want you any more?" She faces him again.

The side door to the dance hall opens and Josie walks in. I take a step forward, deciding to head off disaster before it begins. But before I can speak, she holds open the door and waves to someone. "Come on. It's okay."

Then Hazel Perkins takes a hesitant step inside. She's dressed in typical funeral wear of black dress and limp hat that seems to be weeping. Her umbrella drips on the hardwood floor.

"Um, Mrs. Perkins," I reach to lower the lid on the casket, but Mike puts a restraining hand on my arm.

"Wait," he says.

"Hazel," Mother's brow puckers in that way of hers that says the other person has broken some unwritten social tenet, "you're a little early for the funeral."

"Actually I'm late. I should have done this days ago. But I was too ashamed. Too embarrassed. But—"

"Hazel—" Daddy steps toward her.

"Archie," Josie stands close behind Hazel, "let her speak."

Hazel holds up a hand as if to restrain my father, but her gaze remains fixed on Mother. "Betty Lynne, *I* am the other woman. I didn't intend to be. And as soon as I realized what was happening, I sent Archie right back to you. Or tried to."

"Why, of all the things! My so-called best friend . . ."

"Well, now, you just wait a minute. I've been thinking over the last few days what I might have done wrong. I did not chase after your husband. But I did offer him a kind word. I did listen to him and try to be his friend. But obviously, he took my silence and my kindness to mean something else entirely." She takes three steps toward Mother. "Now, you listen here, Betty Lynne. You have a fine husband there. And he's done nothing wrong."

Mother snorts and looks away.

"Nothing in deed. He poured out his heart to me, yes, but maybe that was because you weren't listening. But he loves *you*. Not me."

Mother crosses her arms over her chest.

"I ain't gonna try to get you to call off this funeral. I've known you long enough to know you're gonna do what you wanna do. But I will tell you this: If you let that man get away from you, you'll regret it till the day they put *you* in one of those caskets. Now, be the woman I know you can be and talk to this man, forgive him, and ask for his forgiveness."

Mother turns back to Hazel, her eyes wide with disbelief. "What do I have to be sorry for?"

"Well, it's the odd person who don't have nothin' to be sorry for. If you can't think of nothin', then maybe the good Lord will give you a hint."

Mother opens her mouth to protest.

"But," Hazel lifts a crooked, arthritic finger, "you gotta be quiet enough to listen to what God's trying to tell you."

"Well, I never!"

"Of course not," Hazel says. "You've manipulated all of us for years. You've kept us all afraid to speak the truth around you for fear we'd be ostracized. Well, if you wanna treat me that way, fine. I'm strong. I can take it. But you are the weak one, Betty Lynne. You are too weak to acknowledge that you are as sinful as the rest of us."

"What are you afraid of, Betty Lynne?" Daddy asks, his voice quiet as a caress.

"Afraid?" Mother puffs up. "I'm not afraid of anything."

"But I think you are. You're afraid I'm going to abandon you. Which makes what I did so much worse. And I'm sorry. So sorry. I had no idea."

"I'm not—"

"Are you afraid I'll abandon you the way your father abandoned you when you were just a girl?"

"My father did *not* abandon me. He died."

"Death is just another form of abandonment, sweetheart. You'd rather leave or bury me before that could happen."

Mother starts to say something, then stops. She turns, grabs her purse off the bench seat. With her shoulders squared, she addresses all of us. "Well, if we're finished with this session of What's Wrong with Betty Lynne, I'd like to get on with the funeral." She pats her purse. "I'll just go freshen up a bit before everyone arrives."

36

꧁꧂

Forty minutes later, accordion music once again swells and throbs through the dance hall. I haven't heard some of these hymns in years. Our church in San Diego sings mostly contemporary praise songs. But "Peace Like a River" doesn't soothe my corkscrewed nerves. Peace would be nice in any form or fashion, but at the moment it seems improbable.

While Mother touched up her lipstick backstage, Daddy, Mike, and Flipper formed their own huddle, discussing options. Then the deputy left to get the squad car ready to lead the empty casket in the crazy black dented hearse to the cemetery to my father's not-so-final resting place. Mike tried to talk one last time to my mother, using legalese that she apparently didn't understand or didn't want to understand.

In the end Mother told us to open the doors and let the mourners enter. Let the festivities commence.

Friends and neighbors fill row upon row of benches. Mother then makes her big entrance, walking past the closed casket, pausing momentarily as if saying good-bye to her not-so-late husband. She even dabs her eyes with her handkerchief. I'm not sure if she's sad that her marriage is really, truly ending or merely play-acting. Finally she takes her seat in the front row, her shoulders squared, her hands clutching a handkerchief in her lap. Cal Henry follows a pace or two behind, then sits next to her.

I feel the gazes of friends settle on me as Mike and I walk past the casket. Oliver was supposed to follow us, but he must already be seated somewhere in the crowded hall. Guilt wraps around me, twisting my insides. Have I been wrong to play along with Mother's mad scheme? Where is the fine line between honoring one's parents and being culpable for their same sins? I haven't actually *lied* to anyone; I didn't tell anyone Daddy was dead. But I didn't speak the truth either. Just as I didn't tell Mike the truth.

Daddy's words come back to me now about the wrongness of hiding sins. For that, I am guilty. I have aided and abetted Mother in her sham. I even tried to make it easier for her, enabled her to go on with her charade. We all did, trying to help her save face or seeking secretive and creative solutions so the truth wouldn't come out. And inside, deep in my spirit, I knew it was wrong. Wrong with a capital *W* that does not rhyme with *S*, which clearly stands for sin. And I know what I have to do.

Mother leans against me now and whispers, "There's a nice turnout, don't you think?"

I start to turn around to look at all those who have gathered, but she puts a restraining hand on my arm. Mother always told me it was rude to turn around in church to look at the people behind us. I'm not exactly sure why.

"Everyone from three towns around is here." She nods as if pleased. But how long will it last?

Josie steps forward then. Accompanied by a guitar, she sings "It Is Well."

Yet I know deep down, it isn't. Not until I fix this.

"The flowers look nice, don't they?" Mother acts like the director of a Broadway play. Maybe she is. She's the star about to make her dramatic debut and final curtain call all at once. I'm not sure how the audience, her neighbors and friends, will react. And the star? What will happen when she discovers the script has been changed? "Is something wrong with the flowers?"

Realizing I didn't answer promptly, I shake my head. "No, they're fine. Beautiful."

"I'm glad I insisted on color coordinating the arrangements."

I take a deep breath as Josie closes with the final notes of the hymn. Slowly, the preacher rises up from his seat. I touch his arm as he passes and whisper a message to him.

"Are you sure?"

I nod.

He walks to the podium and clears his throat. "Thank you for coming here today to celebrate the life of a man we have all known and respected—Archie Davidson. Let's not focus on death," he intones in a somber voice, "but on the life he led . . . and, well, leads even today."

Mother makes a small squeaking sound, then reaches toward me and squeezes my hand. "What is he doing?"

Here we go.

"Archie is loved by everyone in this community, as you can see from all the folks gathered here today. He has mentored young people in high school and coached his daughter's basketball team. He has taught a Sunday school class at this cowboy-and-biker church. Why every farmer and rancher in the area knows him through his feed sales. He traveled much of the time, but his presence has always been very visible. Even now."

"Stop him," Mother whispers. Her eyes are wild. "Mike!" Mother's whisper is on the verge of hysteria. "What is he doing?"

Mike reaches over my shoulder and pats Mother on the back. "It's going to be just fine. He's simply giving his own version of the eulogy."

I hear sniffles beginning behind me.

"Archie's beloved wife, Betty Lynne, has written a little statement about their married life, and I'd like to read it now. I believe it reveals her love for her husband." Again, he clears his throat and pulls a folded paper out of his hip pocket. Slowly, he unfolds it, flattens it out with the palm of his hand.

Mother starts to relax. "Maybe," she takes a slow breath, "he was confused."

"'Archie,'" the preacher intones, reading Mother's written words, "'was always my one and only love. From the first moment I met him, I loved him. I knew we would get . . .'" he pauses as if trying to make out her handwriting, "'married.'"

I glance sideways at Mother who has calmed down. She sits straight and prim, staring up at the preacher.

"'I knew we would have a grave life.'" The pastor stops, frowns, and squints at the paper. "That's not right. Oh! 'Grand life.' They'd have a grand life. Yeah, that makes better sense." He gives the paper a shake and starts again. "'Maybe it wasn't always what we imagined. But I enjoyed making a home for Archie, cooking his meals, cleaning, decorating. I tried to make our life as grand as it could be. And I did a pretty good joke.'" He shakes his head. "'Job. I always tried to take care of Archie, keeping the house, fixing the best meals I knew how. I'm not sure it was enough. But it was all I knew to do. It was my way of telling him every day of our married life that I loved him.'"

Hearing these feminine words coming from the biker-turned-preacher makes me want to laugh out loud. But Mother's sentiment is sweet and caring.

"'Archie traveled so much that I had to raise Suzanne almost like a single mother. But I didn't complain. I worked hard. But we had a good lie.'" Pastor Reese coughs. "I mean, 'life.'" He looks up apologetically. "'We had a good life.'"

"If he couldn't read," Mother whispers, "I wish he'd told me. I'd have bought him some glasses. Or read it myself."

"'Archie was always appreciative of my efforts. He was always quick with a compliment. He made a good, decent living. He was always thoughtful and sweet. He always remembered my birthdays with a rose on my pillow. If he was traveling, he always made it home for my birthday so he could wake me with a kill.'" Pastor Reese's face looks likes he's suddenly suffered a flash sunburn. "It says 'kiss,' not kill. Sorry." He shrugs awkwardly and clears his throat. "Where was I? Oh, yeah, um, 'wake me with a kiss. Archie wasn't always able to say what he felt or what he was thinking, but he did little things that showed his feelings. He swept the porch and kept the yard always looking nice. These were little things, but for a man who was always traveling I know it took effort. Maybe it was his way of telling me he loved me too.'"

Pastor Reese refolds the paper. He leans toward the microphone at the podium. "Now, Suzanne Mullins, Archie and Betty Lynne's daughter, would like to say a word about her father."

I swallow hard. Mike squeezes my hand. Slowly I rise and make my way onto the stage. With heart pounding I face my family's friends and neighbors. Most of these people I've known my whole life. They're here because they love us. I'm here because it's the right thing to do.

"Thank—" The sound system screeches, and faces cringe before me. Many cover their ears. "Sorry. I'm sorry. Okay, well, thank you all for coming today." Mother is glaring at me, frowning as I have diverted from her script. "I just wanted to say a word about my father. It's been a long time since I've been home. A long time. I was remembering this week how my father used to like to play games. He wasn't a card man. He wasn't a gambling man. But he did like a good game of dominoes. He'd sit outside at one of those tables and play with anyone who wanted to play.

"When I was a little girl, he'd sit on the floor with me and line the dominoes up in a long line. Then he'd let me tip one on the end and we'd laugh as the line toppled, one domino knocking down the next, until they all lay flat. As I got older, we'd make little designs, making the dominoes curve around in circles and crisscrossing. Sometimes it worked. Sometimes it didn't."

I pause, look toward Mike who gives me an encouraging nod. "Sometimes life is that way, isn't it? We set things up, and one thing leads to the next. Once started, it's hard to stop. The dominoes speed up, knocking into each other faster and faster until it's out of our control. That's happened in my own life."

My gaze veers toward Mother. She is sitting straighter, leaning forward as if she's ready to bolt.

"Sometimes we make decisions so quickly, just instinct really, self-preservation, and we get in a fix and can't seem to stop the events we set into motion. And that's what's happened here this week." I grip the dais for support. My legs are trembling, but at the same time I feel as if I'm taking flight and soaring on brand-new wings. "My father is not dead."

There's no reaction at first. None. It's like no one heard me. So I say it again.

"My father is not dead. He's alive. And well. He's even here with us."

Someone on the back row calls out, "Amen."

"Suzanne," Mother whispers, her tone harsh, "sit down. You're making a fool of yourself and—"

"No, Mother. It's time someone spoke the truth."

"Betty Lynne." A voice over the sound system bellows out from the speakers. I recognize the voice as my father's. Just off stage, I can see him holding a microphone.

This time there is a reaction. Someone cries out, "It's Archie's ghost!" A couple of people stand. Eyes widen. Gasps sputter through the crowd. I'm glad we didn't let Daddy sit up in the coffin like he wanted—someone might have had a heart attack.

"No, no," I put my hand up to calm everyone. "It's okay. My father is really alive. He's not dead. He's not a ghost. Daddy? Why don't you come on out here?"

My father steps out and gives a slight wave. "Hi there, folks. Don't panic or nothin'."

Mother is the one who gasps now. I quickly step down from the stage to stand beside her. Murmurs of disbelief ripple through the crowd.

"Stay calm." Drew rises from his position halfway back in the dance hall, where Josie is sitting beside him. "There's been a misunderstanding that needs clearing up."

"Don't worry, folks." Dad holds up his hands. "I was lost, but now I'm found." He chuckles to himself. "Sorry, Pastor Reese, that was a rather poor joke."

Mother stands. "Archie Davidson!"

"Betty Lynne," Dad points at Mother, "you just sit on down. I've been listening to you for forty years, and now it's time for you to listen to me."

Mother turns as if she's going to bolt for the door, but I'm blocking one side and Cal Henry the other. I supposed they could make a run for it together. But I remember what she wrote in her eulogy: *Archie was always my one and only love.*

Did Cal Henry hear that too? Did he understand? He seems frozen in place. Slowly Mother sinks back onto the wooden bench. Behind us I hear murmuring and confusion.

Dad holds up his hand. "I'm not a ghost." He clunks the microphone on the podium and claps his hand together to show he's flesh and blood. "Although, my wife here would like it if I were just a ghost. You see, I did something foolish. I've tried to apologize, but Betty Lynne wouldn't listen. I'm hoping she will now."

Mother looks down at her hands. Her knuckles are white.

"But at least I won't be dead. Just like my daughter said, I did something wrong and set a chain reaction in place. See, folks, I cheated on my wife. I did. And I'm awful sorry about it. No, I didn't sleep with another woman. But I stopped loving my wife. I stopped doing all the little things I used to do for Betty Lynne. I let my heart harden against her."

He sticks his hands in his pants pockets. "I didn't realize my wife was afraid of being deserted. And I plainly did that. I made her fears a reality. And she had a knee-jerk reaction. You see, I told her I wanted to leave. And it wasn't until she killed me off—and I know she could've taken a gun and done me in just as easily as she concocted such a lie, and I sorely appreciate the latter—well, it was then I realized how much I'd hurt her, how much she cared.

"Today Pastor Reese showed me that eulogy she wrote. How many men have the privilege of seeing what their wives would say about them after they've gone on to the Pearly Gates? Not many. And it's a humbling experience. Even more so when I realize Betty Lynne was sorely put out with me when she wrote that.

"Betty Lynne could've told you lots more about me. Like when I left my underwear on the floor. But she never complained. Well, not too much anyway. She picked 'em up and washed 'em, folded 'em . . . maybe even ironed 'em, I don't know. I didn't much care. I didn't much pay attention.

"But there's a lot of things I did notice. I noticed how nice she always looked. And that might seem superficial, but I know it takes lots of effort. Women go through a lot to stay so purty. And mine done a lot. I know that, I do."

Out of the corner of my eye, I notice that Mother lifts her chin a smidgen of an inch.

"Now I know she done it all for me. Just like for all these years I went out on the road to provide a living for her, so she could decorate the house and make it nice and welcoming, so she could get all dolled up. I let distance and irritation build up and push us apart. And well, I took all those good times for granted. And there were mighty good times, weren't there, Betty Lynne?"

Mother sniffs but otherwise doesn't move.

"And I'm sorry, Betty Lynne, I truly am. I hope all of you can forgive us for all the inconvenience we've caused. We'll try to make it up to each of you."

I sneak a glance at Mother and see tears flowing. Stunned, I glance at Mike then Daddy.

His face is pale, his hands jittery. "If you folks don't mind, I'd like to talk to my wife now. In private."

Mike stands, and with Drew and Flipper's help, begins to escort all the shocked neighbors and friends out of the dance hall. I give Mother a brief, encouraging embrace. She feels like a stiff board. Cal Henry hasn't left. He stands stone still.

"You too." Dad waves the back of his hand as if shooing away a stinging insect. "You can move along now. Betty Lynne is my wife, and I'm not givin' her up. I'll fight you for her if that's what you're aimin' for. But I must warn you," Dad pushes up his sleeves and makes a boxer's stance, "I know what I'm doing."

"Betty Lynne?" Cal Henry looks lost.

Mother dabs her eyes with her handkerchief. "You best go now, Cal Henry."

Without another word he stiffly trails out the front door behind the other guests.

I walk over and hug my father. I can feel him trembling with emotion.

"Say a prayer, Sugar Beet," he whispers.

I nod, unable to speak. Then I turn toward Mother, expecting recriminations. "I'm sorry, Mother. I hope you'll forgive me. I know what it's like to try to hide something only to find it broadcast to everyone. But uncovering secrets is the only way to find forgiveness." I embrace her, feel her start to lean into me, then resist. "Forgive, Daddy, Mother. Please."

"You're one to talk."

Her words glance off my heart. "It's true. Because I've had to learn to forgive myself the way Mike forgave me, the way God forgave me."

Holding Mike's hand, I walk out the 'Band Only' door with him by my side. The pastor follows after us. Mother and Daddy stand alone, but as the door closes behind me I hear Daddy say, "Will you forgive me?"

WHETHER I WANT them or not, Mother's perfectionist tendencies seem to have rubbed off on me. I find it hard to admit I'm wrong because there is a deep well of insecurity inside me. Is that where perfectionism springs from?

"Are you okay?" Mike asks, stepping down out of the dance hall behind me.

I nod but can't speak for the tears.

He moves forward to hold me, his features pinched with concern. For a long while we just hold onto each other. "It's all going to be okay." He smoothes back the hair from my damp face.

"How do you know? Mother—"

"Not your mother. I meant with us. I'm very proud of you. What you did in there, it was hard. But it was the right thing to do. We're going to be okay."

I burrow my face into his shoulder and hold onto him.

"We're going to get through all of this."

I sniff. "Are you sure?"

"Absolutely. We've weathered worse storms. Sure, some things will change."

"Like?"

He shrugs, the material of his shirt stretching over the muscles in his shoulders. "Oliver will have two dads. But that has to be better than one. Certainly better than none. And I've watched the sheriff. He's a good guy."

I nod, believing him. "And Mother and Daddy?"

"That's up to them. We've done all we can."

Something Mike said suddenly gives me an uneasy feeling. "Where is Oliver? I haven't seen him since before the funeral."

"He's probably around." His voice is calm, but concern tethers his brows.

"This has been a lot for one boy to absorb."

He nods, taking my arm, steering me around the corner of the dance hall. "Let's find him."

37

A quick search of the grounds reveals no Oliver. Mike tries calling him on his cell phone, but he must have turned it off because his voice mail picks up. We search the crowd that has yet to leave Luckenbach and bunches underneath the canopy of trees, waiting for further developments from inside the dance hall. But our son seems to be missing.

Down by the footbridge, not thirty feet from the dance hall, we stumble upon Drew and Josie. My gaze locks on their clasped hands. Is Drew the man she mentioned to me out on Makeout Flats? Is he the one she thinks she could love?

Mike reaches out and shakes Drew's hand as if the two men are coming to a silent understanding. It's Mike's way of saying no apology is necessary. Forgiveness is at the ready.

"Are your folks finished talking?" Josie asks.

"No." Mike answers.

"Is that why everyone is hanging around?" I look back

at the crowd, some of whom are making use of the bar behind the store.

"This is big news," Drew says.

"Bigger than the earthquake?"

Drew frowns. "It wasn't an earthquake."

"Has there been official word?" Mike hooks an arm over my shoulder.

"The geologists left this morning. Said it was a combination of the drought and the underwater aquifer. There are fault lines running all over this county. It makes the ground unpredictable and somewhat unstable. But the seismograph didn't detect an earthquake or aftershocks."

"Just a fluke happening," Josie says.

However I know none of this week has been a fluke. It's all been aftershocks of a long-ago event. I worry there might be another seismic reaction within our own immediate family. Before I can voice my concerns, Mike asks Drew, "Have you seen Oliver?"

Any kid might react in any number of ways to the information Oliver has recently learned about his parentage. And if he inherited any of my mother's propensity for over-reaction, then we could be in for some serious repercussions.

"He doesn't answer his cell phone," I add.

"He could just be out of range," Drew says, but he suddenly seems less relaxed, more official, his posture straightening like a part of him stands at attention, ready to move, ready to take action.

Together we walk up the small rise to where the crowd is gathered, the rumor mill churning out grains of half-truths and speculation. Mother and Daddy are still talking in the dance hall. Should Drew have frisked Mother before leaving them alone?

"It's my fault. I meant to try to talk to him again this morning but . . ." Mike's voice trails off to nothing.

"But Mother, right?"

He shrugs, not looking to pin the blame on anyone but himself. I try to imagine him playing pin-the-tail-on-the-donkey as a kid, but I get the image of a little boy with floppy bangs, tugging off a blindfold and saying, "Mom?"

The disjointed tapping of heels against tile alerts us to someone's approach. Mrs. Hoover bustles toward us, seeming to limp as if her pointy-toed shoes have already given her a blister. "What a day! What a day!" she seems a bit too happy to report the news about my family. "So much going on, I can barely keep up."

I imagine the headlines in the local papers: Davidson Family Cracks Up. The Quake Ain't Nothing.

"Of course, I suspected all along. Why, I'm the one who discovered Archie wasn't even in that casket! I kept quiet about it out of respect for your parents, Suzanne, and my duty as a citizen."

"You're a real Woodward-and-Bernstein clone." Josie elbows Drew.

"Maybe," I touch Mrs. Hoover's arm in a confidential way, "we could keep some of this private. It's going to be awkward enough for my parents to resume their normal life."

She narrows her beady little eyes at me. "And what makes you think that's going to happen?"

I can't tell if she is doubtful or looking for another scoop. But before I can answer, Mike asks, "Have you seen Oliver, Mrs. Hoover?"

"Oliver? Your son?" She takes a step forward, tilting forward as if sniffing out another story. "Why, what is it? Is he missing?"

"Mike . . ." I don't want to reveal anything else to this woman.

Drew claps Mike on the back. "It's worth a shot. If anyone knows—"

"Well, I just may have." Mrs. Hoover cuts straight through our loosely formed circle and hooks an arm around a wooden support beam. Over the din of voices and heavy rain, she calls out. "Excuse me! We have a minor emergency here. We are looking for a minor." She stops and a burble of laughter escapes. "Minor . . . and minor. Get it?" She waves her hand as if to dismiss her thoughts. "Oliver Mullins is missing. Has anyone seen him this morning?"

A rumbling of voices rolls through the crowd. Heads bend together beneath umbrellas. More gossip. More conjecture.

"I seen 'em," a girl toward the back says. I don't recognize the blond hair and blue eyes. "Saw him get in Rick Parker's truck and drive off."

"Rick Parker?" I ask. "Who's that?"

"The kid I arrested with Oliver." Drew's tone is flat and hard as a stone tablet.

My confidence in my son's ability to handle all of these changes and revelations starts to crumble.

WE'RE CRAMMED IN the sheriff's SUV. Drew drives, Mike navigates. Josie and I sit in the backseat, our knees bumping against each other's and the metal gate. With the seat belt holding me in place, I brace one arm against the door and the other along the back of the seat. Josie looks over at me. I watch the rain moving up along the windows. I can hear the windshield wipers slashing at the rain, batting it away, but it continues relentlessly.

My hair is frizzy, one sleeve of my dress damp from sharing an umbrella with Mike. My mind is numb with concern for Oliver. Where could he have gone? And with that wild boy? Why? Is it all my fault? Am I, once again, to blame?

"I'm sorry." Josie's tone is soft yet purposeful.

"For what?"

"I knew there were rumors circulating about your husband and me."

"You don't have to say anything. I trust Mike." Even though I know I did have doubts. And Josie does too.

"I was trying to protect Hazel's reputation. She was very upset by your father's proposal and then your mother's funeral plans. She was, quite frankly, scared your mother would come after her if she knew who the other woman was."

"But why couldn't you have told me that? Didn't you trust me?"

"There was also a private matter I wanted to talk to your husband about."

"Oh?" Even now, after all we've been through, I feel my skin tightening. I release a slow breath. "Some legal matter?"

"Remember I told you about my ex-boss?"

"Yes."

"Well, I wondered if there was any recourse."

"You want to sue him?"

She shakes her head. "No. Not anymore. Your husband helped me see that the situation was as much my fault as that jerk's. Maybe not in eyes of the law. But I have to own my mistakes."

"I know. I've been learning that too."

"So is your mother."

"Yes." I just pray she can.

"You have a good man there."

"Thank you. I think so too." My heart swells with pride. Others look to him for advice. And he's always willing to help.

She gives a little chuckle. "And I was worried you might be interested in Drew again. And he in you." She shakes her head. "I was wrong."

"He's a good man too," I say and reach for Josie's hand. "But it's been over between us for years." I lower my voice. "But what about you two?"

She shrugs but there's a secretive smile tugging at the corner of her mouth. "We'll see."

Drew pulls up to a mobile home. The gravel driveway has pockets of rain. "Wait here." He jumps out of the SUV, leaving the engine running as well as the wipers. In a minute he's back. "No one's home."

"Where now?" Mike asks.

Drew frowns and taps his thumb against the steering wheel. The shoulders of his uniform are soaked. Rain drips along his sideburn. Without explanation, he throws the car in gear and takes off again. He stops at several places—a vineyard, a house that belongs to one of Rick's friends, then finally to some girl Rick dates occasionally.

"She said to try Makeout Flats." Drew turns the wheel, backing the SUV out of the driveway.

"Why there?" I brace my hand against the wire cage.

"Rick likes to go there sometimes to think, get away."

"Seems to be the happenin' place." Mike rubs his jaw. "Isn't there any other place to go in Gillespie County?"

"Since your wife rammed Josie's car into that crack, it's the place to go for tourists and sightseers. More popular than when the Starbucks opened in Fredericksburg."

I hold my cell phone in my lap, hoping Oliver will hear our messages and return our calls.

Ten minutes later Drew veers off the highway. The ground is wet and muddy as we slip and slide along the rough terrain where Josie and I ventured less than a week earlier.

Drew angles the SUV around bushes and rocks. He passes the barriers the sheriff's department set up along the length of the crack. "You know, two kids could be anywhere out here."

"It's going to be hard to find them with this rain." Mike leans forward, trying to see through the windshield. The windshield wipers are working hard, their insistent motion reminding me of the robot on the old television show *Lost in Space* waving its metallic arms and saying, "Warning, warning!"

"Actually," Drew slows down, hits his high beams. "Looks like they might have left a trail for us to follow."

I crane forward. Ahead of the SUV, two parallel trails cut through the mud. Drew fists the steering wheel resolutely. "If they're still out here, we'll find them."

Once the crack is within fifty feet of the SUV, Drew turns and heads north following the twin tire tracks lead.

Mike braces a hand against the dashboard, peering through the driver's window at the crack along the ground. "It looks like the rain is making parts of it cave in."

"Probably pretty unstable around here." But Drew keeps driving, keeping close to the crack. *Danger, Will Robinson!*

But none of us express concern for our own safety. My only thought is Oliver. What is he doing? Where is he? And why did he leave so suddenly? Guilt pulses through me once again. Is this the last domino to fall as a result of my sin?

Trepidation batters my insides as the SUV jounces along the rugged terrain like a Dodge Ram truck commercial in the making. The darkness gives away to a hazy light that streaks through the clouds. The rain lightens, and the clouds begin to lift. Moments later the windshield wipers screech across the glass. The rain has stopped as suddenly as it started. Drew flips a switch and the wipers cease their waving.

"There it is." Relief saturates Drew's voice. "Rick's truck." He pulls up next to the black truck with dirt crusted over the tires and undercarriage and splattered along the back. "You all stay put."

But Mike alights from the vehicle.

Drew hesitates. The two men look at each other over the hood. Mike slams the passenger door shut. "He's my son too."

Drew nods and closes his door. They walk side by side toward Rick's truck. It's a miracle to me, two men so different and yet so honorable that they can set aside their own feelings, fears, and doubts and work together rather than fighting each other every step of the way. They peer inside the truck, then look around as if searching. The back tires are sunk deep in the mud.

"It'll be okay." Josie gives me a quick, encouraging hug. "Drew will find them."

I nod, but inside I pray. This time I know there's nothing I can do or say to make things right. This time I must rely totally on God. Unable to stay locked inside the SUV any longer without helping in some way, I open the back door. I stare at the fracture along the earth only twenty feet away, seeing what Mike meant by the rains making the sides cave in. It looks like the rain has started to heal the split, the dirt filling in the opening like a scab forming. It might leave a scar, with a slight indenture, but maybe it will eventually close.

My foot slips in the mud, and I throw my arms outward to balance myself. The terrain at the moment is a minefield of uncertainty and instability. I know some places in the crevice are deep, and my heart pounds. "Oliver!" I cry.

Drew studies the ground, following footprints. "Looks like they went this way." He points away from the cracked opening in the earth.

"Oliver!" I call out again.

The light dripping of rain and the squishing of boots in mud are the only answer. Josie and I follow the men, picking our way over the muddy landscape. My heels sink into the softened earth.

Then I hear a faint response. Mike must have heard

it because he calls out our son's name. His tone forceful. "Oliver!"

"Over here!"

Josie and I creep up a slight incline, our shoes slipping. Rocks scrape the black leather that are now coated in a chalky mud. Then I see him. Oliver sits on a rock, soaked to the skin, Mike behind him, a hand on his shoulder. Another boy, older but shorter, stands near Drew.

"They're okay," Mike calls to us.

Relief rushes through me like flood waters surging and swelling. I give Josie a hug and race forward. Then I'm hugging Oliver, his wet hair and clothes soaking my dress.

"I'm okay, Mom."

"I know. I know."

"Rick called him and wanted to talk," Mike explains.

"I didn't think you needed me during the funeral." Oliver jams his hands in his pants. "And since it wasn't really Grandpa's funeral, I figured I could miss it."

"Because your friend needed you," I fill in the blanks.

He nods. "I wasn't doing anything wrong, Mom."

"I know." I sit down beside him, put a hand on his thigh. "It's okay. You're okay."

"What about Grandma and Grandpa?" he asks.

"Well, I'm not sure about them yet. We left them at the church."

Drew walks over and claps Oliver on the shoulder. "You okay?"

"Sure. I mean, yes, sir."

I watch as Josie now talks softly to Rick a few feet away.

"Is he okay?"

"Seems Oliver has made quite an impression on Rick. Maybe our boy is helping to lead someone else onto the straight and narrow."

I kiss my son's cheek, then reach for Mike's hand. Somehow I know no matter what winds of change and storms of life may assault our family, with God's help, we'll seek higher ground and come through together.

"THEY'RE COMING OUT," Pastor Reese announces. "Archie and Betty Lynne."

We're back at the dance hall, Rick Parker possibly making his first appearance ever in a house of God, even this makeshift one. Both boys have a sheriff's blanket around their shoulders.

Mother and Daddy step out of the dance hall onto the back steps. Mother looks as if she has powdered her nose and retouched her lipstick. Dad seems calm. They stand next to each other, yet apart, not touching. But not screeching at each other either. They look as though they showed up for church and realized it wasn't Sunday, mildly disappointed and somewhat confused.

"Everything okay?" Mike asks.

"Sure thing." Dad hooks his thumb through his belt loop.

"Mother?" I ask, afraid for her temper to be reignited.

"Oh, yes, dear. All's well." A secretive smile passes between my parents.

Mike and I glance at each other.

"So, can we cancel the funeral?" Pastor Reese asks.

Oliver laughs then looks down at his Nikes. I run a hand over his wet hair and down to his nape. It feels good to know he's okay, that he's handling the family chaos better than the adults.

"Of course. Archie's not dead." Mother speaks as if we should know better, as if she isn't the one who started the whole charade.

I release a taut breath. "Good. Then maybe—"

"We're getting married," Dad blurts out.

"What?"

"We've decided to get *re*married." Mother emphasizes the first syllable.

It's obvious who made that decision. "Right now?"

"Oh, no. That wouldn't be seemly."

"Not in the middle of a funeral," Mike notes.

I elbow him. "But the dance hall is decorated." I cringe inwardly at having to fly back to Texas in a month or two for another family event. I'm not sure my nerves or heart can take it. "And we're already here."

"Kill two birds with one stone." Oliver grins.

"Those flowers are depressing." Mother sniffs indignantly.

"But you picked them out!"

"For a funeral. Not a wedding." She clasps her hands together. "No, it's got to be just right."

I sigh. Not again.

"When?" Mike takes my hand in his.

"Soon." Dad smiles, reaching for Mother's hand.

"As soon as possible," Mother corrects.

"Soon," Dad repeats.

"Can we do this wedding before we go back to California?" I ask.

"Actually," Mother folds her hands together at her waist, "we're thinking of coming to California and getting married—"

"On your balcony," Dad adds, "overlooking the ocean."

"Then maybe going on to Hawaii," Mother continues without missing a beat.

"For our honeymoon." Dad grins.

"We never did get a proper honeymoon," Mother laments, as if all this could be traced back to an improper wedding.

"I want Suzanne to help me plan everything."

Mike looks at me and starts to laugh.

If this funeral was my near undoing, then—who knows?—
my parents' wedding may bring a kind of healing I never
expected.

Acknowledgments

writer is never alone is her work. First and foremost, I have to thank my family. Gary, if it wasn't for you, for your support and encouragement, I wouldn't be able to juggle all I do. Thank you for the glorious vacation in Hawaii where we experienced a real earthquake. How did you plan that? Graham and Caroline, thank you for putting up with meals that never quite measure up to Rachel Ray's. Mom, thanks for always helping out when needed, for buying so many books and for telling bookstores to place my books in more prominent locations.

Thanks to so many supportive friends, both writers and non, who encourage me when the going gets tough: D. Anne, Jane, Hock, Leslie, Maria, Beth. I appreciate the prayers and the support. Thanks to Chris Zygarlicke for answering my geological questions.

I have the best agent! Natasha, thank you for believing in this book.

B&H Publishing has been wonderful! David Webb, you are the best editor I could have ever imagined. Julie, you rock, girl! Karen, Mary Beth, Diana, Kim, Robin, Matt, the sales team—you guys are the best an author could ever envision, and authors have pretty good imaginations! I'm so blessed to work with such talented, enthusiastic folks.